## Praise for Brooks Hansen's *Perlman's Ordeal*

"Admirers of *The Chess Garden* will find similar heady pleasures in *Perlman's Ordeal*. Brooks Hansen continues to display, through richness of his *fin de siècle* fictional territory, a remarkable ability for mapping out how our lives and fates wend through a thicket of symbols."
—*Chicago Tribune*

"Hansen's seriocomic hero is another good poke at the preening self-confidence of science, in this case the budding efforts at the turn of the century to systematize the study of the mind. Hansen deftly conveys these early probings at the border of myth and medicine."
—*Time* magazine

"Brooks Hansen's literary intelligence is present everywhere but never intrusive. His evocation of the turn-of-the-century musical scene is richly inviting. His characters, combustible mixtures of vitality and vulnerability, are compelling. That he gives *Perlman's Ordeal* both the narrative suspense of a mystery and the philosophical depth of a novel of ideas is a testimony to his mastery."
—*Newsday*

"An entrancing tale that mixes psychiatry, hypnotism, and mysticism in turn-of-the-century London."
—*Baltimore Sun*

"The reader, like Perlman himself, is caught eyes wide shut in something grotesquely fascinating and maddeningly entertaining."
—*The Plain Dealer* (Cleveland, Ohio)

"Like the music that Perlman loves, *Perlman's Ordeal* is orchestrated on many levels. In closing, Hansen ingeniously ties its many themes together with a climax that proves—as in his highly acclaimed novel *The Chess Garden*—that narrative trumps all."
—*City Pages*

"Music, hypnosis, and love wrapped in magisterial prose…Mesmerizing."
—*New York Observer*

"The boundary between reason and madness shifts subtly in this psychodrama doubling as a love story. The result is a well-told, heady mix of enchantment and intellectual challenge."
—*Kirkus Reviews* (starred review)

# PERLMAN'S ORDEAL

# PERLMAN'S ORDEAL

## BROOKS HANSEN

PICADOR USA

FARRAR, STRAUS AND GIROUX

NEW YORK

Picador® is a U.S. registered trademark and is used by Farrar, Straus and Giroux under license from Pan Books Limited.

For information on Picador USA Reading Group Guides, as well as ordering, please contact the Trade Marketing department at St. Martin's Press.
Phone: 1-800-221-7945 extension 763
Fax: 212-677-7456
e-mail: trademarketing@stmartins.com

Design by Jonathan D. Lippincott

Library of Congress Cataloging-in-Publication Data

Hansen, Brooks.
    Perlman's ordeal / Brooks Hansen.
        p.    cm.
    ISBN 0-312-26765-7
    I. Title.
    PS3558.A5126P47   1999
    813'.54—dc21                                                    99-14275
                                                                           CIP

First published in the United States by Farrar, Straus and Giroux

First Picador USA Edition: October 2000

10 9 8 7 6 5 4 3 2 1

This work is dedicated to nobody save those who take pleasure in it.

—Franz Schubert, in a letter to the
publisher of his second piano trio

# PROLOGUE

For those who prefer knowing up front, or who may come to wonder along the way, these were the facts of August Perlman's life leading up to the seven days at question:

He was born in 1867 in the Jewish quarter of a small Moravian town called Iglau, the first son of Sophie and Abraham Perlman, a voice teacher. His one and only sibling, Leonard, followed a year later, then in 1871, the family moved to Vienna, where Abraham had been offered a job running a men's clothing store. For the next fifteen years the Perlmans enjoyed a typical urban bourgeois existence—were spoiled enough to feel deprived, and to forge from this some sense of aspiration. In manner, habit, and custom, they were basically like those living around them, with the one difference that while most other families in their neighborhood prayed to the same unnameable God with more or less the same level of devotion, the Perlmans were devout atheists.

This was Abraham's stamp. When he was just a boy, his family had been forced to flee their home in Lithuania by the torchlight of a pogrom. Proud child of the Enlightenment, Abraham eventually concluded that religion was to blame—and not just the religion of his tormentors but that of his own people as well. Of all human contrivances, none had proven more divisive than faith, or more baseless. The point for Abraham, however, was not that God did not exist, it was that He did not need to. Man could write his own laws and do his own good without resort to some Unseen Other. So long as a few basic principles were followed—provided the rights of man were respected, church and state were kept separate, democracy spread, science delved, art flourished, and understanding remained the utmost human pursuit— man could continue to grow and to prosper and to live in peace.

If Abraham was without God, he was not without hope, then, and he passed this distinction on to his two sons, along with the idea that if the secular society they envisioned was to succeed, it was going to re- quire more from its citizens than mere respect or obedience. It would require contribution.

Just what form that contribution should take was a matter deter- mined somewhat by the fact that there were two of them, so close in age. Given that, and given Abraham's priorities, it followed that one son should commit his life to Truth (or science) and that the other should commit his life to Beauty (or art). By the ages of five and six, the roles were cast. Leonard was to be a musician—he always was a gifted pianist; August was to be a doctor—he was not such a gifted pianist. They attended the same Gymnasium in Vienna, were both highly dec- orated students; then, when the time came, each attended the premier Viennese institute in his chosen field. August entered the university in 1885 to concentrate in the field of neuropathology and brain anatomy, while Leonard joined the conservatory a year later, having set his sights on a career as a soloist.

They were both still living at home until 1889, when Leonard left briefly to try his hand in public. It was the first time the brothers had been separated for any length, the first time either one had felt the pull of his own individual trajectory, free from the narrowing influ- ence of the other's rival achievement. Leonard was back within a year, bowed by crushing bouts of stage fright, but by then August's destiny had taken its turn in the direction of a man named Hippolyte Bern- heim.

Director of his own clinic at the Central Hospital in Nancy, France,

Bernheim (1837–1919) had come to Vienna that spring to deliver a series of lectures on the "Therapeutic Application of Hypnosis and Suggestion." His thesis was simple. Suggestion—that is, "the act by which
an idea is introduced into the brain and accepted by it"—was the
great unsung force guiding history. It fueled religion, commerce, ide-
ology, mores—basically all human behavior, from child rearing to nation building, was subject to its power. Bernheim's insight was
twofold: first, he proposed that suggestion could be used therapeuti-
cally, as a means of treating certain psychogenic disorders; second,
that the state of highest suggestibility, what he called *crédivité*, could
be induced through hypnosis. Bernheim was espousing an early brand
of hypnotherapy, in other words, but one, it needs be stressed, that
paid no mind to things like recovered memory, past-life regressions,
or contact with the Beyond. Given his view that the trance state
yielded above all a susceptibility to suggestion, he judged these more
"metaphysical" by-products of hypnosis to be prime examples of
the same—the result of mangled insinuation, subtle intimation, and
wishful thinking, all of which was an obvious distraction to the proper
therapeutic course. Bernheim advised a more direct approach: iden-
tify the most ostensible source of the patient's complaint, induce a hypnotic trance, then suggest a way in which the disorder might be
repaired.

Perlman found this very appealing. There was a simplicity to Bernheim's method, a kind of Machiavellian altruism that echoed many of
the ideas he'd been reared on: that the mind, if consulted directly, had
the means within itself to do "God's work." He introduced himself to
Bernheim, who likewise recognized something of potential in Perlman. When the semester was done, Bernheim invited him back to his
clinic in France. Perlman foresaw no more compelling future in Vienna, and so as soon as he'd convinced his father that he was not aban-
doning science entirely, he finally left the nest. He was twenty-two.
Leonard set off again soon after, this time as accompanist to the conservatory's first soprano. When a year had passed and it was clear that
neither of the boys was coming home again, their heretofore un-

complaining mother, Sophie, also left Vienna for good, to join a Zionist settlement in Palestine. Abraham Perlman was dead within six months.

From 1890 through 1900, the Nancy clinic was August Perlman's home. It was there he learned his craft and came into his own, happily. Bernheim's instincts had been correct. The young Perlman possessed all the natural attributes that make a good hypnotist: superb vocal control, an arresting eye, an assured manner, extremely quick intellectual reflexes, and an instinctive sense of what he could and could not fix. Also, like any adept, he entertained no illusions about the very technical nature of what he was doing. He understood that suggestive therapy was a method. It abided a certain definable logic, as well as cadences and timbres and a myriad of other subtle techniques the final purpose of which was to manipulate confidence. He mastered them all, and within a year had established himself as the best young therapist at Nancy; within two years, Bernheim had appointed him chief of staff.

This turned out to be not quite as astute a determination on the professor's part. As talented as Perlman was—or perhaps *because* he was so talented—he never developed into much of a clinician. He loathed administration and didn't care for research. Studies bored him, and he resisted most of the thornier "psychological" questions that hypnosis roused, on account of their all amounting to theory—precisely what good suggestive therapy was not. Suggestion was a practice. When he was not actually engaged in it, he preferred to be elsewhere, nourishing the other great passion in his life, which was music.

Not to play. That was his brother's purview. Nor to sing; that had been his father's. August was a listener, but listening was a serious business at the close of the nineteenth century. The world of music had survived the transition from church, to court, to concert hall, and was by then a firmly established, increasingly democratic and profitable industry, funded by the fervent appreciation of customers just like Perl-

man. He was among the first real consumers of music, the bourgeois
aficionados, brimming with opinions, preferences, and peeves which,
in Perlman's case, served to bolster a highly involved brand of human-
ism as well as a pleasing sense of cultural assimilation. He patronized
all venues—even the religious ones, reluctantly—and he and Leonard
made semiannual trips together to parts unknown, the purpose of
which was not to ogle the landscape or sample the food or custom, but
to hear the music. He was familiar with the entire concert repertoire,
and his tastes were as distinct as they were unpredictable, excepting the
one bias he brought, which was the unduly high standard he applied
to the work of his fellow German-speakers. He favored melody to
motif, prized subject over treatment. He preferred Bach to Mozart,
Chopin to Schumann, Wagner to Brahms, and even harbored a par-
tiality for Schubert over Beethoven, on account of his being the more
purely "musical" composer (an early appraisal his brother, Leonard,
deemed an expression of irredeemable Philistinism that he was never
fully able to forget, or forgive).

He was hardly making excuses, then, when—to break the monot-
ony of clinic life in Nancy—he and his best friend on staff, Marcel
Parisot, would steal away for weekends in Paris or Leipzig. The problems arose when, as Perlman's years at Nancy rolled one to the next,
these musical excursions grew more and more frequent, and began to
entail more than purely musical indulgences. Perlman's listening ritual
had always entailed a brandy marinade. In Paris, with Parisot, his
tastes expanded to include absinthe, opium, hashish, or whatever else
there was on hand. It was in this same connection that he began to frequent the houses of professional women, and soon was keeping mis-
tresses in nearly every musical capital he could reach by rail.

Ten years into his tenure at Nancy, Perlman's sense of purpose had
gone officially slack, which was unfortunate timing, since it was right
around then that Bernheim decided to expand the empire of clinical
suggestion. In 1899, he began to set up satellite clinics in choice European capitals. Among these, Vienna was the obvious plum, and Perlman could hardly be blamed for thinking it should, and would, go to
him—the staff star—but for all the reasons mentioned, Bernheim

tapped another Wiener, Adolf Werner—by no account as talented a therapist as Perlman, but a much more responsible administrator. Perlman was sent to London.

A definite blow, but Perlman didn't lick his wounds for long. Vienna was no great loss. The bureaucracy was impossible, and the hospital politics were equally vicious. True, there was a vital music life, which answered to a positively magisterial history, but by that same token it could sometimes feel stultified or burdened. Furthermore, Vienna could be an openly hostile place for a Jew.

London, on the other hand, proved to be a town of unexpected charm. Leonard was there, having landed a teaching position at the Royal Academy two years before. Perlman was familiar with the region from childhood visits to one of his father's cousins. He enjoyed the language, and the concert life wasn't as awful as he'd expected. As composers, the English hadn't much to show for themselves, but they did seem to *enjoy* music and liked to be well served. In that regard, the dearth of local repertory turned out to be a kind of advantage for a man of Perlman's taste, since it left the stages open to an even wider array of foreign talent than he'd enjoyed in Paris. As for the quality of English anti-Semitism, Perlman likewise found it to be more palatable than the French or German varieties. In London, the leery eye saw in Perlman not just a Jew but a foreign Jew, a Continental Jew, which somehow seemed to dilute the potency of the prejudice.

London's most pleasing virtue of all, however, was the home it provided his clinic. His official appointment was at St. Bartholomew's Hospital, the oldest and most progressive in the city. They set him up in a small annex across the street—a safe distance—but he proved his worth soon enough. The English, it turned out, were a surprisingly credulous people. They believed anything, and were to that extent an extremely fertile field for the seed he'd been asked to bring. Within a month of his arrival, not only did St. Bartholomew's extend his lease, they contracted him to come and conduct daily rounds at the hospital, which simply meant going from bed to bed, hypnotizing all the patients in need, to ease their aches, their pains, their sleepless nights and surgical wounds. In exchange for this, the Powers That Be were only too happy to furnish Dr. Perlman with an office, a small flat behind, dining privileges, and as many nurses as he required, which was never more than one or two. He ran his clinic as more of a private office, in fact. In five years, he assembled no staff, established no protégés, and conducted no studies. As he saw it, the best advertisement of the suggestive method would be the steady demonstration of its effectiveness—i.e., curing patients, which he could do well enough alone. He was careful never to take a case he didn't have a reasonable expectation of treating successfully, and by his following this one simple rule, his reputation flourished. Patients were soon traveling great distances to see him, and entering his door with a level of hope and expectation that only downright malpractice could disappoint. Perlman never did, and so by the fall of 1906, when our story begins, he had come to be known among a widespread and still-expanding circle as something more than a hypnotist; more than a doctor even. Perlman was a healer.

If his own estimation was more modest—and it was—he still, when he consulted the mirror each morning, was basically pleased. There in the glass was a man who was doing his part. No saint, to be sure—he had his needs—but he could claim his share of noble thoughts as well, and by helping to ease the suffering of his fellow man was surely leaving things better than he found them—every day, undeniably, and on no false pretense.

So sayeth the mirror.

# ACT I

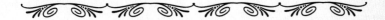

# CHAPTER 1

Perlman's ordeal began at 6:50 p.m., September 24, 1906, a Monday. It ended the following Sunday, late.

A discrete event, then, and brief—though not by comparison to other coups, he supposed, or attempted coups, which this had been, a bid at overturning everything the man had based his life and practice on. For such a radical siege to succeed, it would have to be quick, and thorough, and this was both. For seven days, everything from the weather outside to Perlman's own most private compulsions had seemed to play their parts in perfect concert, so much so that a man of a more credulous temperament might well have construed the hand of an All-Powerful, All-Knowing Being. Perlman, not being so credulous, saw no such sign, but for that same reason was at pains throughout to unmask this thing, expose it for what it was, what it could only have been: a triumph of unlikelihood, in which perfectly commonplace threads of circumstance and coincidence had been woven together by influences all too human—by manners, manipulation, gullibility, hope, shame, desire, hysteria don't forget, and then of course outright idiocy, mostly his.

How long this web was in the making, why it should have chosen him or this moment to descend, all were good questions. Unfortunately, every time Perlman thought he might have hit upon some clue, some insight, he'd turn the next corner to find another explanation waiting, another potential culprit rearing its head to smile and chide him for the presumption. And so in the end he was left with the one impression which had denominated all the others all along, like a keynote striking steadily and repeatedly beneath a wandering melody: He did not know. He did not know. Had no idea with what, or whom, he was dealing. And that had been the real ordeal, hadn't it?

At least one element no one could deny. Requisite to any good storm is the lull that precedes it. In Perlman's case, a lengthy stretch of bland contentment—a blissful stretch, in retrospect—whose wellspring and centerpiece was his own clinic, the London Clinic for Suggestive Therapy, located on the ground level of 38 Little Britain, just across from the East Wing of the four pavilions that comprised St. Bartholomew's Hospital. The clinic was five years old and doing well. That very month, in fact, it had received its first noteworthy press—a feature piece in *The Pall Mall Gazette* which could not have been more glowing, or useful, if Perlman had written it himself, which, owing to his talents for subtle persuasion, he basically had.

On the private front, the doctor's life was just as safely squared away. He had long ago determined his personal preferences—simple matters of what he liked to do, with whom, and when. He kept these few enough and distinct enough that they could be satisfied without compromising too much of his time or reputation. Another way of saying those preferences—on account of their modesty—were liberally served, and by the steady succession of their observance, and the running of the clinic, August Perlman's life had been proceeding at what seemed a pleasing clip—a perfect rhythm, as it would turn out, for disruption.

Two warning notes had sounded, true—two spikes, which stood out in hindsight as having maybe prepared the way. First was the revolt in Moscow the previous December, the riots and subsequent strikes, all of which Perlman had tracked through the *Times* with what even then seemed an unwarranted pang of pity. Second was a thunderstorm which descended on London near the beginning of autumn; September 10, to be exact.

Perlman himself had been at Covent Garden at the time, at a performance of *Don Giovanni*. That evening's principals, Maurel and Lussan, were both in good enough voice that Perlman, settled in his seat like a cat in a basket, remarked the storm outside only passingly. A few thunderclaps had intruded on the wedding scene—humidity had flattened the strings slightly—and then of course there was the inconvenience of being trapped inside the lobby with the rest of the audience for another half hour after the performance had ended. For the delay, he indulged himself in a third brandy until the heavy rain passed. Then, as was his custom, he took the Underground to the Southwark flat of his mistress, Samantha Ronan. There he spent the night, awoke alone—as he preferred—enjoyed an unaccompanied breakfast of tea, toast, and the morning *Times*, and was back home at the clinic by 7:30.

All things considered, not a bad evening. Or hardly the stuff of portent.

**F**ifteen days hence the fury of the summer's final storm did finally reach Perlman's attention, sounding as a set of cautious taps against his office door.

Again, they'd found him in a contented place. His last appointment for the day had been with a Belgian patent clerk named Félix Légère. A relatively simple case, M. Légère had come all the way from Brussels, complaining of a chronic skin rash. Perlman had prescribed a standard regime of counter-suggestion, had eliminated the rash in less than two weeks, and now was working on preventative maintenance.

As always, the metronome was ticking: a standard allegro ($\quarternote$ = 120) had proven to work best for Légère.

"Now, for a third time, Monsieur." Perlman was speaking in the slightly deeper register he invoked for professional use only, at a slower, even cadence. "Do you recall the irritation on your skin?"

Légère gave a willing nod. His eyes were closed, his head was pressed against a small pillow, though he was sitting up in the chair.

"A burning. Itching. An army of red ants, you said."

Légère's face grimaced.

"You can feel it?"

Légère nodded.

"On the inside of your arm, the rash has spread."

Légère grew more agitated and started moaning pitifully.

"It's covering both arms now, a colony of red ants."

"Ooooh." Légère squirmed in the chair.

"Don't scratch them, Monsieur Légère. You know it only makes them angry. You remember what to do."

Légère nodded. "The sun."

"That's right, the sun. They cannot bear the sun, and you can feel it now, shining down in waves. How many waves?"

"Eleven."

"That's right. Eleven waves of sunlight, and you will make them go away, burn them away, as you have proven all this week and the week before—you will make the ants retreat. Even now it has begun. Ten. Breathe . . . Nine."

Perlman let the metronome sound four ticks unaccompanied. Légère's face calmed.

"They are burning away. Seven . . ."

Légère's body relaxed.

"Six . . . Your skin is smooth and cool. You can feel the air. Do you feel?"

Légère nodded.

"How does it feel?"

"Smooth. Cool."

"Good. There's four . . . three . . . two"—he paused—"and all the irritation is gone."

He waited an extra moment to let Légère enjoy the relief. "Very good, Monsieur Légère. Now you will awake." Perlman leaned over and touched him on the shoulder.

Légère's head gave a slight shake, and the pillow fell from behind his neck. His brows lifted and a luxuriant smile stretched across his face, as though he'd wakened from a long nap.

"Well rested?"

Légère took a deep, loud breath. "*Comme toujours*, Dr. Perlman." A child-sized man, he hopped down from the chair and gave his chest two crisp pats. "*Très bon.*"

"You're doing very well."

Légère looked down to inspect the soft undersides of his arms. His sleeves were rolled so he could see the skin, smooth and clear. "Mmm," he toned happily. "Mmm." He kissed his arms, the right and then the left. "*Merci*, Dr. Perlman. I cannot say."

"You needn't." Perlman stood. "It is you, Monsieur Légère."

Légère gave a sly grin. "It was not 'I' with Dr. Arnot. It was not 'I' with Dr. Parent and all his ointments." He looked down at his arms again in wonder. "Mm." He kissed them twice more, then in a fit of gratitude clasped Perlman around the shoulders. "Thank you, thank you, thank you, Dr. Perlman."

Perlman did not protest this time, but as soon as he was able—as soon as he'd been let go—he ushered M. Légère out to the reception area.

Sister Margaret was at her desk—idle, but dutifully posed. She had been with him for two years now and was the best of the nurses the hospital had sent him. Older than most, and taller—taller than Perlman, in fact—she had a long and lean visage that might once have passed for fair but which age had turned more knowing and severe. A bit like a Great Dane, her mere presence served him well—that so commanding a figure as she should nonetheless be answering to him.

Légère presented his arms for her to see. She gave a suitably, but not overly, impressed nod.

"Sister Margaret, I'd like to schedule Monsieur Légère again for Wednesday. Is that all right, Monsieur Légère?"

"Morning?"

"Morning. Shall we say ten?"

"Ten. *Bon.*" Légère clicked his heels.

"Then I think we may be done."

Légère gave a slight swoon, then shot a sly glance at the Sister. "But then when will I see the mademoiselle?" He rounded the desk and kissed her impassive hand.

"That I leave to you."

"Aha, Doctor." He wagged a finger at him, clasped his hand, his wrist, then left with a flourish, sweeping his coat from the stand and bursting out the door, proclaiming his relief to the night air.

Perlman and the Sister shared a quiet smile. "And how much longer will you be holding the fort?"

"Till seven," she said.

"Good. I'll be changing. If I don't see you, Sister Margaret, good night."

"Good night, Dr. Perlman."

Perlman closed the office door behind him and crossed through to his flat, which lay the other side. A modest space for a man of his renown—just a parlor, a kitchenette, a dining area, and a bedroom—but Perlman rarely entertained, and was happy to trade space for the convenience of being so near his place of business. He went straight to the loo to begin his usual ablutions, soaping his cheeks and neck.

Once again he planned to close the day with music, this time the symphony, and this time in the company of Dr. Benjamin. The program was one he'd been looking forward to ever since noting it in his fall subscription letter, an evening of Scandinavian fare—some Nielsen, some Grieg, and as a special treat the London premiere of a tone poem by the Finn, Jean Sibelius, called *The Swan of Tuonela*. Perlman had heard the piece once before, last year in Denmark with Leonard, and he remembered liking it. He couldn't quite recall the themes, though, and so as soon as his hands and face were clean, he returned to his office to consult his Chroniks.

The "Chroniks" stretched across the two top shelves of Perlman's office bookcase—an assortment of journals, cahiers, scrapbooks, folders, and such, more uniform in recent years; he'd found a sturdy black notebook when he first came to London, red-spined, well-bound, and a snug fit in all his coat pockets. In one form or another, he'd been keeping them practically since he was at Gymnasium, recording his impression of every musical performance he attended, every letter he sent or received on the subject of composers, halls, conductors, and so forth. Perlman was filling three or four per year now, and each new entry stoked a quiet hope that when all was done, perhaps when the clinic had passed to the hands of another, he'd go back over the whole collection, clean them up, and publish them for what they were— which was, he trusted, as comprehensive a record of European musical life as probably existed.

He had found the Sibelius notes. June 26 it had been, and he *had* liked it. Four stars. His brother's ranking, two and a half—which was hardly surprising. *Wallpaper*, Leonard had called it. August was more forgiving. *More difficult to listen to, certainly,* read the evening's entry:

*In fact, exhausting—the stamina required. One is never certain, in such a subjective piece, where one is. This, as opposed to the Bruch, where even if one had never heard the thing before, there is still the chance—provided one can distinguish a first subject from a second, tell a rondo from a fantasia—of knowing how close one is to the finish. Not so the* Swan.

*A concern? L frets as ever that less formal music invites the incursion of dilettantes, charlatans. Perhaps. Still, I think one should give the benefit of the doubt—esp. to such becoming "wallpaper" as this— if only because the impulse is inarguable: to let the content of the music dictate the form, and not vice versa. That is all. If Leonard cannot see that—or hear it—he has been in school too long.*

Perlman agreed with himself, and rather liked the last bit. Still, it was a point in Leonard's favor that now, a year later, Perlman's recollection of the music itself was foggy. Fortunately, he'd noted one of the themes in his entry—or Leonard had—a little handwritten

He took the book back to his parlor, straight to his upright, a third-hand Broadwood. He removed the player mechanism and propped it against the wall—useless contraption—consulted his Chronik, and played the *Swan* theme, standing.

He winced at the sound. It had been a humid summer, like living in a bowl of soup. The middle G was sticking, but still he recognized the theme, or thought he might.

He went to finish changing, and ponder the phrase. Shirt first, then pants. He poured himself a glass of brandy and fixed his cuff links at the piano. Three more times he played the theme, standing, then opened the teakwood smoking chest on top. He removed a small clay pipe, an old gift from Dr. Parisot, and then from a smaller interior box, an even more recent gift—a whittled brick of hashish.

He wondered if he should smoke yet, though, or wait. This was a potent batch. Probably he should go ahead. His pocket watch showed 6:30; ten minutes till the carriage would arrive, but this would last the trip. There were no more matches in the chest, so he returned to his office and was rooting through his drawers when the tapping, the aforementioned rapping, sounded the other side of the clinic door.

It was Sister Margaret. "Dr. Perlman?"

Perlman stuffed the pipe into the pocket of the blazer hanging over the back of his desk chair. The drink he kept in his hand. "Yes?"

She cracked the door open. "There's a patient."

"To admit?"

"Yes."

He lifted the watch from his pocket, by way of demonstration. "Did you tell them there are hours?"

She nodded. "They've come over from hospital."

The hospital? That wasn't right. They weren't supposed to do that. He closed the desk drawers firmly. "I'll be right there." He returned his drink back to his flat, swept all the stray papers from his desktop, then headed out to Reception.

There were four figures in the waiting area. A tall, heavyset Jewish man, nervous, holding his hat by the brim. Perlman knew on sight—another Wiener, like himself. The suit looked as if he might have gotten it at Kundhoffer's. Beside him was a slightly older woman of a lower but more pure German stock—a personal nurse or nanny. Dr. Abrams, one of the younger interns from the hospital, was standing next to her, and finally—the subject of their averted attention—a girl lay flat on a hospital carriage. She was unconscious and lanced by three separate rubber tubes—one in her nose, one in her mouth, and one up between her legs—all leading back to a ten-gallon jug of water, which for the time being had been propped on one of the waiting-room chairs.

Perlman approached her first. An early pubescent. Dark brunette; pale olive complexion; expressionless. The Jewish man's daughter. Perlman felt her forehead, which indicated no fever. He pulled open her lids. Hazel-brown iris—or so it appeared; her pupils were button-sized. They'd given her morphine. Perlman fired Abrams an openly contemptuous glance, then turned to the father.

Abrams introduced. "This is Mr. Blum, and Miss Bauer. Mr. Blum, Miss Bauer, this is Dr. Perlman."

Only the man extended his hand. "You were heading out." He indicated the collar of his dress shirt.

"Just a concert. This is your daughter?"

The man nodded. Small eyes, small glasses, even a dainty nose, but still characterized by the downward hook. A tidy crop of curly black hair and delicate lips like a bow. A rather exquisite set of features, all bunched together in the middle of a massive head, broad jowls and neck, well shaven but shaded blue.

He was sweating, breathing heavily. Mr. Blum had been angry not long ago, but the fury had given way to shock and the customary shame people tended to feel by association with a condition such as his daughter's, which Perlman had already concluded was hysterical— probably a mild case exacerbated by idiotic care, as it appeared their own Dr. Abrams had recently administered.

Abrams extended a clipboard. "She came in this afternoon."

"To the hospital?"

"Yes."

"Cause?"

"Dehydration."

"Hydrophobia?"

Abrams shrugged, and Perlman turned back to the girl. He indicated the tube in her nose. "And this is your doing?"

"It's all we could. She hasn't had anything to drink in eleven days." He turned to Mr. Blum to confirm.

"So we are told."

Perlman felt his evening, the Sibelius, slip away. "And this?" He tapped the jug.

"Distilled water."

He turned now to the German woman, who'd been standing beside Herr Blum, silent—or silenced. "And you are not from the hospital?"

"No," said Blum. "Fraulein Bauer works for us."

"How long?"

"Ten years," said the woman, a Pomeranian, it sounded like.

Perlman gave her a welcome nod. "Herr Blum, Fraulein Bauer, if you'll come with me."

Abrams offered his chart, but Perlman pushed it back at him as though it were a mildewed dish towel. "Start her down to one of the rooms. Sister Margaret, you'll help Dr. Abrams. First, though—" He went to the reception desk and dashed a note.

*Arthur—I've been detained. Go on ahead. —A.*

He gave the note to Sister Margaret, who understood—the coach would be out in front of the Priory by now. She went to deliver it, and Perlman escorted Fraulein Bauer and Herr Blum into his office.

**H**e set out two chairs evenly before his desk.

"I apologize about the time," said Blum, sitting. "If we are keeping you."

"Not at all." Perlman took his seat as well. "If I seem scattered, it's that you catch me at the end of a long day." This was an untrue and

entirely unnecessary admission, he knew; he could not have less conveyed preoccupation. His purpose was more to underline the standard
of control he liked to keep. He opened his clinical notebook.

"Now." He looked back up at them and started his pen.
"B-L-U-M?"

Blum nodded.

"And your daughter's name?"

"Sylvie."

*Sylvie*, he wrote, *dark brunette. 5´2˝, 90 lbs. Eyes hazel-brown.
Afebrile.*

"Thirteen years old?"

Blum confirmed.

"Brothers or sisters?"

"No."

Perlman continued to make notes as he proceeded with the inter-
view. "I'll need to know something of her history previous to the crisis. You are from Vienna?"

Blum nodded.

"Is that where Sylvie grew up?"

"Yes," said Blum, "and here. Her mother is English."

"And where is her mother?"

"Switzerland."

This seemed odd, but Blum's head remained so conspicuously still,
Perlman decided for the moment not to press.

"You've come on business?"

"Export."

"*Willkommen. Mit?*"

"East India."

Perlman offered a lift of his brow—he'd heard there was grumbling
at the honorable East India, another German incursion. "When did
you arrive?"

"August. Sylvie went off to school in September."

"What school?"

"Miss Mobley."

Miss Mobley—Perlman's heart quietly went out. That wouldn't be an easy place for a new Jewish girl, or half-Jewish. He added an exclamation point to the note. "That's just outside Bath."

Blum nodded.

"Now, did Sylvie suffer any significant childhood illness I should know about—fevers and such?"

"Typhoid." Miss Bauer spoke up for the first time.

"How long ago?"

"She was eight. Five years."

"And her constitution since?"

"Good."

"Temperament?"

They were slow to answer. He wrote *mixed*.

"Appetite?"

Blum again referred the question to Fraulein Bauer, who shook her head.

"Previous to the crisis?"

"Fine."

"Nightmares?"

Blum answered with a note of irritation. "Like any child."

"Intellect is sharp?"

"Yes."

"Bowels regular?"

Yes, nodded Fraulein Bauer. "Before."

"And her menses began—?"

Blum's eyes descended to the floor. Nurse Bauer answered. "This summer."

Perlman set down his pen finally and sat back. "So this current episode is the result of an aversion to water."

Blum nodded.

"And did this develop gradually or all at once?"

Blum shook his head. "It happened at the school."

"What do you mean?"

"I mean she stopped taking water when she returned to school. She came home from school on Saturday, two weeks ago. After she left again, that is when it began."

"Immediately thereafter?"

Again Blum looked at Fraulein Bauer. Neither of them seemed to know.

"And there was no indication of unusual behavior before she left? Fraulein Bauer?"

She was sitting obediently, hands in her lap. "She was sick."

"How sick?"

"Not so," Blum jumped in. "Not that one wouldn't expect from a child going back to school."

"Fever?"

Not quite, Fraulein Bauer shook her head. "She couldn't eat."

"Wouldn't eat," Blum corrected. "She was scared. It is a new place."

"I understand," said Perlman. "But other than that, nothing else you can think of that might have precipitated or indicated the problem?"

Fraulein Bauer looked down at her hands and shook her head.

"Which is that she stopped drinking—continued to refuse food and water?"

Yes, they nodded.

"Did she bathe?"

They didn't seem to be sure.

"Did you speak with anyone at the school? A physician, any master or sisters."

"Yes," said Blum. "Miss Halsey and another. Their names are written down."

"And what did they say?"

He seemed stumped, exasperated. "They said she wouldn't drink."

"Had she been physically violent?"

"Yes."

"Did you ever observe this?"

"No."

"And did the people at the school say whether she gave any reason for her behavior?"

Blum shook his head, he didn't understand the question.

"Did she express any sort of paranoia or delusion?"

Blum conceded. "They said she was blaming."

"Anything, anyone in particular?"

"That everything was her fault."

Perlman nodded, mostly to reassure them. There was nothing new in the apparent opposition—blaming and guilt; classic hysterical symptoms, in fact. He decided to end the questioning.

"Now, did anyone at the hospital explain what we do here?"

Blum looked skeptical. "You are a hypnotist."

Perlman affected slightly more umbrage at this than he honestly felt. "Suggestive therapy." He paused. "The mind, Herr Blum, Fraulein Bauer, has an effect upon the body. This may not come as news to you, but it has come as news to the medical community—at least that this effect should be so direct, so demonstrable. The mind can stimulate health; it can stimulate illness. Which of these it chooses is a matter subject to suggestion. I'm sure you're aware, Herr Blum— in your business—of the power of suggestion. Here at the clinic, our purpose is to offer, for lack of a better phrase, healing suggestion. *Hypnotism*"—he emphasized the word for Blum's sake—"comes into play simply because the trance state induced through hypnosis happens to be one of heightened suggestibility, what we call *crédivité*. You may even have seen performances of stage hypnotists. I don't approve of such things, but they make the point. If I told Fraulein Bauer now to let me have the pair of spectacles she's holding in her hands, she might resist. If I were to induce in her a hypnotic trance, however"—he now locked his eyes on Fraulein Bauer and spoke the rest more slowly, metrically, and from that precise depth in his chest—"and then told her that those spectacles were mine—those spectacles *are* mine"—he opened his palm to her—"then she might give them to me."

He fluttered his fingers and Fraulein Bauer did, as if on command, start handing them over. Perlman turned his hand and stayed her with a smile.

"With patients, this is not always so simple. We are all different, all susceptible to different suggestions, in different ways. Our work here basically consists of identifying the appropriate suggestions, attaining the state of suggestibility—*crédivité*—and offering them. In your daughter's case, it would seem we should address the question of water. Yes?"

Yes, they both agreed.

"Do you understand?"

Blum cleared the skepticism from the back of his throat. "You will hypnotize her and tell her to drink again."

Perlman smiled. "Something like that."

—Exactly like that—

"Of course, as I say, we are all different. I will have to get to know Sylvie somewhat before I can determine what course and what pace seem appropriate—that is, if you have no objections to my taking your daughter's case myself."

Blum shook his head gratefully, the first good sign.

"Now, it would appear we'll have to keep Sylvie here overnight at least, but as you can see, the hospital is just across the way. We enjoy access to all their facilities and expertise. If at any point you begin to feel uncomfortable, or if you have any questions, you are more than welcome to come and register your concern."

Blum nodded, but there was something else.

"Yes?"

"Would it be acceptable if Fraulein Bauer stayed the night, for when Sylvie awakes?"

Perlman turned back to Fraulein Bauer. Normally he would have refused—any remote challenge to his authority—but in this circumstance, with the girl unconscious, he thought he could at least make use of her faith, which it appeared from the expression on her face he'd already secured. "Certainly." He rose, and escorted them out to the reception area again.

Sister Margaret was back at her desk. The girl was in room 3, she informed him, with Dr. Abrams. Perlman instructed her to prepare room 2 for Fraulein Bauer, and asked if she would spend the night as well. Then he saw Herr Blum to the door.

He still seemed dazed, but relieved—better than when he'd come in, which was all Perlman could have hoped for under the circumstances. He took his hand. "Herr Blum, you've done well, and don't worry. We'll take good care of her." Blum nodded vaguely, and Perlman pointed him in the direction of the cabs up by the Priory.

As soon as the door was closed between them, Perlman started down to room 3, to make sure Dr. Abrams hadn't done any more harm. The girl was in bed, still plugged and inert, now flanked by Fraulein Bauer on one side and Abrams on the other.

"Dr. Abrams, I assume you familiarized Sister Margaret with your system?" Perlman indicated a jug of water, which was propped up on one of the rolling shelves.

"I did."

"Good. You'll do the same for Fraulein Bauer, just so she knows."

Fraulein Bauer nodded blankly. It wasn't clear she understood, which was fine. He addressed Abrams again.

"What ward did you come from?"

"Elizabeth."

"And who was in charge?"

"Mr. Shepard."

"Very good. As soon as Sister Margaret returns, you can go. Fraulein Bauer." He turned. Her eyes were wide with deference. "I'll be back."

She nodded quickly and he left. He started straight down the hall and out into the night, audibly grousing as he crossed Little Britain, as much to prepare for the coming encounter as to vent.

# CHAPTER 2

This was precisely the sort of thing he'd spoken to Shepard about. Shepard was the hospital clerk—not a doctor, not a subtle mind—but Perlman had been clear. You couldn't do this, just trundle someone over out of the blue. This was a delicate business. This wasn't the sort of thing where one could just cut someone open, make a mess, and then tie it up with a needle and thread. These things had to be approached delicately, and from the very first moment. From the very first moment you had to begin establishing the trust, the confidence required.

In fact the first overture should really be the patient's—how many times had he said it?—the patient should be the one to decide to come, or to think he's decided, like M. Légère, because it was the patient, after all, who was going to do the healing. You don't knock them out with morphine and *then* send them over. What was he to do with that? It was the most ridiculous misunderstanding of his office. Just carting her over, insensate.

He climbed the steps to the West Wing and stopped the first nurse he could find. "Has Mr. Shepard left yet?"

"You just missed him," she replied. "I think he was headed home."

Perlman turned right around. As clerk, Shepard kept residence in the administrative building, the North Wing. Perlman used the walk across the square to finish his thought.

They simply didn't seem to appreciate the delicacy, and not just of the particular case but of the whole undertaking, the clinic, the movement. Had they not been watching? Did they not see the care with which he chose the cases? That was as important a part of the craft as any, knowing when and where to strike. Take the cases you know you can treat, establish a reputation for effectiveness, then let word spread. Patients would come with higher hopes—higher hopes meant greater suggestibility—which meant he could afford to admit more challenging cases, enjoy more success and greater faith. To expand little by little, outward—that was the way. Not this. What if the girl turned out to be a hopeless hysteric, what then? One botched case would sow doubt. Doubt would sow more doubt, and then he'd have to start building trust all over again.

He entered the North Wing and made his way down the Great Hall, oblivious to its profligate splendor.

But of course they didn't think about that sort of thing here. Here they just thought—'Send her over to Dr. Perlman. Dr. Perlman will take care of it.' That was the problem. He'd been *too* good, *too* adept, and now they'd begun to treat him like some sort of shaman. It was an outrage. It was an abuse.

Which was to say nothing of the fact that he was now missing the Sibelius.

He knocked three times at Shepard's door. Mrs. Shepard answered. "Dr. Perlman, what a pleasant—?"

"No," he interrupted. "Actually, I was wondering if I could have a word with your husband." An attractive woman—Shepard had done well. A small blond daughter was hiding behind her dress. "I won't be long."

Mrs. Shepard took the girl's hand and went to fetch her husband. Perlman could smell he'd interrupted dinner—brisket. He entered Shepard's study to wait.

His Gramophone was standing proudly between the windows. Perlman sidled over. He'd come very close to getting one of these himself but finally decided that the player piano was the better investment, both financially and musically. The gramophone sound was simply too crude, and the horn an eyesore.

"Good evening, August." Shepard was at the door, in shirtsleeves. Perlman only had to look at him. "Is this about Blum's daughter?"

"Yes, it is."

Shepard entered, extending a glass of Perlman's favorite sherry, Harveys. "Sorry about that."

Perlman accepted—the glass. "And do you apologize to Dr. Benjamin when you send him over one of Dr. Samuel's patients?"

"That's hardly a fair comparison, August. You heard her story, didn't you? All that about water?"

"Yes, the water. So? I agree, perhaps if she had come to me a month ago—if she'd been properly recommended and she had decided to come see me, I agree, I might have been able to do something, but George, have you seen her? Do you know what your residents have done?"

"She was that way on admission, August."

"With a shunt in her nose?"

"She was severely dehydrated. She's in shock."

"Well, I don't blame her. I'd be in shock, too." Perlman took a sip of his sherry, but didn't let the taste distract him. "We've been through this. You have to let them decide. You *recommend*. What do you expect me to do in a case like this, wave a wand?"

Shepard couldn't help a smile. "You say that, August, but you and I both know—"

"We both know that if I can meet a person, yes, but this young woman is going to wake up in my clinic a sick, frightened stranger."

Shepard looked at him, contrite. There was an air, in both their manners, of performance, which he seemed prepared to break. "August, I'm sorry. You're right, and in a perfect world, we would wait. But you are aware there is something of an epidemic in the city. Our beds are full. We could have sent her to the Home for Incurables, I suppose—" He paused on this, knowing the mere mention would win him the exchange. "But we are not going to do that. We are going to

send her to you. Eventually, that was going to happen. We accelerated
the process. As for Dr. Abram's shunt—she hadn't had water in two
weeks—"

"Eleven days."

"Eleven days. Frankly, I think Abrams deserves a great deal of
credit."

Perlman allowed, still simmering. "Well, at the very least, consult
me first. Don't bring them to me after you've sedated them. I
need . . ." What he had intended to say was that he needed confidence,
but he did not finish the thought. "You know what I need." He turned
to the phonograph. "Anything new?"

Shepard stepped over to the stack of recordings. "I'm not sure when
you were here last. There's some Moreschi now. Would you like to
hear?"

The truth was, he would—it looked as if Shepard had bought the
entire G&T catalogue—but Perlman wouldn't give him the satisfaction. He consulted his pocket watch. "No, I should probably get back.
I'm missing the first set at Queen's Hall as it is."

"Ah," Shepard laughed. "So that's what's got you bugged. I thought
it must be something." He paused at the lack of humor that Perlman
took at this. "August, I'll make it up to you. The Borodin is coming to
town—what's it called?"

"*Prince Igor.*"

"There—I'll make it up to you. And don't worry about the girl.
She'll come round in the morning, and you'll fix it. You will." He
winked. "I have faith."

"Not the point."

"No? I thought it was."

Perlman conceded a nod but no smile, handed him the glass, and
departed.

## CHAPTER 3

Fraulein Bauer was still in the chair where Perlman had left her, reading a book now—a Lutheran Bible, which would have been fine, except that her lips seemed to be moving.

Perlman crossed to the girl's bed and took her hand. Still waxy. He checked the jug, which was low. "Perhaps we should refill this."

"Sister Margaret is getting more."

Perlman leaned over the girl. Her eyes were moving beneath the lids. He set his finger in her palm. "Miss Blum?" He spoke into her ear. "Do you hear me?"

He gave a light squeeze with his finger and felt a response.

"Are you comfortable?"

Nothing.

"Are you frightened?"

He thought he felt another squeeze.

"I want you to count, Miss Blum. Count with me. Five—" He touched her eyelids. "Four . . . three . . . two . . . and one." He moved his mouth closer to her ear. "All is well, Miss Blum. Tomorrow you will wake up feeling much better; then you and I will talk. Yes?" He gripped her hand more tightly. "Good. Now sleep."

He stood back up and looked over at Fraulein Bauer, who'd been quietly watching the whole exchange. Her eyes shifted quickly to her book, beneath which Perlman could see that same pair of wire-rimmed spectacles.

"Are those hers?" he asked.

She nodded, and just then Sister Margaret entered with two fresh bottles of distilled water. Perlman took her aside. "Do you know how much morphine they gave her?"

She checked the chart, but shook her head.

"Well, no more. I want her head clear from now on." He turned to leave, and looked to bid Miss Bauer good night. Her lips *were* moving. "Fraulein Bauer." He put his finger to his mouth. "Shshshshsh."

She gave a docile nod, but held his eye. There was something more. He motioned her to the hall. She tasseled her page and joined him just outside the door.

The matter seemed very grave. "Doctor, you say before want to know if there was something—if something changes."

"In German," said Perlman. "And please sit."

They took the hallway chairs. Fraulein Bauer had brought Sylvie's spectacles with her and clutched at them nervously as she spoke. "I don't agree with Herr Blum," she said in her native tongue. "When he says it all happened after she returned to school. No. It happened when she was here." She seemed quite sure.

"Tell me."

"You were here the Saturday, two weeks ago?"

"I was."

"You remember there was a storm?"

Perlman thought back. Saturday before last he would have been at Covent Garden, and yes, he did remember. The *Don Giovanni*. "I do, a thunderstorm."

"Yes." Miss Bauer's eyes began to well. "Sylvie and I were caught. We had gone out to get fish, for Herr Blum, and we were caught." She paused. Her lips were trembling.

"Yes?"

"And there was lightning."

"Yes."

A tear fell onto one of Sylvie's lenses.

"What are you telling me, Fraulein Bauer?"

"I am saying that *that* is when she changed." She pointed vehemently. "Not when she goes back to school. There, in the storm. In the lightning." She pointed at the floor, as if the moment were there beside her feet.

Perlman paused. "Are you saying she was struck?"

"No," she answered firmly. She waved her hand. "But there was a charge in the air."

"A charge?"

"Yes."

Again Perlman waited. "And it was after that—you both went home and she was upset and wouldn't eat."

"Yes. That is when. And then, then the next day she goes back to school, and it begins." She wiped her nose.

"After the lightning storm?"

Yes, she nodded.

Perlman offered her his handkerchief and stood. "Very good, Fraulein Bauer. I know it isn't easy, but I thank you for sharing this with me." He rested his hand on her shoulder and made a mental note to suspend all faith in anything further this woman had to say.

"I'll see you first thing in the morning."

She gave a brave nod, and Perlman started briskly up the corridor. If he hurried, he could still make the second set.

**H**e arrived at Queen's Hall near the end of the interval. Dr. Benjamin was standing by the drinks table, in customary pose, his chosen sherry a sniff's length from that ample and discerning nose.

Benjamin was Perlman's most consistent musical companion in London, and best friend. He also was an import—a French Sephardi, recruited from Paris to serve in the ophthalmology department at Bart's. He wasn't quite as versed as Perlman musically, but his tastes were dead-on, his insights unfailingly keen, humor likewise, and though in almost every particular he was rather unappealing physically—with the perching pince-nez, the faun eyes, fine hair, fragile sloping shoulders—still he possessed a kind of feline grace that let him enter any room and blend right in with no apparent dilution to either his intelligence or his exoticism. It was a fluidity of mind and manners that Perlman envied and considered the luckiest endowment of Benjamin's tribe. Disraeli had been something of a hero in that regard as well.

"How was the Sibelius?" asked Perlman.

"Very nice." Benjamin offered a glass. "But there was trouble in the brass again."

"Kelleher?"

Benjamin nodded with lazy lids. "It's getting to be an embarrassment."

"It's a disservice."

"Yes."

Bells sounded in the distance; the second set was calling. Perlman surrendered his drink, unsipped, and the two men filed to their seats, Perlman's—row G, a step up from last year's and slightly farther to the left, the better to see the hands of a pianist.

Perlman could feel as he settled in, though, he was in no mood. This is no way to go to a concert, just rushing over like this. Shepard's sherry had worn off, and he hadn't been able to smoke. He hadn't had time, which left his mind unfortunately dry, more prone to think than listen, which was too bad. More than ever he'd come to find it a priceless respite, after spending all day guiding other people's minds toward peace, to be able to sit back at night and let his own be guided by the likes of Beethoven, Schubert, Wagner, Saint-Saëns, Fauré. Or here by Grieg.

Alas, the present offering—a selection of excerpts from *Peer Gynt*— provided neither quite the challenge nor the lure to drown out the mastications of his intellect. He was able to listen for moments at a time, when the music served the purpose of his thoughts, but then his thoughts would muscle in again and return him over and over to one of his signature laments, a trusty little jeremiad he'd been honing over the years in his Chroniks and in his mind, and which could sustain an apparently endless number of variations depending upon the music prompting it, but whose basic complaint and basic consolation were always more or less the same.

In digest, this evening's rendition went like this:

Here was Grieg, another of the so-called nationalist composers,
which simply meant he wrote music intended to evoke
the history, the landscape, and the temperament of his
homeland—in this case, Norway. Perlman always liked the
nationalists. He applauded the nationalists, not just because they
defied the yoke of German musical hegemony—bless
them—but because, in borrowing so openly from the folk tunes
of their native countries, they tended to write music that was

more melodic in nature. As opposed to "motivic," that is,
a decidedly more German approach in which entire
thirteen-minute-long sonatas could be wrung from one
completely inconsequential three-note phrase. Obviously, in
certain hands—Beethoven's—the motif had provided for some
of the most astonishing creations ever achieved by man.
Perlman's fear was that, largely because of Beethoven, German
composers had spent so much of the last hundred years
worrying about things like structure and development and
investigation that, with a few notable exceptions (Schubert and
Wagner), they'd completely failed to cultivate the melodic
element that he still considered the essence of the art (Leonard
be damned). Or perhaps he was being too kind. Perhaps the
Hapsburg wells simply weren't as deep as everyone liked to
pretend, and maybe *that* was why the men who drew their
buckets had a growing tendency—a devastating weakness, it
seemed to him—to write moods instead of music.

   Not so Mr. Grieg. Here, for Ibsen's play, he'd provided
a veritable trove of melodies, marched on one after another,
stated once, twice, then ushered off again. Perlman briefly
quieted his mind to listen to an old favorite, "The Dance of the
Mountain King's Daughter," but only long enough to recognize
that this made his point as well. Beethoven never would have
thought of *that*. Perlman wasn't suggesting that Grieg was
anywhere near the composer Beethoven was—God forbid—
only that that gorgeous, slithering, snake of a melody, that
velvet ribbon now unspooling above the orchestra, would never
have occurred to Beethoven. It simply wouldn't have, and in
that respect, Perlman was quite happy to have Mr. Grieg and all
his "catchpenny phrases."* Call them what you will, it was
tunes like *that* that the tradition was built on, and grew by; and
not because of anything so special that Grieg had done *with* it,

*This referred to a line in an article, now ten years old at least, in which London's most en-
tertaining music critic, George Bernard Shaw, had assessed Grieg's music. Perlman still remembered.

mind. No, the reason the daughter's dance would last was because of the line itself, the strange seduction of the path that Grieg had laid. In the end, that was what mattered most—the what-comes-next. That's what brought the people back—the prospect of following a new trail, of being guided through passes they'd never have conceived on their own; braving the wildest contours, the most improbable modulations, but still in the end managing to hear music.

That was how man proceeded, yes? By confronting what might at first seem like chaos and, simply by applying his mind, manage to make sense of it. Tame it. The good modern melodist was like a frontiersman in that respect; the good listener, a settler. One need look no farther than the hallowed Herr Beethoven again to see that very process, the domestication of the wild. For how else was it that all those confounding, maddening stallions he let loose, that so enraged the grandparents of everyone sitting here, had in the course of two generations turned into such reliable war horses? And what better measure of man's progress? What more inspiring idea than that the toddling babies of tomorrow, born unto a world of unimagined dissonance, would hear, say, one of Debussy's *Images* and smile, clap their hands and laugh as though it were a nursery rhyme?

This was Perlman's hope, his desire and his expectation: that melody would keep expanding—always—and take the mind of the generous listener with it. It was the closest thing he knew to faith, and it was somewhere in the heady swoon that always attended its affirmation that Schnéevoigt and his orchestra piped in again. They'd just started up "Anitra's Dance," as if to remind the blushing doctor in row G that of all the peoples currently scouting the frontier, there were none to whom he looked with more yearning than the Russians. "Anitra's Dance" had that Slavic flair, did it not? That rhythm and wit? Enough at any rate to justify the final length of reverie—

Yes, the Russians were the ones. He'd known the moment he

first heard them. Back when he was just a pup at Nancy, he and
Parisot had taken a weekend in Leipzig to hear Rimsky-
Korsakov and his hundred-piece orchestra play an evening of
Russian fare at the Gewandhaus. The entire program was
dedicated to the Mighty Five,* but Perlman knew from the
very first phrase—Mussorgsky's *Khovanshchina*: this was the
music he'd been waiting for. The length of those lines, and the
shape—so strange, so defiant, and yet so lyrical. He felt as if
he'd been peering in on a whole new world, a whole new set of
emotions that music had yet to address—of menace, bitterness,
pride, and irony—and all of it underscored by that unfailing
rhythmic invention, that constant impulse to move, to dance.

There'd been a girl outside the hall, in fact, both nights he'd
gone—a golden-haired Russian girl, dancing for change. It must
have been fifteen years ago, but the image was still crisp in his
brain. How light she'd been, how loose and free, like a scarf,
teasing all the peevish Germans in the street. He could see them
just as well—the brutish, four-square Germans all turning away,
folding their arms and tucking their chins. The girl didn't mind.
She just kept on—taunting them with her ease, the inner rhythm
she possessed. Perlman had gone alone the second night and
tossed a florin in her fiddler's case, just for making it so clear:
how the Russians were drawing on an entirely different source
than their godly German forebears, so much more abundant and
mysterious. The Germans all were straining by comparison,
hammering every ounce of the life out of their tiny little musical
nuggets. The Russians simply let go, spinning endless golden
threads while their lovely daughter, sweet Anitra, danced.

Thereabouts it ended. Perlman's route was run. Once again he'd
managed to lament the death of German melodism, and once again

---

*Five St. Petersburg composers—Cui, Balakirev, Rimsky-Korsakov, Mussorgsky, and
Borodin—none of whom were formally trained, but who in the mid- to-late-nineteenth century took inspiration from the work of Mikhail Glinka, father of Russian music, to forge a
specifically "Russian" sound.

he'd found his solace in the East, where strange and distant melodies were rising from the cold horizon.

Schnéevoigt was nearly done as well. Madame Rolla waddled out onstage to sing the last reprise of "Solveig's Song," and Perlman did his best to listen, but it was still no use. Now that his head was clear again, he realized—all that intellection was nothing but a front, mustered up to distract him from the much more pressing matter which he could see was still there, standing right in front of Madame Rolla's heaving bosom:

The Blum girl.

Damn Shepard. Somewhere in the middle of Solveig's aching plea, Perlman realized he would not be seeing his mistress, Miss Ronan, tonight. If he'd known how much morphine they'd given the girl, then perhaps—probably she wouldn't come out of it till morning—but he simply couldn't risk her waking up with him not there.

He stayed for the second encore—an otherwise inspiring version of *Finlandia,* sunk by the incapacity of the aforementioned hornist, Mr. Kelleher, to hit a good E flat—but paused only briefly outside with Dr. Benjamin.

"Verdict?"

"They're awfully hard on him."

Benjamin agreed. "I thought 'Åse's Death' was a bit slow, though."

"The *tempi* in general."

Benjamin gave a nod in the direction of the Lord Admiral, but Perlman shook his head. "I have to go back to the clinic."

Benjamin's brow lifted. "Trouble?"

"Not trouble. I just think I should probably be there this evening."

Benjamin did not pry; he touched the brim of his top hat. "Mahler Thursday?"

Perlman bowed. "I'll be sure to have taken my nap." And off he went to fetch a cab.

# CHAPTER 5

The moment he entered Reception, Perlman could tell something was amiss, and when he reached the hall, he could smell it, a strange ammonia stench coming from room 3. He hustled down and opened the door. There were towels hanging all about the room, stained pale yellow. Both nurses were there—Sister Margaret soaking washcloths in a basin tub, Fraulein Bauer sitting by the bed, holding the girl's hand. Sylvie was free from Abram's tubes, but arched and trembling now. She'd drenched her gown, her skin was clammy, hair matted to her forehead, eyes open but blank.

Sister Margaret joined him at the bedside. "It began a half hour ago."

She drew back the sheet. The girl's legs were spread, her thighs rashed pink, and the merest trickle of clear urine ran from her urethra. The water was going right through her.

"You haven't given her any more morphine?"

"No." Sister Margaret replaced the towel with another.

Perlman covered the girl again, then leaned down and clasped her by the wrist. "Miss Blum." He spoke into her ear. "Miss Blum, do you hear me?" She gave no indication, she was shaking too frantically. He checked the wall clock and took out his pocket watch to synchronize the two. "It is 11:10, Miss Blum. Do you hear?" He held the watch up to her ear, unclasped it from its chain, and set it flat on the bedside table, beside the eyeglasses. "In two minutes this will end. You will hold your water and awake. Then I want to speak with you."

He stood straight again and released the girl's wrist. "Sister Margaret, remove this." He indicated the jug of water. "And Fraulein Bauer, I want all the sheets and towels out of here. I want the room clear."

He threw open the window himself, then stormed back to his office, down the hallway and through Reception. Damn Shepard. This was exactly the sort of thing he didn't want. He found his tobacco pipe on the office mantel and packed himself a bowl. Exactly the sort of thing—cleaning up other people's messes. He grabbed the matches from the desk and headed back.

Fraulein Bauer and Sister Margaret stood waiting, side by side. The towels were gone. The girl was ready. Perlman took her hand and checked his pocket watch. The two nurses consulted the wall clock. The second hand was passing the nine. They watched it tick up and up, and as it flicked over the twelve, the girl's trembling at that moment subsided; her body relaxed and her back touched the mattress again.

Perlman lifted the sheet. She'd stopped.

Fraulein Bauer looked up at Perlman and crossed herself.

"If you will excuse us, Fraulein Bauer. Sister Margaret, help her. She looks as if she could use a cup of tea."

Sister Margaret took Fraulein Bauer's hand and escorted her from the room, closing the door behind them.

Now it was just Perlman and the girl. She looked up at him, groggy, fawnlike. She seemed young.

"I am Dr. Perlman." He lit the bowl of his pipe.

"Hello." She smiled; her voice was weak.

"Do you know where you are?"

As she looked around the room, Perlman noticed her spectacles were on the side table again. "Would you like those?"

She shook her head. "I'm thirsty."

Perlman straightened. He didn't remember giving any instructions to drink. He poured her a glass from the pitcher at her bedside, and she sat up.

"Thank you."

Perlman watched her gulp it down. "Careful," he said. "Slow." She flatly disobeyed. "You're at a house I run. Your father brought you here last night. Your nurse, Fraulein Bauer, is down the hall."

She held the glass out, empty. He filled it, and she drank in gulps again, then said something he didn't understand, some foreign utterance: "*An-ey-oona.*"

"I'm sorry?"

She nodded over at the open window. "Oona would like a glass as well."

"Oona?"

"Would like some water." She gestured toward the window now. "You can leave it on the sill."

Perlman thought it best not to introduce any conflict, so he did as he was told. He set a glass of water on the sill and returned. "How are you feeling?" He palmed her forehead, which was cool.

"Not well. I think I'd like to take a bath." She noticed the basin. "Is that for me?" She stood up from the bed, in the same motion pulling the hospital gown over her head.

It was an arresting display, the sudden presence of such young flesh, and slender—he could see her ribs—but she stood before him unashamed, with the self-possession of spoiled aristocracy.

"But I'm not sure it's clean," he said. "There's your robe in the closet. I'll fetch your nurse."

"Thank you."

As Perlman started down the hall, he tried to think. He didn't remember giving her any instructions about drinking or bathing. Her compliance didn't quite make sense.

Sister Margaret and Fraulein Bauer were sitting in the reception area. Fraulein Bauer had a cup of tea in one hand and Sister Margaret's consoling hand in the other. "You may go in," he said.

Fraulein Bauer looked up at him, bewildered. "Doctor?"

"She says she'd like a bath."

Sister Margaret took the teacup from Fraulein Bauer's hand and helped her stand. The Fraulein looked back up at her, but Sister Margaret answered with an expression native to her features—faith. She'd been working here too long to question.

Fraulein Bauer started down the hall, on small and wary feet.

Perlman returned to his office, still troubled. Of course, he shared the Sister's view. He had performed enough "miracles" in the past five years for this evening's episode to seem a mere 'nother. The difference was that in the past he'd always understood how he'd done it. This time, he didn't—quite. Why was she being so agreeable? He lit the bowl of his pipe and went to check his office files, to see what he could find on the subject of water, hydrophobia.

He'd hardly begun when there came another knock at the office door. It was Sister Margaret again.

"Doctor?"

The door opened, and the Sister stepped aside for him to see: Fraulein Bauer was back in Reception, sitting in her chair again, staring blankly at the floor.

"Fraulein Bauer?" He went straight to her side. "Is something wrong?"

She didn't answer, but he knew already what it was.

"Sister Margaret, go check on the girl. Fraulein Bauer." Perlman knelt. "What is it? Tell me."

Her face was ashen. "*Das ist nicht Sylvie.*"

"What? What did she say?"

"*Das ist nicht sie.*"

Perlman stood again—he knew it. "Fraulein Bauer, stay here. Sister Margaret." He started down the hall and caught her at the door. "Sister Margaret, go see if you can calm Fraulein Bauer down."

She turned. "Is something wrong?"

"We seem to have an impostor."

Through the door, they both could hear the girl's voice, speaking that language again, a singsong gibberish. Perlman motioned the Sister away, knocked twice, and entered.

"Hello again." She was sitting on top of the covers in a pink and white robe, looking content, if anemic.

"Hello." He stopped a pace away and looked her in the eyes—blue, the color of the sea, and equally self-possessed. "Fraulein Bauer tells me you are not Sylvie Blum."

She shook her head. "Who is Sylvie Blum?"

"That is Sylvie Blum's robe you're wearing. And those are her glasses." He pointed to the bed table. She didn't seem to care. "What is your name?"

She answered with something impossibly long and garbled—Welsh-sounding, or Arabic, all *l*'s and *y*'s and *n*'s.

"Would it be all right if I called you Nina?"

She agreed.

"Nina, can you tell me where Sylvie Blum is?"

She thought. She seemed to be on the verge of shaking her head when she suddenly turned, distinctly as if the glass on the sill had said something. She spoke another line of gibberish.

"What is that?"

"Oona says why do you want to know."

"Does Oona know where she is?"

"Why do you want to know?"

"Because, we need to get Sylvie Blum bet—" He stopped himself. There was no need to engage her like this. "Lie back," he said. She did. He reached across and touched her forehead. "I'm going to count to three. When I come to three, you will let me see Sylvie Blum. Understood?"

She nodded, and lay back down against the pillow.

"One . . ."

She rested her arms.

"Two . . ."

She turned up her palms, and as she did, Perlman was shot through with an apprehension—he knew what was about to happen, but he could not stop himself, as if compelled by the cadence of his own order.

"Three."

The girl's spine fell slack. All wind, all breath of air seemed to leave her. Her chest slumped. Her skin burst out wet, but she still had so little fluid to give that a deathly yellow pallor swept over her, and her sockets darkened to a pale green. He looked down below the tie of her robe and pulled it open just enough to see the water spreading again, soaking the flannel beneath her.

"Blast."

He took the girl's wrist and spoke into her ear again. "Miss Blum, you will stop. You will stop on three." She was beginning to shiver, to quake. "One—two—three."

Her body remained taut, seized, ill, and now drenching the bed beneath her.

"Miss Blum?"

There was no response.

"Blast." He paused, as on the edge of a high rock overlooking black water, then leaned forward and spoke into her ear. "Nina."

The trembling stopped at once. She relaxed on the bed. Her head turned against the pillow weakly and looked up at him with those same blue eyes, now blaming. She was as pale as the sheet beneath her, but stable again.

Perlman said nothing at first. He poured her another glass of water from the bedside pitcher and held it out, but she was too weak to take it. She turned on her side and covered her mouth.

"Are you all right?" he asked.

She nodded, whimpering, and Perlman was surprised by his remorse. He felt almost ashamed for what he'd done, or tried to do. She slipped her arms out from the robe and slid beneath the covers. He took a towel from the chair and spread it beneath her.

"Will you sleep?"

She blinked slowly, not looking at him. He tapped the face of his

watch; it lay flat on her bedside table. "It's almost half-past eleven. You
may sleep until nine o'clock. Do you understand?"

She nodded.

"We'll count together, down from ten. I'll touch your shoulder and
you will fall asleep—a deep, dreamless sleep. Are you ready? Ten."

She echoed faintly from beneath her hands.

". . . nine . . . eight . . ."

They counted down to one together; then Perlman touched her
shoulder—she was asleep. He lifted the cover to her chin and turned
down the light.

Fraulein Bauer and Sister Margaret were back in Reception, the
Fraulein still in a stupor.

"Fraulein Bauer, I need to know. Have you no experience of this
kind of behavior?"

She looked him straight in the eye and shook her head.

"Absolutely?"

She shook her head.

"Very well. I've put her to sleep. I'd like you to do the same."

"But what about Sylvie?"

"We'll see about Sylvie in the morning, but don't worry. Sister Margaret will tell you—nothing here is uncommon." He looked to the Sister. "Does Fraulein Bauer have a bag?"

"It's in her room."

"Good. You'll see her down."

Perlman returned to his office. His medical journal was waiting
there, opened to the page of notes he'd already begun. He wrote the
time—11:30—but then he paused. His pen hesitated above the paper,
as if to commit this evening's episode to ink were to lend it a credence
it might not merit, and credence was the first step down many a wayward path. Better to wait. He closed the book.

Instead, he stole the Chronik from his coat pocket and returned to his flat. He poured himself a shot of brandy and then climbed into bed, propping himself up against his pillow.

*25 September*

*No Sibelius tonight. Perhaps tomorrow: forgo Bernheim presentation. But it is more clear than ever—only the Russians will satisfy. Perhaps a trip in the spring, if matters there have settled.*

He leaned over to take a last sip of brandy, then darkened his lamp to wait for sleep.

# TUESDAY

# CHAPTER 6

First thing in the morning, even before his tea, Perlman went to check on the girl. All was silent in the hall. Fraulein Bauer's door was closed. He entered room 3 quietly and found the girl on her stomach, dead away—she wasn't due to wake for another two hours. He brushed the hair away from her face. Still a girl, her head was pressed so hard into her pillow, her lips were slightly parted. Her cheek was round and blemishless but for a tiny star-shaped scar just down from her left eye. A small and slightly receding chin; brows firm, dark, solid. A more than capable mask. He pulled her left lid open. Her eyeball rolled, still sea-blue.

That was all he needed to see. He returned to his flat and fixed himself breakfast—tea and toast with marmalade. He read the morning *Gazette*, only grazing the words, while in a deeper register he reminded himself that he hadn't really been expecting Sylvie Blum to wake up in room 3. Sleep had been a stopgap measure, to allow more time for the morphine to clear her system, but he'd known that the problem wasn't just going to fix itself.

He conducted his eight o'clock with Mrs. Dillenbeck, a justly anxious woman from Liverpool who had been suffering chronic diarrhea for the last year. She took an unusually long time to hypnotize, so it was half past nine before Perlman returned to room 3 again.

He met Sister Margaret coming out. "She's awake?"

"She still wants her bath. Shall I heat the water?"

Sister Margaret didn't look well. Her eyes were glassy, but before Perlman could ask, the girl's voice came babbling through the door, in the same conversational tone as yesterday.

"Yes, a bath will be fine." He motioned the Sister away, then cleared his throat before knocking.

"Come in."

The girl was lying back against her pillow in a light blue hospital gown, alert in manner but still sickly in appearance—sallow and fragile, with dark circles beneath her eyes and the slightly furrowed brow that comes from prolonged languor.

"Good morning."

"Good morning."

"You slept well?"

"Yes, thank you."

He felt her forehead.

"Oona says good morning."

He checked her eyes again. The whites were a pale yellow. The iris still blue. "Have you eaten?"

"I had a glass of water. Do I have to have these?" She made a sour face in the direction of the black iron guardrails on the sides of her bed.

"We can keep them down where you won't see. I'll mention it to Sister Margaret. I'd like you to begin trying to eat, though."

The girl agreed. "Did the other nurse leave? The shorter one?"

Fraulein Bauer, she meant. "I don't think so. Would you like me to get her?"

No. She shook her head. "She didn't look very well."

"When did you see her?"

"This morning." She looked at him. She seemed to be on the verge of a sweet smile.

"Could you excuse me?"

He went and checked room 2 directly. The floor was bare, the bed stripped. Sister Margaret was coming back with clean towels now. Perlman intercepted her in the hall.

"Have you seen Fraulein Bauer?"

"Not this morning."

"Do you think she could have left?"

"I'd have thought she might come see you first."

"Yes." He pressed his lips. That was not good. He'd like to have had the chance to reassure the Fraulein. "Very well. Give the girl her bath, then see that she gets something to eat—fruit, some soup, toast, that sort of thing. Also, at some point, if you could head over to the library. Check Bernheim's files for everything relating to dissociative disorders." He paused. "That is, if you're up to it. You don't look entirely well, Sister."

"Tickle in the throat," she dismissed.

"All right. Then check Bleuler, too. He'll have something."

"Yes, Doctor."

"And when is my next appointment?"

"The rest of the morning is free for rounds, then you have a two o'clock, with Mrs. Woolsey."

"Good." He started for his office. "Do not disturb."

Perlman closed himself in and confronted his notebook. It was as he'd left it, open on his desk. He wrote quickly and decisively:

*25 September, 10:00*
*Two identities:*
   *1. Sylvie, "parent/root" hysterical catatonia*
      *—will not hold her water.*
   *2. "Nina," auditory and visual hallucination ("Oona")*
      *eager to recover*
      *disdains her condition.*
   *A paradox:*
   *—Nina (false) healthy*
   *—Sylvie (true) infirm.*
      *Feed the body,*
      *starve the mind.*

"Feed the body, starve the mind." It was a prescription which seemed fairly obvious. First things first: see to the well-being of the corpus, make sure that it's properly fed, bathed, and rested, while at the same time providing as little stimulus to the incumbent personality as possible, for a simple reason based on much experience: Dissociative personalities were highly, highly suggestible creatures. "*Miroirs brisés*," Bernheim called them, and it was true. Absent any real history, they tended to reflect whatever was put in front of them. The more they were exposed to, the more they would become, which made it very difficult to unmake them. By that same token, if they were given basically nothing to process or reflect, they tended to wither and fall, like the leaves outside.

The problem was this. This "Feed and Starve" approach took as its premise something that Perlman didn't really believe—namely, that the girl's physical recovery and "Nina" were two separable phenomena. Clearly they were not. He paid her three more visits that day, kept them deliberately brief and to the point, but each made it more clear than the last: "Nina" was the author of the girl's recovery. She ate everything that was brought her, slept like a cat, and bathed like a hippopotamus—four meals, two naps, and three baths, to be specific, not to mention the three liters of juice and water she drank, with no apparent protest from her previously fickle bladder. She did not ever seem to grow bored or restless as would any other child left so alone. She didn't ask for books or puzzles, but contented herself with the gobbledygook conversations she conducted with her imaginary friend, whom for that reason Perlman was willing to abide.

His last call came at six o'clock, an hour before he was to leave for this evening's concert—the Sibelius again.

He found her in bed, still wan, but her eyes were more clear. She'd lowered the guardrails and draped them with two blue blankets, to make it look as if the bed were skirted.

"And how are we feeling?"

"Better."

He palmed her forehead. "Good."

There was a pitcher of lemonade on her side table, half-filled, and an empty glass. "Did Sister Margaret bring you this?"

She nodded. "Would you like some? It's delicious."

"No, thank you. When did you last have a glass?"

She looked at him curiously. She could tell he was up to something, which was his intention. "Before you came."

"And that was delicious, you say?"

She nodded.

He took the pitcher and poured her another glass. "Have you ever tasted lemonade with salt?"

Her face soured. "Sounds awful."

"I agree, but sometimes at hospital I could swear they put salt in."

"I don't believe you."

"That's what it tastes like."

She shook her head. "But if they put salt in, then it's not lemonade."

"That may be, but I am telling you that sometimes I taste salt." He held out the glass to her, but she only looked at him suspiciously.

"Did you do something?"

"What do you mean?"

"Are you playing some kind of trick?"

He offered a deliberately vague expression and extended the glass farther.

She took it this time and sniffed the rim. "I can't tell." She tilted the lemonade to her lips, but kept them purposely closed. She licked them first, detected nothing peculiar, then downed two hearty gulps. "No. No salt." She set the glass back down on her side table.

"Very good," said Perlman. "Now listen to me. If I said to you that all men are mortal, would you know what that means?"

"What game is this?"

"No game, but would you know what that means—'All men are mortal'?"

"Yes."

"I am a man."

She nodded.

"So?"

She smiled. "You are a mortal."

He straightened. "Very good. Very good. Now, if I say 'No gods are mortal,' what would that mean?"

"No gods are men," she answered directly.

He straightened again. "That's right. Very clever."

At that moment Sister Margaret entered with the girl's supper on a tray—soup, broiled chicken, grapes. The girl plucked one from its stem. "Sister Margaret, do you know anyone who puts salt in their lemonade?"

The Sister spread a linen napkin across the girl's lap. "I'm not aware of anyone who would do such a thing."

"But the doctor says he knows people who do."

The Sister glanced at Perlman with a conspicuous but customary lack of expression. "If Dr. Perlman says so, it must be true."

The girl pursed her lips. "You're both very silly."

"Sister Margaret, will you be staying over this evening?"

"I expect so."

"Good. I'm going out again—"

"Where?" The girl sat up, excited.

"Just out," he said. "If you need anything, you know to ask the Sister."

"But where are you going?"

He looked at her. "Just out. Good night, Nina."

"Good night, Dr. Pearl Man." She spoke his name as two words. He was at the door when she called after him. "But, Dr. Pearl Man?"

"Yes."

"Oona says you're wrong, you know."

He offered only a twitch of a smile.


Back in his office, Perlman found himself facing his open notebook once again, stumped. The case was making less and less sense. His assumption from the outset—or from the moment of the girl's dissociation—had been that "Nina" was the product of an unconscious state, most probably induced by him, inadvertently, at some point early on.

He did not remember having hypnotized her, but that didn't mean he hadn't, and that's what dissociative disorders were in his experience—and Bernheim's, and Bleuler's and everyone else in the field—a side effect of hypnosis.

What troubled him was the fact that Nina did not really behave like a side effect or someone in a trance. Perlman could normally peg a dissociative personality in a glance. Certainly they could be dynamic, expressive, but they were shallow creatures; there were never very many notes in their scale, and what there were they tended to strike hard and loud, for attention. Not so Nina. This rather appealing, aristocratic child sitting patiently in her bed down in room 3 represented a performance of such polish, such composure and authenticity, he was inclined to think she must be some fantasy that Sylvie Blum had cultivated over time, without her nanny's knowing. Nina was simply too functional; too—to put it bluntly—conscious.

Which had been the purpose of this whole exchange about the lemonade and gods and immortality. One of Perlman's own published observations—his one clinical assertion—was that deduction and, to a lesser extent, induction were functions of the conscious mind. In other words, a patient who was in a trance or in a dream state would not be so quick to attest that this evening's lemonade had tasted the same as this afternoon's; and under no circumstance would she have been able to reason through the immortality of gods.*

The girl had had no trouble with either, obviously. In fact, in the case of the lemonade, she'd proven herself rather staunchly unsuggestible—the inference being that she, this figment of Sylvie Blum's hysteria, not only behaved like a fully conscious entity, she reasoned like one, too.

---

*The reason for these two deficits, in Perlman's view, was the tendency of the subconscious to impose an alternate set of conditions on its environment—laws of a different nature. In dreams, for instance, one inherited all sorts of false assumptions—that the weather depends on one's ability to capture the bees in a jar; or that one's grandmother is still alive and has been living secretly on the island of Crete. Such "alternate ontologies," as Perlman had dubbed them, were so fundamentally distinct from that of the conscious mind that the normal devices of reason simply did not obtain.

He wrote:

> *19:10. "Nina" holding strong.*
>   *appetite* ✓
>   *bladder function* ✓
>   *induction* ✓
>   *deduction* ✓

That was all. Again, he didn't want to stain the page with wild hypotheses. He closed the book, but wondered if he shouldn't skip the Sibelius tonight as well. Go see Bernheim instead.

# CHAPTER 7

Hippolyte Bernheim was the man most responsible for Perlman's career. It was Bernheim who had discovered him, back when Perlman was still studying brain anatomy at the University of Vienna. Bernheim invited him back to the clinic in Nancy, France, and there initiated him in the craft of hypnosis and suggestion. It was under Bernheim's tutelage that Perlman had developed into one of the best young hypnotherapists on the Continent, and it was also Bernheim who, after ten years' guidance, had arranged for Perlman's position at St. Bartholomew's—having passed him over for the spot in Vienna.

The years since had rendered justice—Perlman was thriving, Werner failing miserably—but Perlman's relationship with Bernheim had never quite recovered. He had yet to return to Nancy since leaving, and he didn't particularly like it when Bernheim came to London, as now. He felt as if he was being checked up on or, worse, upstaged, for they both knew that Perlman should have been the one giving lectures like this evening's—"The Use of Hypnosis and Suggestion in the Treatment of War Trauma." Really, it was only in an instance like the present one—caught flat-footed by such a confounding case—that he would ever seek Bernheim out.

This evening's talk had been at the Royal Hospital. The reception was at the home of their chief of staff, Dr. Kingston. Perlman arrived at a quarter past eight, and was reminded in a glance of why he'd initially intended not to come. Bernheim was over in a corner, surrounded by a covey of well-wishers, very much in his element. He noted Perlman's entrance with a broad smile and a nod; his white whiskers spread like wings. Drinking, thought Perlman.

He decided to let the old man have his moment and headed for the bar, where he bumped into Dr. Sulka, a generalist at the Royal Hospital, Hungarian, and an incorrigible proponent of Janáček.

"Dr. Perlman. Congratulations." He raised a glass of red wine to Perlman's brandy.

"On?"

"Oh, everything I hear. Good press. And I assume you've heard about Werner?"

Perlman pretended ignorance.

"They're closing him down," said Sulka. "Trial's over, and here look at you. Word is you're stealing some of the old man's business."

Perlman smiled humbly. "Easier territory, the English."

Sulka gave a good-humored nod, then propped up. "Oh, oh, thought of you. You haven't been getting *Die Freie Presse*, have you?"

Perlman shook his head. He could tell Sulka was about to launch in on one of his tirades about Eduard Hanslick's legacy, when from the corner of his eye he caught sight of someone across the room, a woman.

He touched Sulka's sleeve. "Is that Alexander Barrett's sister?"

"Who?" Sulka turned.

"There."

She was over by the window, holding court with a group of four.

"Why, yes. Yes, I think so."

Perlman knew it was. He'd recognized her instantly, though it must have been ten years since he'd last seen her—in Vienna, up in the first balcony of the Hofoper.

She looked older, but the years seemed to suit her. Her hair was still piled the same way, a lighter, slightly faded shade. Same posture: the raised chin, long neck, low elbows, and the grin, at once generous and mischievous. Handsome woman. Madame Helena. Helena Sophia.

"What is she doing here?"

"I wonder." Dr. Sulka clucked his tongue. "Wasn't she involved with the theosophists?"*

"Oh."

The logic here went without saying. Theosophists were flies upon the body scientific, buzzing around its nether regions out of a purported interest in rejoining reason and faith again. Hypnosis had long been of interest to them because of their mistaken but highly expedient belief that the trance state represented a kind of gateway to hidden realms, untold histories, and the like. In other words, they understood hypnosis to be a good way of *getting at* information, as opposed to being what it was—a good way of planting it.

Perlman did the Madame the favor of not mulling the farce, his mind turned so quickly to the likely cause of her wayward interest—which was her brother's sudden death, now seven years ago. Even as he stood there, Perlman could feel his heart throb, an echo of the helpless rage he'd felt himself—toward death which comes too early, and to talent; the death which deprives.

Strange, though. He felt as if he'd just been thinking about Alexander Barrett. He had—last night during the Grieg—or he'd summoned the spirit, at least, because Barrett was one of those Russians he'd been so keen for.

Which wasn't as incongruous as it sounded. Barrett's mother was from Moscow—Maddalena Nemirovich, the novelist—and one could hear it in his music. Those overlong, odd-angled melodies, that strange admixture of beauty and irony which was the Russian stock-in-trade. The last time Perlman had actually heard any Barrett must have been a year ago spring, at St. James's Hall. They'd played the chamber symphony. The young Mr. Beecham had conducted, and fairly well missed the point—where the humor, where the splendor. But the music had still managed to eke through, enough at least to reconfirm the rightful place of its composer.

---

*The Theosophical Society was founded in 1875 by Madame Helena Petrovna Blavatsky and Colonel Henry Olcott. Its purpose was to promote "scientific" research into all major religious doctrines, to create a synthesis of esoteric truths of the same, to promote the formation of universal human brotherhood, and to investigate all unexplained laws of nature and the powers latent in man. The first English lodge was established in 1888, and the European headquarters was located at 19 Avenue Road, London.

The question was why it had come to that. For it was true—ever since his passing, Barrett's work had been fading from the repertoire, so much so that now even his most popular pieces were having to serve as a reminder of themselves, a memorial to the man's appeal and promise. That had been the sense last spring, at least—the abiding impression throughout the hall—almost of having been scolded. *So there*, the symphony had wagged its finger back through the murk of Thomas Beecham's wand. *And don't forget again. I was the one. I was the hope.*

Perlman took a sip of brandy and let the warmth suffuse his body. The Madame—the composer's lovely, extravagantly elegant older sister—was over by the staircase now, listening indulgently as Dr. Wesley held forth on the subject of either magnets or butterflies.

Now, the reasons for Alexander Barrett's neglect were several, in fact, and not really so difficult to cite. Perlman had done so many times, on walks home from concert halls and in his Chroniks, often enough that on an occasion such as this, public and rife with distraction, he was still able to run them down in roughly the time it took him to finish his brandy.

He took a second sip and began:

### The Elegy of Alexander Barrett

First, of course, was the matter of the name, for though most everyone understood that Alexander Barrett was Russian, or half-Russian, there still remained—if only because of the name—the hovering scent of English blood; an odor which, however misleading, did lump Alexander Barrett in with a legacy to which no serious or self-respecting composer would willingly admit association—there with the likes of Charles Stanford, Granville Bantock, Frank Bridge. It was a grievous insult, even the comparisons to Elgar. Elgar. Such a pathetic display on the part of the English, this desperate need of theirs to put forward someone, anyone. Alexander Barrett was much more talented than Edward Elgar.

But entirely different, that was the point. The problem was that no one—not the English or the Russians—could really

claim him as their own, his life was so hither and yon. Son of
Henry Barrett, iron magnate and onetime ambassador to
Russia, the young Alexander would seem by all accounts to
have spent his childhood shuttling back and forth from manor
to dacha to manor again. It was an upbringing which almost
put one in mind of Mendelssohn or Mozart, or would have, if
Barrett hadn't spent the better half of it in a country forever
destined to struggle beneath the long slope of Western Europe's
nose. Even so, Barrett was another of those golden boys, those
prodigal fonts of music, about whom all the same sorts of stories
were told—of performances he'd given this queen here, that
duke there; of the oratorio by Saint-Saëns which was written
with the young Barrett's soprano specifically in mind; of the
march he composed at the age of six, which would crop up
again as the second theme in the *moderato* of the piano concerto.

He was that sort, and whether any of these notes and  anecdotes
were true or not, they still conveyed a probably accurate sense
that Alexander Barrett had known little in the way of want or
hardship. Not that Perlman would ever have held this against him,
but it did seem that Barrett's was precisely the sort of privilege that
an increasingly populist, democratic, and (in certain corners)
socialist world was beginning to resent. At least to judge from the
aspersions that now attended the mere mention of his name. The
more forgiving chose to damn with the faint praise that the young
Mr. Barrett had done all that one could ask of him really: to a
rarefied and vanishing existence he had provided an equally
rarefied and vanishing score. Others less kind questioned outright
the legitimacy of his standing, such as it was. The only reason his
work had found a place in the repertoire was favoritism, said they,
elitist-aristocratic patronage. That and the fact that his more
popular pieces were of a light enough, confectionery nature that
they did make a nice addition to most evenings' menus.

Not work of substance, though. It was common knowledge
that he'd never graduated from any conservatory, that he'd
withdrawn from the Free School after only two years. Perlman

had always understood this to have been the principled protest
of a young man who was an avowed enemy of all musical
rhetoric, which he (and Perlman) believed the conservatory
education only propagated. In the minds of his detractors,
however, such complaints were deemed excuses. Barrett was an
essentially lazy composer, as nearly all the music that proceeded
from his pen thereafter testified—so sensually extravagant, so
technically lax. It simply hadn't the weight, said they, neither the
grand emotions nor the formal discipline. It lacked ambition.

But of course, this was all just the German bias again. All
these critics were only restating in the most unflattering terms
what no thinking ear could miss. Young Barrett composed
within a tradition—Slavic or French, if you will—that openly
prized color over constructional logic, entertainment and
sensual beauty over philosophical depth. Moreover, Barrett was
an essentially programmatic composer—best, or happiest, when
called upon to depict. His oeuvre was stuffed with all sorts of
poems, ballets, essays—"Music for petting a cat," "Music for
walking the dog." All those Blake songs. Gebrauchsmusik.
Hausmusik, Barge music. He suffered from an English
weakness for ceremonies and commemorations, from teas to
consecrations. The bell hymn of St. Paul's was an example.*
Even the "Nonsense" scrolls,† when you thought of it.

The point being, there probably wasn't enough of the

---

*St. Paul's had been Barrett's English alma mater. Not the most diligent of students, Barret had,
as a parting gift and in exchange for a diploma which would not have been forthcoming otherwise, composed a hymn for the famous campus bells, even going so far as to purchase the B flat
necessary to complete it. Perlman had gone up to hear it two or three times—they still played
it every year at graduation. Elgar with a twist, and well worth the trip, but impossible to hear
anywhere else.

†The story went that Barrett had been under contract with the people at Welte-Mignon, mak-
ers of the premier reproducing pianos. They'd commissioned him to record some of his own
pieces—pastorales and songs without words. During the session no one had been the wiser.
Barrett recorded over forty rolls of music. It wasn't until they sent him the masters for his cor-
rections that he revealed he'd extemporized the whole thing. Welte was furious and canceled
the contract. He wasn't going to go to the trouble and the expense of printing forty rolls of nonsense, and vowed never to work with Barrett again. So just the masters existed, and the tragi-
cally elite circle who'd actually heard them.

sturdy stuff, the traditional forms—symphonies, sonatas, concertos, and such. For despite the efforts of Barrett and his contemporaries to stretch the forms, there still remained, in the cringingly conservative world of the listening public, a yearning for Absolute Music. Barrett simply hadn't provided much on that score: one concerto Perlman could think of, two or three trios, and three symphonies, two of which were a single movement and therefore of questionable stock.

Even worse for the sake of his standing, this fixation with the more open setting of program music encouraged Barrett to cultivate a melodic and harmonic idiom of unforeseen, and to that degree, baffling, ingenuity. Left to his own devices, Alexander Barrett wrote *the* longest, the most spontaneous and downright defiant melodic lines of any composer of his generation. This was probably his signature, in fact—the endlessly tumbling, evolving subject, a kind of horizontal indulgence which was both an affront to musical academe— investigation being the watchword of True Art—and a frustration to the public, if for no other reason than it made his later work very difficult to familiarize oneself with. As opposed to a Tchaikovsky, for instance, who settled upon much simpler themes and then pounded them at you eleven different ways, Barrett was more inclined to let his subjects go, like a kite at the end of an endless spool. The first theme of his first piano sonata took eighty-eight bars to state, for instance, and then never recurred, imagine.

The impression that such work left upon an audience could not help but seem fleeting, at least on first hearing. And somehow this, the experience of the virgin listener, came unfairly to reflect on the efforts and methods of the composer. There had been a cartoon in *Punch* that captured the perception: a boyish Barrett perched on a high stool beside a giant scroll of sheet music, marking it madly as it unfurled. That was the trouble, it seemed—never looking back, never giving shape. A spinner of ephemera. Victim of his own good fortune was Alexander Barrett—composer of undeniable gifts but deniable substance.

Perlman took another small sip, but barely tasted it.

For then, of course, there was his personal life, which didn't help matters. Subject of no nation, student of no school, Barrett was the original decadent. Overly generous, probably a touch naïve, epicurean, reveler in all things fine (as well as some degenerate), he was known to have exercised a kind of moral autonomy nowhere better evinced than in the relationship he shared with his sister, Helena, the woman standing across the room right now—

Now by the stairs.
Now raising a glass of red wine to her lips.
"But she hasn't been in London?"
"Who?" Dr. Sulka awoke from his neglect.
"Madame Barrett."
"Oh." He looked back across the room. "No, I think you're right—I think this is her first time back. I believe she spent some time in India."
"India?"

A poet in her own right, librettist and unofficial dramaturge of all her brother's narrative efforts, Madame Helena was also his principal companion and muse. No less an authority than Solovyov (the philosopher and apparent spurned suitor) had written that if Alexander Barrett turned out to be the great composer of his generation, it was no wonder. He had Helena Sophia to write for.

And she, him to care for. That was the generally accepted understanding. Though protean in his art, Alexander had not been a robust specimen physically. Perlman wasn't exactly certain of the cause—polio, scarlet fever, collapsed lung.

Whichever, he was not a well man, nor one who apparently respected his limitations. This was left to the Madame. Wherever he toured, she went, too. Where he taught, she followed. They shared suites. They kept townhouses in several artistic capitals—Paris, Leipzig. The one in London was over in Chelsea, the largest home at Charles Place.

The question was whether they ever shared the same bed. The cognizenti liked to whisper—*sp-sp-sp*—but Perlman never paid the rumor much mind. Life was more complicated than that, more obscure and ultimately mundane. And the only real "evidence" anyone ever seemed to point to was the *adagio* of the piano concerto that Alexander had dedicated to her. Perlman knew the piece well and agreed that in certain hands it might seem a tad passionate, perhaps not the most appropriate lyric to be dedicating to one's sister, but hardly proof of any carnal longing. Really, it was just a lovely theme.

Like all Barrett's themes, damn it. Really, the whole business—the whispers, the condescension, the insinuations— Perlman found very irritating. Alexander Barrett didn't lack ambition. He'd simply pursued a different kind of ambition: to play at the outskirts, to scout the frontier. If he sometimes failed to explore a theme as fully as he might, that was only because he had so much more to get to—more of the stuff itself.

Alas, he hadn't had more time. He died at thirty-two, not long after Perlman's own thirty-second birthday.

Perlman had been in Paris when he heard, at one of the Société des Nouveaux Concerts at La Place de la République. Camille Chevillard was conducting. He'd led a basically French evening—Franck, d'Indy, Chabrier. But then at the end of the first encore he had turned and spoken. "A la mémoire d'un cher ami." The orchestra began, the cellos wreathed them all in the opening statement of the famous *adagio*, and Perlman understood right away. He supposed it was because the gift, the always unexpected pleasure of his music was right there filling the hall around them, but the realization had hit with an unexpected force. No more of this. By the time the French horn took up the second theme, Perlman was weeping in his seat, as he'd not wept at the death of his own father.

He would not repeat the performance now but, on the strength of its memory, act. He drained the last of his glass, plucked a fresh brandy from the bar, and started across the room.

**M**adame Helena was standing by the window again, a silhouette against the light of the streetlamp. She was holding court among a group of four, one woman and three men, none of whom Perlman quite recognized. He stopped just outside their circle, near enough to hear, not so close as to interrupt.

She was saying something about gold.

"But was it mined?" asked an older gentleman—and strangely familiar, this one—with a ruddy complexion, and a bushy, cheery mustache, which spread to an equally cheery set of muttonchops.

"No, that's just what he was suggesting," the Madame replied, "that they were able to produce it from some other mineral."

"Alchemy?"

"I suppose." She noted Perlman out of the corner of her eye and flexed her brow slightly, invitingly. "That's why he was saying the capital should have been called the Golden City—it might literally have been."

The coterie nodded. "Interesting," said the muttonchops. "Midas and all."

"Yes. My thoughts." Again she glanced at Perlman, smiling this time. "Ah, but Dr. Perlman thinks we are fooling ourselves."

Perlman straightened—pleasantly goosed by this, the mention of his name by such a renowned stranger. "Hardly." He gave a faint bow of introduction. "I only wonder about these stories, how gold would retain its value among a people such as you describe."

The Madame turned the circle to face him. "How do you mean?"

"Well, the value of gold consists in large part upon its rarity, does it not, in which case it strikes me that in a society such as you describe, capable of creating it at will, to gild the city would be a bit like hammering tin everywhere."

The coterie turned its attention to Madame Helena. She stood back with a clever smile, a charming smile, caught somewhere between admiration and dismay. "Have you ever looked at gold, Dr. Perlman?"

"From time to time," he punned, instinctively reaching for the pocket of his vest; not that he would have removed his watch—to produce such a handsome instance, on cue, would have been a bit showy. Still, he'd made the gesture. She saw, too. The watch was not there.

"Allow me." She lifted her right hand out between them—ungloved, a slender hand, of age and culture and breeding, and on whose third finger rested a simple golden band. "The value of gold consists not in its rarity, Doctor, but in the fact that it resembles the sun, which more cultures than not have regarded as a godhead, the symbol chosen to express God to those who could not see God. Therefore, to gild the city would not have been to hammer tin everywhere. Rather, it would have been to offer praise and thanks to God, and to surround themselves in His glory."

"Ah." For the first time he noticed her skin. Luminous. Like a purebred dog, he thought: gorgeous coat, and completely mad.

He took her fingers. "August Perlman."

"Madame Helena Barrett."

The rest of the company politely receded to the mantel.

"I didn't see you at the lecture, Doctor."

"No." Again he was struck by the level of attention she seemed already to have paid his existence. It relaxed him. "I'm afraid I couldn't make it, but I wanted to see Professor Bernheim before he left."

"You were a student of the Professor's?"

"Of a kind. I was his chief of staff."

"I wasn't aware. Does that mean you're an adherent, then?"

Perlman paused. "I'm not sure I know what you mean."

"*Que tout est suggestion,*" she offered quickly, "*crédivité*—all that?"

"Well, I'm not sure I like to think of it in terms of 'adherence,' but yes, I believe there's a great deal to be said for the power of suggestion."

"Oh, no one could deny that."

She looked at him. There had been a note of pleasant skepticism in this remark. "And what could they deny, Madame?"

"Well." She took a moment to choose her tack. "I mean, I think it's as you say. Suggestion is pervasive and powerful. In fact, there's so much suggestion in the air, I wonder how one would propose to control it."

This seemed an odd question, given the lecture she'd just attended. "Hypnosis," he answered simply.

"Yes, but as I understand, the value of hypnosis is simply that it leaves the patient that much more prone to suggestion—more open."

"Yes, that's right."

"So?"

He hesitated. "I'm afraid I don't understand the question."

"So? Who is doing the suggesting?" She looked at him—her eyes, a teal blue, beneath hillen lids, and uncommonly opaque. "Who is doing the suggesting, Doctor?"

At that moment the answer seemed so clear he could barely keep from speaking it: The one doing the suggesting, Madame, is you.

"You smile."

He shrugged, caught, and retreated to his glass for another sip. "So you haven't been here in a while?"

She sobered. "Seven years."

"Do I understand you were in India?"

"Oh, ages ago. Six years, I suppose."

"Didn't suit you?"

She nodded. "Too hot. And ultimately I suppose one has to play the hand one is dealt."

"Does that mean you've been in Russia?"

She nodded. There was a perceptible twinge at the corners of her eyes. He wondered if she'd been there in December for the uprising. He wondered if that was what she was doing here now.

"Well, welcome back. Are you finding it as you remembered?"

"A bit lonelier," she said, confiding an intimacy which seemed almost inappropriate, and yet her eyes remained so open, so welcoming, he replied in kind.

"That's part of the reason I came over, actually. I don't mean to kindle grief, but I just wanted to say, to confess— I don't think I ever expressed to anyone how upset I was when your brother passed away."

Her eyes flared. "Did you know him?"

"No. Just his music."

"Oh," she calmed. "Well, that's very kind."

"I wish I could say, but no, it's pure selfishness. I wanted to hear more."

She agreed. "You are a music lover, Dr. Perlman?"

And here he swelled a moment, savoring the prospect of a modest answer—"Somewhat"—but just as he opened his mouth, the two of them were suddenly clamped in the outstretched arms of another. "Is he a music lover?" Bernheim burst in, his breath sweet with port. "*Dr. Perlman est un connoisseur. Il etait le plus grand amateur de musique en France, et puis maintenant en Angleterre.*" He laughed. "*Oui?*"

The Madame looked back at Perlman with a new regard. "Is that so?"

"I try to keep up."

"Do you play?"

"The piano?" The question surprised him. "Some. Not as well as I should. I have a brother who's a pianist."

"Leonard," Bernheim growled. "How is Leonard?"

"He's well. He's teaching now at the Royal College."

Madame Helena seemed not uninterested in this, but took the diversion as an opportunity to pry herself free of Bernheim's lingering grasp. "Do you know? I should probably be going."

"Oooh," Bernheim soured his face.

"I'm afraid, yes. But, Professor, an enlightening talk. Much food for thought."

She turned. "And, Dr. Perlman, a pleasure meeting you."

"My pleasure." Perlman held her eye. They touched hands again, and she withdrew. The older gentleman was waiting for her. She offered her arm, and they started across the room for their coats.

As Perlman watched her go, Bernheim let out a low, guttural murmur of appreciation; then his eyes began darting about the room again. "Did you read the book I sent?"

"The book?"

"Yes. On dreams; the Freud. You remember him."

"Oh yes." He did, barely.* "I'm sorry, I haven't had the chance."

Bernheim gave a stung smile. "All's well at the clinic?"

Perlman hesitated. This was the reason he'd come, after all—to seek advice about the Blum girl—but as he looked at Bernheim now, punchy from wine and attention, he realized that he had no real interest in anything his old mentor had to say.

"All's well. How long are you staying?"

Bernheim proceeded to detail his schedule for the next several days: more talks and presentations. They agreed he would come by Monday afternoon for their annual exchange of paperwork, then Bernheim followed his nose back to the bar. Sulka was waving him over to meet another young lady.

Pearlman noticed there was a captain's clock on the mantel. It read 9:30. He thought perhaps he might go see Miss Ronan.

/

---

*A young Sigmund Freud had paid a visit to Nancy in 1889. They'd shown him some of their techniques, but Perlman hadn't thought of him since: another Wien Juden, with a taste for theorizing. He had published a couple of books recently, whose modest ripples had apparently finally reached Nancy. Bernheim had sent Perlman a copy about a month before, but Perlman hadn't bothered to open it, sensing only hostility in the gesture—as now.

# CHAPTER 8

Tuesdays she worked at Kennerly's, the pub beneath her flat in Southwark, waiting tables while she awaited parts. Miss Ronan was an actress and a singer in addition, though Perlman had never heard her singing voice.

The Underground took twenty minutes getting there. They saw each other as he entered, but offered no greeting. He sat at the bar. If tonight was a problem, she'd tell him there. He ordered a plate of bangers and mash from the publican, a pint of ale, and the *Gazette*. Miss Ronan came and took his plate when he was done. She'd be off soon. He ordered a second pint and started upstairs with the paper.

Her flat was on the third level. Perlman used his key and went directly to his place on her sofa, his back to the streetlamp. In its inadvertent light, he could see that the room was cluttered with more pillows and sundries than any amount of tidying could ever straighten, heavy with drapes and blankets and curtains to muffle the street noise. There was a new chair, a boudoir chair, set on the other side of the rug, and a Chinese curtain. Her bank was in its place on the side table, a blue ceramic box beside a small German clock he'd given her. It was 10:55. Perlman took a twenty-pound note and tucked it underneath. He set his pint down on the floor, opened the paper at his feet, and waited.

Miss Ronan was Dr. Perlman's fifth mistress—of note. He'd been keeping one ever since his first year at Nancy, the same year as the scandal with Dr. Guignol. Guignol had abused his position with a young hysteric—a male. Bernheim had managed to control the damage, public and private, but the point was made. Men of their profession, of their cultivated ability to manipulate, should not be tempted. They should be sated. Most of the unmarried members of the staff began using the professional women in town. Perlman and Parisot established contacts in Paris and Leipzig as well, as they often went to concerts on weekends and liked to have a place to go when the music was over. Perlman kept only one in Leipzig—the opera was in transition, and Perlman couldn't stand Reinecke, the conductor. In Paris, though, Lamoureux had just been getting started, so Perlman had had two women there, Mmes Negron and Giustine, the one he'd taken to hear the Berlioz. He shuddered to think of it now. She'd clicked her teeth through the *Carnival* overture and slept through the remainder. He could still see the expression on Parisot's face. A lesson learned: Never mix pleasure with pleasure.

Miss Ronan would never ask such a thing. She understood—hers was a simple role, to serve a simple need.

And he could hear her now, her feet in the hall. As the key slid in the lock, he felt a faint rise in his loins—Pavlov's most reliable dog.

The bedroom was on the other side of a black velvet curtain. She lit a lamp and was there a few minutes. He followed the sound of her feet. Into her loo. He heard the water run in her basin, then she stepped out a moment later in her white dressing gown and stockings, her hair a wild red frazzle. For the first time she looked at him, with tired eyes but game; he asked so little. She walked up slowly and stopped on the newspaper, an arm's length away. Perlman sat back slightly and Miss Ronan simply lifted her robe for him. The hem rose past her knee, past the top of her stockings, her skin a mottled pink and white. She paused a moment before lifting it the final length, then there she was, ablaze in the gaslight.

She set her hands on her waist while he unbuttoned himself. He never let them see until he was like this, full and indistinguishable.

Miss Ronan didn't seem to notice. She took a step forward, from the paper to the floor, and Perlman slid to his knees. She widened her stance to make room for him, but he still kept his distance and reached down between his rumpled shirttails to take himself in hand.

This was all he wanted. This was all he asked.

He shut his eyes and leaned in slightly to where he could almost feel her warmth. He tightened his grip, found his rhythm, and his brain began to pump with urges, images.

The first right off, and not for the first time—that this was not Miss Ronan here in front of him. Not Miss Ronan's mottled skin beneath a flannel gown, but smooth, lithe thighs, swimming beneath something much more sheer and gossamer. Her hips not full and round like Miss Ronan's, but narrow and slung forward—left knee open and crooked, heels together, a casual rendering of first position. He could even feel her scarf across his face, and another surge within him. Without his meaning to, his cheek pressed against Miss Ronan's lap, and he felt a quick slap on the top of his head.

"Sorry."

She resumed her pose. He closed his eyes again, quickened his pace, and imagined the legs. He could see their slender outline against the backlight of the kitchen—but there was someone else now, too, stepping out from behind the Chinese curtain, nude. Standing there so straight and unashamed—that sterling immodesty. It was the Blum girl, taking a step this way to see more clearly.

He felt another surge, and now there was a third figure, sitting in Miss Ronan's boudoir chair, shifting, lifting a gloved hand to her chin, as if it were the first box at the Paris Opera and he the show. And the girl now joining her. The two of them, the Madame in all her jewels and finery, the girl with nothing on, but not a care—invited guests in the first box, both openly watching him, as he knelt before the street girl, lost inside her veils, arching up beneath her like a hook. He felt their eyes upon him, another surge, and the onset of his final pleasure. The Madame was grinning contentedly, the girl more curious; the Madame turning out her hand, the girl replying in kind, and finally

Perlman could not contain himself any longer. As their fingers touched, he shuddered twice and then released—a brief fleck on page 3 of the *Gazette*.

A dizzy, pounding silence. Then he felt Miss Ronan's hand on the bald patch at the top of his head. She was pushing him back onto the couch. Perlman swung his legs up and laid his head against the armrest pillow. She unlaced his shoes and slid them off. She used his shirttail to tuck him back inside his pants, then covered him with his blanket.

He was only vaguely aware of her movements after that. She knelt down quickly to retrieve the paper, folded it over, and made her way back to the kitchen first, to snuff the lamp, then to her room behind the curtain—her sanctuary.

In the thin light it shed, piercing the drape and casting itself an arrow on the floor, Perlman drifted, not surprised. Two new women had entered his imagination. This was to be expected, but now was done. Now was to forget again, to "parenthesize," as Parisot had liked to say. In his mind, Perlman summoned the voice. *Now rest*, it said. *Let sleep erase the memory of this, as waking pushes away all memory of dreams.*

It was 11:09.

*Go to a dreamless sleep and awake at 7:00.*

He counted down from twelve. He did not come to one. His last conscious thought was of Miss Ronan's light, still on.

# WEDNESDAY

# CHAPTER 9

There had been a fire in the Underground, so Perlman didn't get back to the clinic until 9:30, barely time to wash up and change his clothes before his appointment with Monsieur Légère, the little Belgian. In Reception he found a younger, moon-faced nurse sitting in Sister Margaret's chair—a Sister Antoinette, whom he didn't like the looks of; too young and skittish, her round brown eyes primed for admonishment.

She confirmed Perlman's suspicion. Sister Margaret had awakened with a slight fever and would try to come in later. In the meantime, was there anything he needed? She'd fed the girl breakfast, observed nothing untoward.

Perlman left her there without instruction—the less she knew the better—then went to take at least some fleeting relief in his session with Légère—*le petit* fellow, whose psoriatic arms were now bathed in the golden light of suitability, of how-this-was-all-supposed-to-work. He was under by 10:05. They ran through their exercises three times without a hitch, and *au revoir.*

Then back to room 3. He found the girl sitting on the bed on her knees. There was a bowl of fruit on her side table and a half-eaten pear on her pillow, but she was focused on something down in front of her, a smooth pond amid the green rumple of her blanket. He saw her fingers dark with color and realized it was a sketch pad. Beside it was a jar of pastels.

"How are we feeling today?"

"Better." She didn't look up. He came around beside her to see what she was drawing. A fairy-tale image—a maiden in a golden tower, overlooking a blue river, winding through green hills, beneath a moonless midnight sky.

"Where did you get the pad?"

"The Sister. Can you tell who it is?" She sat up to assess the whole. He shook his head.

"Oona."

He looked again. The figure in the tower was leaning over her rail to see what appeared to be a whale in the water below. The colors were all deep and solid. The lines were certain, the perspective true, though that was hardly surprising. Dissociative personalities were notorious for their artistic talent. Back at Nancy, Perlman had had a patient who, during one particular episode, demanded to see a piano, then sat down and played the *Goldberg Variations* by ear, despite having had no previous musical training. So the girl's facility was nothing new. It was the conception that troubled him, quite literally an inventiveness he thought it best to discourage, and quickly.

The bowl of fruit was at her bedside—a second pear, a bunch of grapes, and a yellow orange.

"Do you know what a still-life is?"

The girl shook her head.

"That's when you draw what you see. The fruit, for example." He took her pitcher of water and set it beside the bowl. "It's good practice."

She gave an only mildly interested nod, and there was a knock at the door.

"Dr. Perlman?"

"Yes, Sister."

She spoke from the other side. "There's someone to see you, who wants to talk to you."

He knew right away it was Herr Blum. He set the pad back down on the bed. "Try drawing the fruit. I'll come back and see how you've done."

The girl tilted her head graciously and took another bite of pear.

From the far end of the hall, Perlman could see Blum down in Reception, pacing. Quickly he ushered Sister Antoinette through to room 2 and closed the door.

"Did you give the girl that sketch pad?"

"From the children's ward." She cringed. "The girl said—was that wrong?"

"Sister Antoinette, listen to me. All I want is for that girl to eat, to drink, and to rest. Do not talk to her. Do not play with her. Do not ask or answer any undue questions. If she must draw pictures, I'd prefer she confine herself to still-lifes. Do you think you can see to that?"

She nodded. "She mentioned wanting a bath."

"Well then, give her a bath. Just wait until I've shown her father into my office."

"Yes, Doctor."

He waved her out of his way, took a moment to brace himself, then started down the hall.

## CHAPTER 10

**D**r. Perlman, what is happening here?"

Perlman extended his hand, but Blum didn't take it. He was much more impressive than the night before last—clean-shaven and wearing a black wool suit that broadened his shoulders and narrowed his waist—but he was as restless as a caged animal. Perlman showed him into his office and closed the door behind them.

Blum refused a chair. "I have a mind to take her right now, Dr. Perlman. I don't like this. I don't like what I'm hearing."

"What are you hearing, Herr Blum?"

"Fraulein Bauer was very distressed when I came home last night."

"Well, Herr Blum, there was an episode. Nothing out of the ordinary, but I'd doubt it's the sort of thing that she is used to."

"She said you did something, Doctor. She said that Sylvie was not herself."

"Herr Blum, I haven't done anything. I haven't even begun the therapy, and I will not until Sylvie has her strength back."

"Don't lie to me, Perlman." Blum was looking at him intensely now, Jew to Jew—but there was something in his eyes, a dodge. Perlman's instinct told him—Blum was not seeking answers, he was holding them.

"Herr Blum, please sit down."

He waited for Blum to comply, then crossed behind his desk and took a seat himself. "You need to understand, your daughter is in a very delicate condition. She is still severely dehydrated and anemic. She is a full stone underweight, which on her frame is a considerable deficit, and she has been heavily sedated. My point, Herr Blum, is that in such a vulnerable state she may be prone to all kinds of unusual behavior—but none of it uncommon, I assure you."

He tapped the folders on his desk to indicate the wealth of precedent, and noticed there was something new—a long brown envelope on top, with his name on it.

He continued. "We can be thankful that she is young, though, and resilient. I can see that already."

"Where is she?"

"She's in her room, but I'd have to insist, I don't think it's a good idea your seeing her."

"And why is that?"

"Because you are her father. You are worried about her, which I understand, but worry is contagious. I don't want that for her. I want her trying to get better. You understand."

He seemed to, for the moment. "But then tell me what Fraulein Bauer was saying."

"Fraulein Bauer saw something she did not recognize. I don't blame her for being upset, but I assure you, the ship will right itself just as soon as Sylvie has had a few more days to regain her strength, to eat and drink—"

"She's eating?"

"And drinking, yes. So let's all just try to be patient, wait until she's regained her strength, and then I think you should come and see her. Absolutely, I think it would be good for her, and for you."

Blum's posture slackened. "I cannot lose her, Doctor." He sat like a sack of grain, eyes bereft, looking out the office window, which opened to nothing in particular.

"Herr Blum, may I ask—why is Sylvie's mother not here?"

Blum's lids winced painfully, and for a moment it looked as if his expression might break, but he caught himself.

"Is she not well?"

"Doctor, this cannot happen again. I don't deserve this."

"Where is your wife, Herr Blum?"

He was looking down at his hands, shaking his head faintly. He could not say it.

"Is she at Burghölzli?"*

Blum's head stilled. "Bellevue," he said quietly, and Perlman felt a ghostly blow to the abdomen. Fortunately, Blum was not looking, and so did not see his reaction, a brief flutter in the eyes. He pretended to make a note, then stood and rounded the desk again. "Herr Blum"— he spoke low, and slow—"you've done the very best thing you could have, bringing your daughter here. You're just going to have to trust me."

Blum looked up. His eyes were swimming.

"Will you? Trust me?" Perlman set his hand on the thick, round hump of Blum's shoulder and summoned every last ounce of his assurance. Finally Blum nodded. "Good." Perlman gave his shoulder a faint squeeze, and Blum stood.

Quickly, but not hastily, Perlman escorted him back to Reception and helped him with his coat. "Herr Blum, I appreciate your coming by, and you should feel free. But do remember, patience. Shall we say Monday morning?"

Blum nodded. He looked exhausted.

"And don't worry. You'll have your Sylvie back." He spoke the last in German.

Blum exhaled a long blue mist, and made his way out into the midday drizzle.


**P**erlman started down the hall again, wondering if he shouldn't have bought more time. Monday Bernheim was coming as well, which meant a great deal of paperwork, which meant less focus than he'd have liked, though he supposed it hardly mattered. Sylvie's mother at

*The Burghölzli University Psychiatric Hospital in Zurich, Switzerland.

the Bellevue Sanitorium—that meant nervous degeneration most likely, which had a nasty way of passing down. He was almost certain now, this was all a function of brain lesions—biology's intractable scowl at a bit of ill-conceived breeding—and there wasn't much he could do about that.

He knocked and opened the door. Sister Antoinette was sitting straight in her chair, back a way from the tub. There was a candle on the sill, lit.

"Hello!" The girl splashed.

"Hello. Sister, three things. Appointment Monday morning. Write it down in Sister Margaret's book. Also, Professor Bernheim is going to be here that afternoon, so we'll be needing to get the files ready. Sister Margaret will understand, but if you could just let her know."

"Yes, Doctor."

"Good." He took hold of the knob. He was about to excuse himself, but the girl splashed again for his attention.

"What?"

"You said three things."

"Oh. Yes. Sister Antoinette, I see there's a large envelope on my desk. When did that come in?"

"This morning. You were with your 10:00."

"By post?"

"Messenger."

"Hm. Thank you, Sister."

He was just about to close the door behind him when the girl called: "Goodbye, Dr. Pearl-Man."

"Goodbye—Nina."

## CHAPTER 11

**H**e took up the envelope first thing and examined the hand, an elegant, slanted cursive. Of course, he didn't want to jump to any conclusions, but he knew from years of living with Leonard, there were only so many things that required an envelope of this size. He opened it carefully and saw that he was right—the staves, the dots—it was sheet music. And a note on top, in elegant script.

*Dear Dr. Perlman,*
    *So touched by your condolence. I thought you might find this of interest. An old songbook, for the instruction of a young cousin.*

                                           *HB*

*P.S. Don't worry. This is not the only copy. We've others—somewhere in the heaps, I'm sure.*

Perlman could barely read the postscript, his hands were shaking so. Not the only copy? This looked to be the original manuscript.

He held the sheets up to the light. No opus number. F pp. The first, 2/4. B minor. He checked the back. There were dates. *Sept. 1881, Pskov.* He could not believe his eyes.

A songbook. Of Alexander Barrett's.

A gift from Madame Helena, in her brother's hand.

Perlman began bobbing, hopping, then spontaneously prancing out from behind his desk, ankles high, manuscript held out front. An original songbook. He goose-stepped one time around his desk and stopped again. He scanned the first page, a jumble of black hatches. He only wished he could play it right now—sight-read like Leonard—but he could tell already, this would take some doing. He'd probably have to wait until tonight, and now it was only noon. He was due to meet Benjamin at Fortunes of War, so he gathered up the pages in their envelope again and removed them to his flat. He took them to his private letter desk, laid them flat inside the long drawer, locked it, then floated off to lunch.

What would you say if I told you that back in my office right now I had the original manuscript of a songbook by Alexander Barrett?"

They'd both ordered sausages and mash, but Perlman was hardly touching his.

"How do you mean original?"

"Handwritten. His sister sent them over, just today."

"I didn't know you and the Madame were acquainted."

"We weren't. We only met at Bernheim's last night. Then this."

"Well, that's nicely done."

"Thank you, yes."

Benjamin forked a small bite, thinking. "You know, I could never quite make up my mind about him—Barrett. Somewhere between irresistible and facile."

Perlman agreed. "When he was younger. Did you hear much of the later work?"

"Well, there you see—I didn't know there was 'late Barrett.'"

Perlman smiled. It was a bit much. "He died here in London, didn't he?"

"I think so."

"Do you remember the cause?"

Benjamin chewed. "Syphilis?"

"Never a bad guess."

Benjamin offered another congratulatory smile and took a sip from his pint. "So have you decided how you're going to thank the Madame? I'd say you owe her."

Perlman hadn't thought, but Benjamin was right, and what a thrilling notion—to "owe" Helena Barrett. But before he could enjoy the burden for even a moment, the most unwelcome nose of Mr. Shepard poked in between them.

"Mind if I join?"

Benjamin slid down. Perlman arched.

"Not still cross, are you?" Shepard tried prying a smile, but Perlman's eyes deadened. "I trust it's all under control."

Perlman could see the slight panic that just his brief hesitation had caused. He let it for one more moment, then released his grip. "She'll be fine."

"There's a fellow." Shepard gave a cheeky look at Benjamin and a chummy nod back Perlman's way. "Magician."

No more was said of the Barrett matter until Shepard had bid them both good day in the hospital square.

"Did he saddle you again?" Benjamin had noticed Perlman's mood swing.

"Something like that. A tight knot, that's all."

"So when can I come by and see this songbook?"

"Any time. This weekend. I'll be seeing you tomorrow night, though. The Mahler?"

"Oh, did I not mention?" Benjamin stopped. They'd come to their crossroads. "I've a dinner. Completely escaped me. I'm afraid I won't be able to make it."

"Won't be able to, or don't want to?"

"Won't be able to. I don't think I have it in for him quite the way you do."

"You've never seen him conduct."

"True." Benjamin smiled. "This weekend, then?"

"Yes. Say Sunday."

They parted—Benjamin off to Ophthalmology; Perlman back to the clinic, first at a walk, then a brisker walk, then an outright trot.

**H**e wrote two letters as soon as he got back to his desk, both on office stationery. The first was addressed to the Bellevue Sanitorium in Kreuzlingen, inquiring about any available information regarding the case of Herr Irving Blum's English wife.

The second was as follows:

*Dear Madame Barrett,*

*Your gift is much too kind, falls on ungainly hands but receptive ears. I would very much enjoy talking to you about it. Wondered whether you'll be at Queen's Hall tomorrow, for the Mahler premiere. If not, another time.*

*In insurmountable debt,*
*August Perlman*

So the axes were set. He delivered both envelopes to the hospital couriers—they were most reliable—then spent the rest of the afternoon traipsing back and forth between these same two subjects, the girl and the songbook, whose effects upon him could not have been more disparate if the one had been a glass of brandy, the other castor oil.

Not surprisingly, he visited the brandy more liberally. Five trips in all, back to the long drawer of his letter desk, and each time he unlocked his prize he was more amazed at his good fortune. Just to have the manuscript itself, the artifact, filled him with a kind of giddy inner gladness he hadn't felt since his first train ride to Bayreuth.

There were six pieces in all, as was customary for books of this type, all of varying length and clearly pedagogic: a speed exercise, two waltzes, a march, and two less definable miniatures. Based on the various stages of completion, Perlman assumed that this must have been a penultimate draft of the book that Barrett intended to offer as a gift. The pages were strewn with all sorts of last-minute changes and notes, most of which he couldn't read, but that's what made them so valuable, was the human evidence. Perlman wondered if the Madame was even aware of the financial prospect, because from that perspective, it seemed almost showy of her, and extremely irresponsible.

He pondered how he should treat the pages, though. Should he bind them? Should he frame them? Lock them away in a safe? He should probably insure them, and make a copy as well—not just for safety's sake, but to use, to play from, for there was that whole aspect as well—really, the most thrilling of all: the music, the code he'd been given to break.

He refrained from applying himself in any practical way that afternoon. The piano was criminally off-key, and he'd have only made a shambles, but Leonard was coming over Friday and Leonard could play this at a glance. With that in mind, he began drawing up some fresh manuscript pages, tracing the staves from his Chopin book with a pen and a ruler. And he made an appointment for a tuner as well. He was very excited. He'd never known life to respond so quickly, and so precisely, to his desires.

There was, of course, that ninety-pound spoon of castor oil waiting for him back in room 3, to allay any fear he might have had that something altogether too pleasant had occurred. He visited the girl three times that afternoon, to confirm the fact that matters there were not improving—which was to say, they were improving a bit too rapidly. The girl was getting better, yes—physically. What he hadn't anticipated (though watching it happen, he wondered what else he could have been thinking) was the fact that every ounce she was gaining, every breath she took, every deeper shade of pink in her cheek only seemed to be tightening Nina's purchase on the body, the mind, the space. The prospect slightly withered him, but he realized he should probably try contacting Sylvie Blum again himself. The only real question was how soon.

He paid his last call at dusk, just before supper. The girl was having a bowl of soup.

"Feeling?"

"Better."

She was looking better. The skin around her eyes had all but lost its pale green hue. Even her hair had begun to take a sheen, and to confirm an impression he'd formed early yesterday that Nina was somehow prettier than Sylvie. He didn't think Sylvie would carry herself the same way—that she would eat her pears in such small, well-bred bites; or would spoon the soup into her mouth as Nina was doing here, so evenly.

He checked her sketch pad. She'd finished three more drawings, all of which bore the same vibrance as the first, the same depth of tone, but were of pears and pitchers, eggs on dishes.

"These are very nice." He turned to her. "Open your mouth." She opened. Her tongue, her throat were pink and healthy.

"Do you not like me, Dr. Pearl-Man?"

He checked the glands in her neck. "What makes you say that?"

"Well, you don't talk to me, really." Her tone was absent self-pity, more curious than sulking. "And you don't ever say hello to Oona."

He came around behind her to unlace the tie of her gown, and as it fell open he took cowardly relief at the sight of her ribs and scapulae. Improved though she may be, these lean wings attested she was by no means yet robust. If she should react to Sylvie's invocation as she had before—by evacuating—it would only undo all the strides she'd made to date. He would wait.

"Is it true you live next door?" she asked.

He set his palm against her back. "Yes. Breathe for me."

She did. Her lungs were clear.

"May I see?"

"No." He turned her around again and listened to her heart—thumping away contentedly; no objection to the new regime.

"You don't like me." She looked at him with smiling, sparkling eyes, intent on catching his. He had done his best all day not to meet them, to deny a natural inclination to return their affection. He did again.

"That's not true." He began lacing her gown. "Sister Antoinette should be in soon. Did you get enough to eat?"

"Maybe," she said.

"Did you? I'm sure there's more."

"For who?"

"For you."

"And who?"

And Oona, she meant. "Don't be silly. I'll see you in the morning."

Perlman ate his dinner in a dozen bites, he was so anxious to get back to the songbook. Now that there was time, he wanted to try his hand, actually to hear these things he'd been studying all day. He put a pillow on the bench for comfort, and he had to stand the manuscript pages against his lamp, they were so tall. He poured himself a brandy. He was very excited.

Unfortunately, he was also a terrible piano player. He'd forgotten how awful. He'd simply never practiced when he was young, out of respect to his brother. One summer while Leonard was away, he'd taught himself "Träumerei" and could still call upon it in a pinch, but that, he now discovered—that minute's worth of ability—was not piano playing, that was a parlor trick. Actually sitting in front of strange sheet music and trying to siphon the meaning through his hands was another matter altogether.

He began with the first song, which was far and away the simplest of the collection—Barrett in his elegiac mode—but even there, it took Perlman ten minutes just to pick out the chord progression, his hands trembling above the keys like a pair of baby deer. It was an embarrassment, that pedagogy for a little girl should have stopped him up this way. He skipped ahead, looking for the simplest passages he could find. For a while he applied himself to just the melody line of song #3, but there again—it started out simply enough, but the second half lost him completely. Without the supporting chords, it was a keyless wisp of inchoate phrases.

He had the most luck with one of the more "vertical" passages—somewhere near the middle of the second piece, entitled "Overture." It was just a progression, eight chords marching in succession, but he even might have said he "heard" Barrett in there, all the qualities one associated—playful, mocking, pretty, sad, subversive, and absurd. He could imagine the birthday girl, the cousin, finally coming to it in her lessons; her father rooms away, lowering the page of his evening paper to wonder a moment at cousin Alexander's influence.

With that image his lone reward—and about as good as he could have hoped for—he covered the keys at half past eight and turned over the rest of his evening to the much less humiliating task of transcription. He'd prepared six pages of blank staves earlier in the day. Now he resumed his seat at his letter desk and went to work; very happily, hunched there inside his little bubble of light, sipping and scratching away. His brain was soon a-swirl with all the dots and staffs, the signatures and decrescendos, the triplets and quadruplets, *meno mossos, poco più sostenutos*, and little snatches of melody floating above him like jewels in a whirling crown, serenading him and him alone, the only one in all the world to know; or him and some pretty cousin somewhere, and her well-posted father.

It was a wearying task, though. His lids were just beginning to fail beneath their weight when he became aware of her presence, standing in the vestibule leading back to his office. She was barely visible—a murky blue, from the coarse-cloth gowns they issued over at hospital, echoed somewhere near her eyes, and her long dark hair hanging down past her shoulders.

She rubbed her heel against her shin. "I couldn't sleep."

Perlman turned the manuscript pages facedown. "Where's Sister Antoinette?"

She shrugged her shoulders.

Just then a light came on behind her and the moon-faced naïf appeared, in her robe and nightcap, cupping her cheeks in relief—and then chagrin. "Oh, Dr. Perlman, I am sorry! I only stepped away—"

"That's all right."

"Naughty girl. I'll take her straight back."

"It's all right, Sister." Perlman stood. "I'll take her."

This met with the girl's approval. All she wanted was some attention. Perlman escorted her back through Reception. They dropped off
the Sister in her room—#1—and headed down the hall, just the two of
them.

Outside her door, she put her finger to her lips. Oona was asleep.
They entered quietly.

Her sketch pad was on the bed, with a new drawing face up: the
moon outside her window, a silver crescent peering through the
branches of the alder tree. As with the others, there was a bold and
beaming quality about her colors. Her pastels were down to their nubs.

"This is very nice."

"I'm bored," she said.

Perlman took a chair and set it beside the bed. "I understand." He
poured her some water. "But you're doing very well. All the rest
you've been getting, and the food and drink." He held out the glass,
but she refused. "Why don't you make yourself comfortable."

"Why? What are you going to do?"

"I'm just going to relax you."

"How?"

"We're just going to talk."

"What about?"

"Nothing so much. Do you know how to count backwards?"

"Five-four-three-two-one."

"Yes, but slower."

"What for?"

"I just want you to relax."

She shook her head. "But I don't want to do that. Tell me a story."

He smiled. "No."

"Why not? Please?"

"No."

"But that's what I'd prefer."

"Well, that's not what we're doing. Now come, we'll begin at
eleven."

"I don't want to do that. Tell me a story."

He smiled again, despite himself. "I don't know any."

"Yes, you do. Of course you do."

"Not bedtime stories."

"It doesn't have to be a bedtime story. Make one up."

The conversation was reminding him of something Parisot had once said, after a weekend visiting a band of nephews: one shouldn't take lightly a game of checkers with an eight-year-old.

"I'm not going to make up a story."

"Why not?"

"Because I just don't have much of an imagination."

"Then I'll make one up."

"No."

"Why not? You're mean. Why not?"

"Because." He looked at her. Her eyes were cross, but inside she was smiling, enjoying this. And for a moment Perlman let himself forget that she was nothing but a scar. He wondered, Who was this girl—this strange and charming creature—to be treating him this way, so comfortably? So sweetly? Where had she come from? And why had she come to him? But then, through her blanket, he felt the cool iron of her side rail against his knee, and he remembered again.

"Because," he said, "if you tell the story, you'll be wide awake when it's through. I'll be the one asleep, and that's not what we need."

"But I've been sleeping ever since I came." She fell back against her pillow and kicked at the pad. "Please?"

He shook his head.

"Please?"

"No."

She crossed her arms and made a face—he was too stubborn. Then she said something he didn't understand.

"What was that?"

"Nothing." She said something else.

"Excuse me?"

"Nothing. Oona's up. You can go."

He stood—too quickly—almost as if he were intruding now. "Is there anything you need?"

"No. Thank you." She seemed authentically disappointed, as if an overture had been refused. And Perlman, for his part, did feel contrite.

Sister Antoinette was waiting for him back in Reception, still in her robe and cap. She tried apologizing again for before. She'd only stepped away a moment—

"It's all right," said Perlman. "You might check on her in an hour or so. Just to see that she's asleep."

"Yes, Doctor." She turned, but stopped. "She is a sweet girl, though, isn't she?"

This was not an appropriate thing for her to have asked. Sister Margaret would have known better—but he replied, "She is, yes."

Then he returned to his flat. He took his brandy, his songbook, and the copies that he'd made to bed with him, and stayed awake another hour or so, making sure that there were no mistakes.

# THURSDAY

# CHAPTER 12

The twenty-seventh was the day of the Mahler premiere, which Perlman had been looking forward to, all previous remonstrations aside.
Premieres always tinged the air with a certain electricity, but this one
in particular, since Mahler's was a career in whose failure Perlman had
long entertained a rooting interest. Mahler was from the same home-
town as the Perlmans, and he and Leonard had attended the conservatory at the same time. An unsavory, pretentious character, the young
Maestro had been doing very well for himself even so. He'd worked as
second conductor to Nikisch in Leipzig, enjoyed a brief stint in Budapest, and was the current conductor at the Vienna Court Opera,
in addition to which he clearly fancied himself a composer. He'd
completed three symphonies already, of which this evening's title—
*Titan*—had been the first. The point being, he was a man of extraordinary ambition who actually seemed to be fulfilling it, or near enough
that one couldn't help a certain pang of envy—and its cousin, resentment—at the mention of his name, the local boy who was making so
good.

This evening's program tendered the occasion for some good and
hearty payback, in other words—brother sticking up for brother. Perlman was primed, but bridled. Between now and then other matters
loomed.

He went to check on the Blum girl just before heading over for his morning rounds at the hospital. He found her kneeling rump-high on her bed, drawing a portrait—of him—which he supposed had been inevitable. This was a slightly expressionist version. She'd put a great deal of effort into the background, a smoky swirl of dark greens, black, and purple, against which his head appeared a pearly white orb.

"The nose isn't right," she said.

The nose he rather liked. It was the eyes that troubled him. A bit large, and shaped like fish.

"We'll have to ask the Sister what she thinks."

Nina agreed, tilting her head the other way.

"Nina, do you remember my asking you about someone named Sylvie Blum?"

He was standing behind her, but as with nearly everything she did, her reaction was instantaneous and transparent: here, an aversion which bordered on shame. "Yes," she murmured.

"Do you think it's possible I might see her again?"

Her body slumped, burdened. "But I'm feeling so much better."

"Do you mean to say she's still the same?"

She shrugged. "I don't know."

"You don't know?"

"No. But I am feeling so much better." She craned to look at him, first with pleading eyes, then squinting—the artist's scrutiny. He decided to let the question hang.

"You don't think he looks a bit frightened?" He gestured to the portrait.

She considered—him first, then the drawing, then him again. "No."

He left her in the same pose as he'd found her, rubbing out the nose with the side of her palm.

Rounds lasted through the morning, and after lunch Sister Margaret returned from her sickbed, still pale, but armed with all the files he'd been asking for. Perlman checked twice on the girl, and twice found her napping—or pretending to. He wondered if she might be avoiding him, now that he'd broached the 'Sylvie' subject. Otherwise, he spent most of the afternoon behind his office door, conducting his scheduled appointments, reading the case studies that Sister Margaret had found—none of which seemed particularly pertinent—and intermittently slipping away to his piano to drill his fingers.

He was doing just that, late afternoon—practicing the left hand of a brief contrapuntal passage in the third piece—when he heard the sound of a little Indian creeping into his office.

He lifted his wrist. "Hello?"

There was no answer.

"Hello?" He opened the door.

"Shshsh." She hushed him from underneath his desk. She was crouched down, head tucked in.

"What are you doing down there?"

"Hiding."

"From whom?"

"Oona. Shsh."

Perlman looked at her. She wasn't wearing any socks. The soles of her feet were blue and shiny with dirt.

"I'm not sure this is a good place for you to hide."

She looked up at him angrily, set to shush him again, when suddenly she turned to the door, gasped, screamed, and fled the room like a jackrabbit, slamming the door behind her.

Perlman could hear her squealing through Reception, her feet scampering down the hall. When he opened the door again, Sister Margaret was leaning around from behind her desk. "She's getting a bit restless."

"Yes."

Down at the end of the hall, the girl flashed by again, darting from room 3 across to room 2.

Yes. No more excuses, he thought. Tomorrow he'd roll up his sleeves and speak to Sylvie Blum, come what may.

To that end, he used the rest of the time before the concert to script an induction. It had been years since he'd felt the need, but in this case, he wanted to be certain of his course.

First, he'd have to gain her consent. He found a fresh page in his medical journal and began:

1. *Consent, before.*
2. *Induction:*
   *Affirmation.*
   *Stone staircase, spiral.*
   *First landing.*
   *Reaffirmation.*
   *Acclimate.*
   *Stairs.*
   *Second landing.*
   *Chair = Sylvie.*
*Plant amnesia?*
*Plant signal for Nina's return?*

Good questions, these last two. The first concerned whether, before lifting the girl from her trance, presuming he'd managed to induce one, he should instruct her to forget whatever might have happened therein—that was a decision he could probably wait to make. The second was a bit trickier. Specifically, should he, somewhere in the course of the session, plant a suggestion to return to 'Nina' when they were through? The argument against was obvious. Why, if he did manage to contact Sylvie, should he give 'Nina' the opportunity to recur? In planting the signal for her return, did he not thereby ensure it? He did, he knew, and yet not to plant the signal would be just as clearly reckless, like climbing without a rope.

This would take some thinking, but it was time to get ready for the concert now. He returned to his flat, lit the oven, and prepared a light plate of sausage and boiled potatoes. While they were warming, he washed up—shaved, waxed his mustache, slicked his hair, tweezed all strays—and for the first time let himself indulge the hope the Madame might be in attendance this evening. He understood she'd given him absolutely no reason to think she would be, but somehow the fact that he'd mentioned it in his note seemed to substantiate the possibility, and this was a concert not without draw: Mahler's first audience in London.

As soon as he was through at the mirror, he returned to his office and unshelved the Chronik from his trip to Vienna three years ago. That's where he'd first heard the Mahler himself. He ate his dinner, book beside plate, but the notes were damningly brief.

> 'Titan' indeed. Four movements, 52 min. (!)
> 1. . . . and?
> 2. Waltz.
> 3. Frère Jacques, and Jewish theme. Naught of his own.
> 4. L is right. Mahler is an insufferably pretentious megalomaniac.

Next he changed to his evening clothes—socks, garters, shirt, pants, collar, tie, cuff links, spats, swallow-tail coat—and fetched the current Chronik from his bedside and his favorite pen. The only deviation from his customary routine came last. He did not smoke his hashish, for three reasons not equally reasonable. First, the Mahler wasn't to come until after intermission, by which time the effects of any mood would be long gone. Second, there remained the off chance he might be seeing Madame Barrett there—

Hah.

Third, he could not find it.

His carriage arrived at 6:30. He was at Queen's Hall by 7:00. He proceeded to the bar and ordered a brandy and a coffee to wait. It wasn't a bad crowd. There was Charles Graves, from the *Spectator*, and Loomis, the *Times* critic. Mrs. Wood. Maestro Beecham. Mr. E. A. Baughan, who'd just published a book of essays. Lord Morley. Dr. Evans from the Royal Hospital.

He didn't really *expect* to see the Madame, of course. It was laughable, in fact, the idea that she was going to emerge from the crowd, glide over and greet him with outstretched arm. Better she wasn't there. They'd only have pleasantries and part. Then he'd have to slink off to his seat in the orchestra, while she ascended to a box with whomever.

He downed the last of his glass and was about to go take his seat, when one of the ushers approached.

"Dr. Perlman?"

"Yes?"

"For you." He extended a small envelope, like the one she'd included in her package yesterday. His heart recognized it, too, and was thumping loudly as he read the note inside:

> *Dear Dr. Perlman,*
>
> *Thank you for your kind reply, but I am otherwise engaged to the early evening. Do come to the party after, though—Café Royale— armed with suitable, or passable, approbation.*
>
> *Your insurmountable creditor,*
>
> *HB*

Café Royale. That was where the orchestra often retreated after a performance of note. The Madame had invited him to the premiere party.

The gong sounded. Perlman started for his seat, euphoric.

## CHAPTER 13

The feeling prevailed, more or less, during the first set—a serving of suitably small and simple appetizers to precede a main course as demanding as this evening's. Some Strauss, some Wolf, an orchestral variation by Granville Bantock entitled, of all things, "Helena." Common English tripe, but in the company of a premiere audience it was conferred an undue glint, and was certainly well enough played to keep Perlman's generous mood afloat.

Then, however, came the entrée. *Titan.*

What could one say? It was Mahler. On the one hand, so bogglingly, maddeningly, resentment provokingly brilliant. The resources upon which this man drew, the facility he demonstrated in "playing" an entire orchestra so unashamedly. This was very much a conductor's piece, and Maestro Mahler was a virtuoso in the very best, the most accurate, sense.

And yet, on the other hand, did this music itself not lack a certain something? A certain Music? This was an impression he'd formed the first time hearing the piece and no doubt related to the frustrations he'd been feeling with the Viennese tide, but was it not particularly true of Mahler—that for all the mastery, all the *Sturm und Drang,* one was still left with a yearning for more of the Stuff Itself?

The first movement was as good an example as any, impressive in the sense that Mahler may have been the only composer alive who could write that many notes and still not get around to it. The waltz scherzo left Perlman feeling much the same: a lush and tasteful presentation of nothing in particular. The third movement, the funeral business, was a bit more bite-size and tasty, but even there, that Jewish theme. Perlman wouldn't have minded if it had been a *new* Jewish theme, but this—like so much of what Mahler put forward—like the counter-theme in this very movement, the "Frère Jacques"—was a direct quotation. Did he not see? Was there no one with the gumption to tell him that this would not do, that in offering these same old tunes he was abnegating the primary responsibility of the artist? Mahler wasn't a composer really so much as an assembler—an occasionally tasteful quilt maker, choosing which patches to include and where to put them but providing no patches of his own, at least that Perlman could hear. These were all gestures elsewhere, which was even more irritating when one took account of the number, the length. Oh, but that enormity itself were a virtue, Mahler might be on to something, but what was one to do with a piece this size? It was an embarrassment. Well before the end, Perlman was quite done with it. He tried setting his mind elsewhere—counting the gold hatches in the carpet design—but as the finale broke and boomed like tidal waves over his frazzled brain, his restlessness turned to outright fury. The idea. Where did Gustav Mahler get off being so high and bloody mighty? Perlman had half a mind to stand and shout, "I know this man, I know the streets he's walked, the stores he's bought his penny candy in, he knows naught of this. He is a child with a cannon." It was an outrage. And just as well that Mahler wasn't there, for if he were, if Perlman actually had the chance to meet the man afterward, would he have any choice but to grab him by the ear and throttle him, tell him to shut up, shut up, shut up.

He might even have left, if not for his engagement afterward. As it was, he suffered through the last thousand measures of bombast, then bolted his seat as soon as the final chord sounded, to wait in the lobby.

He wasn't exactly sure about the timing of the reception—whether

they all went over immediately after the concert or gathered somewhere on the premises to make a group exodus. He lingered out front,
looking for some clue. The entire audience passed by, but like a reed
in the stream, Perlman held his ground; then, when they were all gone
but the ushers with their brooms, he decided to walk down Regent
Street alone.

He was there in ten minutes, but didn't enter right away. He stood
across the street and watched the guests come trickling in, in groups
of five and six. One couldn't be sure they were from Queen's Hall,
of course, and the only real question was whether she had arrived
yet.

He took out his Chronik to make a note:

*Sept. 27. Mahler's first. Wood. QH. The second time now, and for the
second time seems nothing but a colossal pedestal. Proceeding from the
same premise: that all the melodies have been written.*
    *Cowards.*

With that, he closed his pen, stuffed the Chronik back in his pocket,
and ventured across.

He'd actually never been inside the café. It struck him at once as being more intimate than he'd have thought, even a bit musty. He passed
through to the Domino Room. It was three-quarters full, maybe a
hundred guests, murmuring like a flock of pigeons. A portly maître d'
noted his entrance, but Perlman swept by, past a table of food, a stack
of plates. Roast beef. He recognized several of the players crammed
in booths. Groups of two and three huddled in corners, clogging
aisles. Some of the Queen's Hall people. There was Wood and Mrs.
Wood. The first violinist, Godwyn. Mostly it appeared to be the orchestra.

He made one circuit around, then exited to the lobby, past
the maître d' again, and straight through the rotating door to the
street.

Perhaps she wasn't coming. Perhaps she was in one of the private rooms upstairs. He walked a half block down to the archway of the fire station, took out his Chronik again, found a fresh page, and wrote:

*SB.*
  *To plant Nina or not?*

"SB" stood for Sylvie Blum. The question was the same as before: Should he plant a signal for Nina's return during tomorrow's session? For whatever reason—a woods-clearing blast of music—the answer seemed evident now. Sylvie Blum, authentic though she may be, remained an unknown entity to Perlman. Nina was not. She had made the body well. She was conscious—responsible, reasonably compliant, game. It was no wonder she wouldn't want to yield the body, least of all to an uprooted Jewess, yanked from her home and carted off to Miss Mobley's.

  *Definitely. Plant signal.*
  *Sylvie = Necklace.*
  *Nape = Ni—*

"Dr. Perlman?"
He jolted from the page as if a shot had sounded.
It was Madame Helena, standing in front of him. In a tilted, broad-brimmed hat, swathed in velvet, and for cover something which looked awfully like a great black cape. Magnificent, and alone.
"What are you doing out here?" she asked. Her manner was disarmingly open, friendly.
"Nothing." He closed the book. "Just making a note."
"Don't let me interrupt your inspiration." She nodded toward the café. "You're coming in, though."
"Yes. I'm done, in fact." He screwed the top back on his pen and stepped out to join her.
She turned slightly, extending her elbow for him to come. Awfully forward, but a reminder as well that there was something blessedly un-English about this woman. He hurried the Chronik back into his

coat, and then a bit too awkwardly—for he supposed he would really rather not have—hooked her arm.

It was getting cold now, so they hustled.

"So?" She squeezed his elbow. "You'll have to tell me, how was the Mahler?"

Perlman laughed. An awfully small question for such an overlarge subject. "Have you not heard it?"

"No."

"Well . . ." They were at the door. Much too little time. "It's a rather large guilt."

She nodded, girding for their entrance. Perlman felt something like a handbag as she passed a porter at the door. The maître d' bowed. A young woman came and took their coats and hats. Again the Madame hooked his arm and guided them through to the Domino Room.

The drinks were set out in glasses. Perlman took a sherry; she, red wine.

"I'm glad you decided to come," she toasted.

"My pleasure. Thank you for the invitation."

They looked about the room.

"Will you be hearing the symphony tomorrow?" asked Perlman.

"Oh, I don't think so." She sounded distinctly unappetized.

"Do you not attend anymore?"

"Not really. A chamber piece here and there. One has obligations." She scanned the crowd again, conspicuously.

"Is that what brings you here this evening?"

"I suppose. It's an opportunity to kill some birds with a stone."

"I trust I'm not a bird."

"No, of course not." She took a sip of her drink and looked back at him with those willful eyes.

Extraordinary creature, thought Perlman. Such confidence for a woman, and such a handsome face. Her features were an embarrassment of riches; her skull should be cased in glass when all was done.

"I was reading about your clinic today," she said, "in the *Gazette*. That was a very nice piece."

"Yes."

"I guess I wasn't aware you were so closely affiliated with the hospital. I think that's extraordinary, don't you?"

"How do you mean?"

"Well, that an institution like St. Bartholomew's would be willing to sanction what you do. It isn't exactly mainstream practice." Her eyes glinted. "But who can argue with success?"

He gave a slight bow of appreciation.

"I didn't quite understand, though. Is that how most of your clients come to you, through the hospital?"

"Clients?"

"Sorry. Patients."

Again, her eyes. "No. I conduct rounds at the hospital, but most of the clinic patients come to us directly."

"I see." She paused, thinking. He couldn't decide if he found her curiosity more mysterious or charming. "And how many are there at any given time? Right now, say?"

"Myself or the clinic?"

"Is there a difference?"

He smiled. Clever woman. "Not much. At present, I think a dozen or so."

"A dozen staying with you?"

"Oh no. Staying with us, just one." He stiffened slightly at the reminder. The Madame noticed and seemed willing to let the matter pass. It was Perlman who took the next step, tossed all principles aside for the pitifully modest purpose of keeping her extraordinary eyes on his. "She's been drawing pictures, in fact, of golden temples. I thought of you."

*I thought of you.*

The valiancy of the phrase seemed lost, however. The Madame looked more puzzled than touched. "I wasn't aware you had your patients draw pictures."

"Well, we don't. This is a special case."

He tried meeting her eyes again, but suddenly they flashed over his shoulder. "Signor Bassetto!"

He turned. Standing beside them now was a bearded gentleman, with impish, sparkling eyes. "Signora Barrett."

It was George Bernard Shaw.* "*Ecco. Quando sei tornata.*"

"*Questa semana,*" she replied in a far superior accent. "*Corno. Dr. August Perlman, Corno di Bassetto.*"

Shaw bowed. "*Un dottore. Sono sempre malato.*" He gripped his hip and grimaced.

"Suggestive therapy."

Madame Helena touched his arm. She was touching both their arms. "Dr. Perlman runs the clinic at St. Bartholomew's."

Shaw's eyes sparked with mischief. "*Un hypnotiste? Come Dr. Dahl?*"†

The tips of Perlman's ears flared. "*Si.*"

Suddenly another gentleman—a dashing Englishman of roughly Perlman's age—swept up next to them as if the waltz had just begun and he was asking the Madame's hand.

"Madame Helena Barrett."

"Andrew." She modulated the name to convey a good-humored wariness about this one, who appeared to be another one of those impossibly handsome Englishmen, pretty really, with a luxurious swath of hair, paper-thin nose, bright eyes, and an irritating overabundance of charm.

"How could you not come straight?" he said. "I'm hurt."

"I've only been here a week."

"Still, a week. That's a while." He noticed Perlman.

"Andrew Allan Rowe. August Perlman."

"Careful, Andrew." Shaw leaned in, Irish again. "He's a hypnotist."

"Not the Rachmaninoff fellow?"

Perlman waited. "No."

---

*Corno di Bassetto was the pen name Shaw used while writing as a music critic for *The Star.*
†Three years earlier, the young Sergei Rachmaninoff, despondent at the critical rejection of his first symphony, sought help from a Russian hypnotist, a Dr. Nikolai Dahl, whom Perlman had never heard of. Dahl treated him for two weeks, immediately following which Rachmaninoff composed his second piano concerto. Perlman had been intensely jealous. After hearing the concerto for the first time, he commented to his friend Parisot that he might have prescribed a few more sessions.

Wrong answer apparently. Rowe turned back to the Madame. "You're here for how long?"

"I'm not sure."

"A while, though."

"I've some work to do."

"A show?"

"No. No no. Just some clean-up."

"Sounds like drudgery."

"Drudgery may be just the thing."

Rowe glanced at Perlman again, distinctly as if he'd been referred by the word. "So what did we think of the concert?"

"Wasn't there," said Shaw.

"Nor I," the Madame conceded.

"Nor I," Rowe followed sheepishly.

Perlman's silence was conspicuous. Rowe reached into his pocket and pulled out a silver cigarette case. "You were there, Dr. Perlman?"

"I was."

"And?"

Perlman couldn't help a smile. How Benjamin would have loved this—G. B. Shaw leaning in to hear his opinion of the Mahler. He demurred. "A great deal to admire."

He hadn't meant this to be particularly cutting, but Shaw reacted, on Mahler's behalf, as if he'd been jabbed in the stomach.

"But what about to enjoy?" Rowe offered the cigarettes around.

All refused.

"I'm afraid I'd have to know a bit more about your affiliations," replied Perlman.

"Oh, none."

"Mr. Rowe is a director," the Madame explained.

"His opinions couldn't matter less," added Shaw.

*Yes, sir, but yours.* "The truth is, my brother attended the Vienna Conservatory at the same time as the Maestro, so I suspect my opinion may be somewhat slanted."

"But slanted which way?" Rowe smiled. "Come on, Doctor. You're not getting off that easy." He chose a fag and returned the case to his pocket. "You have to give us *something*. Yea or nay?"

Perlman hesitated again, and finally the Madame answered for him. "The doctor was comparing it to a . . . tapestry?"

"Quilt, actually." She knew that.

Shaw nodded knowingly, but Rowe was lost. "Help me."

"A quilt is made of borrowed fabrics," Shaw explained.

"Ah, so you think it was derivative, Dr. Perlman?"

And there Rowe tipped his hand; he didn't know what he was talking about. "Patently," said Perlman. "I don't think even Mahler would deny that."

"Well, yes, all right." Rowe took a rather dramatic pull from his cigarette. "But aren't they all." He blew over his shoulder. "I mean, isn't that the point—how to cop off each other, give it a spin?"

This was a rhetorical question, obviously, but for some reason it piqued Perlman, the stupid cynicism of the remark. He answered: "To a degree. On the other hand, it's nice when a composer thinks to offer something new."

"You don't think Mahler is offering anything new?"

"Oh, on the whole, I suppose." Perlman could feel himself loosening. "I mean, I can't think of another composer who'd have presumed to write that entire symphony, but note for note . . ." He looked at the others; Shaw's silence was making him nervous. "It's a long piece, of course, and I'd like to hear it a few more times—but I'm afraid that note for note, the music itself just doesn't stir me."

"Hm." Rowe liked this. "And whose music does stir you, Dr. Perlman? Just so I know whose taste I'll be passing along."

That was putting him on the spot. Who? The Madame was standing right next to him. "Well, I always enjoyed the Madame's brother."

He regretted this answer the moment it left his mouth, the shamelessness of it. They all looked down at their shoes in agreement.

"But I have a weakness for Russian fare." He tried to save himself.

" 'A good Russian tune,' " Shaw quoted helpfully.

"Yes."

"But you're not Russian," said Rowe.

"No." Shaw turned. "Vienna, yes?"

Perlman conceded.

"Hn." Rowe took another long drag. "One doesn't hear that every day, a Wiener preferring the Russian school. Why do you suppose that is?"

Perlman paused. "Why do I suppose you haven't heard this, or why do I prefer Russian music?"

Smiles.

"Perhaps the doctor doesn't like C sharps," said the Madame.

"Or F sharps," added Shaw.

Perlman turned. Charming as this had sounded, he didn't know what they meant.

"The Lydian scale," Shaw informed. "That's what most of the Russian folk tunes are composed on."

"Lydian?" Perlman scoured his brain. "That's old Greek?"

"It's an old Greek church," the Madame replied.

He'd never thought of that.

"Any old Greeks in the family?" asked Rowe.

"Not that I'm aware of."

"Interesting, though, isn't it?" Rowe clearly wasn't ready to let his thought go, whatever it was. "Why a person develops a preference like that, for one tune over another."

They all nodded expectantly.

"Not the sort of thing one can explain," said the Madame finally. "Unless you've some theory you're hiding up your sleeve."

"Oh, not a theory really. I just wonder if it isn't all to do with association, do you know? The reason I like one thing over another is that it reminds me of a time I enjoyed when I was young and impressionable."

Shaw shook his head disappointedly. "You've been reading again, haven't you, Andrew?"

"Some. Perhaps. But living life, too. You can't deny."

"No, it's true," the Madame came to Rowe's defense. "I know, Lexei and I went to see *La Traviata* after an uncle of ours passed away. I don't think either of us ever forgave Verdi. Music is like smell that way. So associative."

"Exactly," said Rowe. "So all I'm suggesting is that if Dr. Perlman does like a Russian tune—"

"—it's because his mother sang him Russian lullabies in his crib," Shaw finished the thought.

"There you go."

Perlman cleared his throat. "Yes. Well, clearly you've not heard my mother sing."

The others bounced at the humor. Perlman flat-footedly abstained. Madame Helena noticed. "I sense dissent."

"Not dissent." Perlman tried to remain polite. "I take Mr. Rowe's point. Associations are certainly important. I just find it interesting, the reluctance we seem to have developed these days to judging the thing itself."

No one seemed to understand. Rowe bit. "How's that, Doctor?"

"Well, just that one hears so much talk about the construction of a piece, or the program, or the biographical context in which it was written; and now we have this, what you're suggesting here, that it's all a matter of association. All this discussion, the purpose of which—I would assume—is to assess the value of the thing, when it seems to me no one ever mentions the one element upon which that value almost entirely depends."

Rowe's brows arched. "Which is what exactly?"

"The music."

"The music?"

"Yes."

"But that's a slightly foggy area, wouldn't you say?"

"I don't see why it should be," said Perlman. "It all still comes down to what comes next. If what comes next in a given piece pleases us musically, or moves us in some way, then that is good. If what comes next strikes us as trite or arbitrary—then that is not good."

"But you don't think those are awfully subjective assessments?"

What a tiresome reply. "To a degree," said Perlman. "But you tell me, why is Beethoven's seventh better than Beethoven's eighth? Is it because we'd all just had a delicious cup of custard before hearing it? No. It's because those themes in the seventh are good themes, and those themes in the eighth"—he paused for effect—"aren't. Great composer, not great themes."

Brash, but who could deny? He was right.

"The problem is, we're not even allowed to discuss such things."

"Like politics," agreed Shaw.

"Or religion," said the Madame.

"Exactly," said Perlman, encouraged. "But that's a danger, I think. Because you see, if no one's willing to stand and make these judgments—if no one is willing to say that this is *inherently superior material,* or that there's even such a thing as inherently superior material—well, then we find ourselves in situations like tonight, where such an extraordinary mountain of genius and sound and resource is brought to bear upon this . . . completely trodden territory."

"Ohp." Rowe grinned. "The gloves have come off."

"Well, I do think it's an ugly feature of the modernist mentality—this idea that all the tunes have already been written and that what remains for the contemporary composer is to quote the old melodies, or twist them, or reconfigure them somehow."

"Oh, it's worse than that." The Madame shook her head ruefully. "In Paris, they speak of getting beyond melody altogether."

"Exactly!" Perlman was actually rocked on his heels by this phrase—what a perfect distillation of the prevailing idiocy. "That's what I'm saying. 'Beyond melody'? You can't get beyond melody."

Rowe was looking round at them; he seemed happy enough to play the fool for now. "I'm sorry, why not?"

Perlman paused to give the others a chance to answer, but they didn't seem inclined to. "Because," he said, "melody expands. It's been expanding for the last three thousand years. I should think it will keep doing so for a little while longer at least. Really, it's the most ridiculous hubris to think that we should be the ones to bring it to a close. Imagine the arrogance in that."

"Cowardice," the Madame murmured.

"Yes, *my* word. 'Cowards.'" He was flushed; he tried to calm himself. "But not everyone, fortunately. There'll be someone to step forward and push it along."

"The only question is who," said Rowe, with mock intrigue.

"And will we know it when we hear it?" the Madame asked.

"Probably not," answered Perlman. "But that's why we go back. That's why we keep exposing ourselves to the difficult pieces, isn't it? In hopes that maybe we'll get to know these things, and that when we do, perhaps we'll hear the music, too. And then *we'll* have expanded along with it."

He looked at them and stopped. He remembered now—he was speaking to three people who hadn't even attended the concert this evening. They, in turn, were all looking at each other with high, impressed, if somewhat embarrassed brows.

Finally Rowe cleared his throat. "I wasn't aware I was speaking to such an avid listener."

"And an idealist," said Shaw.

"Yes." The Madame looked up at him. "Dr. Perlman is full of surprises." She held his eye a moment, then turned back to the others with a deep, regretful, but clearly adjourning breath. "I'm afraid you three are going to have to excuse me, though. I have to tear myself away."

"We understand," said Shaw. "You've been missed."

Rowe took her hand. "You'll be back, though. We're not through."

"Oh, I'll be here awhile." She turned to Perlman, touched his wrist, and drew him close to whisper in his ear. "You don't mind?"

He shook his head.

"There, you see?" She was so close, he could feel her breath on his neck. "You're not the bird. You're the stone."

She turned and made her way off into the milling crowd.

The three men watched her go, mutually aware that their conversation had just, for all intents and purposes, lost its motive.

"I have a question," asked Rowe, still keeping her in sight. "Why do we call her Madame? Was she married?"

"I believe she was," said Shaw—news to Perlman. "Very briefly, when she was younger. Back in Russia."

"A youthful indiscretion," observed Rowe.

They smiled.

"And yet we also call her Barrett."

Shaw nodded. "That was Alexander, I think, never letting her forget."

"Forget she'd married or forget she was Barrett?"

Shaw thought. "Good point. I'm not sure." He turned. "So who is your brother, Dr. Perlman?"

Perlman answered as though it were a question. "Leonard Perlman?"

Shaw thought, then shook his head. He hadn't heard of him.

"That's probably a good sign," said Rowe.

Perlman smiled, and they all tucked their feathers again.

"Well, I think I'm going to freshen my drink." Perlman lifted his glass, now empty. "A pleasure."

"A pleasure, Dr. Perlman." Shaw gave a bow, Rowe a nod.

All there was at the drinks table was champagne. Perlman took one, against his principles, and toured a bit. He felt the effect of his drink almost immediately, but he was more comfortable now, satisfied with his performance. He helped himself to a plate of beets, some potatoes, and beef. He ate standing, happily preoccupied.

Across the room he saw the hornist, Kelleher, sitting alone. Sorry dog. Perlman and Benjamin had often joked, if they ever got the chance they should tell him he didn't *have* to be a hornist, there were any number of things he could probably do with himself. But of course, face-to-face, seeing the man sulking over his plate of potatoes, all was forgiven.

Madame Helena was talking to Henry Wood.

"Good evening" came a strange voice. The maître d', the portly man who'd eyed him so suspiciously before, had noticed him watching.

"Good evening."

"Did I see you come in with Madame Barrett?"

"Yes."

"She hasn't been here in a while."

"No."

"Have we met?"

"I don't think so. Dr. August Perlman."

"Perlman." He pretended to rummage through his mind. "Of Royal Hospital?"

"Bart's."

"And what do you do there?"

"Suggestive therapy."

"Hypnotism?"

"Yes."

"You must be familiar with Dr. Dahl's work?"

"Dr. Dahl, yes."

"There's a piece."

"Yes."

Another moment passed, of awkward teetering. "So, you must have been pleased about the pardon."

Perlman looked down at him. Stupid man. He meant Dreyfus. That summer the civilian court of appeals had finally reversed all convictions, but Perlman made him say it.

"Which?"

"The Frenchman. Dreyfus. Terrible business."

"Yes."

Madame Helena was pulling away from Wood. "If you'll excuse me." Perlman toasted their parting and left abruptly.

He made straight to her side before anyone else could grab hold.

"Madame Barrett."

"Helena."

"I should probably be going."

"So soon?"

"I'm afraid so. I wanted to thank you, though, for inviting me, but also for the songbook. I have to tell you, it is the most generous gift I've ever received."

"Oh." She whisked away the gesture. "Better they should go to someone who'll appreciate them. Were you able to have a go?"

"Tried. I did my best."

"Well, I hope they weren't an insult."

"No, you did well. I'd say they're right at my limit."

"Good," she said, slowing, sly. "You'll have to give us a recital."

"Only if patience is another of your virtues."

She looked at him—thank heavens she seemed to have found this charming. She shook her head. "It isn't." She extended her hand. "A pleasure."

"Mine." He took it, bowed, then made his way.

He decided to walk to Oxford Circus and take the Underground from there. It was a cool night, but he was barely aware, reviewing all the evening's conversations. With the Madame, then Shaw and Rowe. For shame, holding forth like that, and yet he wished he'd said more, or made himself more clear.

He wanted to make some notes. He reached into his pocket for the Chronik, but then stopped cold. It wasn't there. Nor in any of his other pockets. He must have left it back at the café, which he wouldn't have minded so much—it was hardly the first time he'd left a Chronik behind—except that the last note he'd written had been about the girl. He thought of going back, but the Madame was probably still there, and he didn't want to ruin the effect of their parting. He'd send a message to the café in the morning.

For now he uncapped his pen and unrolled the evening's program. *"Beyond melody,"* he scrawled along the top, then *"Lydian,"* then *"Def.,"* meaning "definitely."

*Plant the signal.*
*Necklace. Nape.*

# FRIDAY

## CHAPTER 14

The girl was just finishing breakfast when Perlman went to pay his first visit that day, to gain her consent. Sister Margaret was there as well. She'd brought a stack of case files with her and was wading through them. The girl had pulled her side table out to the middle of the floor, to enjoy a more proper meal. She was seated upright in her chair, and though with the shades rolled the room was perfectly bright, there was that lit candle standing across from her.

"Good morning, Dr. Pearl-Man." Her hair was in a braid.

"How long have we been up?"

"Hours," replied the Sister. "Before I came, and that was seven o'clock." She handed him her chart, which offered only what the girl had had for breakfast—an egg, toast, tea. "She's been asking about a walk outside."

"I was thinking the same thing." He turned. "I thought we might take a stroll around the square."

"When?" The girl bounced in her seat.

"Right now, if you like. Are you done with that?"

She pushed away her plate, and Perlman went to get the coat from her closet, a sky-blue wool, skirt-length and flared.

"Not that one," she said. Her tone was perfectly reasonable.

"But it's cold, I think. You'll need a coat."

She shook her head. "Not that one."

An obvious repudiation of Sylvie. Perlman chose not to contest it. "Sister Margaret, have you a coat that Nina can borrow?"

"Out on the stand."

"Thank you. If we're not back in a quarter hour, come get us. I'll be doing rounds at the hospital this morning."

"Yes, Doctor."

He noticed a pair of boots in the closet. "I'm going to assume these are all right?"

The girl allowed; she'd made her point, and these were more to her taste apparently—red overboots with a rounded toe. He knelt down before her like a salesman, and she slipped her feet inside, with just her socks on underneath. Then she took his hand and stood, blowing out the candle before they headed for the door. Oona was coming too apparently.


It was blustery morning, but oddly warm. Sister Margaret's brown mackintosh fit the girl like a glove on a twig, but she was pleased, skipping beside him across Little Britain. As they entered the low tunnel which led to the main square of the hospital, she called out a couplet in her private language to hear the echo. It was an eerie effect, her voice chattering against the brick—like two people speaking but making no sense, in well-rounded locutions that sounded purposeful and true but never flagged toward anything sensible.

She fell suddenly silent as they came upon the square, an open space, bordered by the four wings of the hospital. There were patches of green here and there, four sheltered benches, and a fountain in the middle, but the sight of the other patients seemed to subdue her, all out in their wheelchairs or taking fragile, guided steps.

"Everyone here is sick," she said.

"Yes. This is a hospital."

"But I am better, you said."

"You are, but there are still some things we need to see about."

She said something else, not for his benefit. He decided to act.

"Nina, do you think I could talk to you alone? Without Oona."

"I was just telling her—"

"I understand. I'm just wondering if you could leave her some-where while we spoke."

She did not appreciate this, but then noticed that one of the tiers of the fountain was a large stone shell. This appealed. Nina directed her friend with a nod, and then turned back to Perlman. "What?"

He started them in an anti-clockwise direction, but waited before speaking, to let their steps assume a rhythm.

"First, I wanted to commend you for being such a good patient—eating, sleeping. You've done an excellent job, and I want you to know that I appreciate it." As they rounded the first corner, Perlman was aware that the other patients in the square were watching them.

"You know, however, that I need to see Sylvie Blum, which means I'll need your help. I'd like us to try this afternoon."

She was silent a while, considering. She walked slowly, nodding faintly at each appearance of her boot tips peeking out from beneath the hem of her coat.

"What are you going to do?"

"It's very simple, actually. It's a bit like telling stories. I'm going to ask you to imagine some things with me; then we're going to talk to Sylvie, just to see how well you've made her."

"What if she doesn't want to speak to you?"

"Then I need to find that out. It's my hope that she's feeling better now, though, thanks to you. I expect she might even want to thank you."

The girl pursed her lips; she doubted that, but was silent again, counting her steps. Finally she asked, "What about Oona?"

"What about Oona?"

"Can she come?"

"Frankly, Nina, you're the one whose help I need. Not Oona." He stopped, and turned to look at her. "Will you? Help me?"

Her eyes stayed low. "Yes," she murmured; her lips barely moved.

"Good. That's all I need."

He touched her shoulder, and they finished rounding the square in silence. The other patients all seemed to have lost interest now, and as they came around to their starting point again, Sister Margaret appeared from behind the East Wing to collect Nina.

"She'll sleep now, I suspect," said Perlman. "I'll be back at 1:30 or so. Bring her to my office, say at 2:00."

"Yes, Doctor. Two o'clock."

He turned to the girl. "After lunch, you and I, we'll have our talk, yes?"

She nodded nobly, the good soldier, then took Sister Margaret's hand and headed back down the low tunnel to Little Britain, in her mackintosh and boots, and with her head tilted to the side again as if her friend were hovering beside her like an invisible helium balloon.

## CHAPTER 15

Rounds were uneventful, comfortingly so. Over at the hospital, everything was the management of physical pain, the bread and butter of Perlman's trade. This was where he'd taken the *Pall Mall Gazette* man, to show him what a useful purpose suggestive therapy could serve. They'd gone from ward to ward, bed to bed, as he did every day, meeting patients spastic with pain—with severed limbs and surgical wounds and 105° temperatures—and leaving behind him a wake of peace and quiet. Perlman turned the turbulent waters still again, and did again today.

He lunched alone at the Fortunes of War, and was back at the clinic by half past one. Sister Margaret was waiting for him, her desk inundated with files. The Bernheim request had clearly swamped her. She said she needed to step out to the North Wing to pick up more stationery. The girl was asleep, so Perlman let her go and returned to his office to prepare for the session. The high bookshelf reminded him, though, he still needed to write the Café Royale about his Chronik. He was rooting through his drawers, looking for an envelope, when the doorbell rang in Reception. In the absence of the Sister, he answered it himself and had to check the peephole twice before opening the door.

"Madame Barrett?"

There she stood, grinning, enjoying his surprise. She was in a trim waistcoat; a more conservative attire than the night before, with the exception of her headdress, which was sprouting three great black feathers, all grazing the vaulted gray silks of an open umbrella.

She extended her hand, but there was something in it—a book. It took him a moment to recognize it in the calf-skinned grip of someone else: his Chronik.

"*You* have it? I was just going to write a note to the café."

"Yes." She smiled. "The man at the coat check handed it to me. I recognized it was yours."

"Well, thank you. I hope you didn't go out of your way."

"No. I was in the neighborhood. I've a meeting at Trench & Vernon & all the rest"—a legal firm just a few blocks down. "This isn't a bad time?"

"Oh. No. Come in."

He took her coat and umbrella, and hustled her past Sister Margaret's desk into his office. "Can I get you anything? Tea?"

"No, I can't stay long."

"Yes, sorry. Trench & Vernon. That can't be fun."

"No." Her feathers swayed. "I'm afraid we left quite a mess."

Perlman did not probe. Instead, he crossed to the far wall and set the Chronik on its shelf, where the Madame could not help but note its likeness to the whole row of other Chroniks stretching end to end.

"My-my."

"Yes." He pretended embarrassment. "I've been keeping them for some time."

She walked up and stood a moment before them, gazing. "They're not medical, though?"

"Musical."

She touched one of the spines. His body tingled. "May I?"

He'd never shown his Chroniks to anyone, least of all a woman, but he felt oddly willing. "Of course."

She tipped it down into her hand, and it fell open somewhere in the middle. She covered her mouth. "Oh, your handwriting."

"Yes, I suppose I believe in maintaining a certain degree of inscrutability."

"You must." She turned a page and squinted. Her lips moved slightly. "T-c-h. That's for Tchaikovsky?"

"Yes." He looked over her shoulder; could smell a trace of jasmine in her hair.

" 'The truth about T-c-h,' " she tried, " 'the h . . .' "

". . . 'the blessing and the curse,' " he assisted.

" 'The blessing and the curse, colon: he is only ever as good as the themes.' Hm." She looked back at him. "There you go again."

"Yes, there I go."

She handed the Chronik over, and he slid it back into its slot on the shelf. He was very happy. Then he felt her touch. Her hand was on his wrist, but as he turned back in hopes, the glowing ember in his stomach suddenly flared. She was looking toward Reception.

"Why, hello," she said, tapping him again. "Doctor, is this the artist you were telling me about?"

He turned. The Blum girl was standing at the threshold of his office, with her sketch pad tucked beneath her arm.

"Yes," he said vaguely. "Madame Barrett, this is Nina. Nina, Madame Barrett."

"Nina." The Madame removed her hand. "I had a cousin with that name. She was very beautiful, too."

The girl gave a curtsy. She did look particularly pretty. Her hair was still in its braid, and she'd stolen the belt from Sylvie's coat to give the hospital gown a more pleasing, feminine shape.

Perlman stepped up and spoke in a tone perhaps too terse—"Nina, what are you doing up?"

"I woke," she said simply. She was looking at Madame Helena. "And you didn't introduce Oona."

"Oona?" the Madame returned.

The girl nodded at the bookshelf. "She's right next to you."

Madame Helena turned to see. She surveyed the entire collection again. "Hn. My eyes must be getting old. I can't seem to see her." She glanced at Perlman and winked. "What does Oona look like?"

"Nina"—Perlman remained calm—"was there something you needed?"

"No." She stepped in. "Blond."

Just then the clinic door clanged open, and Perlman could see Sister Margaret stomping in out of the rain, canopied beneath the shawl of her habit. He excused himself quickly, holding the office door ajar behind him. "Sister Margaret"—he lowered his voice—"the girl is awake. I'd like you to come get her—for a bath."

She was dripping on the floor, but gathered his urgency. "Is she all right?"

"She's fine, but I'd appreciate your haste. We've a guest."

"I'll start the water."

He re-entered his office to find the girl and Madame Helena beside each other now, looking startlingly like a portrait. The Madame was seated in the leather wing-back chair, black feathers blooming from her head; the girl beside her, half-standing, half-balanced on the arm-rest. The sketch pad was open on the Madame's knee.

"Doctor." She turned the pad around for him to see. "Did you know this was Oona here in Nina's picture?"

The ember flared again. It was the first drawing the girl had done, of the maiden in the golden tower.

"I did actually, yes."

"Don't you think that's interesting?" She looked at him. He wasn't sure, but there seemed something mildly goading in her expression.

"I suppose. Nina, Sister Margaret is drawing your bath."

The girl nodded, distracted by the Madame's feathers.

"Well, I think that's very interesting." The Madame turned the painting around again to look at. "And is this where she lives?"

"No." The girl edged farther over onto the arm of the chair. "It's her uncle's. Her father sent her there for safekeeping."

"Ah, so there was danger."

"Her father said. He said there was sorcery in the hillsides."

"Excuse me," Perlman interjected. "What are we doing?"

"Just asking about the painting," said the Madame, all innocence. But she saw now, she could tell from his expression that she might have transgressed. "Oh, I'm sorry. I assumed the two of you had discussed this."

"No," said the girl. "Dr. Pearl-Man only likes the ones he can see."

The Madame didn't seem to understand exactly what she meant by this, but yielded. "Well, it's a lovely picture, in any case. I thank you for showing me." She offered the pad back to the girl, but Nina didn't take it. She wasn't through.

"It's the night she first saw Thaire," she said.

"Thaire?" The Madame leaned in.

"Yes, can you tell where he is?"

The Madame consulted the drawing again, but with a slower, more pointed interest now. "Well, I think maybe I can, but really I wonder if this isn't a question you should take up with the doctor."

"But I told you," said the girl, "he isn't interested."

The Madame looked over at him with the same puckered brow. "This doesn't interest you?" She turned the drawing around to face him: a tower, a maiden, a whale below.

He shook his head.

"See," said the girl. "So where do you think he is?"

And even then, the Madame gave him one last chance. All he had to do was shake his head, but for some reason he could not bring himself to—as if he were ashamed of his incuriosity—and that was all the Madame needed. She pointed a pair of slender, calf-skinned fingers down toward the bottom of the picture, at a shadow in the water. "I suspect this is him here."

"That's right," said the girl.

"But is Thaire a whale, then, or does he live inside the whale?"

"Lives inside." The girl was beaming. "At least that's what Porphyry said. She said he slept down there and he ate down there, but the only time you ever got to see him was at night, because then the whale would swim up near the surface so Thaire could build himself a fire."

The Madame observed the logic with a nod. "So this is smoke, then?" She indicated the silvery-gray plume above the shadow.

Yes, the girl nodded. "And that's how come they knew it must be him, because what other fish breathes smoke like that?"

" 'What other *mammal.*' "

"What other *mammal,*" the girl repeated. She didn't mind. She was in heaven. "And do you know what happened then?"

"Excuse me," Perlman tried again. "But, Nina, I worry your water is getting cold."

She looked back at him, glaring. "Sister Margaret will come and get me. And besides, there isn't much more."

He laughed nervously. "More what?"

"What happened," she said, obviously.

Oh, but where was Sister Margaret? They both were looking at him now, waiting for his consent, which he knew he should not give. This was a fruitless vine—or poison—and yet the Madame's eyes. What anaesthetic did she keep within those two blue orbs? What weakness was it she tapped in him that for a second time in less than twenty-four hours he should forsake his better judgment and submit like this—his only defense, again, that one could hardly be expected to refuse such attention, could one?

"Quickly," he said.

The girl turned to the Madame. "She jumped!"

"I'm sorry, what? Who?"

"Oona. When she saw the smoke, she jumped from the tower and dived down next to it, and when she looked inside, she saw there *was* a man!"

The Madame stopped her. "She looked inside the *whale?*"

"But it wasn't a whale. It was a boat, with a window, and when she looked inside she saw there was a man—"

Just then the office door clicked open and Sister Margaret ducked in. "Ready."

Rescued, thought Perlman. "Nina, your bath."

"Just a moment." Madame Helena held up her hand, to stay them. "This man—Thaire—did he see Oona?"

"He did," said the girl. "He turned and he saw her, too, but then she got so frightened, she flew back up to her tower."

The Madame paused, sensing his impatience. "Well, I don't blame her." She sat back. She looked at the picture again, admired it for one last moment, then offered it back to the girl.

But the girl still would not take it. "Do you want it?"

"Oh no. I really think the doctor should keep hold of all your pictures, don't you?"

The girl didn't see why. She turned the question to Perlman, who turned his answer back to the Madame.

"Yours," he said.

The girl acted. She tore the page out and presented it to the Madame.

"Well, lucky me," she answered graciously. "I do a good deed and look at my reward. Will you sign it?"

Perlman offered the pen from his own pocket—anything to get them apart—but the Madame refused. "Oh, a pencil. Ink will fade." She found one in her purse, and Nina leaned over her to sign the picture at the bottom right: *N-I-N-A*.

"Well, thank you." The Madame held it up again. "And Oona as well."

"Nina." Perlman stepped forward.

"You're welcome," she replied, unrushed. She smiled. "I like your hat."

"Thank you. I do, too." The Madame turned her head proudly. "They're ostrich, you know."

With his eyes Perlman signaled for Sister Margaret to come get the girl. Nina managed a curtsy before being wrapped in her towel and pulled away.


**H**ave the lamps dimmed?" The Madame was looking up at him, her large blue eyes as round as a pair of coins. "What a remarkable child."

"Yes."

"Don't you think?"

He paused. "Yes." He'd handled that very badly.

"Is there something wrong, Doctor?"

"No, it's just—I'm just reminded of some things I need to do."

She took her cue and stood. "And I as well. Much less pleasurable things. You're sure you don't want this, though?" She offered the picture, but again he refused, and she tucked it inside a large black leather folder she'd brought.

They conducted a stilted goodbye out in Reception. He could tell she was disappointed that their visit should end this way—or confused—but he was too distracted now to care. He handed her umbrella, she gave a nod, and without their having touched again, she stepped out into the rain and turned left on Little Britain, umbrella high above her headdress.

Perlman started for the girl's room, thinking of the time when he and Leonard had visited the photographic laboratory of a friend in Cambridge. They'd watched some pictures being printed—he remembered the effect, how beneath the chemical solution the image had suddenly appeared from nowhere, by deeper and deeper shades of clarity: a tree on a hillside. He felt as if he'd just watched the same thing—been watching it all week—only the subject was Nina.

He could hear her now behind the door, splashing, singing a bold marching song in her private tongue. She barely noticed him enter, she was calling out so proudly.

He cleared his throat for quiet. The Sister touched the girl's bare shoulder and she turned, the water swishing around her in abeyance.

"We're running a bit late."

*"We're running a bit laaaate,"* the girl sang heroically.

"Nina, please. Sister Margaret, if you could bring Nina around at half past."

*"Half paaaast!"* she bellowed, chest jutting.

"And I think perhaps some quiet time might be in order."

*"Quieeeeeet!"* The girl crescendoed, and swept a splashful of water down onto the tile floor. Sister Margaret scolded with a light tug on her hair, and Perlman closed the door again, holding the knob for just an extra moment, as if it were a cane or a banister.

She was done. What was the word they used in Cambridge? She was "developed."

But there was no point in thinking of that now, not with the task ahead. He returned to his flat and tried putting all this out of his mind.

It was two o'clock. He sat awhile in his reading chair, then moved over to the bench before his Broadwood, and for the next half hour drilled his left hand, repeating measures 12–16 of Barrett's second song over and over and over again, so that eventually his fingers would know it by rote.

## CHAPTER 16

Sister Margaret brought Nina to his office at 2:30 precisely. She appeared clean and rosy, but the heady inebriation of the Madame's visit seemed to have worn off. She'd washed her hair; it hung lank about her shoulders, a quieting shroud, and she'd brought the blanket from her bed as well.

He escorted her into room H, which was behind his office, just off the small vestibule that connected the clinic to his flat.

"It's small," she said, which it was, 7′ by 9′. He turned on the shaded lamp in the corner, and she looked around. Two chairs facing the window, one behind the other. A little stove, an etching of a windmill, and a drainpipe just outside. She touched the walls, which were a light, light gray.

"Like Pearl," she observed, "for Dr. Pearl-Man."

"Yes. You can sit if you like."

She did, with her arms up on the rests. Her feet didn't quite touch the floor. He slid over the footstool, and she covered her legs with the blanket. Then he sat behind her, where he could see her reflection in the window.

"It's quiet," she said.

"It's my quiet room. Safe and sound." He started the metronome ($\quarternote = 90$), then opened his journal and wrote the time. "Now what we're going to do here, it's very simple. As I said before, we're just going to try to imagine some things. But to begin, I want us to breathe. Can you see my hand?"

She nodded.

"Follow my hand—breathing in . . . and out . . ."

He guided her for five deep breaths. She obeyed precisely.

"That's good," he said. The metronome had established its rhythm by now. He counted five more tocks, then began.

"Nina, I want you to think of a spiral staircase . . . made of stone . . . Not steep . . . but smooth and round . . . You are walking down, step by step . . . You can see your feet . . . They're in slippers, and you're counting the steps . . . There's twelve . . . eleven . . . ten . . . nine . . ."

She was nodding as he counted.

"There's seven . . . six . . . five."

She sounded the steps with him—"four."

". . . three

". . . two

". . . and one."

Her breathing was slow and steady. He let her take three full breaths, and proceeded.

". . . We've come to a landing . . . There is a slim window, it's sunny outside . . . You take a breath . . . You can feel your body, full and well inside . . . You feel your chest . . . the sun on your face . . . your hands, your legs, your arms, your middle . . . all full and well . . . You can smell the grass outside, and wet stone."

She nodded.

"You are relaxed."

She nodded.

". . . Now I want you to continue down the stairs . . . We are going to keep going down the tower . . . You turn from the window and start . . . We are at the twelfth step again. There's eleven . . . ten . . . nine . . . You are going down. Eight . . . seven . . . breathing deep . . . five . . . smooth beneath your feet . . . three and two and one . . .

"We are at the next landing. Breathe. You are relaxed, comfortable . . . There is a chair by a window, looking out over a green meadow

. . . The sky is blue . . . The clouds are white. You stand behind the chair. There in the seat, you can see, is a necklace."

She nodded. She saw it.

"Do you know whose necklace that is?"

She nodded.

"The necklace is Sylvie Blum's. I am going to ask you to put on the necklace, so I can talk to Sylvie. Do you understand?"

She nodded.

"You wear the necklace, and I can talk to Sylvie Blum . . . And she will hold her water . . . and we can see how well you have made her, nursing her to health . . . We can see how thankful she is. But listen to me, Nina. If Sylvie should become frightened or uncomfortable, all I have to do is touch the nape of your neck. The necklace will fall, and I can speak to you again. Do you understand?"

She nodded.

"So I want you to sit down in the chair now."

He gave five more tocks to the metronome.

". . . Are you sitting?"

"Yes."

"Now I want you to take the necklace, lift it up and over your head." She was doing as told. Her hands were rising. "That's right. Now down. That's good. It is hanging from your neck."

Her head twitched.

"Calm. All is well. You can smell the meadow. You can see the sky."

She was beginning to tremble, her entire body.

"Is that Sylvie?"

Her breathing was growing more strained.

"Sylvie, everything is all right. I want you to feel your body." But she wasn't listening. Her eyes were rolling; then all of a sudden her breathing stopped. She gagged. Her neck puffed out.

"Sylvie?"

Her legs began kicking spastically. Her arms were flailing, beating the rests of the chair.

"Sylvie!" Perlman stood. She was in full seizure. "Breathe."

But she could not. She was choking. Her face was turning purple, as if Nina's well-being were somehow gorging Sylvie. He had to stop it. He reached down and touched the nape of her neck.

"Nina."

Her eyes were bugging.

"Nina, breathe."

Then suddenly she released. She drew in a lungful of air, much too quickly, and began coughing. She looked terrified, but all Perlman could do was kneel beside her, stroking her arm. She kept heaving; her eyes were wet and wild with fear. He lowered her head between her legs, then as soon as she had caught her breath again, her throat thickened and she began to cry.

"Here." Perlman tried helping her up from the seat, but she pushed him away, the spit stringing down from her lips. He called for Sister Margaret, who'd been waiting in Reception. She had only to open her arms and the girl folded into her. She stood up from the chair, and with her face buried in the Sister's breast, she hobbled pigeon-toed from the room.

Perlman was still standing there, alone, when he heard the door. Someone was knocking at the front door of his flat, he had no idea who. For a fleeting moment he thought of the Madame and was angry, but when he came to the window he saw it was a man, in a pinch-brim cap.

"Who is it?"

"Mr. Ramsey."

"Who?"

"Mr. Ramsey. For the piano."

It was the tuner. Perlman let him in and conducted their exchange in a complete haze. He'd been meaning to ask him about the player mechanism, but he was too undone by what had just taken place. He showed him to the piano, apologized for the condition, and left him there to work, all without register.

He went to her room then, briefly. The girl was in bed, still whimpering, holding Sister Margaret's hand.

"Nina." He stood beside them. "I'm sorry that was so difficult." She pulled away. "I want to thank you, though. You did very well."

She said nothing, but looked at him through thin, glassy eyes, the same as the first night she'd appeared—simmering, reproachful eyes.

Perlman returned to his office and sat at his desk. Just through the door, Mr. Ramsey was striking chords and individual keys, tuning them up and down.

The journal awaited his words. *First session, 2:30,* he wrote.

*Sylvie still in seizure.*
*A ransom captive.*
*What for?*

He sat awhile, looking at the words; then finally tore the whole page out. He closed the book and continued sitting, still only barely aware of Mr. Ramsey's efforts, sharpening the C, then the C sharp, the D and the D sharp, and on and on, till all the keys were in agreement.

# CHAPTER 17

Leonard arrived at six o'clock sharp with a bottle of Hartley & Gibson's and the warning that he could not stay long, his meeting was at 7:30 tonight. Perlman poured two glasses; Leonard refused his.

He didn't look well, or he didn't look good, which wasn't entirely his fault. Leonard had inherited more in the way of ugliness from their father's side than August, who counted as the one welcome bestowal of his mother's clan, a basic trimness. Leonard had been beefing up and down seasonally for years, but it really did look as if the fat had settled in this time—and early. His neck was massive. The surplus flesh on his face was effecting a permanent scowl. He was frankly looking an awful lot like Herr Blum, except that Leonard was also losing his hair in fistfuls.

"So?" said Perlman.

"*Wie geht's?*"

This was always an unacknowledged battle between them, whether to speak English or German. Leonard preferred German; he spoke English with a thick accent. Perlman did not—had worked hard not to—and did not think it appropriate to speak in foreign tongues, even for expatriate brothers.

"All's well."

"I got a letter from your mother—" Leonard strained to pronounce the *th*.

"Did you?"

"Yes. I wrote her."

"She's still at the settlement, I assume?"

"Yes. She sounds happy."

"Well, good." Perlman hadn't meant to sound quite so peremptory, but this was a sensitive subject between the brothers. Unspoken was the charge that their mother's departure had hastened their father's death. Less tacit was their disdain for the place she'd gone to, Palestine. Vienna had never seen a more cultured Jew than Theodor Herzl, and for him to turn around and proffer the snake oil of Zionism—revolting enough on its own, but then the image of their own mother down there, picking olives—ridiculous and pathetic. Perlman hadn't seen her since, or written.

He took a sip; foul brand. "And school?"

"Fine. The recital is coming up."

"Remind me the date. I know I wrote it down."

"Then I shouldn't have to remind you."

"The sixteenth. At St. John's?"

Perlman held his wince. He didn't like having to enter churches to hear music, and Leonard would never fill the space.

"Which ones are you playing?"—that it would be Beethoven went without saying—"90?"

"No. You want me to play 90, 110, and 111."

The last two. Again Perlman contained himself, but still, the way he'd said it. Leonard was becoming Arnold Müller. Müller had been Leonard's teacher back at the conservatory in Vienna, the one who'd imparted this unseemly reverence for the Beethoven sonatas. And the ruinous teaching style. Perlman remembered how Leonard used to complain, but now he was doing all the same things—confining his students' repertory; dissecting their playing, note by note, to the point that even the most robust talents would wither of self-consciousness. The brightest students all eventually fled, leaving a small harem of pianistic cripples whose only remaining purpose was to testify as to their master's brilliance, which was of such sensitive and refined nature that he was only ever able to express it in their classes—that is, in the confines of the adoring, spirit-broken gaze of ruined prospects. The public performances were another matter, and increasingly excruciating affairs—empty benches creaking up to vaulted ceilings, scattered pockets of old students all holding their breath, visibly swelling with pride at well-done passages, then just as visibly puncturing at Leonard's flubs, which there always, always, always were, one or two awful moments that shattered the illusion and ruined everything. The whole business finally made Perlman's stomach turn.

"Speaking of which. Do you know . . . I have something."

"So I suspect. What?"

"You tell me." He stood up and led his brother over to the piano. The pages he'd copied were waiting on the stand.

Leonard squinted at them dubiously. "Who did this? You?"

"I copied them, but can you tell who it is?"

Leonard scanned the top page grudgingly. He did not sit down. "I don't know," he said finally, then threw out "Alexander Barrett."

"Why, yes."

"Well, that's the bell hymn right there, isn't it?"

Perlman looked at the first piece. He hadn't even recognized, but Leonard was probably right.

"They're for a songbook." Perlman showed him the envelope. "I have the originals, but I didn't want any harm to come to them."

Leonard smiled smugly. "It's only Alexander Barrett, August. What are you doing with them?"

"His sister sent them to me."

"Madame Helena's a friend?"

"We met the other day at a reception for Professor Bernheim. We spoke, and the next day I received this from her."

"Must have been quite a conversation." Leonard glowered down at the copies again, like their father checking a hem. "Have you played anything?"

"Tried. But you can feel free." He pulled out the chair.

Leonard knew—they both did—how desperate August was for his help here. He lifted the skirt of his jacket and seated himself. Warily he set his hands on the keys and tried a chord. "Well, well. Did they come with a free tuning?" He set his hands back down and read through the first page. "Tsk, tsk, tsk. What was this for anyway, cousin Magda's birthday?"

Perlman sighed. "I don't know. It's just for a songbook. It's peda-gogy—"

"Oh, don't go apologizing for him." Leonard adjusted the bench.

He was in such an irritating mood, Perlman was tempted to stop him right there, yet as his brother began—the second piece—there was an instantly pleasing effect. A mock opening (Beethoven loosed upon Chopin's raindrop) seemed to welcome Leonard's condescension, striking an attitude that somehow reconciled the player's derision with the composer's delight. Likewise the gleeful dance of thirds that followed; that is, until Leonard actually began bobbing his head from side to side.

"Leonard, please."

"What?"

"Without the choreography."

Leonard refrained, merely rolling his eyes through the next section, a light-spirited amble that summoned up for Perlman the unchaperoned excursion of a curious two-year-old, seeking and finding, tripping and catching itself. Again, Barrett defied with charm: The harder Leonard tried to tease the piece, the harder the piece teased back. The dissonant chord progression followed on—the one that Perlman had worked so hard to figure out—and here Leonard did offer a smirk of respect, but really it was a pathetic display. As Perlman looked down at his brother, he felt something like pity, or shame. It had been cruel of him, he supposed, making Leonard play.

The last passage was the most lyrical. Leonard managed it dutifully, then returned to the opening, which could serve either as a coda or as a bridge to a second run-through.

"Need I?"

"No."

Leonard pointed back to the end. "Wish he'd gone with that a bit longer."

"Well, he may have, somewhere else." Perlman turned the page to reveal the third piece. "There's another."

Leonard gave a sigh. "How many?"

"Six altogether, but the one I have the most trouble with is this." He flipped ahead to the sixth and longest. "I'd just like to hear." He pointed at bar 12. "And that's a cross-over, if you like."

Leonard looked up at him, heavy-lidded. "I think I can manage."

He began, once again treating Perlman to an infuriating display of live disapproval and grudging consent, until finally all the facial histrionics caused him to flub a chord. His hands rested and he muttered, "I do hate this."

Perlman agreed. He snatched the pages from their place. "All right, Leonard. Thank you. You've been very kind."

"Oh, what is it, August? Am I insulting your new friend?"

"Leonard. I don't understand why you take this attitude."

"It just makes me ill. Alexander Barrett."

"What's wrong with Alexander Barrett?"

For momentary lack of words, Leonard soured his face and waved dismissively at the sheets that Perlman was now clutching protectively to his chest. "August, I'm sorry, but you and your notebooks and all your little opinions—the truth is, you know nothing."

Perlman stood back, momentarily stung. There was something in this phrase that excited a hot swell of rage within him. "I know nothing?"

"Yes. You listen to this decadent, parlor-room *debris* as if . . ." He paused, shaking his head, just long enough for that word to echo: decadent. "As if they'd ever invite *you* to their salons. That's what you want, isn't it? *Entrée.* That's the point of all this." He looked up and around, generally, clinic-ways.

"Leonard, I don't know what you're saying."

"Helena Barrett. What would Father think?"

"What would Father think about what?"

"About what you're doing, August, about what's becoming of you. And the sad fact is, you don't even see it. August, you could hypnotize all the Mrs. Flibbertigibbets in London—you could cure every case of hiccoughs from here to Budapest, and they still wouldn't let you in." He stopped, exasperated, at the limits of his own disgust withal. "Or maybe they would. Who knows? Maybe it would be fun to have a hypnotist around. A Hebrew hypnotist."

Leonard was staring down at the keyboard now, his face red and burning. Perlman stood above him, not so much offended as astounded—how someone as vulnerable as Leonard could be so hostile. For what was this display but envy? Alexander Barrett was a creator. Leonard knew that. And Leonard was not. Leonard was a destroyer.

"Leonard, it's half past. Doesn't your meeting start at 7:00?"

"Seven-thirty." Leonard stood up. "But I should get there early."

Perlman saw him to the door. Neither would look the other in the eye.

"Concert on the sixteenth, then."

"Yes," said Leonard, putting on his hat. "I'll send your best to Mother."

"Do."

With their hands on opposite knobs, August pushed and Leonard pulled the door closed between them.

# SATURDAY

# CHAPTER 18

$P$erlman took an unusually leisurely breakfast on Saturday morning—second helpings of toast and jam, and a more thorough perusal of the paper than he normally allowed. He'd awakened in a slightly different mood today, to an almost healthy fatalism about the Blum girl. All week he'd been laboring under the notion that if he simply handled things correctly, more deftly, he might actually have been able to meet his deadline. Herr Blum would come in Monday to find his daughter intact, physically robust, and they could proceed with the water question. This morning, however—or really since his session with the girl late yesterday—he'd come to accept that the case was more complicated than that. Whether it was a condition the girl brought with her or the result of his own mishandling—perhaps just a rash of bad luck—he realized he wasn't going to be able to solve this so quickly. He'd have to wait now, gain Nina's trust again, then see—not act so much as react.

He was pouring himself a third cup of coffee when the first opportunity presented itself. A disconcerting thud in the distance, then the girl's voice shouting.

He rushed out to find the moon-faced nurse they'd sent him Wednesday, Sister Antoinette, racing down the hall to get him, holding the shards of the fruit bowl. She looked overwhelmed.

"She wants you."

"What did she say?"

"I didn't understand. Something about her friend Oona, and is there some Madame Someone?"

He nodded. "I'll talk to her. Has Sister Margaret taken ill again?"

Before she could answer, there came another crash from inside the room. Perlman motioned Sister Antoinette away and started down the corridor.

Nina was on her bed, on her knees, taking a moment's break from a tantrum which was clearly exhausting her. Her gown was twisted around her waist. Her face was red and strewn with wild strands of hair, but when she saw him through the brunette tangle, she scowled with a mythic intensity and barked—"You take me to her!"

"Take you to whom?"

"Oona! She left because you're so mean to her."

He looked about the room. Her pad was on the floor, her water jar spilled, her brushes flung in every corner. "You're sure she isn't just hiding somewhere?"

"You know she isn't. She's with that woman. That lady."

"Madame Barrett."

"That's where she is, and that's where you're taking me."

Perlman paused. He'd never seen her act this way, but it was no less she, the Princess Nina, showing the flip side of her good breeding—spoiled insolence, and not without its charm.

"Nina." He approached the bed and spoke in a calm, measured voice. "You know that isn't possible. Besides, what makes you so certain she's gone? When did you last see her?"

"Last night."

"And you're sure she's not here now?"

The girl did not humor this attempt. "She's with Madame Barrett." She eyed the door and, knowing full well that she could not make it, started from the bed, obliging Perlman to grab hold of her by the arms.

"Let go!"

"I want you to calm down."

"No. I hate you."

"Nina, calm down. Now, I am not taking you to Madame Helena's."

"You are, too. If you don't take me, I'll . . ." She couldn't think, she was too angry. She wrested free, grabbed the iron rail of her bed and began shaking it.

"Nina, stop that. You'll hurt yourself."

"You don't care if I hurt myself. All you care about is Sylvie. Well, I hate Sylvie and I hate you, and I don't care what happens to Sylvie Blum!" She smacked herself on the side of the head.

"Nina, *don't* do that!"

She looked at him, and her eyes swelled fiendishly at the effect that this little inspiration of hers had had. She smacked herself again on the ear, and Perlman grabbed hold of her wrists.

"You will stop that this instant."

"I will not."

"You will. I will tie your hands."

"Doesn't matter," she sneered. "It doesn't matter what you say. Then I won't eat. I won't eat, and I won't sleep. I'll make myself as sick as Sylvie." Her arms fell suddenly slack and her eyes rolled back in her head as though she was having a seizure.

"Nina, stop that."

She slumped over and began to dry heave in the direction of his lap.

"Nina!" He shook her by the arm. "I want you to stop."

"No." She wrestled free and glared at him. "You can't tell me what to do! I'm the one who tells you what to do, because *I* say what happens to Sylvie, not you. *I'm* the one who says when she eats. *I'm* the one who says when she sleeps, and if you don't let me out of here—" Her face was red and trembling with rage. "If you don't, I'm going to—" she began hitting herself in the head again.

Perlman reached for her, but she was too quick. She jumped down to the floor on the other side of the bed and then hurled herself against the wall, much harder than she'd intended. The thud resounded horrendously. For a moment she was dazed; she couldn't choose between crying or rage. Then she began flailing against the wall again.

Perlman was stunned. "I'll kill her!" she was saying. She was thrashing herself, pulling her hair. "I'll kill her, because I don't care." She began scratching at her face.

"Stop," said Perlman. "Stop!" he cried. He lifted the bed up by its frame and dropped it on the floor. The room shook, and she turned, suddenly still.

"What is it you want?" He glared.

She looked back at him, flushed and woozy, even bashful. It didn't seem she expected he'd yield so quickly. "Just to see Oona." She coughed meekly.

"Oona. And you think she's at Madame Barrett's."

"I know she is—"

"All right," he stopped her. "We'll try," he said, only now considering the consequences of what he was saying.

"When?"

When? He could hardly believe his own ears, but in just that moment of hesitation, that look entered the girl's eye again, that frankly murderous glare.

"WHEN?"

"I'll have to see. But, Nina, let me be clear. If we go, it's to find Oona; then we leave. Do you understand?"

"Yes."

"And no more of that hitting or scratching or hair pulling. Are you all right?"

She felt her elbow. "Yes."

"I don't want to see that anymore."

"Fine."

"All right." He patted the bed. "Wait here."

As he made his way down the hall, Perlman felt numb. He couldn't remember ever having lost control like this, but he wasn't sure what else he could do—aside from sedating her, which he would never do, and which wouldn't have worked, in any case. This girl wasn't going anywhere. Really, it had only been a matter of time before she figured it out: that she controlled Sylvie Blum and Sylvie Blum controlled him.

Sister Antoinette was back at the desk in Reception, her round white face still flexed with fear. "Doctor, are you all right?"

"I'm fine. Who else do I have today?"

She checked the schedule. "A Mrs. Woolsey at two and Colonel Hicks at three."

The colonel was an insomniac, hadn't slept a full night since returning from South Africa. "Hicks is still at Royal Hospital?"

"Yes, I think so."

"Cancel that." He thought. "And how ill is Sister Margaret, did you say? Will she be coming in later?"

"She said she'd try, but I wouldn't expect her. She's white as a sheet."

He nodded, thinking.

"I could send someone else."

"No, that won't be necessary. Cancel Mrs. Woolsey as well; then let me get Sister Margaret's paperwork together. You can drop it off when you're through here. But tell her she doesn't need to come in today. Tell her to rest, that I've got things under control."

"But the girl—"

"The girl is fine." He held her eye to plant the idea. "Don't worry about the girl. I'll have all the files by three, then you can be on your way."

Perlman said no more. No more was necessary—Sister Antoinette was clearly terrified of him, and Nina. As he headed back down the hall, he supposed he was lucky in a way that Sister Margaret should have taken ill. He could never have smuggled the girl out with Sister Margaret looking on.

Nina was sitting up on her bed again, demure, victorious.

"We'll go this afternoon."

"This after*noon*?"

"Yes, as soon as the Sister leaves. In the meantime, you can clean up here."

"Whose coat am I going to wear?"

" 'Whose coat.' Nina, do you know the expression 'looking a gift horse in the mouth'?"

She shook her head.

"It means you shouldn't be so demanding when you're already getting your way. You will wear the coat in the closet."

She pursed her lips.

"You can bathe, have a bite to eat, then we'll go."

"Fine."

"And, Nina, listen to me—I don't want you mentioning this to Sister Antoinette, do you understand? This is our secret. If I find you've told her, then we're not going."

She hugged her pillow to her chest. "Fine."

Back in Reception, Perlman informed Sister Antoinette that the girl would take her bath now; then he returned to his office and began organizing files for Sister Margaret. He thought of his errand only to reassure himself: a brief trip across town, that was all, to show the girl that he was not her enemy. He would need the girl, and sometimes unusual conditions required unusual measures.

He realized he should probably try to warn the Madame, though. He was on with the operator for a quarter of an hour before he remembered that the Madame hadn't been in London since 1900. She probably wasn't even wired. He thought to send a messenger, but it was Saturday. They'd have to go blind.

He devoted the remainder of Sister Antoinette's shift to the files, and by three o'clock was able to present her with the lot of them. The Sister was out the door by 3:05, none the wiser.

He was a half hour at the mirror then, washing, slicking, snipping. He chose his four-button jacket, brown hound's-tooth scarf, and suede gloves, topped by his favorite bowler hat.

The girl was waiting for him in Reception, wearing a prim white dress, ruffled and high-waisted, shiny black shoes, white socks, and the sky-blue overcoat.

"I hate these clothes."

"You look very nice," he said, though he more or less agreed. She rose and took the pad beneath her arm.

"What's that for?"

"Just in case."

"Put it back."

Grudgingly she obeyed, then they left.

The fog was coming in, fast and thick, but Perlman welcomed it for once.

"Take my hand."

They hustled down Little Britain. He could barely see the cab in front of the Priory. As they emerged from the soup, the coachman tipped his cap in approval—more fathers should take their daughters out for tea.

"Charles Place," said Perlman. "And take the river, if you would." He pressed two shillings into the coachman's glove and closed the door behind them. The reins shook, the horse replied with a snigger, and they were on their way.

# ACT II

# CHAPTER 19

Perlman and the girl rode in silence, like a pair of feuding newly-weds: she with the upper hand, looking out contentedly at the fog; he hounded into submission, eyes straight ahead, uncomprehending, and with a complexion slightly blanched from the burden of responsibility he'd just taken on.

He knew this was wrong. This was madness, in fact—taking his patient away from the controlled setting of the clinic, escorting her all the way across town to a basically unknown destination, there to engage in an extremely delicate improvisation with a woman he barely knew, in hopes—that is, if all went well—of fetching the girl's imaginary friend. In all his years as a therapist, he'd never participated in anything nearly as confounded or reckless as this.

But what else could he do? As the fog ushered them deeper and deeper into its twilit folds, he kept going over his dilemma from every different angle, and each time reached the same conclusion: he had no choice. The girl, sitting so prim and superior at the far end of the seat, had found the key and she knew it. It would be her leverage over him for as long as she chose to use it: "Do as I say, or just as I have protected your patient up to now, I shall harm her; just as I have sustained and nourished her, I shall starve her till she withers before your eyes. Or I shall beat her against the wall." The simplicity of it, the obviousness, had Perlman scolding himself now—for not carting her right back to the hospital that first night; for not snuffing Oona the first chance he got; for letting Nina keep the drawing pad; for letting the Madame have the picture. What could he have been thinking? His whole approach, the entire "Feed and Starve" canard, had been sheer idiocy. And not just that it should find him, four days later, engaged in this perfectly absurd mission, but that as he sat here now he could think of nothing else they *should* be doing instead. For even if all went well— if he should "retrieve" Oona and return directly to the clinic—all they'd do there was wait and wait and try again, induce her again, to ask after Sylvie, to watch her seize again, bloat, choke. He knew that's what would happen. He just didn't see any other way.

"I hope you're prepared for the possibility that Madame Barrett may not even be there," he asked midway, his lone question.

She simply looked at him with a kind of bewildered disgust, as if he'd used a verb tense she didn't understand. The Madame would be there.

He thought so, too. He could feel it, like a ball of twine in his lap; there was more line to go, and Helena Barrett, of all people, seemed to be holding the other end.

At length it led them to the southeast corner of Charles Place, just off the Kings Road in Chelsea. The cab left them in front, but the fog was so thick they could barely see: a three-story Georgian terrace house, its white-stone exterior suggesting to Perlman that this was a holding of the family's English—i.e., moneyed—side, as opposed to its more artistic Russian strain, which doubtless would have preferred one of the more distinctive houses down by the river. Still, this one stood out from the others in its line. Because it was the last in the row, there was a side path leading to the back garden, and western light. Also, it was wider than the others by half; whereas its neighbors all presented a uniform front—a terraced door on the right, broad windows to the left—the Barrett house boasted wings on each side of the door.

"We're supposed to bring her something," said Nina. She spied a bed of flowers two houses down, a white blot of lilies, through the mist. Perlman waited for her to pick one; then they ascended the steps hand in hand.

It wasn't clear if anyone was home. All the windows were dark but for the ground floor on the left side—a faint lamplight sifted through the lace curtains. He tried peering in, but Nina was pulling him too fast.

"Hello!" She took the knocker and pounded it four times. *Alloo.*"

"Quiet." He squeezed her hand. "They'll come."

There was no answer for a while, which Perlman found curious. The girl took up the knocker and was about to strike again, when they heard the sound of feet padding to the door, and a voice, bright and curious—"Hello?" The lock turned, the door swung open, and there stood the Madame herself.

"Why, hello. Dr. Perlman. Nina." She addressed them both with pleasant surprise.

She was dressed in as simple an ensemble as he'd yet seen: a black shawl over her shoulder; a dark brown gown, one piece, tucked at the waist, with long, open sleeves. Her hair was up but relaxed; the only hint of the exotic was hanging from her neck, a long strand of beads and stones looped three times around. He assumed he'd caught her alone.

"Madame, I'm sorry just to appear unannounced, but—you remember Nina."

"Of course. How are you, Nina?"

"I'm very well, thank you." The girl produced the lily from behind her back.

"Why, thank you." The Madame took it, glancing two doors down. "How kind."

"I tried phoning ahead," said Perlman.

"Oh, I'm afraid we're still a bit Victorian around here."

"Enviably, I'm sure, but I wanted to make—"

"Where's Oona?" asked the girl.

The Madame looked at her. "Oona?"

"Yes," said Perlman. "It seems we've lost track of Nina's friend. You remember. She suspects she might have come here."

He tried catching her eye, but the Madame was steps ahead. She looked down at Nina and, without missing a beat, "Why, yes," she replied. "Yes, she's in the parlor." Then she stepped aside—cunning woman. Nina bolted like a colt.

"Thank you," mouthed Perlman.

He crossed the threshold to a narrow entry, dimly lit. He could feel it instantly, though, a stillness in the air, a tincture of old incense hovering in the ambiance of every leaf and vine that crawled across the wallpaper, every post along the banister. The house was not yet fully resuscitated.

He deposited his gloves and scarf on the shelf of a walk-in closet, which seemed almost deliberately to resemble the one at St. James's Hall, with a Dutch door. "I appreciate your help here." He kept his voice low. "I don't expect we'll be long."

With her lily she waved this away as a needless attempt at courtesy, which it only was in part. "You're very welcome." She took his arm and started them down the front hall, her necklace gently clicking. They passed a dining room on the right. "You'll just have to forgive our appearance. I've been in the Cotswolds since getting back, so I haven't gotten round to much. Al?"

Al? To the left they entered a parlor facing the street. There was a man there already—the aforementioned—standing to greet them. Older, with an exuberant red complexion beneath white hair, a bushy mustache, and ample muttonchops. It was the gentleman from Bernheim's reception.

"Dr. Perlman, you've met Lord Stanley."

"Yes." He bowed. "Sorry to intrude like this."

"Not at all." Lord Stanley bowed in return, unopposed. They'd been having tea, just the two of them, though Stanley looked a bit old for a suitor. Maybe not. Rather Johnny-on-the-spot, though, for as Perlman looked around now, he saw the Madame had meant what she'd said. This was the front room of two, divided midway by French doors, but most of the furniture was still draped in white sheets. Only a rolltop desk and the seats immediately surrounding the hearth had been unsheathed. That and a small drinks cabinet by the dividing wall.

The girl had availed herself of the love seat by the fire. She was holding her blue coat closed and directing a fierce glare in the general direction of the mantel. She and Oona would have words later.

The Madame joined her, standing. "And did Nina introduce herself?"

"Not quite, no," said Stanley, good-humored.

"Nina, would you say hello to Lord Stanley?"

"Hello to Lord Stanley."

"She's a bit upset with a friend," the Madame explained.

"These things happen."

"Nina, may I take your coat?"

She hunched her shoulders.

"Are you cold? I can put on another log."

She shook her head.

"I'm afraid she's not very pleased with her wardrobe either," said Perlman.

The girl looked to the Madame. "You don't have anything, do you?"

"Nina"—Perlman was quick on this. "We're just here to pick up Oona and go. You understand that?"

"But we're having tea, aren't we?" She pointed to the table in front of her. A plate of crackers, jam, and a crock of pâté—a gift from Stanley, it looked like—and an exquisite silver samovar stood watch beside the couch.

"Of course you are," said the Madame. She looked over at Perlman to make sure.

"Very well. A cup of tea. But the Madame is being very kind."

The girl agreed; she swung her legs. "But I still need something to wear."

"Nina. Don't be silly."

"It's all right," said the Madame. "I think I can probably find something."

"No, Madame, really—"

"It's no trouble," she said. "And I'll get some more cups. Sit." She smiled, and then was gone.

Odd, he thought, the absence of help. He took a moment to look around. Even draped, he could tell this was the room for conversation.

Through the French doors was more of a performance space. There was a small stage at the far end, and a piano. Two, in fact. A baby grand and a second full-, he wasn't sure what kind. He thought he might even see a spool box above the keys, but before he could take a closer look, there was Stanley, mistaking his curiosity for criticism.

"It is a bit of a mess," he said.

"Well, I wasn't aware; she must have just returned."

"Week or so. She was out in the Cotswolds. I've been trying to get one of our housekeepers to come over, but they're all so skittish."

"You two are old friends?"

"Oh no. I'm her uncle," said Stanley, smiling at the relief this freed in Perlman's posture. "Yes, Uncle Al. Her father was my cousin. But how is it *you* know Helena?"

"I don't really. At the reception the other night, that's the first we met."

Stanley was impressed by this, though there might have been something else in his expression, the recognition of another stray cat who'd followed his niece home.

"What's this?" The girl was over on the far side of the room, by the streetside windows. She'd been conducting a survey of her own apparently and was now standing before a team of smaller furnishings, all clustered together in the corner—lampstands and statuettes which must have been taken from their places before the covers were laid. There was one in particular, though, taller than the others and draped in a gray-white linen. She took the fringe between her fingers, and Stanley's posture visibly stiffened.

"Nina," called Perlman, "get away from there."

She stood straight. "But what is it?"

"Something the Madame apparently wants covered."

The girl was hardly dissuaded, but Stanley chose a friendlier tack. He rounded to the couch by the hearth again. "Come sit," he said. "You need to explain to me—who is this friend you're having trouble with?"

"Oona." She turned.

"And she's meeting you here?"

Perlman thought of stepping in, but frankly couldn't think of what to say.

"She's here already," said the girl.

Stanley straightened. "Helena didn't mention anything."

Perlman couldn't tell whether he was playing or not, but Nina smiled. She seemed to think he was.

"Is she upstairs?" he asked.

Nina shook her head. "She's in here."

"In here?" he blustered. "Where?"

She pointed to the mantel.

Stanley set his hands on his knees and gave the shelf a good long squint; he was indeed the Madame's uncle. "How big is she?"

"Right now?" the girl asked.

"Yes, now."

The girl considered, then showed with her hands, setting them about a yard apart, high and low.

Stanley tried again to see if he could discern some small creature sitting above the fire, but finally gave up; just like the Madame, he was too old. "I used to have a friend no one else could see," he said. "Did you ever, Doctor?"

"No, I never did," he answered, glancing back toward the Music Room, at the larger of the two pianos, the one with the spool box.

"What was his name?" asked the girl.

"Tom," said Stanley fondly, sadly. "Tom."

"What happened to him?"

"I suppose I'm not exactly sure. I saw less and less of him. I still suspect that from time to time he pays a visit. Maybe we've just grown quiet with one another. When you've known someone that long, there really isn't much left to say."

Nina nodded. She agreed.

Just then the Madame stuck her head through the doorway leading to the front hall. She was hoping for just Nina to see, but Stanley caught her.

"Helena, why didn't you mention anything about this Oona?"

"Oh." She stepped out into the frame, contrite. "Sorry about that. I didn't want to alarm you."

"Wouldn't have been alarmed. Sounds charming."

"She is—very charming. And in fact, I did tell you." She stepped over to the rolltop desk. Perlman hadn't seen, but the girl's picture was right there, lying flat. Madame Helena brought it over to her uncle. "That's Oona there." She indicated the figure in the tower.

"Oh." Stanley had to hold the drawing out at arm's length. "Well, I suppose that gives a better sense."

The Madame motioned Nina to the door—she'd found something for her. While Stanley continued his examination, Nina snuck by, pulling tight the collar of her coat.

There were just the two of them now. Stanley set down the picture and grinned. "Enchanting young lady. Yours?"

"No. No, no, no. She's . . . in my care for the time being." Perlman nodded through to the next room. "May I ask, is that a performer in there?"

"The Welte, you mean?"

A Welte. Perlman literally swayed. "A Welte-Mignon. Really? Do you think I could take a look?"

"Certainly." Stanley stood up to escort him, which was hardly necessary. Perlman glided through the open door like a charmed snake. He took quiet note of the other pieces: a five-string cello, gray with dust; a psaltery; timpani. More draped lamps and chairs, but it was the Welte that called him over.

"Oh my."

What a gorgeous piece. An original Welte-built, Welte-Mignon reperforming grand. Victorian make. He'd been reading about these for years, but he'd never actually seen one in person. These were the vanguard, and just now coming on the open market, to blast away the old pianolas, the chief difference (aside from price) being that the older models hadn't any real shading or nuance; their hammers all struck with the same dumb heft. Not the Weltes. They could vary their dynamic—or so they claimed—note to note, and on that basis offered more than a mere rendering of the pieces in their catalogue. They

promised actual *performances,* which was why there'd been the rush to
sign up all the most celebrated players and composers—Grieg, Strauss,
Mottl, and Barrett, too. Now one could hear the virtuosos play with
"photographic likeness," as the Welte people liked to advertise, *"in
your very own parlor!"*

"This must be one of the first," said Perlman.

"Prototype." Stanley had followed him over. "Spectacular piece of
machinery."

"But was this his? He didn't leave Welte on very good terms, as I
understand."*

"No." Stanley smiled. "I'm sure he paid."

And a pretty penny, thought Perlman. He ran his hand along the
case. Lacquered mahogany. "Do you think I can have a look inside?"

"Of course."

He slid back the casing. They both peered in.

"My word, look at that." He was practically drooling. "I have an in-
sertible of my own, so I'm somewhat familiar with the mechanism, but
this—this must be for the dynamics."

"I suppose. They do a remarkable job."

"I've heard—tell."

"Maintenance is key, though."

"Do you know about this one?"

"No. I sent over a tuner before Helena arrived, for the Pleyel. I
imagine he may have taken a look."

"Probably couldn't resist." Oh, but to hear it play. Perlman cast a
stealthy glance around the room to see if there might be a collection of
rolls somewhere—perhaps even the "Nonsense" themselves. Just the
idea started the back of his neck tingling—

"Hello?" the Madame's voice called from the parlor again. "Where
did you go?"

Perlman and Stanley both rushed back to help. She had a fully
loaded tray in her arms.

"We'll need another chair." She directed Perlman to one against the

* See p. 56.

wall, still covered. He removed the sheet carefully, and well he did. Underneath was a very unusual piece, with a Middle Eastern print and tasseled fringe.

"Where is this from?" asked Perlman.

"Baghdad. Somewhere." She set down the tray.

"May I?"

"It's a chair."

He set it down in their circle and sat gingerly, with privilege.

Madame Helena had brought three cups on saucers—three gold-rimmed English teacups, a silver sugar shell and matching creamer, a jar of honey, a dish of dark jam, and the lily that Nina had given her, in a slender glass vase.

"And where is our fourth?" asked Stanley.

"Our fifth," the Madame corrected.

"Yes, our fifth."

The Madame turned, and the girl just then stepped into the door frame. "Oh, look at you."

They'd found a white lace dress, a picnic gown. Perfect fit; Perlman dreaded getting that off. But the image stilled him, not just because she looked so pretty—she had an ivory comb in her hair, and slippers. It was more the aptness. She'd found her element, and the swiftness with which she'd done so, turned into this enchantment standing before them now—the niece, was it?—was frankly unsettling.

"Oh, very pretty," Stanley commended them both. "Much better."

The girl gave a slight curtsy and entered. She took her place at the love seat, her cheeks gleaming like apples. This was much better.

## CHAPTER 20

The girl addressed the Madame: "So what did you and Oona do all day?"

"Well, I'm afraid I've been a bit of a bore." The Madame held a cup to the samovar. "Unhappily, I have returned to find a great deal of homework waiting for me, so I actually spent most of the morning with that." She set down the first cup, full now, and started a second. "But Oona didn't seem to mind. She was very good company. Sugar, Doctor?"

"No. Thank you."

"Nina?"

"Two, please." She frowned. "She didn't say anything, did she?"

"She said a great deal." The Madame handed over the cup and began a third. "Unfortunately, that language you two speak—exquisite, but I'm afraid I couldn't make heads or tails." She gave a faint nod toward the mantel. "I am assuming Oona does not take cream."

"No."

"Honey?"

"Yes."

The Madame obliged. She dunked a spoon of honey in the third cup and carried it to the mantel, which was overdoing it just a bit, thought Perlman.

The girl was suitably encouraged. As soon as the Madame took her seat again, Nina sat up like a rooster and called out a singsong couplet in that "exquisite" language—*"Rea lono lylo, ila layama."*

Perlman felt slightly embarrassed watching her, but Stanley perked up his ears. "What was that?"

"It means 'Why must I be here,'" said the girl, "'when I can do whatever I want?'"

The Madame grinned into the steam of her tea. "I bet I know where that's from."

Stanley turned. "No fair secrets. Where?"

"Well," the Madame glanced at Perlman, playfully almost, convivially. "Nina was telling the doctor and me a story the other day. The picture's an illustration, in fact." She tapped it; it was lying beside the tea tray now. "I suspect that that line—'Why must I be here?'—belongs somewhere in there."

Stanley spun the image around to see better. "This was Oona's lament."

"Something like that."

"So was she trapped up here, in this tower?"

"In a manner of speaking," said the Madame. "Not bad, Al."

"Well, I can still put two and two together on occasion." He gave the picture another squint. "And what's this, then—a whale?"

The Madame and Nina shared a smile. "It looks like one, doesn't it?"

"Yes. What's it doing in a river, though? Is it lost?"

The Madame set down her tea. "I suppose we could just tell you the story, if you like. I think you might find it very interesting, in fact."

Stanley handed over his cup for a refill, but the Madame glanced at Perlman first. "Do you mind?"

He looked back at her. Was this his chance, then? Was he supposed to say no now, while they were all being so charming? Again, it was his impulse to nip this in the bud, but as he looked at the three of them, looking back at him, the drawing in Lord Stanley's hand, the solitary teacup cooling on the mantel, he realized that the bud was in bloom. And this *was* why they'd come, wasn't it? Because Dr. Pearl-Man didn't listen and the Madame did.

As faintly as his neck would allow, he nodded.

"Good." The Madame sat forward and let the shawl slip from her shoulders. "And Nina, you'll help?"

Nina nodded.

"Good." The Madame gave her a wink, then sat back with her cup. "Now, my sense is that this happened some time ago, yes?"

The girl confirmed, absolutely.

"How long, if you don't mind my asking?"

"Very long. Longer than you know."

The Madame smiled. "Well, that could mean a number of things. How long?"

"Long."

"Before Jesus–long?"

"Longer."

"Before Noah–long?"

The girl nodded. "Before that."

"Well there, yes." The Madame attended to her tea, to veil a reaction, it seemed to Perlman, of undue interest. She took lemon. "Very, very, very long ago, when Oona was . . ." Again she turned to the girl. "How old would you say?"

"Well, it's not the same."

"But for our purposes."

The girl glanced up at the mantel to consider. "Not a girl, but not a woman either."

"All right." The Madame turned back to Stanley again. "Very, very, very long ago, when Oona was not quite yet a woman, it seems the land was embroiled in a conflict of some kind, some sort of schism—I am not certain of the reason. I assume that if it becomes pertinent, we will learn. In any case, because of this unrest, there had begun to circulate talk of sorcery in the hillsides."

Stanley grunted, sounded grave. The girl was very happy.

"Fearing which, Oona's father—a priest named Mmmm-

"—alachai," the girl finished.

"Malachai—sent his daughter, Oona, to the Temple of . . ."

"Aram, her uncle."

"... the temple of her uncle Aram. Malachai sent her there for safe-keeping."

Lord Stanley shook his head. "Always a mistake."

"Yes." The Madame tapped his knee. "For, you see, Oona was, among other things, a demigoddess."

Perlman jolted in his seat as if he'd burnt his tongue.

"Doctor?"

"Demigoddess?"

The Madame seemed legitimately surprised. "I thought that was the first thing she said. No?"

"I didn't hear anything about a demigoddess."

"I could have sworn." The Madame opened a nephrite box and took out a cigarette. She plucked a match from a small stone bowl, struck it against the side, and lit the fag. "Well, in any case"—she tossed the matter aside with the burnt stick—"the point is, divine or no, she seems to have been able to do whatever she liked. Fly like a bird, swim like a fish, and so forth. Yes?"

Yes, Nina nodded.

"The reason it bears mention"—the Madame now took the ash-tray from the table and set it, for no apparent reason, down on the floor at her feet—"is to make clear that as our story begins, Oona is a free spirit, someone capable of doing almost anything she can conceive, but who finds herself confined, by obedience, at her uncle's temple. Agreed?" She consulted Nina, the mantel briefly, and then Perlman.

This woman was much too clever. "Agreed."

"In fact," she said, "every night she used to go out onto the balcony of her uncle's tower, look up at the stars, and lament . . ." She waited.

The girl sat up and repeated the line. " '*Rea lono lylo, ila layama.*' "

" 'Why must I be here alone,' " the Madame translated, "when I can do whatever I want?' " She took a pull on her cigarette.

Much too clever.

"One night"—she swiped the air clear again and set the cigarette down in the ashtray at her feet—"Oona was out on her balcony."

She turned her attention to the tea service now, to the lily in particular—a white stargazer, as it happened. In its slender vase, she set it near the edge of the table. "She was taking her evening bath, with her nurse Porphyry attending"—she stood the stout creamer faithfully beside—"when out of nowhere she noticed something very strange."

The Madame turned, drawing all their attention—the lily's included—beyond the table's edge, where just now the first plumes of her burning cigarette were wafting into view.

"A trail of smoke was rising above the balustrade." The Madame glanced at Nina, then the flower.

Nina understood. She lifted the lily from its vase and rushed it to the brass bar at the edge of the table. " 'Porphyry, look! There it is again.' "

The Madame slid the creamer beside the flower and tilted it slightly to look down over the edge. " 'Why, child, you're right.' " She turned to Stanley: "An enormous black shadow was sliding through the water."

What on earth? thought Perlman.

" 'But do you think that's really him?' " asked the girl, bobbing the flower like a puppet.

" 'I think it must be,' " the Madame replied, tilting the pitcher. " 'What other fish breathes smoke like that?' "

" 'A whale isn't a fish,' " said the girl. " 'It's a mammal.' "

Even Stanley couldn't help a slight head stammer.

The flower looked down. " 'But do you think he really lives inside?' "

" 'So they say.' "

" 'And eats down there?' "

Yes, the pitcher nodded.

" 'And sleeps down there?' "

" 'Ay, and builds a fire at night . . .' "

They both took a moment to observe the smoke, which continued drifting up and dispersing.

" 'Must be cold,' " said the girl.

" 'Yes.' "

" 'And lonely.' "

" 'Yes.' " The Madame tipped the creamer even farther, as if it were leaning to keep the whale in sight. " 'Very lonely.' "

Nina turned to Stanley now. "And do you know what Oona did?"

"I haven't the faintest." He grinned at Perlman. "You, Doctor?"

They all three looked over at him. What else could he do? He nodded.

Stanley faced the girl again, but she was still smiling at Perlman.
"What did she do, Dr. Pearl-Man? You say."

She waited, the manipulative little imp. They all waited. He saw no
other way. "She jumped," he said.

"And she flew!" The girl lifted up the flower and started it in a high,
graceful arc. "And she dove down into the water beside him." She
plunged the flower down below the tabletop.

"Yes, but up close," the Madame put in, "up close she saw that it
wasn't a whale. It was a boat, gliding *under* the surface."

This was news to Perlman, but Stanley didn't know any better. He
seemed to like the idea.

"With a glass window!" said the girl. "And Oona swam up, and she
looked inside, and she saw there was a man." She glanced at the
Madame, just to make sure she hadn't missed anything. "And the man
saw her, too."

The Madame nodded.

"And what did she do?" asked Stanley, ever-game.

"She got so frightened, she swam away. She flew back up to her balcony."

Again the Madame obliged. She picked up the flower and set it back
inside the vase, but there was something lacking now, something that
did not satisfy. She took up the cigarette as well and treated herself to
a long, glowing drag, squinting. "Yes, you mentioned that before," she
said, her breath blue and smoky, "how she became so frightened. I'm
still not entirely sure why, though. Was there something about his appearance?"

Stanley seconded the question.

The girl took a moment. She hadn't counted on this, but seemed to
acknowledge that some further explanation was in order. "Well, it was
dark," she said, clearly buying time, "so she couldn't really see him
well at first. All there was was the fire. But she looked and she looked,

and then she did see . . ." She paused, but only to heighten the suspense;
she had it now. "There were two eyes staring straight back at her, and
she'd never seen eyes like that—that color."

"What color?" asked the Madame.

The girl leaned in. "They were like ashes."

"Ashes?" said Stanley.

"Ashes," she repeated, breathless.

Stanley looked over at the Madame, who flicked a clump into the
tray.

Perlman had watched all this from an oddly detached perspective,
not really listening so much as marveling—how these two raced together. Every sentence they spoke was like another dash into the
thicket, another loop in the knot he knew he would eventually have to
untie. And yet he'd just sat there. In the weeks and months to come,
he'd have ample time to wonder why—why he couldn't at least have
tried to rein them in—and, in more forgiving moods, would point to
the nature of the performance itself, which had been so arrestingly
strange and adept, and which seemed to flow of its own so naturally, it
effectively forbade any aggressive intrusions from the outside. Also,
the setting hadn't helped. That strange draped museum would probably have lent *anything* that took place in its midst a certain perspective-
leveling surreality. That is, a game of hearts might have seemed just as
odd; or just as distracting, frankly, for there was that, too—the fact
that Perlman's foremost quelled desire since entering this place hadn't
been to shut these people up. It was to explore the place in peace, without Stanley peering over his shoulder like some lonely docent. They
could have talked all they liked, quite frankly, if he could simply have
been excused to go peek beneath the drapes, along the shelves, inside
the frames.

Now that the Madame and Nina had finished with their scene,
however—now that the curtain had fallen, so to speak—the brief lull
did permit Perlman to reflect on the one respect in which he really did

have to say, all apologies and excuses aside, he'd found this more than a bit peculiar.

Not the girl. The girl's behavior was fairly obvious. This garish fairy tale she'd concocted was nothing but a kind of revenge on him, for having tried to bridle her all week. It was the flag she'd planted in the curious land her ill imagination had stumbled on—this world of doctors, clinics, limestone *pieds-à-terre*, and aesthetes. That was clear.

What was not so clear was the Madame's aim. Hospitality was one thing—creativity, imagination, intrigue—all were one thing. But this. There'd been an element of determination here, a sense of purpose he couldn't quite figure. It was almost as if she was trying to teach a lesson of some kind, he simply couldn't tell for whose benefit, because this certainly wasn't just for Stanley, to bring him up to speed. This had been for the girl, too, to show her how we like to tell our stories in this house. And Perlman couldn't help feeling it had been partially directed at *him* as well, just to show the good doctor what a little encouragement could yield; what happened if you said 'yes' rather than 'no.'

For that was the real and final wonder, was the power and the subtlety of the Madame's persuasions; her technique. And he wasn't thinking here of the cigarettes and milk pitchers—that was flourish, that was coloratura. It was more the tones of voice, the glances, the rhythm she'd managed to sustain. The woman was a master, and her effect upon the girl was sun and water. It was as Perlman looked at her, in fact, at the girl—watching the Madame, waiting for her cues—that's what started the first distant tremors of alarm, for there was no missing it in her eye: He'd brought his patient—his livelihood, his career—directly to the one person in all London with whom, for control of her attention, even *he* might not be able to compete. Bravo.

**D**octor"—she was looking at him right now—"do you not like your tea?"

"No, it's fine," he answered stiffly. "Just waiting for it to cool."

She turned to Stanley again. "So that is what we know."

"Well, it's very interesting. Quite intriguing, actually."

"May I have a biscuit?" asked the girl.

"Oh, I'm sorry." Madame Helena sat forward, shamed hostess, and took up one of the crackers. "Doctor, is it all right if she has pâté?"

"Jam, please," said the girl.

"Jam?"

Perlman nearly had to laugh. She asks about the jam? He offered a nod, from which his hostess, needless to say, inferred a more universal consent than he could ever intend.

"Now, but, Nina, if I remember"—she spread an ample slab of blackberry preserve across the toast—"you said before that this was the *first* time they saw each other."

"Yes."

The Madame handed the toast across. "So would I be right in assuming they did so again?"

Here Perlman did clear his throat; not more. The Madame looked over, oblivious.

He chose to speak in French. "*J'espère que vous comprenez que vous n'êtes aucunement obligée d'envisager tout ceci.*"

"*Aucunement obligée. En fait, je trouve tout cela fascinant.*" Fluent. Gorgeous accent, like his; not native, but true.

"*Oui, mais Lord Stanley est venu prendre le thé, et nous, nous nous sommes imposés, et je ne voudrais surtout pas que vous vous sentiez obligée . . .*"

"*Mais, Doctor, j'insiste. Détendez-vous.* We are enjoying our tea."

Stanley agreed. "*Beaucoup, même.*"

Nina took a bite of her toast and slid her eyes over at Perlman, sly and victorious.

(This was a foolish thing he'd done.)

"So when was next?" asked Stanley.

(A very foolish thing.)

"Next was the next day," said Nina.

(This made taking Mlle Giustine to the Nouveaux Concerts look like an absolute stroke of genius.)

"The next night, you mean?"

"The next day," the girl holds firm. "except she couldn't tell if it was him."

"Thayer?" the Madame makes sure.

"Is that his name," asks Stanley, "Thayer?"

"Thaire," the girl pronounces.

"One syllable," the Madame advises. "Thaire."

"And the boat's name is *Y'aromel,*" the girl adds.

"*Yarmel,*" tries Stanley.

"*E-yar-o-mel,*" the girl corrects.

"*Yarumul,*" he tries again.

"*Iyaromel,*" the Madame improves.

Yes, the girl nods, or that would do. She takes a bite of cracker.

The Madame proceeds. "But what do you mean she didn't know it was him? The following day."

Nina's mouth is full now. She glances up at the mantel where Oona's cup sits, untouched. She appears to listen, to agree, then covers her mouth to speak. "Did we mention her father was coming?"

"Her father?" The Madame ponders. "I don't think so. Do you remember, Doctor?"

(For it wasn't as if he'd just brought the girl to a park, or a pub. That would have been reason enough to revoke his license—absolutely. But no, he'd brought her here, to 97 Charles Place, one of the most notorious addresses in all of London, it was only now occurring to him why. Not the depravity of the people inside. Listen to them . . .

. . . It was their freedom—their idleness, quite frankly—which permitted them to do what they were doing here, to pursue whatever thread presented itself, the merest whiff of intrigue.

And not that he blamed them. That's who they were, he supposed; that's what they did. If their lives should be so blessed as to allow for these sorts of teatime goose chases, then by all means. But could they not see what was happening here?

Right there—"her father"— was it not clear? She was like a little girl who doesn't want to go to bed, asking for one more glass of wa—

"Hm?"

"Do you remember her saying anything about her father coming?"

"I don't remember her mentioning it, no."

"Well, he was," says the girl. "Because it was time for the feast."

"Ah, the feast." The Madame leans forward to prepare another cracker. "Spring or summer, just out of curiosity?"

Nina hesitates; she isn't sure, and once again consults the mantel.

"Harvest or Thaw?" Madame Helena spreads the jam.

"Oh, Thaw," says Nina, "which was Oona's favorite. She'd been looking forward to it, because it meant all the people would be coming."

The Madame hands the cracker over. "The temple is where they held the feast?"

Again she checks the mantel. "Not exactly," Nina says, "but it was nearby, and Aram would always open the gates so the people could bring their gifts inside and he could bless them."

"What sort of gifts?" asks Stanley, curious.

Nina has taken another bite, so

"Spring or Summer?" What was the meaning of a question like that?

"Harvest or Thaw?" What was she doing? No, there was definitely something he was not seeing here . . .

. . . The strange part was that he'd encountered this sort of thing before, many times back at Nancy. Dr. Racine used to do this, test his patients this way, drawing out their delusions just to see what the mind, if pressed, could yield. Perlman always detested the practice, thought it cruel and gratuitous. What was the mystery, after all? The more you pressed, the more the mind would yield.

the Madame suggests, "Offerings?"

The girl nods, and once again she covers her mouth to speak . . .

"They brought flowers," she says,

". . . and grain . . .

. . . and fruit."

Stanley looks confused. "But I thought we'd said this was a festival of the Thaw?"

The Madame and the girl both nod.

"But don't those sound more like harvest offerings?"

"Not necessarily," says the Madame. "The harvest offerings would simply be the *first* grain and the *first* fruits. At the Thaw, I assume they were offering the last, the last of their winter store."

"So they'd begin with nothing again?"

The Madame nods. The girl nods, too.

"Rather ascetic," says Stanley.

"Rather faithful," answers the Madame. She turns back to the girl. "So you were saying, they brought their gifts to Aram, for his blessing."

"Yes." She sits up again. "They all did, so it was like a parade. There was even music and danc-

*A chaque question, sa réponse.* Never was the maxim more on display.

Look at her now, consulting the teatray—

The flower was in its vase.

The crackers were on the plate, the jam beside.

Good girl.

The difference here, of course—from Dr. Racine's old game—was that neither the Madame nor Lord Stanley knew what they were dealing with. They didn't know the girl was split—that was their excuse, after all. It was their alibi, but it was also what made their behavior so completely baffling, why should the Madame be egging her on this way . . .

The girl could hardly get a word in edgewise.

But there, a gentle tap was all she needed. A little nudge, and she was off again, like some

ing, and Oona got to stand next to him, because she could bless the gifts, too."

"Sounds lovely," says the Madame.

The girl agrees. "It was her favorite time."

For a moment the two of them simply look at each other . . .

"And?" Madame Helena says finally.

"And that was when it happened," the girl replies. "She was on the steps with Aram, and the sun was shining, and all the people were showing their gifts, but then she saw there was one man standing in the middle." She looks at Perlman

spoiled showhorse, prancing for the Madame, the one who listens, the one who nods, the one who winks and prods . . .

Perlman could hardly bear to watch. They were like two young lovers, enjoying the silence.

And there, another touch, and off she goes. He was a fool. The woman had cast her spell right in front of him, while he was watching. Just look at the girl's eyes. They were beaming.

. . . and turning this way now

—or just over his shoulder.

"She couldn't see who it was, but he was staring right back at her."

She was looking at something in the room, so intently that both Lord Stanley and the Madame were compelled to turn as well. Perlman was prepared not to. He hadn't really been listening to what the girl was saying, but when he saw the expressions on their two faces— the Madame blanched, Stanley blinked—he knew what it must be.

He turned, and there it was—the covered something, the lamp or statue that Lord Stanley had warned the girl away from before, hiding beneath its drape. Perlman did not wonder what was underneath. He too enjoyed the warm wave of retribution, that someone else should finally feel the sting of Nina's defiance, these two in particular.

" 'Who is that man?' " she said, in a deeper register, play-acting. Perlman turned back around to watch.

". . . 'What man?' " she answered softly.

". . . 'That one.' " She put her chin to her chest and pointed. " 'There in the hood. Why does he look at you that way?'

". . . 'I don't know how he's looking. I can't see his eyes.'

". . . 'You've never seen him before?' "

She shook her head, innocent.

". . . 'You tell me if you see this man again. Your father would not be happy to see this man looking at you.' "

Then her face relaxed again. She sat back and looked at the Madame with glassy eyes.

"That was Aram she was talking to?"

Yes, she nodded.

"That must have been rather upsetting."

Yes, the girl agreed. "She'd never seen him act that way."

"Did she ask why?"

"She was going to," said Nina, "but that's when her father came." She glanced up at the mantel again and smiled. "And do you know how?"

The Madame wasn't sure what she meant. "Some sort of grand processional, I'd imagine."

No, the girl shook her head—better.

"A giant flotilla," tried Stanley.

No, she shook her head again—even better. "Balloons," she said. "So everyone could see. And they all cheered and raised their hands."

"Even the one in the hood?" the Madame asked.

"No. He was gone."

Correct, the Madame sat back.

Stanley still wasn't quite clear, though. "And just so I understand, that fellow in the hood, that was Thaire?"

Nina looked at him. It was kind of her, in fact, for she could, if she had wanted to, have subjected the old man to any measure of derision here, his question betrayed such a slow grasp of what she'd been up to. But she didn't. She simply nodded and took a sip of tea.

Stanley turned to Perlman, eyes aglow. "The plot thickens, doesn't it, Doctor?"

"Yes, it does. Very thick plot." He set down his cup. "Would this be a stopping point?"

"Seems so." The Madame looked up. "Did you need to excuse yourself?"

She meant to the loo. "No." He stood. "I don't mean to put a damper on things, but I think that Nina and I should probably be heading back."

"So soon?"

"We've imposed enough."

"Well, don't rush on our account." She checked with Stanley to make sure. "We are free."

Yes, much too, thought Perlman. "No. It's just that it's getting dark, and we do have a curfew of sorts."

Madame Helena looked straight at him. He could see she didn't quite believe this—was right not to—but offered no further protest. "I understand."

She conveyed her deference to Lord Stanley, who answered with an expression of authentic disappointment. "So we don't even get to find out what happens?"

Perlman offered an only mildly apologetic smile. "Sorry."

"Perhaps another time," the Madame tried.

The girl leaned forward for her cup again, not seeming to have taken any of this very seriously. "Lord Stanley could even be in it," she said. "Oona says you look like Malachai."

Perlman felt a dull throb in his head.

"Well, there's an idea." The Madame turned to Stanley. "A new role."

"High time."

"Excellent choice, Nina. Lord Stanley is quite a superior player." The Madame gave Perlman a wink here. He wasn't sure why at first, but then he looked at Stanley again and finally it came to him. That's where he'd seen him before—last year, at the Lyric; Benjamin had dragged him. Stanley was Polonius. He was Alfred Stanley, the actor.

The old man looked up, eyes twinkling, as if he'd sensed the recognition, but the realization hit Perlman like a stiff wind—what a pawn, what a puppet he was!—not only had he gone and delivered the girl to one of the best fantasists in all of London, he'd introduced her to one of its most esteemed actors as well.

"Do you want to?" Nina was still waiting, gazing at Stanley with an almost adoring expression, such as no behearted man could refuse, least of all this one.

"I suppose I might be able to clear the calendar. When were you thinking of?"

"Tonight," said the girl.

"Nina, no." Perlman stepped forward. "Really, you've both been very kind, but I'm afraid we have to be getting back."

"No, we don't," said Nina calmly, confidently.

"Yes. Yes, we do."

"Why?"

"Because we don't want to abuse the Madame's hospitality."

"She doesn't mind." The girl turned to the Madame. "Do you?"

"Of course not. But you are in Dr. Perlman's care."

"No, I'm not. I want to stay here. I want Lord Stanley to play Malachai tonight."

Perlman stood his ground. "Nina, we had an understanding. We came to find Oona. We have succeeded. Now we need to go back."

"But I don't want to." She spoke with a defiant calm. "I hate it there."

"Tsk," the Madame chided. "That's not very nice, Nina, especially when the doctor has done so much."

"But I do hate it. You've been." She looked around the room. "We prefer it here. We want Lord Stanley to play—"

"Nina." Perlman invoked a deeper, more commanding voice, of a tone and timbre which was capable, under normal circumstances, of reducing military leaders to well-trained dogs, but which in the present context only prompted a look of withering contempt. Nina was stronger than ever—and no wonder, with the encouragement she'd been getting the last half hour. "You're tired," he said, speaking of himself. "We need for you to eat and then rest."

"But I'm not hungry." She gestured to the table before them. "I just ate."

"Nina, stop." He stepped in front of her. "Perhaps some other time we can—"

"No!" she shouted and, with that sudden rise in volume, launched them all into the foul atmosphere of a misbehaving child. "I don't want to!"

"Nina—" He placed his hand on her shoulder. "Now listen to me. Calm down." He was trying his best, summoning as much authority as he could, but in this place he might have been a pet mouse. "I want you to count with me." He felt embarrassed even demonstrating his technique; it seemed so crude in comparison to the Madame's. "Nine." And impotent. "Eight." It was clearly getting him nowhere. As she looked at him, a startlingly invidious smile spoiled her features. "Seven."

"Doctor—" Stanley interrupted.

Perlman ignored him. "Come again, seven."

"Doctor—" Madame Helena stood up now, with a more urgent expression. She was gesturing to his upper lip. "Your nose."

Perlman felt his mustache. It was wet. He lifted his fingers and saw red. He was bleeding.

"Here, Doctor. Come with me." Madame Helena was quick to his side.

The girl sat back.

"Stanley, take care of our guest-s"—she added the final *s*.

Perlman tilted back his head and was escorted from the room on the Madame's arm.

## CHAPTER 21

In fact, Perlman's blood had always run thin, particularly as a boy, so what had just happened was not half as alarming as it might have been. The problem with blood, however, is that it takes instant priority over all else, no matter how urgent the all-else may be. As he followed the Madame back around to a small eating area at what he gauged must be the northeast corner of the house, he was therefore more annoyed than anything else. And embarrassed.

He took a seat by the window and tilted his head back against the cool pane. From the corner of his eye he could see the Madame holding a towel beneath a tap. It seemed an oddly common gesture.

"Does this happen often," she asked, "with your nose?"

"No. Yes. It used to. I'm sure it's just the dry air of the fire."

She gave him the cloth to administer himself.

"But really, as soon as it's stopped, Nina and I should say good evening."

"I understand." She dried her hands on another hanging linen. "Then again, I'm not sure I'm the one you need to talk to. She is an astonishing young lady."

He bristled. This was the second time she'd made a comment like this, and for the second time he had to remind himself that the woman did not know that the girl was sick—or sick in what way—and therefore had no idea of the situation into which she had so craftily inserted

herself. He resolved that it was not a position he should put her in
again.

"Madame." He sat up slightly to speak, but felt his blood run and
quickly tilted back his head. "I'm afraid there's something you don't
entirely understand, and I wouldn't normally divulge such information—it's a strict violation, frankly—" This was an awkward position,
holding a cloth to one's bleeding nose. "And yet under the circumstances, I think you should probably know that Nina . . ." He hesitated
again. He wasn't quite sure how to put it.

". . . is not Nina," the Madame finished the thought for him.

He turned his eye.

"It occurred to me."

It occurred to her? He moved on. "Well, but in any case, you can see
there's really no point in pursuing this fantasy."

"What's that?"

"All this business about Oona and the whale." With his head still
tilted, he couldn't see her expression, but felt a singe of censure.

"You don't think so?" she asked.

"Well, Madame, she is not she. She is a shard; she's a broken mirror."

The Madame reached for his towel and took it back to the tap,
where she stood a moment, skeptical. "I don't know, Doctor. I certainly wouldn't claim your level of expertise, but I think I can tell the
difference between something that's been broken and something that's
been replaced." She wrung the cloth dry again and brought it back, but
Perlman was too stricken by the impertinence of this last comment to
take it. *Replaced.* Before he could think to reply, there came the sound
of feet tramping above them upstairs. "Where are they going?"

"The closets, I suspect."

"No. I really can't have this." He stood up, much too quickly. He
could taste the blood, dark and thick in the back of his throat. He felt
suddenly dizzy and sat back down.

"Doctor." Madame Helena palmed his forehead. "I'm not entirely
sure you're well. Would you like to lie down somewhere?"

"I'll be fine," he said. His head was swimming, though, and now he was beginning to feel a queasiness in his stomach. "Perhaps for just a moment."

"I think that's a good idea. And don't worry about the girl. Stanley's harmless."

She helped him stand again—more slowly this time—and led him into a smaller, darker room just through the door. Her necklace clicked gently, and he thought he felt a loose wisp of her hair tickle his cheek. She sat him down in an easy chair, and he rested his head against a small embroidered pillow.

"I'll get you your tea."

"Just the water's fine," he said. "And lemon. Thank you."

She left.

Perlman tried not to think. There was nothing he could do about the girl until he calmed down, got this bleeding under control. He put out of his mind what the Madame had said, or what might be happening upstairs, and tried simply to breathe, to focus, to feel the chair beneath him. It was darker now, and quiet.

Out of the corner of his eye he could see her desk, submerged in files and letters, legal and financial documents. The drudgery she'd spoken of. A lithograph hung above, its image half-illumined by the small puddle of light surrounding the desk lamp. He could just barely make out a mansion. A great lawn, sloping up to a pine forest—

"Here." Madame Helena was back, a silhouette in the door frame. She'd recovered her shawl, and with the light behind her, her hair was a glowing crown. She brought him his cup.

"Thank you." He sipped. It tasted odd—bitter.

"It's just some valerian root," she said. "It will calm you down, slow your blood."

"My blood is fine. I'm sure it's stopped."

She nodded unconvincingly and picked up a stack of papers from the desk. "Let me get these out of here, though."

"You needn't."

"No, I should. It's terrible. I should . . . burn these." She shook her head and left again.

He hadn't liked that, her putting the valerian in his water without asking, but perhaps it wasn't a bad idea. He took a few more sips, sat back and tried to focus on breathing again—but as he set his head against the pillow, his eyes for a second time slanted over to the lithograph.

That must be their dacha, he thought. Grand stone manor, wraparound porch, and a single spire, onion dome. He'd seen pictures of these, the country estates of Russian aristocracy. It saddened him usually, the sight of one country trying so hard to be like another. There was something about this one, though—the dome, he supposed—that suggested a deeper, more native root than normal.

There was a second framed picture as well now. It must have been behind the stack the Madame took away—a photograph, of people. Two dozen, all bunched together like a rowing team. He leaned closer, but all he could make out were two borzoi hounds lounging in front. A hunt? It was too far away, and the valerian was beginning to take effect.

He leaned his head back. He felt soothed, slowed. The Madame was right. Stanley was harmless, and so was she. Well-intentioned people. They just happened to be very entertaining people, that was all—enjoying their tea. There was nothing to worry about. He'd simply rest here another moment, then when he was ready, he'd fetch the girl, and they'd be on their way. Then tomorrow, or the next day, or however long it would take, he and the girl would simply have to do what they would have to do. There was no rush. He'd get Sylvie back. Herr Blum would just have to be patient. Trust him and be calm, as Perlman was feeling right now. If Herr Blum could feel this—

"How are you doing, Doctor?" It was the Madame again. She had a light tread. "Are you awake?" And a soothing voice.

"Yes. I'm feeling much better, thank you."

She palmed his forehead.

"Is that Russia?" He glanced over at the pictures.

He hadn't meant for her to take her hand away. "Yes," she said. "Both." She took the photograph from the desktop—the one of all the people—and brought it to him. "Sonskovo. That's by the river."

They were children, all dressed up—costumed—in old Russian garb: a wizened old woman, a burly huntsman, a monk.

"Who are they?" His own voice was unusually soft, like the light.

"Cousins."

"Are you in there?"

She tapped the back row. He might have guessed. The face was a blur, but there was a resemblance in the posture—the high-chinned pride. She was holding a long spear.

"And that's Lexei." She pointed to a boy up front, squinting in the sun, beneath a long, floppy crown of blond hair. The picture magnified their difference in age. She must have been fifteen or so, the eldest of her generation, and ravishing. He a boy, a little golden boy—"gift from God," as they liked to say.

"Why are you all dressed this way?"

"For a play. An opera. That's the stage behind. You can just barely see it."

You could; scaffolding. "Looks like quite a production."

"Oh yes." She smiled slowly. "In the summers, when all the cousins came, we'd put on two or three shows for the parents. Orchestras and all."

"Orchestras?" Perlman hushed a laugh. "Where did you get the players?"

"The serfs, the ones who stayed. Some very fine musicians."

Perlman didn't doubt. Still, the idea—grown men brought in to play for a child's opera—Leonard would have gagged.

"Which one was this? I'm not sure I recognize."

"Well, you wouldn't," she said. "We made them up."

Of course. "Your brother wrote the scores?"

"And sang."

"And you?"

"Oh, I was more of a dancer—and tyrant, I'm afraid. I was in charge of exits and entrances." Her eyes rested on the image and the memory. "Those were fun, though."

"Did you prefer it there?" he asked, and wished he hadn't, her expression changed so quickly—that tug at the corners of her eyes.

"I did," she said. "But those days are over, I'm afraid." She set the photograph back on the table, laying it flat this time. "It is the strangest country. You've no idea."

Everything seemed to slow then—the trees outside, the grandfather clock keeping time in the parlor, and their words. "Well," said Perlman, "she sits between two different worlds."

"And two different centuries," the Madame answered, gazing straight ahead at nothing. "Do you think countries are like people, Doctor?"

Perlman thought, unrushed. "They have traits," he said finally. "They have histories. Yes."

"I wonder sometimes—it's wrong of me, but I do—why Russia can't be more like England, or Austria. Why can't she allow herself to evolve, grow naturally. Why must she go from this"—she indicated the two framed pictures—"to . . ." she couldn't bring herself to say it. "Can you imagine? It's all going to be horrendous, I fear. I really do. Only the beginning."

She spoke of her native land like an unfortunate, damned sister, thought Perlman.

"Do you imagine Russia is a woman?" he asked.

They were speaking very softly now, using more silence than words. "I suppose I don't know. Did I say 'she'?"

He nodded. "Because if she's a woman, then you've hope." His eyes were out ahead as well—glazing the shadows in the corner—and his voice felt smooth and even as it left his throat. "A woman can endure the darkest swings and still return. A woman can lose everything she knows, all reason and memory, and somehow find them again; and resume her life. A man is not so quick to break. He'll fight longer to keep hold of what he knows—his mind—but if he should ever lose it, it's gone forever. Did you know that?"

Again they could hear the clock all the way in the parlor.

"I suppose that's true," she said.

"It is." He thought of Mrs. Blum and felt hope.

"Well, that's good news, then."

Her right hand was resting on the back of the chair; the other was against her dress, her thigh. He could see it out of the corner of his eye, and he felt an urge to take it, to touch it. In a different world he would have—a different life—but here it rested against her hip, and Perlman accepted his lot. Best, if he could not take it, was to feel its nearness, and offer his nearness to her by remaining silent, by turning his head and closing his eyes, to feel that extra hue of warmth hovering everywhere around her.

How long they stayed like that he had no idea, but that he'd have remained forever in that perfect soft light, with the breeze stroking the trees outside and the two of them so close. Finally, though, they were lifted from their stillness gently, as gently as they had entered, by a soft knell coming from somewhere high.

"I believe that's our cue," the Madame murmured. "Can you make it all right?"

"Where?"

"The library, it sounds like."

She offered her hand. Perlman stood gingerly, and they started, arm in arm, just as they had walked across the street to the café, clinging for warmth, though here inside it was warm already.

# CHAPTER 22

Nina was waiting for them at the top of the stairs. She was in the same white dress, and she hadn't changed her hair—it was parted in the middle and hanging down past her shoulders—yet there was something different. Perlman could sense with each ascending step that this was a more refined creature than the one they'd left downstairs. That one had been almost puppylike, so stimulated by attention that she'd had to vent her excitement in little uncontrolled bursts—bouncing seats and swinging her legs. This one here, waiting intently with her hand upon the banister, was clearly just as thrilled, but had managed to contain her energy within an exterior of perfect calm—calm eyes, calm wrists, calm feet—and was as a result imbued with a kind of glow, so clear and so magnetic that Perlman was all the way to the second level before it occurred to him that he still had no idea what they were doing here, or what the knelling bell had been a summons to.

With a gently lifted arm, she directed the two of them to the first room on the right: a reading room. The walls were all books. There was a small idle hearth, a second interior door, and two western windows, between which stood a cherrywood cabinet with glass doors, as tall as a man.

Two easy chairs had been pulled out from their corners, a pace or two. The Madame entered first and took one, but Perlman hung back.

"The moment this is over," he whispered, "we go."

The girl did not answer, but her eyes flashed with a kind of bored contempt. They would leave when she was ready and not a moment sooner, and her leverage was the same as it had been since breakfast. The hostage Sylvie.

He entered and took his seat beside the Madame.

The hearth would frame the scene. A small burgundy divan stood directly in front, facing out. Before it was an open steamer trunk.

Nina took her place in the left-hand corner and addressed them, standing. "It is the library of Aram's temple."

She stepped back and dimmed the gas lamps. The Madame took the moment to clear her throat. Outside the window, the evening shone a hazy blue. There was the sound of someone entering, and when the lamps fired up again, Lord Stanley was standing before the cabinet. He was wearing a purple silk cassock over his shirt and pants, and his hair was swept forward as if he'd just awakened from a nap.

The doors of the cabinet were open wide before him. As the scene began, he was taking down something the size and heft of a bottle of wine but swaddled in black velvet, so Perlman couldn't tell what it was. Stanley handled it with great care, though. He took down a second bundle and carried them both back to the divan like a pair of infants, one on each arm. He set them inside the trunk, then repeated this opening direction, returning to the wall cabinet and taking down two more.

He was about to set these inside the trunk as well when Nina spoke from the corner.

" 'Father.' "

Stanley turned, but not to her. He looked back at the doorway to the right of the hearth, an empty threshold, and a warm smile crossed his face. "Oona." He sat. "Come. Sit."

His eyes then traced an even line from the door to his side, precisely as if some invisible figure had entered the room and taken the seat next to him.

Nina spoke. " 'I've missed you, Father.' "

"And I you." He was speaking directly to the absence again, and

Perlman felt slightly betrayed, watching him. The stagelights seemed to have the same effect upon the Madame's uncle as the Madame had upon the girl. He had been transformed, from the bumbling play-along at tea into this evidently well-honed dramatic instrument, his movements all distinct and clear, his voice both effortless and resonant.

"Aram has treated you well, I hope."

" 'Yes,' " replied Nina, pausing just the right interval to let the unseen player finish her lines. " 'What are you doing with the arcana?' "

The *arcana*. Stanley looked down at the two bundles in his arms and took a deep, grim breath. This was the reason he'd summoned her, no doubt. "Oona, my light. You recall the augur's prophesy?"

Nina answered, quoting, " 'Whose father's fate was fire, shall know a fate of flood.' "

This was correct. Stanley stood. "The augur has had the dream again. He says a Lord of Darkness shall soon descend upon the earth. The form that it should take, I do not know, and I am glad I don't, but the augur leaves no doubt: the life we've known will not survive the season." He looked down at the divan. "I'll be sending some of the others away. I'd like you to go east with Aram."

" 'But, Father—' " Nina took a moment, or Oona did, to digest the enormity of the news. " 'I don't understand. Is there nothing we can do to stop it?' "

Stanley shook his head. "I suspect we've done what we can, and it has not been enough." He turned and crossed to the cabinet again, but paused at the window. He looked out between the shutter slats, a picture of defeat. Stanley was a marvel. "All is one, Oona. Never forget."

" 'I won't, Father.' "

"One."

" 'I know,' " she tried consoling him. " 'But you know, it's only that it does not seem so sometimes—' "

"Oona, don't. They don't deserve your pity."

" 'I am only saying, if there are some who forget, it's because they look around and they see a world that's filled with difference, and they—"

"Oona, just because they see something doesn't mean they have to

worship it. It's a wayward path." He turned to the cabinet now and
was about to take down another pair of black bundles, but stopped. "It
is true, you know, what they say is happening at the western temple—
I have gone and seen myself. At every station now there stands a statue
made of gold, and do you know whose images they bear? All the rich-
est men! Their servants come and leave fresh flowers every day." He
shook his head in amazement. "Must they march us all right into the
sea?"

" 'That's only one temple, Father.' "

"But they're everywhere, Oona. They're down there right now, sell-
ing their trinkets." He glanced through the shutters again, presumably
at Aram's courtyard. "And this Lord of Darkness the augur sees? Your
uncle Timmon says there are some who've already begun *praying* to it,
seeking its favor before it descends. 'Light from Light,' they call it."
He took a deep breath and removed the last two bundles from the
shelf, but even then he stood a moment, lost.

" 'Don't be sad, Father," said Nina, and her voice had caught the
tone exactly, a child frightened by her parent's anguish. " 'I remember
what you told me when I first learned the augur's dream.' "

"What did I tell you?"

" 'You said darkness harkens dawn; that the fire had come to purify
the land, and that the waters will wash it clean again.' "

Stanley turned, and a slow proud grin crossed his face. "Wise child.
You're right." He started back to the divan, holding out the two last
bundles. "Still, there are some things we must keep safe."

" 'May I see?' "

Stanley obliged. He set one bundle down inside the trunk but kept
the last for her. He tugged at the string tie, and Perlman watched—as
he'd watched all the preceding—bewildered. How exactly were they
doing this? Was this a scene from some play he didn't know? Some
one-act that both the girl and Stanley knew by heart? That's all he
could think, or that's what he *was* thinking as Stanley worked the tie,
but now as the velvet sheath slid down to reveal what was hiding inside, Perlman's pupils bloomed.

It was a piano roll.

" 'Where are you going to put them?' " asked Nina.

A red Welte.

"The catacombs beneath the stones," said Stanley.

It was—a roll, for the Welte-Mignon downstairs. Stanley held it out an extra moment to make sure they'd seen, then he slipped it back inside the velvet cover and set it in the trunk with the others. Perlman counted six.

" 'But, Father,' " Nina went on, " 'there's still something I don't understand. If what the scrolls say is true, why don't we share them with everyone? What harm could they be?' "

"And what harm might a sickle be?" he answered. "In the farmer's hand, no harm at all. But would you give that same sickle to a child, or a thief? Everything in time, my light. For those who seek, good seed will keep. For now, it is best that the sun be their guide. The sun is all. The sun is One, and One is all they need remember—as you will remind them tomorrow."

" 'Then we are all still going?' "

"Of course. As long as there is a sun, there shall be a feast. You will go with Aram, though, afterward."

" 'But what about you? Where will you go, Father?' "

Stanley's expression darkened, but tenderly. "Take my hand." He extended his, turning up his palm. "You know I am not like you."

" 'Father, don't speak this way. I hate it when you speak this way.' "

"But you know it's true. I am more of flesh than you, and flesh grows tired."

" 'Don't speak of it, Father.' "

"Don't fear it, Daughter. It is not death which stalks us. It is defilement." He searched for her eye again. "And we can never truly be apart, you know that. All *is* one." He waited.

Then, " 'All is one,' " she replied, with somewhat less conviction.

"Come." He closed the trunk. "The sun has gone to bed; so should we."

He rose, and with an open arm escorted the invisible figure to the door. Just before stepping out, though, he stopped. He turned to his audience and spoke, *sotto voce*, so his daughter wouldn't hear: "And would that I could, I'd place that girl in a chest as safe and tight, in a catacomb twice as deep. Or better, I would summon her mother, Artemis, this very night—if I'd not made my vow. I'd bid her come and steal her daughter now, take her somewhere free from all these shadows. But then I look upon the people sleeping, I think of the evil lurking in the hills, and I am reminded how our nature does need Oona, more now than ever."

Nina lowered the gas again. The lamps fell dim; then she crossed behind the divan and left by the same door as Stanley, closing it softly behind her.

# CHAPTER 23

In the dim light Madame Helena looked across at Perlman, brows high. "Perhaps we should head back down," she whispered. "Give the players a moment."

Perlman agreed in a perhaps too casual manner, to veil a state of puzzled delirium. How they'd managed the scene he still had no idea, but it was the rolls—those six gold bricks stacked inside the steamer trunk—that had seized his imagination. From the moment he'd identified them, he hadn't heard a word that either the girl or Stanley said.

Back in the parlor, the Madame poured them both snifters of brandy; she offered his in silence, took a sip from her own, and only then, with the vapors settling in their chests, did she speak.

"Quite impressive. I know it bothers you when I say that, but—" She conveyed the rest with her eyes.

"He was very good."

"Oh, Uncle Al, he's wonderful. But she . . ." Again she let the thought trail to convey her admiration. "I've seen some fairly remarkable things in my day, but that girl—she's a fountain."

Perlman looked at her. Had she not understood what he'd been saying before, while his nose was bleeding? This refusal to admit the girl's true condition was troubling—it reminded him that there were aspects to the Madame's personality that he'd yet fully to countenance; but before this worry could take root, Stanley entered from the Music Room. There must have been another set of stairs in back.

"Bravo." Madame Helena lifted her glass.

He was in his pedestrian garb again, a dark gray tweed that now seemed to confine him slightly. He gave a humble bow and proceeded to the bar. "Just following directions." He helped himself to two fat fingers of port.

"Is she coming down, too?" asked Perlman.

"I believe so." He seemed even more chipper than before, evidently invigorated by the performance. He joined them by the nascent fire.

The Madame shook her head in wonder. "I have questions."

"I assume you do. I have a few of my own. But first—" He raised his finger. "She said to let you know—very important." He reached inside his pocket for something. "That night, when Oona went to bed, the smoke did not appear outside her balcony—"

"Did *not*," the Madame checked.

"No, but she found this beneath her pillow." He opened his palm to show them a small white shell, crescent-shaped, with smooth, rounded edges.

The Madame leaned in. "Where did she find that?"

"I don't know. The walk outside? She just handed it to me."

Perlman sensed a possible trespass here. "I'm sorry, was this yours? I—"

"No." She took the shell to examine. He couldn't tell if she was being truthful or not. "So Oona found this beneath her pillow, you say?"

"That's right."

She let Perlman see. Again, an unusual shell; not so unusual.

"But let me ask"—she turned to Stanley again. "I don't want to ruin the effect, of course, but your parabasis there at the end, did I hear you say Artemis?"

Stanley nodded. The Madame glanced at Perlman, pleasantly vindicated. "And did she come up with that?"

He touched his heart. "Strike me down."

"I'm sorry," Perlman interrupted. "Is there a reason Nina didn't want to come down and show us this herself?"

Stanley thought as if he hadn't thought.

"Did she *say* she was coming down?"

"I think so. I suppose I'm not absolutely sure."

They all three looked up at the ceiling now. There was no sound. The Madame touched Perlman's wrist. "Why don't I go check?" she whispered.

She'd beat him to the punch. Perlman had wanted to go himself—should go—but before he could insist, the Madame was off, once again leaving Perlman alone with her uncle.

They rocked on their heels for an awkward moment. Stanley's eyes were twinkling, though. "How's your nose?" he asked.

"Fine, thank you." Another moment passed. "Well, I suppose *I* don't mind ruining the effect." Perlman nodded in the direction of the library. "What was all that from up there?"

"How do you mean?"

"Was it some play or a story I should know?"

Stanley shrugged. "You'd have to ask the girl."

"No, but you can tell me. I'm really not that interested."

"Honestly, Doctor, I don't know."

Perlman smiled. "You're saying she told you to do all that?"

"More or less. Gave me some bells to ring."

Liar. "You're an awfully quick study."

"Well, it's easy remembering the good stuff." He grinned.

Perlman did not appreciate this, as her doctor, being treated as if he'd just asked how they sawed the lady in half—but clearly he was getting nowhere. He changed the subject. "And were those piano rolls for the Welte, by the way?"

"I suspected you'd pick up on that."

"They wouldn't be the 'Nonsense'?"

"Oh, I assume they were," said Stanley. "I think that's all there are."

They were. Perlman took a long sip of brandy. "Have you ever heard them?"

"Not those, *per se*. But that was something he used to do." Stanley wiggled his fingers.

"What do you mean—improvise?"

"Well, not really 'improvise.' You can ask Helena, but the 'Nonsense' was something he used to do for the sake of his composing, I believe."

Perlman shook his head; he would need more.

"Well, Alexander was always very concerned about his hands," said Stanley, consulting his own. "Like any composer, I suppose, but particularly one who plays as much as he did—afraid his hands might be influencing the music too much, foisting their own habits."

"I see."

"He actually broke them once—his left hand—riding. Couldn't use it for six months. Best work he ever did."

"All he could do was listen."

"To what was in his head, yes—fingers couldn't get in the way. So for somewhat the same reason, he used every so often to sit down and just flop about the keys, not for any musical purpose, I never got the sense, so much as to punish his hands in a way, or break whatever habits they might be forming."

"So that's what 'Nonsense' meant?"

Stanley nodded.

"And that's what he did for Welte?"

"So I gather."

Perlman laughed. That was even better than he'd thought. "And you actually heard him do this?"

"Sometimes. Rooms away."

Perlman took another sip. "And what did it sound like?"

Stanley thought back, now with a distinctly avuncular air. "Nonsense." He winked. "But who knows how they've aged?"

Wasn't it true, though? And what he would give to hear, he was so close. He glanced up at the ceiling again, and as if on cue, there came the wooden moan and sigh of someone coming down the stairs. The Madame entered.

"Sound asleep," she said.

"Asleep?" said Perlman.

"In Alexander's room, dead away. She looks quite comfortable, in fact."

"Which room?"

She pointed up. "End of the hall. You're not going to wake her?"

"Madame, we have to go."

"You don't," she said simply. "There's a guest bed, all made up."

"No, Madame, it isn't a matter—you're very kind, but really, I need to get back."

"You're aware it's about to pour."

"Is it?" Stanley set his snifter on the mantel. "I should go."

"And I should, too," said Perlman, setting his brandy beside.

"Well, all right." The Madame sounded reluctant. "I'm just not sure how I feel sending you out in your condition."

"I'm fine. We'll be fine."

"You're still a little pale, Doctor. And as I say, she looks very comfortable—"

Stanley leaned in quickly. "I'm going to leave you two to debate this. Dr. Perlman, good luck."

"Where are you headed?"

"Just around the corner. Wellington."

Damn—they might have shared a cab. And outside now the distant sky was clearing its throat, like rumbling boulders. Stanley winced.

"Will you be coming tomorrow?" asked the Madame.

"I suspect so. I suspect I may be called for." He turned. "Dr. Perlman, again a pleasure. And perhaps I'll see you before the weekend is through."

"Oh, I doubt that, but yes, a pleasure. And thank you—for the performance, I mean."

Stanley bowed, and the Madame escorted him to the door. Perlman wondered if he shouldn't run up and wake the girl while he had the chance, but just then another roll of thunder grumbled and cracked. Stanley bellowed. He was braving it, but now the first wet streaks were splintering against the front windows, hard and forbidding. Devil. The grandfather clock showed eight—and Saturday evening, too. Cabs would be impossible.

The Madame returned from the front hall with a still pleasant but suddenly tired countenance. "So, Doctor, have you decided?"

"I suppose we probably should wait it out. But don't worry, the girl never sleeps long."

"I think that's a good idea. Unfortunately, I've some things I need to do for tomorrow. I've another meeting."

"On Sunday?"

"I know. But, the sooner it's done with, the better. In any case, I'm afraid I do have to prepare."

"You won't know I'm here."

"Let me show you the guest room, though."

"No. No, I wouldn't think—as soon as the shower's passed, we'll be on our way. Do you think I could see where she is, though?"

"Of course. Is your drink all right?"

Perlman eyed his snifter—it was a bit shallow.

"Why don't you freshen it?"

He did, rather casually; poured another finger, then the two of them headed upstairs, the Madame leading the way with a lantern.

Alexander's room was at the far end, garden side, across the hall from the library. Just outside the door the Madame pointed at the floor. "Above the Music Room," she whispered. "So the only person he'd be keeping up was himself."

She turned the knob and they both leaned in.

Not surprisingly, the girl had chosen for herself what appeared to be the most ostentatious room in the house. Even in the dark Perlman could make out a grand armoire, billowy lace curtains, a four-poster bed. He could hardly see Nina for all the pillows, but she lay on her stomach, sprawled above the covers, the tan of her left leg peeking through. He'd have bet she wasn't even asleep, that if he'd gone right up and given her a spank, she'd have laughed out loud. She shifted slightly and resumed her pose—a little wag of her tail—and the Madame closed the door again.

The only light in the hall was coming from her lantern and the amber glow upon her face.

"I hope you understand," he whispered, "this is not the way that I generally work."

"I wouldn't think so." She moved them away from the door.

"What I mean is, it's not the way I'd *choose* to."

"I understand." He didn't think she did. "But this is an unusual case, wouldn't you say?"

"Increasingly."

She held the lantern up. "I can't see your eyes, Doctor. Are you being ironic?"

Just then another blot of light outside bleached the hallway a whitish blue, and there followed a less distant rumble in the sky. The Madame touched his wrist. "Why don't I show you the guest room. It will make me feel better."

She started them for the second flight, past another room at the foot of the stairs, which could only have been hers. For the first time it occurred to Perlman that she might actually want the company.

The guest room was the first door on the third level. The Madame leaned in with her lantern. "Sorry about the condition."

It looked very nice, actually. Dark red and gold wallpaper, striped. A small fireplace. A standing armoire. Brass bed.

She set the lantern on the side table. "I'm going to leave you this." She slid open the drawer and removed a candle. "There's a loo down at the end of the hall, and I trust you'll let me know if there's anything you need."

"Only for you to go do what you need to do. I'll be fine. I may do some reading."

"As you wish." She lit her candle by the lantern flame. He could see its reflection in her eyes; her skin was dewy. "You know where the library is."

"Thank you." She was leaving. "Madame—"

She stopped, her hand on the doorknob.

"Lord Stanley and I were speaking downstairs about the rolls. I hope you don't mind."

She shook her head.

"Well, he was saying that all your brother was really doing there was playing at random, that it wasn't music-making so much as an exercise at untraining his hands. Does that make sense to you?"

"A bit." She smiled. "But sometimes Al just says things." She lifted her light. "Good night, Dr. Perlman." She left the door halfway closed and started back down the stairs.

She really was the most attractive woman.

# CHAPTER 24

**A** quick shudder at the window apprised him, the initial torrent of rain had settled into more of a blustery shower—not violent, but still not the sort of thing one would want to dare. It was better he'd waited. The weather would pass.

He wanted to give the Madame a head start downstairs, so he went and checked the armoire. There were two pairs of men's shoes, some slippers, a dressing gown. Strays. A door closed downstairs—the Madame was back on the first level—so Perlman took his brandy and descended to the library.

The room was as they'd left it, dim. He flared the lamps. The glass cabinet was still ajar, the steamer trunk still shut. He wasted no time. He took a seat on the divan, set his snifter on the floor, and flipped the brass latch open.

There were six rolls inside; he'd counted right. Huddled together in their velvet sheaths, they looked like a litter of black Labradors. But there beside them, lying flat on the bottom of the trunk, was a leaf of stationery.

He held it to the light. Beneath the monogram *ATB* was an outline, looking very much like something Perlman himself might have written. *Seven Bells* read the heading, with seven lines below. He could make out the word *arcana*, then *augur's prophesy*. The rest was barely legible—*God of Night, E w/ A*—and the last word appeared to be *Artemis*.

These were Stanley's notes, he realized, his crib sheet for the scene that he and the girl had played, and Perlman felt a tincture of relief at seeing it—that there had, in fact, been some method to their madness. It was difficult to tell much more than that, though. Like his own, this was a private hand, and the phrases were far too cryptic to tell just how much preparation, as opposed to improvisation, they implied. So for the moment, he set the page aside, and turned back to his vices—the snifter first, then the stack of rolls.

He lifted out the topmost. It was heavy, heavier than his, and wider. That was the problem with the pianola industry. Nothing was standard. You couldn't run an Ampico roll on an Aeolian piano, or an Aeolian roll on a Welte-Mignon. He loosened the tie and slid the cover down, scarcely breathing. Right away he could see the reason for the difference: an extra column of holes running down the side. Those were what controlled the dynamics, what made this so much more than a mere piano roll; what made this a "reproducing" roll.

He traced his fingertips along the wax, felt the perforations. For each of these holes a note; for each note an accent, all precisely chosen and precisely placed, to catch the proper pin, to open the valve, to start the hammer, to strike the intended wire with just the right heft and value, and in this way—this perfectly pneumatic, unthinking way—take a moment seven years dead and reproduce it so exactly that to the listening ear no difference could be heard. Bless this century. What a noble and ingenious creature was man.

The tempo markings were on the bottom side, handwritten:

*Lento—37''*
*Allegro ma non troppo—1'11''*
*Con moto—45'' eleganza—1'13''*
*Agitato Robusto—43''*
           4'29''

Awfully precise instructions for someone who was just trying to punish his hands. Of course, 'Sometimes Stanley just says things.' The

Madame was probably right. Who knew what this roll might represent, the intention it reflected? He'd have given anything to hear it, to judge for himself. But perhaps another time. She'd said that as well, hadn't she?

He permitted himself one last caress, then dressed the roll in its velvet sheath again and set it back inside the trunk. He wanted to make a note.

He hadn't brought his Chronik, but there was Stanley's crib sheet on the pillow. He used the blank side. *"Nonsense" rolls*, he wrote.

*Stanley: "Something he used to do." To break hand habit. Anti-music (broke hand > best work [which?])*
   *MH: "Stanley says things."*

He turned his attention to the book shelves next. He took his brandy over to the western wall, and right away he could see there was no order. Books on botany stood beside those on poetry, history, a row of Bibles, orthodox theologica, a rhyming dictionary.

Just to his right, however, on the northern wall, his eye caught the spine of a Grove dictionary. And there were all the Burney histories as well, *The Present States*. Perlman leaned in slightly, scenting prey. This was the musical library. There was the Breuning on Beethoven, and the Czerny, and the Schindler. Perlman put his hands behind his back and openly leered:

C.P.E. Bach, yes; *The Life of Johann Sebastian Bach*; Beaumarchais's *Le Mariage de Figaro*; the Berlioz memoirs (he'd gotten that for Professor Bernheim, years ago); the Carlyle collection, *Musician's Wit, Humour & Anecdote*. The *Memoires* of Gounod; *Alexander Borodin, Borodin and Liszt;* Cui's *La Musique en Russie*. Tolstoy, *The Kreutzer Sonata;* Turgenev; the Rimsky-Korsakov *Histoire de Ma Vie Musicale*. Glinka. Gluck. The Grétry essays.

It surprised Perlman—even disappointed him slightly—that a primary source like Barrett should be so well versed in secondary literature. One preferred to think of him as oblivious to all this. Not to say that Perlman wouldn't have spent a happy month in here, tucked away in the corner of the divan with a snifter and a lamp. Some of these books he'd had his eye on for years, in shops: the *Handel* by Rockstro; the *Chopin* by Liszt; Letters of Liszt; some Hanslick; Haydn; Heine; Hoffmann; *Musick's Monument* by Thomas Mace. Perlman pulled this one out, to remind himself of the subtitle—

> *A Remembrance of the Best Practical Music,*
> *Both Divine and Civil,*
> *That Has Ever Been Known, to Have Been in the World.*

Very touching. He replaced it next to Mendelssohn's letters. There was North's *Musical Grammarian*; Praetorius' *Syntagma Musicum*; the Rameau, needless to say; Stendhal's *Vie de Rossini;* the autobiography of Louis Spohr; and then the Wagner section: *My Life, Prose Works, Nietzsche contra Wagner, The Pleasures of Music*; the Wille; and there at the end, *The Perfect Wagnerite.*

Perlman plucked it out.

> *A Commentary on the Nibelung*
> by
> George Bernard Shaw

His new friend. Leonard had brought this to Bayreuth once, so Perlman had read bits and pieces. He opened to the title page. There was an inscription.

> *H & L,*
> *This also is dedicated to nobody. Save those who take pleasure in it.*
> *Fondly,   GBS*

He started back to the divan with the book and snifter, but just as he sat down, a postcard fluttered out onto the cushion, picture side up—an etching of a dance garden in Paris.

Perlman glanced at the other side. Had they been words, he would not have looked further, but they were not. They were this:

*Paris, 9 Jan. 1891*
*H,*

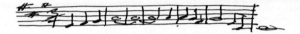

*L*

Alexander's hand—he recognized it from the slant of the quarter notes. *L* for Lexei, to his sister, *H*—this musical phrase. In A major.

Was this a note-to-self, he wondered, a reminder of some phrase he should remember when he got home again?

3/4 time. A waltz.

Or perhaps they'd heard it together—danced it together at this place in Paris. Lexei was there without her, was reminded of the dance, sent her the memory here in London. 1891. He would have been twenty. She, twenty-five or so. Eight years later, he would be dead.

Perlman took out his pen and Stanley's crib sheet and copied down the phrase beneath the notes he'd already made. Three measures. No harm in that.

He tucked the card back inside the pages and for the next three-quarters of an hour read the Shaw. He began with "The Preliminary Encouragement," which he'd always liked. It was the commentary itself that slowed him down. Shaw's aim had been to educate the interested English audience as to the political, economic, and intellectual revolutions that were rocking Germany at the time Wagner was composing, and of which the *Ring,* in Shaw's opinion, represented a kind of allegory. Perlman did not disagree but, being more abreast of this

information than Shaw's average reader, found the commentary alter-
nately obvious and much too precise; worse, it distracted from the one
aspect of Wagner's art that recommended it above all others—which
was, of course, the music. He therefore skipped ahead to the last six
chapters of the book, and it was somewhere in there—in the middle of
Shaw's plaintive call for more provincial musical festivals like the Rut-
land Boughton venture in Glastonbury—that the day, the brandy, and
the Madame's divan finally got the better of him.

He wasn't out for long. He was roused by the sound of his own
snore, but his pocketwatch had stopped, so he couldn't be sure of the
time—only that the rain seemed to have let up, and the lamps had
dimmed. He checked the hall.

It was dark. The girl's door was still closed. Downstairs was entirely
black; the crack beneath the Madame's door likewise. The only light at
all was coming from upstairs, a faint glow sifting down from the guest
room.

## CHAPTER 25

There were several sprigs of bittersweet on the bureau. The shutters had been closed, and a plate of food was waiting on the mantel— cheese, bread, a small dish of mustard, and some red grapes. Perlman helped himself to a stem, and noticed that the door of the armoire was open. A nightshirt was on a hanger, hanging from the hook above the mirror, cleaned and pressed. Again the monogram, *ABT*. He inspected the collar—Swan and Edgar Ltd.

He decided to try it on, not because he had any intention of sleeping in it—he kept his trousers on—but one didn't often get the chance to wear Alexander Barrett's sleeping gown. He wrestled it over his head and checked the mirror. The shoulders were a bit tight, but still it was an image worth keeping: August Perlman clad in Alexander Barrett's nightshirt, Barrett guest room, September 29, 1906.

Take that, Leonard.

He plucked a grape with his teeth, gave himself two congratulatory pats on the chest, then noticed behind him in the glass there was a small stack of books waiting on the bedside table. The lamp was shining down, and there was a note on top, in the Madame's hand:

*More bells? Sleep well. HB.*

He glanced at the spines. On top was Plato, a volume of the Dialogues; then something by someone named Donnelly; a slimmer volume by a W. Scott-Elliot; then at the bottom two more familiar, if more worrisome, names—Steiner and H. P. Blavatsky, *The Secret Doctrine*.

That was a daunting pile. He was curious that the Madame should make the gesture, though, and distantly troubled. He took up the Plato. There was a slip of paper sticking out, which opened to the first page of a Dialogue called the *Timaeus*. The opening paragraph had been marked by a straight line down the margin, in fresh ink.

He sat warily on the edge of the bed and began:

*Thereupon, one of the priests, who was of very great age, said, "O Solon, Solon, you Hellenes are but children, and there is never an old man who is an Hellene." . . . There have been, and there will be again, many destructions of mankind arising out of many causes. There is a story which even you have preserved, that once upon a time Phaethon, the son of Helios, having yoked the steeds in his father's chariot, because he was not able to drive them in the path of his father, burnt up all that was upon the earth, and was himself destroyed by a thunderbolt. Now, this has the form of a myth, but really signifies a declination of the bodies moving around the earth and in the heavens, and a great conflagration of things upon the earth recurring at long intervals of time: When, on the other hand, the gods purge the earth with a deluge of water, among you herdsmen and shepherds on the mountain are the survivors, whereas those of you who live in the cities are carried by the rivers into the sea . . .*

Perlman had read the last sentence slowly, retarded by a sinking sense—the slow dawn of a most unwelcome realization. The room, the armoire, the shutters all withdrew, while the title of the next book in the stack gazed up at him knowingly.

Atlantis: The Antediluvian World
*by Ignatius Donnelly.*

He looked back at the Plato and skipped down to the end of the passage.

*and there was an island . . . for this sea which is within the Straits of Heracles is only a harbor, having a narrow entrance, but that other is a real sea, and the surrounding land may be most truly called a continent. Now in the island of Atlantis there was a great and wonderful empire . . .*

*"The island of Atlantis"*? Oh, what was she thinking?

He set down the Plato and gingerly took up the Donnelly. It opened straight to the table of contents. He more scanned than read what was there:

As his eyes flicked down the page, the expression on Perlman's face muscle by muscle soured. What could the motives of this man be? What perverse desire was it that could put this much effort into deliberately misleading people? He began flipping through. The text was littered with charts and illustrations—maps, diagrams, ancient Mayan alphabets, comparisons of arrowheads, skull types, vases, daggers. Was it simply mischief? Did the man derive some sense of power from fooling people this way, or was it possible that he actually believed this nonsense?

Perlman came upon another loose slip of paper like the one in the Plato, this one under the heading "The Kings of Atlantis become the Gods of the Greeks." As before, a block of text had been marked:

*The Greeks, too young to have shared in the religion of Atlantis, but preserving some memory of that great country and its history, proceeded to convert its kings into Gods, and to depict Atlantis itself as the heaven of the human race . . .*

He supposed he must have, on some level. That was the only explanation really that at some point along the way this Donnelly fellow must have convinced himself of his own lie.

*. . . Where was Olympus? It was in Atlantis.*

And yet of course it wasn't really Donnelly that Perlman cared about. The next several pages were a hash of marginal inscriptions, stars and arrows, little sketches, cross references to "Chronos," "The Garden of Hesperides" and so forth, none of which had been made for his benefit, he didn't think. The Madame had come through here a while ago for some purpose of her own, some ballet or play or poem. But each of her little hatches was like a knife stroke to Perlman, the image they summoned was so excruciating—of his hostess curled over this tripe, beneath her midnight lamplight, marking it fiendishly with her quill.

Here a star:

*The Nymphs were plainly the female inhabitants of Atlantis, dwelling on plains, while the aristocracy lived on the higher lands.*

He supposed he should have known, though. It was the first thing Sulka had said—theosophy, and all that business about gold, alchemy, Midas. He looked back down at the stack—Steiner. That was Rudolf Steiner, yes? Designated Gypsy to Germany's elite. And there on the bottom, Madame Blavatsky, maddest Hatter of them all. He'd just been pretending it wasn't there, this hole in the woman's head, but here she'd gone and thrust it before his eyes.

He picked up the top book—Scott-Elliot, *The Story of Atlantis*. This one was slimmer, but it too was strewn with little notes and slips of paper, the first of which directed him to page 92, under the heading "Sorcery versus the Good Law."

> *Personal aggrandisement, the attainment of wealth and authority, the humiliation and ruin of their enemies became more and more the objects towards which their occult powers were directed: and thus turned from their lawful use, and practiced for all sorts of selfish and malevolent purposes, they inevitably led to what we must call by the name of sorcery.*

She'd underlined the last word twice, and exclamation-pointed the margin: *"sorcery!"*

Perlman had to stand.

> *Surrounded as this word is with the odium which credulity on the one hand and imposture on the other have, during many centuries of superstition and ignorance, gradually caused it to be associated, let us consider for a moment its real meaning and the terrible effects which its practice is ever destined to bring on the world. Partly through their psychic faculties, which were not yet quenched in the depths of materiality to which the race afterwards descended, and partly through their scientific attainments during this culmination of Atlantean civilization, the most intellectual and energetic members of the race gradually obtained more and more insight into the working of Nature's laws, and more and more control over some of her hidden forces. Now the desecration of this knowledge and its use for selfish ends is what constitutes sorcery. The awful effects, too, of such desecration are well enough exemplified in the terrible catastrophes that overtook the race. For when once the black practice was inaugurated it was destined to spread in ever widening circles . . .*

Perlman was stunned. He supposed it was a relief, in a way, just to know, because he had to admit that for a while there he had found the whole thing a bit—he could say it now—unassimilable, how the Madame and her uncle could possibly have been so deft. "Seven bells," indeed. He'd known there was something he was not getting, some piece to the puzzle he simply hadn't been given yet. Here it was, and seeing it finally, he had to say it didn't seem they'd been very deft at all. All they'd done was taken this Atlantean hoax—the hook, the line, and the sinker—and jammed it in the poor girl's mouth.

Page 37.

> . . . These events took place about 50,000 years before the first great catastrophe . . . The great "City of the Golden Gates" had by this time become a perfect den of iniquity. The waves swept over it and destroyed its inhabitants, and the "black" emperor and his dynasty fell to rise no more. The emperor of the north as well as the initiated priests throughout the whole continent had long been fully aware of the evil days at hand, and subsequent pages will tell of the many priest-led emigrations which preceded this catastrophe, as well as those of later date.

It was all here. He'd venture there wasn't a thing he'd heard the last twenty-four hours that he couldn't find some basis for in these books. And yet as the realization settled in, of what exactly had been going on this evening, he could feel that initial draft of relief turning fast into something much darker and less digestible.

To think that she would do this, and do it so obliviously, so conscience-free—that was the staggering part, for Perlman didn't suspect the woman of malice. Probably she thought that in finding the girl and drawing her out, she was operating by some sort of "intuition," as if that were anything but a veiled expression of a person's need. But why would she need this? It didn't make sense, how she could be so blind to her own devices—so stubborn, so desperate as to think that . . . Well, he didn't want to presume what she was thinking—wouldn't want to sully anyone with such gross assumptions—except to say that the madness of it, the true mal-adjustment to reality, was right here in front of him, in the fact that she'd seen fit to show this to *him*, as if it weren't perfectly clear how he would react; how clear it would be to Dr. Perlman that the girl was only throwing the Madame's own rubbish right back at her. Could the woman not at least have known what *he* would think?

He was pacing now. He flipped past another five pages of Toltec history, his eyes grazing the words so as not to let the meaning seep too deep. "Fourth Root Races," "Akkadians," "Turanians," Air-Ships. Maps: "Atlantis at Its Prime," "Atlantis in Its Decadence." Even the headings were absurd. *Architecture. Education. Food. Manners and Customs. Arts and Sciences.* They sped past like trees through a train window, but his eyes couldn't help snagging here and there:

> *The original Semites, who were a quarrelsome, marauding and energetic race, always leant towards a patriarchal form of government.*

Perlman didn't even want to consider the implications—the evil, insidious shadow this cast upon the day's proceedings. Still, he flipped back to the introduction, just to make sure he understood the rationale—the basis, that is, on which this miscreant had been moved to offer up such corruption—for no doubt his methods would shed light on the girl's condition as well.

It was written by someone named A. P. Sinnett. "A. P." Did that mean woman? Alice Penelope?

He stopped in front of the wardrobe, propped his arm upon the door, and read:

> *. . . For anyone who will have the patience to study the published results of psychic investigation during the last fifty years, the reality of clairvoyance as an occasional phenomenon of human intelligence must establish itself on an immovable foundation . . . In truth the records of Nature are not separate collections of individual property, but constitute the all embracing memory of Nature herself, on which different people are in a position to make drafts according to their several capacities.*

There it was. So Nina was some sort of antediluvian prophet, then? Or what was the term they were suggesting? "Astral clairvoyance . . ."

*. . . which, in some of its more magnificent developments, has been employed to carry out the investigations on the basis of which the present account of Atlantis has been compiled . . . Without this knowledge all speculations concerning ethnology are futile and misleading. The course of race development is chaos and confusion without the key furnished by the character of Atlantean civilization and the configuration of the earth at Atlantean periods . . .*

That was as much as he could take. Perlman stood there a moment, literally numbed by the influx of every dark emotion he possessed— scorn and fury, fury at himself, humiliation, betrayal at what was happening here. This woman. These people.

Up to this point in his life, his connection to their world—the world of mystics, theosophists, the occult—had been purely peripheral, and rightly so. Of course one encountered them on the fringe of any discussion involving hypnotherapy, for the very reason just laid out by Mr. or Mrs. Sinnett here—hypnosis lent their fantasies a kind of unimpeachable authority. But Perlman never paid them any mind. He knew of them through the newspapers more than anything else. Whenever the *Gazette* ran a piece, he and Benjamin would read it over lunch, he'd clip it for Parisot, for the humor—the image of these rich English morons, gathered round hushed tables, gasping at bumps on the wall. It was all too pathetic, and a point of quiet pride too, because both Parisot and Perlman knew, the money that men of their abilities could have made on these imbeciles—it was Perlman's saving grace that he resisted.

And yet look what had happened here. These so-called imbeciles had gone and captured one of his patients. They'd sent their most beguiling envoy, who in less than two days had managed to insinuate herself between Perlman and the girl, and now had basically won her. She had beaten him at his own game, and in so doing had managed to fill this empty vessel "Nina" with the rankest horseshit that idle minds could muster.

And she *knew* it. That was the criminal part. The woman had admitted that she knew the girl was split. She'd said so when his nose was bleeding, which only made all the business with the cigarette and the milk pitcher completely unconscionable, how she could be so . . . there wasn't even a word. It seemed to him an unprecedented combination of cunning, manipulativeness—genius, for heaven's sake—but also complete obliviousness to the truth and to common decency and to the covenant that must exist between a doctor and his patient and the society in which they live. The sheer level of contempt for another human's well-being, he could hardly fathom—these stupid, frivolous, self-indulgent, idle . . . idle, idle, idle, wanton, reckless, overprivileged idiots, with their lodges and ridiculous fur hats and handshakes.

The book flipped open to offer him one last glimpse:

*The battle of Armageddon is fought over and over again in every age of the world's history.*

He was in the midst of an absolute professional catastrophe.

He looked at himself in the mirror. Fool, utter fool—standing there with Alexander Barrett's nightshirt clenching his armpits. Leonard was right. What was he doing here?

He had to get the girl. He wrestled the nightshirt back over his head, but the shoulders were so tight he split the seams. Infuriating too-tight nightshirt, he thrashed the bedpost three times with it, and then flung it into the bottom of the armoire.

He had to get out of this place, this den, this playpen. He threw on his shirt. Get back to the clinic, back to sanity. Go wake the girl, throw her over his shoulder. Hear nothing of it. There'd be cabs on King's Road. Or something. Carry her the whole way back.

He grabbed his dress coat.

And tell no one. No one should ever know. Blast her full of morphine, if that's what it took—plant her on a goddamned lightning rod—just get her away from here and start the whole thing over on Monday, Sunday. He didn't even know what day it was.

He took up the lantern and started for the stairs, but he was so agitated he bumped the knob and the flame went out. All fell dark. His ears were pounding. He felt his way down the banister, past the Madame's bedroom and then along the wall. The floorboards winced at every step, but finally he came to her door again, Alexander's.

It was open. The lights were still out. He got down on his knees and crawled in the direction of the bed, felt for the post and up over a lace blanket.

"Nina."

He ran his hands over the sheets for her, satin sheets, searching for warmth—a leg, a hip—but all was flat and cool. There was nothing. She wasn't here, and now his mind began to cloud with panic.

The girl was not even here.

## CHAPTER 26

Then Perlman heard a strange chiming sound coming from below—a quiet, instantly calming sound. Music. Someone was playing the piano.

His eyes had adjusted. He could see the black silhouette of the spiral staircase leading down. He crawled over and gripped the iron rail, and now he heard a familiar phrase calling up. Was that from the songbook?

Carefully, as quietly as he was able, he started down toward the melody, rounded one and a half times, and came face-to-face with the small door separating the stairwell from the Music Room. The piano was just the other side. He stood there in the dark, listening, and now he was quite sure. It was—the longer waltz, the *dolce tristezza*—but played so fluently. All the different lines which beneath Perlman's hands had been like slowly tied knots here were slipping, smoothing, braiding. Only the Madame could know the piece this well, and yet he knew, he could hear, this was not the Madame.

It was coming to the end now, a high reprise of the opening melody, concluding with an acceptable dissonance. It sounded for a full measure, then with an expert conviction the sustain pedal lifted, and he could feel the player waiting, knowing he was there.

With his fingertips he pushed the door open. It bumped the tail of the Pleyel. He leaned around and there she was, looking back at him, she and her reflection in the varnished top of the piano, both of them still wearing the white dress the Madame had found for her, with the lace collar.

"We have to go," he said.

They shook their heads. He looked at the higher one, the right-side-up one. Her eyes seemed unnaturally wide. There was a lamp on behind him, but her pupils nearly eclipsed her irises, black with a faint blue halo.

"Are you awake, Dr. Pearl-Man?" She spoke with an almost mocking prettiness.

"Yes. Now come. We're leaving."

She shook her head. "But we're not finished yet."

"Yes, we are. We have to leave this place."

He knew he should just go get her, but the way she was looking back at him, with those wide eyes and that strange smile, with the strings still warm between them and the air still sighing, finally he let himself ask his question—the one which had been hovering in the back of his mind all week.

"Who are you?"

She smiled, as if she'd been expecting this, as if it were long overdue. "Who do you think?" She waited, waited, then struck a single note to clue him.

"The cousin?" he said.

"That's one. Who else?"

He didn't know.

"I'll give you the next. I'm the one who was spared."

"I don't know what that means."

"You will—"

"No." He shook his head. "Why are you doing this?"

"For you," she answered. "It's all for you, Dr. Pearl-Man. There's nothing to be so angry about. Now who else? There's only one more, and you should be able to guess it now." They tilted their heads, the girls in white dresses. "Who else could I be? Who else *must* I be? Says you."

No, he shook his head again. "We're not playing this. We have to leave. Now, either you're going to come with me or I'm going to take you, do you understand?"

They said nothing. They didn't seem very worried, though.

"Will you go quietly? Or will I have to come around there?"

He intended to, but now he couldn't move his feet. He looked down at the pair of them. "Nina, stop that."

"Stop what?"

"You know very well. Now come, we have to go."

*No.*

And Perlman's entire body stilled, was suffused by a chilling, numbing poison—

*No,* came the voice again, and it wasn't the girl's—he was looking at the girl—nor was it a voice exactly. It was more a thought, a presence behind him, speaking to him not in words.

*We're not finished yet.*

And now he knew, that was no lamp back there. That was a gleaming, golden-haired young thing, seated on top of the Welte-Mignon. He could feel her round blue eyes piercing the back of his skull.

*Did you hear me, Dr. Perlman?*

"Nina, we have to go. Now."

"But what about Oona?"

He shook his head. "There is no Oona. She isn't here. Now come."

*Doctor, are you listening?*

"Nina. Tell her to come."

"Who?"

"We're all going. Whoever you think needs to come. We just have to leave this place. We have to get Sylvie back."

*But I am not afraid of the water.*

Perlman said nothing for a moment. He was lost. "No, but Sylvie is, and we have to get her back."

*Then go.*

The girls tilted their heads. "Are you sure you're awake, Dr. Pearl-Man? How does the lemonade taste?"

"Nina, don't."

"Answer, Dr. Pearl-Man. Are all the gods mortal?"

"Stop. Now we have to get Oona and go."

*But I am not here.*

He looked at the girl again. She smiled. "I don't think you're awake, Dr. Pearl-Man. I don't think you could be."

He eased. It was true. How could he be?

"Is this a dream, Dr. Pearl-Man?"

This must be, he thought. "This is a dream—"

*Then I was never here,* said the voice.

"Then you must go up to bed," said the girl. She was teasing, and yet the words were soothing. He turned.

*Now is to forget,* came the voice more slowly.

And she was right. He stepped through the small doorway again and into the darkness, with the wrought-iron rail spiraling up.

*to wipe away deliberately,* she continued. *Now is to parenthesize.*

"To sleep," the girl returned.

*And let sleep erase all memory of this.*

They both were teasing now. "Go to a dreamless sleep, Dr. Pearl-Man."

*and awake at nine*

"Say ten."

*Yes, awake at ten*

"Up the stairs, Dr. Pearl-Man."

He started up.

*"Count with us."* They spoke together as he ascended step by step. *"Now ten . . . now nine . . . now eight."*

"That's right, Dr. Pearl-Man."

*Good night, Dr. Perlman.*

The last he heard was the two of them giggling; then he did as they said.

# SUNDAY

# CHAPTER 27

Perlman awoke with his trousers on and his head buried in an avalanche of down and white linen. He smashed down one of the pillows low enough to reveal the bedside lamp and the books. He saw the blurry word *Atlantis* and it all came swarming back.

He was out of bed and down the hall in moments. He threw on his shirt, his shoes, made a quick stop in the loo, and headed down.

All was quiet on the second floor. The door to the girl's room was open, the bed unmade. "Hello?" No answer. He descended again, by the front stairs.

He called into the parlor. "Hello? Good morning?"

"Morning," Madame Helena's voice answered from the back end of the house. He followed by way of the Music Room and found her in the small office where he'd taken his nosebleed yesterday.

"Madame."

She was sitting at the desk, chair turned out, dressed as she'd been the day of her visit to the clinic—a white high-collar shirt and the same gray flannel dress, her business suit. She was surrounded by boxes, files, and leaning stacks of paper, making piles—what to keep, what to throw away, what, thought Perlman, to send to other Dr. Perlmans.

She addressed him from over the rims of her reading glasses. "And how did you sleep?"

"Where is she?"

The Madame tilted her head in the direction of the garden, and Perlman stepped to the window. The girl was down at the far end of the lot, beneath a willow, wearing a straw hat not her own. "How long has she been up?"

"Not so long. We had a nice breakfast, then she headed out."

Perlman looked again. She was standing at a picnic table.

"What's she doing?"

"I'm not sure." The Madame had to lean back to see. "It looks as if she's setting places."

So it did.

"Did you see there are scones," she said, "sausages?" She nodded through to the far side of the office, to the breakfast nook. "And do you take coffee or tea this time of day?"

"What time is it?"

"Half past ten."

Half past *ten*? What had overcome him?

"Coffee or tea, Doctor?"

Perlman looked at her. He wasn't quite sure how to respond, having heaped such scorn on her the night before. He felt his rage like a raw throat after shouting, yet something about her manner, the ease with which she was treating him, had a calming effect upon him.

"Coffee," he answered.

"It should still be warm. Make yourself comfortable. It's Sunday."

He passed through to the nook. There was a bay window facing the garden and a small square table with a yellow cloth. Sausages had been set out on a warming dish and some scones. He helped himself to a plate and poured himself a cup, black.

To keep an eye on the girl, he took a seat at the window. Yesterday's *Times* was on the sill, folded open to the international page, which was also the concert page.

His instinct was to read:

*If proof were required of the great superiority of the average English composer of the day over the average German composer, it would be*

*supplied by the two new works played at the Promenade Concerts last*
*night and the night before. Mr. Granville Bantock's orchestral varia-*
*tions, called "Helena," are constructed upon a rather unpromising*
*theme of three notes, B natural, F, and B flat, concerning the applica-*
*tion of which the programme is perhaps a little too explicit, giving at*
*length a dedication to the composer's wife with which the public is, of*
*course, not concerned. The theme is handled with very remarkable*
*skill, and subjected to all kinds of transformations, the result being a*
*piece of distinct value, although a theme more easy to follow might*
*perhaps have increased the pleasure of many hearers. The composer*
*was enthusiastically cheered at the end.*

"You were up late last night," the Madame called through the open
door. He leaned back. All he could see was her feet beneath her desk.
"Yes, I'm afraid I lost track."

"Well, you're a beautiful player. Very modest."

"Sorry?"

"No. It was rather nice." She returned to her sorting. He hadn't the
faintest.

He looked down at the paper again.

*The so-called symphony played on Wednesday evening is the first of*
*five composed by Herr Gustav Mahler, one of which has already been*
*heard in England before. The composer is a conductor of high repute,*
*but his writings have not as yet won him undisputed success . . . All*
*the subjects are studiedly, not to say affectedly, simple to the verge of*
*baldness, but when it comes to the question of developing them, the*
*composer has little to offer but a series of noises in the manner of*
*Richard Strauss, which assort so ill with the themes themselves as to*
*produce a most incongruous impression. When one thinks how the*
*same kind of ideal has been realized by Humperdinck—not to men-*
*tion Wagner or Brahms—one is at a loss to conceive why this piece*
*was chosen for performance, although the finale, as performed on*
*Wednesday, justified itself entirely. Mr. Wood conducted both pieces*
*with great care and ability.*

Perlman shoved the page away. It dampened the spirit of his own misgivings about Mahler that he should find himself allied with such a provincial nincompoop as the *Times* critic.

"Doctor?" It was the Madame again. "Did you happen to read any of the books I left out?"

He leaned over to see her fully. She was intent on some financial statement, studying it like a hieroglyph.

"I did, yes."

"And?" She tossed the page on the largest pile.

He found it odd that she should be the one to bring the matter up, but he supposed now was as good a time as any. He took his cup and saucer to the threshold of her office, and leaned gently against the frame. "Madame, may I ask, how long have you been entertaining this interest—in Atlantis?"

"Oh, I don't know, a while." She held another letter up to the light. "Whenever it comes up."

"Comes up?"

"You know, when there's talk."

Again, he looked at her. What to make of this woman, whose mind could be by turns so keen, then so susceptible?

"You're staring, Doctor."

"Madame, may I be frank?"

"Of course."

He turned to face her squarely. "You are a very impressive woman—"

"Thank you, Doctor."

"—with an evidently excellent mind, which is why I have to tell you: some of the ideas you entertain, they do not befit you." She smiled at this. "You must be aware—Madame Blavatsky, Ignatius Donnelly—these people are notorious frauds."

She laughed lightly. "Oh, I am aware."

"Well then, how can you take the interest you seem to?"

"I suppose it all depends upon what one means by interest." She put down her work to consider the question. "I mean, I think you're right, one needs to be careful. There are a great many lies out there, but there's also a great deal of truth to be found in certain lies, don't you think?"

"If you're confident you can tell the difference."

She agreed. "It's tricky sometimes, and I'll admit it doesn't help that people like Helena Blavatsky do the things they do—or did—because you're right. She was a fraud, and a liar and cheat. And yet she also happened to be one of the most gifted people I've ever met, in that way. What her mind encompassed, and the things she could do with it. You'd never look at a letter opener the same way." She shook her head, pleasantly puzzled. "It's just too bad, I suppose, how often it's the very people who have the most to share, the most light to shed, who'd just as soon try tricking you for the fun of it." She smiled at him. "An unfortunate quirk of human nature, yes—how sorcerers tend to be so good at sleight of hand."

"I should think it would make one very suspicious."

"Oh indeed, but I'm not sure we can always pick and choose our sources, do you know? I mean, if we just dismissed the ideas of every person we didn't completely trust—or who harbored a, shall we say, renegade opinion—we'd still be drawing on cave walls." She looked at him curiously now. "But perhaps I'm not taking your point."

"My point—" He stopped to gather himself. He hadn't expected the conversation to take quite such a theoretical turn. "My point, Madame, is that these people are not harboring 'renegade' opinions. They are knowingly perpetrating falsehoods—in certain cases for clearly nefarious purposes. That would be bad enough, but that their efforts should go and trample the work of the really well-intentioned people—I'm speaking here of historians and scientists and archaeologists—that may be what disturbs me most of all. Madame, we are very fortunate to be the children of an age when so much time and effort has gone into determining what we know, what may be held as true on account of good things like reason and evidence and scientific understanding. I should think you'd agree, we are very lucky."

She nodded, she did.

"Which is why I have to say I find it such an outrage that a person of your intelligence and advantage should be promulgating these patently ridiculous whims and ravings."

"I see I've touched a nerve."

"Well, I shouldn't think there's anything so sensitive or strident in what I say, but if there is, perhaps it's because of the really rather difficult position you've put me in."

"That I've put you in?" She lowered the folder to her lap. "What have I done, Doctor?"

This piqued him, this innocence. He wanted to be careful, though. He could sense he was beginning to abuse her hospitality. "Well, I gather your purpose in leaving those books out for me last night was to suggest a connection between these Atlantean legends and the story that Nina is telling us."

"I thought you might find it interesting, yes."

"Yes, well, I did find it interesting—but not for the reasons you do, I don't suspect."

She waited.

"I mean, I hardly think it coincidental that she should be telling *you* these stories."

She looked at him and shook her head for some further explanation. It was an expression he was growing used to—this innocent inquiry—but as many times as he'd seen it now, he still couldn't tell if it was a purely rhetorical device or not. "I'm still not sure I follow, Doctor."

"Madame, she is a sick girl, in the middle of an acute hysterical episode. You choose to forget this. Let me remind you: 'Nina' is not a person. She has no past. She has no future. She is a spontaneous concoction of a mind in a state of great depletion and disarray, such as which, I am telling you from experience, is more prone to suggestion than you can possibly imagine. Trust me, Madame. If we talk to her of ancient demigoddesses, she will tell us about ancient demigoddesses. Is this not perfectly clear?"

She sat back, eyes opened wide. "Why, Doctor, you make it sound as if this is all my doing."

She waited a moment, in hopes he might rescind the suggestion. He did not.

"Oh." She turned her head.

To her credit, she did seem—for a moment—to consider the possibility, but finally rejected the idea with a shake of her head. "But, Doctor, you've been here. You've seen."

He nodded.

"Then you know. I've opened my door. I've served her tea."

"Madame, you've done a good deal more than serve that young lady tea."

"I've asked her some questions."

"Yes. Some very clever questions, which she has answered by telling us tales about sorcery and demigoddesses and golden temples—"

"Which she was painting before we even met." She pointed in the direction of the parlor. "You know as well as I—"

"Oh, Madame, come." This seemed a silly tack. "A restless child paints a picture. It's hardly difficult for an adult of your powers to foist a story on it."

"My 'powers'?" She was astonished. "Doctor, you are not giving her anywhere near enough credit, and you know it."

"I am not giving anyone credit—or blame, I hope. You have been a very kind hostess, it's true. You have been generous and open. Just the same, you cannot deny that you've given much life and luster to this little delusion of hers, so much so that she demanded to come here. She has taken to you, Madame, and I can't say that I blame her. I'm sure I'm not the first to tell you, you've a mesmerizing presence."

This admission sent an unexpected frisson up Perlman's spine, so ticklish he wondered if he'd not counted it as his excuse, the license to his sudden antagonism, that its object should be this—as he was now openly admitting—the fact that he found her beguiling.

She was not so moved. "Let me just understand, Doctor. You're saying that because I own these books, and because you've seen what's inside them now, you believe that I must be responsible for what the girl is saying?"

"You and Stanley, yes."

"That we have somehow managed to insinuate their contents into the girl's imagination."

"Absolutely."

She sat back, stunned. "You are a puzzle, Doctor."

"Madame, what would you have me believe? Really now, what is the alternative? That the body of my patient has been engaged by the spirit of some mysterious 'Nina' who has befriended an invisible Atlantean goddess named 'Oona,' who for some reason insists that we hear the story of her first love? Is that what I'm to think? Or am I to suspect that an hysterical young woman has, by virtue of my own regrettable laxity, been exposed to someone who believes all this?"

The Madame removed her spectacles. It was a strangely exciting gesture. "Doctor, I think there are some things we need to get straight. I am sorry if I've misled you. I can see it was wrong of me just to leave those books out with no explanation—but you seem to be assuming an interest on my part that I'm not sure I entertain. In the first place, you have me as caring whether this story actually happened or not. I do not. If you have me a proponent of ghosts and reincarnation, I am not. I don't rule out the possibility. I don't see this necessarily as evidence. This I see as evidence of the very idea that I know you yourself believe, what would seem to be your guiding faith: that man is a very suggestible little creature. I agree.

"Our difference is simply over what we think might be responsible for these suggestions. You seem to think the choices are few. You think we should be able to point at them, and in this case, you are pointing at me, which coming from the man who brought her here, esteemed director of the London Clinic for whatever-you-call-it—suggestive therapy—I suppose I should find a compliment.

"The problem, Dr. Perlman, is that I do not share your confidence. What is making the girl act this way? I have no idea. To me, the possibilities seem rather endless, and obscure. I'll say this, though. Whatever it is, I'd wager it's more powerful than either you or I, and that we'd do well just to get out of its way and let it have its say."

Perlman nearly had to laugh. "And so that's all you're doing, getting out of the way?"

"Clearing the way. Yes."

Ridiculous. In all his life he had never encountered such a thoroughgoing degree of self-deception. She almost outdid the girl.

"And so the fact that you've a small library of material on this very subject—the fact that I've heard you speak of it, Madame, independently—that's just coincidence? What's happening here is no reflection of what you believe or what you'd like others to believe?"

She smiled at his persistence. "Believe," she murmured, in an oddly derisive manner. She rolled the question around for a moment, then sat up and, with a high chin, replied. *"A i raz v gudu tserkaf'chudnaja pandnimajettsa k sin 'a mor'a."*

"I'm sorry. I don't speak Russian."

*"Sadko,* Doctor. 'A wondrous church rises from the blue waves.' That is what I believe." She set her spectacles on the desktop. "A wondrous church arises, and we call this church Atlantis. Whether this place actually existed or not, or where—I'm sure I don't care. Better we never find out. That's the point, isn't it? That's what distinguishes Atlantis—from Athens or Lux or the Isle of Man—that there *aren't* any pots or ruins, nothing to confine our thinking."

"Madame, you cannot be serious."

"I'm deadly serious. I think that's what makes Atlantis so interesting, the fact that it should be the one place about which we are free to think anything we like. Tell any story. It's no wonder it keeps bobbing up to the surface like this."

"Madame, please."

"No. Frankly, I should think you'd see the appeal. You talk of how melody expands. Well, so do stories, Doctor. This one does. If Atlantis never lived, it also never died. It keeps coming back, over and over again, and every time it's the same—the same ideas, the same characters—but every time there's something different, too. Something new gets added."

"Madame." He shook his head, he could barely listen to her. "There's really no point. You know what I think."

"Yes, that we're all making it up. To which one might ask, What don't you think we're making up, Doctor?"

"Madame, I cannot have this conversation."

"Fine. Don't. But please don't accuse me of having some hidden purpose here. All I have done is open my door. All I am doing is listening, and I'll admit, wondering why—why here, why now, why at this time?"

"But, Madame"—he growled through clenched teeth. For some reason, this last bit had pushed him over the edge, her utter disregard for what was utmost here. "She is MY PATIENT!"

The last two words in particular had been unexpectedly loud, and Perlman felt instantly ashamed. He'd never spoken to a woman this way.

The Madame could see this. She stood, and more out of respect to his chagrin than her own offense, she yielded. "Very well, Doctor." She gathered up the pile of papers she'd been making. "I understand if that's the way you feel, but then why don't you just leave? Take the girl and go."

"Madame, I've been trying. I feel as if that's all I've been doing."

"You're not saying I've kept you against your will?"

"No," he lied.

"Then what? She's just a girl. Go get her. I myself have to be leaving. I've an appointment—" She stuffed the papers inside a leather envelope, then looked at him, his hesitation. "What?"

"Well, it's not as easy as you suppose."

"Why not?"

"Because"—he could hardly bring himself to say it—"she's made threats."

"What kind of threats?"

"Against the girl—the 'host.' She's said she'll starve her or harm her. She could do any number of things, quite frankly—"

"Oh, Doctor, please. Listen to yourself." She looked out the window again. "She's not going to harm anyone. She's one of the healthiest children I've ever met."

"Yes, as long as she gets her way, as long as she's allowed to tell her little story."

"Well, then *let her tell her little story.*" Her eyes were beaming with impatience. "Dear God, man. This will end if you let it. Just allow the girl to finish." She looked at him intently for one last plea, but then seemed to realize she was asking the wrong man. She took a deep breath. "Very well, Doctor, what would you like me to do?"

He was caught short by this. She seemed to have given up.

"Speak," she said. "What would you have me do?"

"I think it's a bit late for us to *do* anything."

"Well, you're going to have to figure out something." She glanced out at the garden again. "She's coming up here right now."

Perlman stepped to the window. She was—blast it—contentedly climbing the back steps in her new straw hat, humming.

The Madame waited, but Perlman's mind was a fog. There seemed no good answer, and now the back door was clanging open.

# CHAPTER 28

Good morning, Dr. Pearl-Man!" Her voice was a singsong, and a bright white-yellow light was pouring in behind her.

"Good morning, Nina."

She looked well rested, and she'd found another linen dress for herself, also white, but with a slimmer line and a square collar. "Did you tell him?" She looked through at the Madame.

"Tell him what, dear?"

"You have to come see, both of you."

The Madame answered. "Actually, Nina, I was just saying to Dr. Perlman, I have to be going out."

"It won't take long. But you have to come now. Oona says she's ready."

"Nina," tried Perlman, "we really can't keep imposing like this. As the Madame says, she has things she needs to do."

"What?" the girl addressed her directly.

"Service," the Madame replied, "and then to go talk to some people. Lawyers. No fun."

"No fun at all," said Perlman. "Now, come along. Let's get our things."

"But it will be quick. I promise." She looked at them both. "Two minutes. Please?" Her eyes were darting between them, looking for a chink in their armor. "I promise."

Perlman turned back to the Madame, but she seemed to be waiting for his answer.

"Two minutes, you say?"

"Yes. And right now. We're ready."

"Madame, have you two minutes?"

She granted.

"All right," said Perlman, "but then we have to get our things and go."

By no means accepting these terms, the girl took his hand and began pulling him toward the door. The Madame tucked the leather folder beneath her arm, and the three of them headed out.

They descended a set of wooden stairs to the garden. The entire lot was submerged in a jungle of tall grass and dandelions, honeysuckle pouring over the fence. Some work had begun—there were piles of weed over to the side—but the overall appearance was further evidence of the Madame's divided nature. No proper Englishwoman would have let this garden be, even a week.

Nina led them back to the table beneath the willow—square, with a black wrought-iron frame, Parisian-style, and a clean glass top. There was a hammock as well, a stone pool, and a sundial, which Perlman could already sense would serve as Oona's perch. In fact, he could see that the crescent shell which Stanley had shown them yesterday was balanced against the stile.

Nina rounded to the far side of the table and remained standing. The Madame and Perlman took the two chairs opposite. Between them, shifting in the dappled light that needled through the willow braids, three wooden bowls were set on three ascending levels. The first was on the glass itself, the second was on a pair of books laid flat, the third was sitting in the open mouth of an earthenware pitcher. Three matching dishes were set in a row before Nina. On these, successively, were a pile of dry oatmeal, a pile of black currants, and a pile of dried flowers.

"Do you remember," asked the girl, "where we are?"

The Madame answered. "Malachai had put Oona to bed. She found the gift beneath her pillow"—she glanced to the shell on the sundial. "And the next day was the day of the feast."

"Yes," said Nina. "but first they had to make the offerings." She tapped the bowls—one, two, three—and Perlman realized they'd been brought out to observe a trick. "The first came at dawn. All the people gathered at the altar nearest to the temple, and Malachai led them in prayer:

" *'There is one light that lets us see,*
*one spirit, and one source of life.'* "

Perlman glanced at the books beneath the second bowl, to see if they might have provided her liturgy, but the spines were turned away.

" *'As you rise again,*
*that the earth may be reborn,*
*hear our thanks and praise:*
*All is One.'* "

She looked at them. The Madame, more accustomed to responsorial liturgy, answered, "All is One."

"And the grains were offered." The girl poured the oatmeal into the first bowl and covered it with the dish.

"Oona led the people up to the second altar, which was beside a lake. Malachai sang:

" *'There is one light that lets us grow,*
*one spirit, and one source of life;*
*as you shed your warmth and glory*
*that all your children may flourish,*
*hear our thanks and praise:*
*All is One.'* "

"All is One," the Madame said again.

"And the fruits were offered." The girl took the currants and dumped them into the second bowl, the one on top of the books, and covered it with the dish as well.

"For the third prayer, they all climbed up to a bed of stones. Malachai sang:

> " *'There is One Truth*
> *one center, one spirit, one source of life—'* "

Here she dropped a handful of the dried flowers into the third and highest bowl, perched in the mouth of the pitcher. Like the others, she covered it.

> " *'As we offer our thanks and praise,*
> *let the fast end,*
> *that we may hold within us,*
> *the memory of this truth.'* "

"All is One," the Madame offered.

"One one one," Perlman murmured.

"Then all the people looked at Oona," said the girl. "And just the same as every year since she was girl, Oona climbed up to the first stone of the bed. She opened her hand in front of it, and the first spring water came flowing out."

Nina nodded to the third bowl again and looked at the Madame— a party magician, asking that she blow on her hand. The Madame obliged. She removed the dish and they all three looked in.

The flowers were gone. The bowl was filled with water and three large white petals, floating—from yesterday's lily.

The Madame gave an impressed coo and glanced up at Perlman.

"What an unfortunate quirk of human nature," he replied.

Nina continued: "And all the people drank the water and ate the blossoms." She handed the bowl to the Madame, who once again—if more remarkably—obliged. She placed the rim to her lips, but as the first petal approached her open mouth, Perlman cleared his throat. He wasn't sure that was such a good idea.

She turned her eye; the petal hovered patiently. It was fine. She tilted the bowl, and Oona's eucharist floated into her mouth.

The girl looked at Perlman now. He thought better than to fight. He took a mouthful of water and the second petal. The Madame seemed to have swallowed hers, so he did the same, gulping for the girl's benefit.

Gratified, she continued. "When all the people had had their share, Oona filled a bowl for her father." She removed the plate from the second of the wooden bowls, the one she'd put the currants in. It too was filled with water now and lily petals. "But she couldn't find him anywhere. She asked her uncle, Where is Malachai? But he looked very upset. 'Malachai is in the catacombs,' he said, 'but you should stay up here.' "

" 'But why?' asked Oona. 'Has something happened? Is something wrong?'

"And Aram said there was. He said that they'd been followed, and that a prisoner had been taken."

Nina waited a moment, then looked at them both. "That's all." She poured the water from the third bowl into the earthenware pitcher, then did the same with the second.

"Well," said the Madame, "that's very interesting, and a lovely service, too. I'd almost say you've saved me my trip, but I'm afraid I do have to be on my way."

The girl nodded, she didn't object. She went and sat in the hammock, in fact, looking very tired all of a sudden.

"Doctor." The Madame lowered her voice, cold again. "As I was saying, the door is open either way. If you should decide to stay, be warned that I am having guests this evening for dinner. You are both welcome, just know that some of Lord Stanley's maidservants may begin to appear."

"I understand."

"Good day."

"Good day."

"Nina, you'll convey my appreciation to Oona."

Nina nodded from the hammock. "She knows."

Then Madame Helena turned and left by the slate path that bordered the house, sidestepping the piles of weed.

The girl spoke. "I'm tired, Dr. Pearl-Man. What does one say when one is going to nap, me to you?"

He turned. Her eyes were already closed. "I'm not exactly sure."

"What about you to me?"

He hesitated. Her hands were folded across her belly; her narrow chest rose and fell in the shifting light. This wasn't life as he'd come to know it. As he watched her drifting off, he felt something like a lost explorer, caught halfway across an arid desert or through a deadly jungle, so far inside that to turn back now was probably just as dangerous as pressing on.

He looked down at the table again. The first of the three bowls was still hidden beneath its dish. With his finger Perlman lifted the plate to look inside: nothing but a pile of oatmeal.

"Nina? Where are your clothes? In the bedroom?"

She nodded faintly.

"Shall I go get them?"

She didn't say yes, but she didn't say no.

"I'm going to get them."

He started for the back steps, prepared for her to object. He looked back once, but she just lay there, lids placid, cheeks flushed. Perhaps he wouldn't even have to wake her. Perhaps he could simply carry her to a cab.

He ascended the steps, trying to think of what she'd brought—the dress, her coat, the shoes—though it occurred to him there might be just one more thing he had to do before they left. He was beginning to suspect he might not have the chance again.

## CHAPTER 29

The steamer trunk was still up in the library, all six rolls still inside. He chose the one he'd looked at the night before, No. 6, and took it back downstairs. Better to go with just the one, he thought, rather than try hearing them all. He carried it in two hands.

The grandfather clock was tocking in the parlor. It read a quarter past eleven. Gently he laid the roll down on the floor, opened the case, and stilled the pendulum. Then into the Music Room.

He'd never worked a Welte-Mignon, obviously, but the procedure was fairly self-evident. There were three levers below the keyboard. The one marked Tempo he set for *lento*—as indicated on the roll— then he inspected the mechanism. All seemed clean and ready. He inserted the scroll into the spool box; it snapped right into place. He adjusted the pegs to make sure they met the side holes, and that seemed to be all. His heart was thumping. As if to quiet its rhythm, he placed his hand to his chest, then set his feet on the foot pedals and began pumping. The roll descended, the holes passed down to meet the pins, and Perlman closed his eyes to listen.

A soft, sustained chord to begin—struck so gently he'd have sworn there was a hand there, resting. A second more unusual array sounded, then a third—whole tones each, and yet Perlman hadn't the sense that this was a statement of any kind or a theme. The effect was more sen-

sual than that: a sounding of the instrument, intervals felt for their effect—some troubling, some soothing—each heard, considered, then
discarded for the next.

Then a shift. A subtle syncopation, and in two measures this basically vertical meditation toppled into a much more streaming, horizontal thing; almost a toccata, but smoother than that—like a river or
a flight, which Perlman had the vivid sense of propelling with his feet.
He switched the tempo lever to *allegro* and quickened his pace, *ma non
troppo.*

He thought of what Stanley had said—about Barrett always wanting to "untrain" his hands. Certainly there were respects in which
what he was hearing now answered to that description. There was no
discernible key, for instance, and what few moments of intelligible
melody did manage to glimmer through were just as quickly rejected
for the sense they made. Yet the overall effect wasn't really so dissonant
or defiant, for there still remained a distinct rhythmic intelligence to
this, as if to make the point that a great deal of nonsense could be tol-
erated thematically so long as a piece behaved itself rhythmically—so
long as it flowed. And this did flow, so tumblingly and faultlessly that
Perlman was inclined to think the Madame was right. Maybe these
shifting contours were just a matter of getting used to. Perhaps the two
lines playing against each other right now, whose pairing sounded
merely arbitrary to Perlman's virgin ears, might on a third or fourth
hearing prove to be a handsome counterpoint. Who knew?

And now the river slowed again, opened to a broader, calmer, almost lyrical space, but Perlman still found himself listening more in
awe than in appreciation. That the casual meandering of this man's
hands could conjure melodies so effortlessly and let them go—right
there, a glowing phrase, climbing up and down and gone forever—
was a kind of exquisite torture for Perlman to be hovering so near.
What he'd give to be able to express himself like this—so freely, so immediately. There was simply nothing in the world like musical genius.
No gift quite so glaring.

And now another shift. The roll had entered an even quieter moment, and slower, to offer up an unusually simple statement. Perlman let it play once through, then stopped his feet. He wanted to hear that again. And to make a note as well.

He hit the re-scroll and began searching his pockets for Stanley's crib sheet. He checked in his breast pocket first—it wasn't there—but then in his side pocket he felt something odd, a tacky lump between his fingers, the size of a pea. He wasn't sure what it was at first, but then he felt his pipe as well, the clay pipe, and now he remembered—*that's* where he'd put it.

He'd brought his hashish.

The roll thunked to a stop and wavered a moment like a roulette wheel. The opening trail of perforations climbing up and over the cylinder looked almost like a half-grin, daring him.

He couldn't help a smile back, at the simple fact that he should find this now, just exactly what he needed in a way, given the task at hand—to focus. He knew better, of course. Could hear the chorus in his brain already, singing no. No, for so many obvious reasons, not the least of which that this was Parisot's Tunisian connection, remember—a potent extract from the first, which age had only turned hairier, and scarier. And in this setting? Absolutely not. No.

And therefore obviously, *yes.*

He removed the brick and the pipe. The Madame wouldn't be back till three at the earliest. The girl was ten minutes into her nap. Ample time. He'd simply have to be careful, was all. There was a stone cup filled with matches right there. Without another thought, he struck one, held it to the bowl, and drew in.

The brick was dry. He could feel the smoke almost instantly. The hash glowed, then suddenly flared orange. His throat burned; he coughed. That was more than he'd intended. He coughed again, another burst of blue. His eyes watered, his salivary glands began to ooze, and only then, of course, did it occur to him how little he'd had to eat—nothing last night, and a half a scone just now, and a sausage. He'd given the smoke free rein, and he could feel it taking advantage even now. The first wisps had reached his brain already, like a family of ghosts in the attic, opening their usual drawers and cupboards, closing others.

He needed a glass of water. He started for the breakfast nook, but stopped short. Through the Madame's office he could see the light flooding in the bay window. It seemed unusually bright outside all of a sudden, and unusually dark within, but he knew he should not go there, not with the window looking out onto the garden.

He checked the drinks cabinet. There was a row of clean snifters but no water. On the coffee table was the slim glass vase the Madame had brought in yesterday—sans lily. He supposed there might be a filthy sip or two there, but then he noticed Oona's tea was still sitting on the mantel, her cup from yesterday.

He went directly. The bowl was nearly full. Without even thinking, he began to drink, and it wasn't so awful—cooled and stale, and slightly sweet from honey—but as he stood there gulping, from over the rim of his cup he could see all the hooded furniture, the chairs, the lamps, like sleeping bodies beneath their sheets, awakened now and looking back at him curiously. Who was this man, and what exactly was he doing here?

He lowered the cup. What *was* he doing here? For just a moment the reality of the situation asserted itself; not comprehensively, and not even in any particular detail. More like a dog on a chain, it took a lunge at Perlman—just to remind him that there was a broader circumstance that he was choosing for the moment not to think of. And that was enough. That released an adrenal charge that felt to Perlman like poison, and now he wasn't feeling very well at all. Clammy, dizzy, and his heart was beating too fast again. He pressed the soft flesh between his left clavicle and shoulder. No, this had not been a good idea, exposing himself this way, if only because of this—this fickle pump inside his ribs, this ever-clenching fist that always seemed to listen in this way, and care. He could practically see it beneath his lapel *k-thunk-k-thunk-k-thunking.*

Then an arrow shot him high through the chest, so piercing he had to bend over. Damn, this was not good. He was feeling nauseous now. He thought he might even throw up, but then a second blade lanced him up nearer his shoulder and he nearly dropped his cup. He set it down on the floor and tried to breathe—not to panic—though this was a fear of Perlman's, a recurrent dread, that he might actually end his life this way; not by ingesting the finally lethal dose of resin, but by doing precisely this, what he'd just been doing: focusing such rapt attention on his own heart—the physical presence of it drumming away inside his breast—and wondering so brazenly at the mystery of its unflagging stamina, that the thing might, of spite, simply stop; clench once and for all and never unclench again. Far from absurd to a man of his profession. Even now, he could feel his whole chest tightening, and his left arm growing numb; tingly—

But no—enough. He stopped himself and stood up straight. Now was not the time. His arm, his heart, the room (the girl)—he could not think of these. But breathe. Just breathe and drink your tea and this shall pass, it always does.

He took a sip, not to taste; he gulped it down. He was here for a purpose, was reckless reckless Perlman, and the purpose was in the other room, loaded and ready to go. He took a deep breath. Better. The drumming in his chest was slowing down. Just a brief flutter was all; gas, most likely. He squared his shoulders, set his eyes straight ahead, and ventured through the French doors again.

The roll was still grinning on its spool, waiting. Perlman wondered if he shouldn't try another—he should probably listen to them all while he had the chance—but there again he stopped himself. Eyes too big for your stomach, August. This was the one you've started. This is the one you're to finish.

He sat down, and before his mind could be lured away in some other ill-advised direction, he set his feet on the pedals, lowered his head, and began pumping. It felt better, the movement. The scroll began to turn again. The holes descended, and the "Nonsense" began anew.

But had he closed his eyes before? He must have, because this time, as the flat ivory slats began curtsying before him, he found himself very nearly mesmerized. They looked so much like players in a dance, entering in two and threes, bowing, stepping back and waiting their turn again. He tried guessing which would enter next—would it be the middle C, or the high F sharp where the hands had gone to hover and then descend? But he was wrong, and wrong again. The veil between now and then—between the doctor and the artist—was absolute.

But now it was time for the flight—the river shifting, turning—and this was easier to follow. Perlman remembered this, the one about the man who kept trying to escape himself but never quite made it. As hard as Barrett tried, you could still hear him—there in that turn, that modulation, the spark of humor and arrogance, as one key after another came forward to make its appeal, only to be whisked aside with all the rest, like another lopped head.

It was frustrating, in a way. One could well imagine Welte's reaction. (Was it he who'd dubbed it "Nonsense"? Had the siblings laughed?) All the man had wanted was another "Für Elise," a quaint piece of salon music his customers could recognize, nod their heads along to. But no, Barrett had known better. He'd seen, the real opportunity here wasn't to play a "known" piece. It was to capture the moment—to record the artist engaged in his most basic task: unlearning, unknowing, becoming a vessel for the music just to pour through—from the sky inside his mind out through his hands and down onto these eighty-eight well-tempered wires. The hammers were pummeling them now, devouring the board with unheard-of runs and counterruns, and as Perlman watched, he had to admit it did look awfully close to freedom.

He smiled, to think of the impression his two hands would leave—Perlman's "Nonsense." He could just see the furtive chords, stumbling one to the next, hesitating, flubbing, starting over. What a lowly beast he was, compared to this one here. The notes were glancing everywhere now, like light on water, and for a moment, Perlman simply gazed at them . . .

—but then he realized he was doing it again. The roll had come back to the primitive passage—he recognized the drumbeat bass—but once again he'd missed the transition. He'd have to go back—for a third time, imagine. He lifted his feet and looked away in disgust, but then he stopped. The notes retarded, but he barely heard.

There across the room was something he hadn't seen before. Standing on the seat of a pretzel-back chair was the draped statuette—the one that Stanley had warned the girl away from yesterday, and that she'd subsequently cast as the hero of her story—Thaire. Someone must have moved it. Stranger than that, though, Perlman thought he could tell what it was now, or what those were.

The room was silent. The silence urged him from the bench, but he felt oddly detached from his body—eerie and euphoric—as if he were the subject of some invisible intention, an exasperated angel who finally had enough and chose now to intervene, to nudge him across the floor and make him see this thing, this mystery—though it was hardly any mystery at all.

He stood a moment before it. The drape was nothing but an old linen dustcloth. He took the fringe between his thumb and index finger—just as the girl had done, as if to feel how soft—and just as the girl had wanted to do, he pulled. The flax slid silently over the bronze, and there they were:

Alexander Barrett's hands. And even though he'd known, Perlman's breath still caught in his throat; they were so relaxed. Neither large nor small, they rose up from the pedestal, wrist against wrist, palm grazing palm, fingers barely touching—poised the perfect equidistance between prayer and applause.

And just then an image flashed to Perlman's mind—of the Madame's face as she'd looked over at these yesterday, when the girl was pointing. There'd been a sequence in her eyes—of grief, consoled by love, ruined by grief again. He'd seen it at Bernheim's reception as well, when he'd first offered his condolence. And as he pictured it now—how she'd grown young, then old again—for the first time it occurred to him:

Perhaps they had been. Perhaps they were.

And a strange thing happened inside Perlman as this thought first took root. Standing there beside the hands, he felt somehow humbled, or chided even. He wasn't sure why at first, except that there must be something awfully small and sad about a mind that could spend so much time dismissing a notion which, now that he actually considered it, should seem so obvious, so natural.

They lived in a different world, these two, by different rules. He'd been here less than a day and he could feel how just the air was changing him. The Barretts enjoyed a wealth few would ever know, an intelligence, a beauty, and, above all, a talent few others would ever know. That was their lot, and Perlman thought he finally understood now, that for someone who has been blessed already with everything to which a person might aspire, the only remaining purpose—the only challenge, the only hope—is to create. The Barretts had been doing so since they were children, making heroes out of drapes, monsters out of nursemaids, music from thin air. And growing up in such a peculiar place—the world of their invention—how could they not eventually have looked to one another with a special intimacy, that glint reserved for the only other one who truly knows, who speaks the language, too? Perlman had seen it in her eyes, twice now, and having seen it, he was more than willing to concede, if these two had broken a few hearts along the way, or if they'd known a moment of transgression, not only would that not have surprised him very much, that—it now struck him—would have been one of the few truly honest acts.

Of course they had.

The fact he'd never considered it before—that was the real indictment. For what was that but fear, some vestigial bourgeois moralism that can think only in terms it can personally abide? He felt ashamed of himself, like one of those wretched little Englishmen who plodded by his windows every night at dusk, all hunched and buttoned beneath their gray umbrellas of common sense, common knowledge, common decency. How he liked to pity them their invisible oppression, but he was no better—standing here, forgiving the Barretts their trespasses. What did it matter what he thought? They were a pair, and that was as it should be—as it must be—for reasons Perlman knew as well as anyone: where different conditions exist, and different rules are followed for long enough, different laws shall eventually obtain. This was how one soldier could kill another on the battlefield and never think himself a murderer, and this was how Monsieur Légère could once again enjoy the baby-smooth underarms of his youth; because Dr. Perlman had convinced him—that rash was an army of red ants, those ants hated the sun, and Félix Légère controlled the sun. Simple as that. Introduce another truth, see that this truth is accepted in the mind, and the world outside would follow on. For some reason, this was more clear to Perlman now than ever before.

What was not so clear to him was how a man who'd staked his living on this very insight, who'd been applying it on a daily basis for the last fifteen years, had never once dared to test it beyond the most chastened boundaries of medical science. What fear had he been protecting? That the mind might wield some influence beyond the body? But of course it did. Look at his life—the drab little flat behind his office, the grimy gray kitchen he almost never used, the warped cottage piano shoved against the wall; he could hardly bear to think of it. And yet it made perfect sense, that for him who permitted no untoward suggestions, who accepted no hidden possibility, his world should be accordingly barren: a chair for sitting, a table for eating, a window he opened in the spring and closed in the fall. What was his life but that? An old gray veil, hiding nothing underneath.

While here, here within the gleaming limestone of 97 Charles Place—where the books whispered every known and unknown rumor from cover to cover, where the piano danced at the outskirts of melody, and every little girl was welcomed in, was fed and clothed and offered tea—who was to say who should touch whom, or what might be conjured along the way? For here when you peeked beneath the veil, you most certainly did find something.

The hands again. He looked back down at them—brilliant, ungoverned creatures—and there again was the Madame's face. He couldn't get the image out of his mind, of her eyes in the middle moment, of succumbing. How blind had he been not to see? This was all about the two of them, wasn't it?

"Oh, Doctor," she smiled. The hands were on her face now, and neck. The fingers were grazing her lips. "Doctor, you know nothing."

She turned away, and Perlman's skull was like a basin, like an ocean floor, spilling in with rage—humiliation, shame, and envy—furies he didn't understand, except that she, this woman, was the cause; for simply having known him, for tainting him, for claiming him as well. Must she have everything? Was it not enough she'd stolen the girl?

His heart was racing now, pounding in his temples. He should stop this, he knew, but all he could think to do was to cover the hands. He took the dustcloth and lifted it over the top again, and he meant to leave it there, be done with it, but then he felt the firmness underneath, the fingers rising up, and for a moment Perlman let the linen be his alibi. He let his knuckles graze the knuckles, let his hand slide down to feel the softer, rounder flesh of the palms. And though it wasn't flesh—though it could not have been more cold, or heavy, or hard—still he gave himself away. For even as he stood there, caressing the bronze, he could feel that useless little knot between his legs ever so slightly beginning to slip.

His heart shuddered then, as violently as if he'd been kicked in the chest. He fell to his knees. He couldn't breathe, and his mind went white with terror. Was this It, then? Had he committed the suicidal thought? He even had a vision of himself, as from the corner of the ceiling. He could see his body on the floor, fallen beside the hands—the little green monster who'd strayed too far inside a kingdom of golden-haired gods; a devil lost in heaven, cupping his ears against the din.

But it did not come to that, for just then a bilious vapor rose up from his stomach, and he began to heave—once, twice, then on just his third attempt, out plupped a little gray mulch of sausage, scones, and lily, doused in day-old tea—a catlike deposit on the fringe of the rug.

And all he wanted now was air, but he couldn't go outside. She was still there, so he pulled himself across the floor. Like a soft-shelled turtle he crawled into the parlor again, leaving behind him a thin gray smear, from the cast of Barrett's hands to the brick of the Madame's fireplace; the safest place. There was air up there at the top of the flue, and so there he remained, with his knees pulled up and his arms above

his head, waiting for this fear, this trembling, this terrible loathing to
burn itself away.


Hello?"

He hadn't even heard the front door open, but someone was there.
"Miss Barrett?"

Another woman, but all Perlman could see from his vantage were
her feet, a beefy pair of ankles pinched inside black Murphy shoes—

"Miss Barrett? The do—" She stopped—she'd spotted him, or his
trail. For a moment the two of them were perfectly still. Then like a
stalking beast she started over, inch by inch, by tiny side steps closing
in on him, but Perlman couldn't move. He cowered down inside his
coat, even as she stood directly over him. He could feel her shadow, her
arm now rising up. She had something long and heavy in her hand,
earmarked for his skull, but all Perlman could think was yes, yes, give
it a good pounding.

And she did.

# CHAPTER 30

The rest of the afternoon was something of a blur. Nina came in from her nap shortly after the beating and calmly cleared up all misunderstanding. She and Miss McCumber, Lord Stanley's unforeseeably estimable housekeeper, both helped Perlman upstairs to his bed and dressed his wounds, the most pointed of which was a small but welting laceration above his left ear. Miss McCumber had insisted on calling a doctor, which Perlman's groggy reply, that he *was* a doctor, did little to dissuade.

He did not feel so terrible, in fact, or low. Almost from the moment his head touched the pillow again—his pillow—he began to enjoy the typical lightness of spirit that always follows a good purging. Also, he had a vague sense that somewhere deep inside the twisted labyrinth they'd all been groping their way through, a light had been lit, a track had been switched. He wasn't sure how or why, but he felt it distinctly, a confidence all the more pleasing for its mystery, that everything which had seemed so dire before was in fact proceeding according to plan, and by that token licensed him, from his high white throne, to an almost girlish flippancy toward everything that was happening below.

Madame Helena came home earlier than expected and did not share his post-regurgitory rosiness of cheek. She agreed with Miss McCumber.

Professor Bernheim? she suggested.

"Oh, God, no. No. No, no, no, no, no."

"Well, but someone. I'm worried about you, Dr. Perlman."

"I'll be fine. It's just a bump."

"It's not the outside of your head that concerns me." She'd snapped this, but then he felt her touch, her hand against his forehead. "And you're warm. Miss McCumber, could you go chip some of the ice into a towel?"

He gathered the reason for her pique. She probably knew the moment she opened the door: someone had been playing her brother's music. She'd smelled it in the air. And of course she also must have known who was responsible. Who else but the bedridden guest, the nose-bleeding, lily-vomiting, book-snooping, finger-pointing, and always slightly hysterical Dr. Perlman. What a beast he was. Of course it was he, and probably she'd construed his invasion as a vengeful act, to get her back for tampering with his patient—which, come to think of it, may have been entirely correct.

He noticed the girl was there, sitting in a chair against the wall, in white canvas shoes, to match her dress. The calmest presence in all this. Her hair was wet, the linen on her shoulders was slightly damp; Perlman felt an oddly sentimental pang. He would miss her.

"Well, if not Professor Bernheim, then who?" the Madame pressed. "Is there someone else with whom you'd feel more comfortable?"

"Dr. Benjamin?"

"Where?"

"St. Bartholomew's. The ophthalmology office."

"It's Sunday," mentioned the girl.

"At home, then. Yes."

As soon as the Madame could get the address out of him, a messenger was dispatched.

He asked that they not let him sleep too long. Every twenty minutes or so, either Miss McCumber or the Madame came up to freshen his cup with some more hot water or another drop of valerian. As a result, he spent the better part of the day drifting woundedly, but agreeably, between proper sleep and proper waking—in the "hypnargogic" state was the medical term—which for that period exposed his mind to an unremitting, but again not-so-unpleasant, pageant of everything that had crossed his path the last six days; or more of a masquerade, where meanings and limbs were traded like hats or masks; where bronze hands fell on starless skies; where towers drowned in stone pools and different voices spoke in loops—the girl's, the Madame's, Herr Blum's—all chiming in with a word or two. Some he tried to remember, or the syntax of certain images—that the key to it all was the Madame's hat, the ostrich feathers!—but then it would rush away again on the wind of the next epiphany, so quickly and irretrievably forgotten he could only think it was utter gibberish or the absolute truth.

At one point, he became aware that the Madame was sitting in the chair.

"How are you feeling?" She was still cool.

"Sorry."

"How are you feeling?" she said louder, misunderstanding.

"Better, thank you."

"Your friend Dr. Benjamin is on his way."

"Thank you. You're very kind." His smile ached. "Madame, I hope you understand—" He paused; he hadn't thought this through—*understand that it was only out of respect he would ever have done such a thing; that he'd meant no harm*—but the light was low already, casting a broad shadow of her profile against the wall, slipping between her lashes and seeming to light her pupils from inside, to make them seem to glow.

She spoke: "You should probably know—Stanley is here."

"Is he?"

"He's with the girl."

"Stanley." His head rolled against the pillow. "He is an interesting fellow, isn't he?"

"Would you like me to separate them?"

Perlman hadn't even considered; one could sooner reverse the spin of earth. "No."

She stood. "You should rest, then."

And before he could say any more, engage her as he'd have liked—

asked how her meeting with the solicitors had gone—she closed the door behind her, and once again Perlman was swept away into a bleary swarm of towers and whale spouts, wooden bowls and piano rolls, and the random return of epiphanies past—the Madame's hat! The ostrich feathers! All nonsense, he knew—a function of his state, which would simply have to pass but which, while it lasted, he would not be so foolish or ungrateful as to resist. The Madame was right. Just shut up and listen. Only bear in mind the . . . well, he couldn't remember what to bear in mind, and drifted off to sleep again.

The next he knew, the sun had begun its wintry-early descent, the window was a simmering blue rhombus, and there was Arthur Benjamin leaning over his bed, looking down at him with such heavy-lidded bemusement it was almost worth the flogging.

"Arthur, you're here." He sat up. "It's good to see you."

"Good to see you." He swirled his brandy. "Are you comfortable?"

"Yes."

"Do you know where you are?"

"Yes."

"Do you know how you got here?"

"Do you mean *here* here?" Perlman chuckled and felt his head. "I suppose I'm not exactly sure. I was overcome." He gestured to his coat. "You might want to get rid of what's in the pocket, though."

Benjamin felt inside, then smiled. "Gone bad, has it?" He sniffed his fingers.

"Gone evil."

Benjamin folded the evidence inside his handkerchief.

"You've met Madame Helena?" asked Perlman.

"Yes." He check Perlman's eyes. "And your patient. Nina?"

Perlman nodded.

"Is that the one that Shepard was worried about?"

"The same."

"August, what on earth are you doing here?"

"I don't know." He began to laugh again, and his skull throbbed. He reached up and felt the bandage. "Ow. That woman. What did she do?"

"She beat you with the fire bellows, as I understand."

"Or the poker, I thought."

"And the Madame tells me you had a nosebleed yesterday."

"Yes. That's true."

"And you vomited this morning."

"Yes. I'm not a very good guest, I'm afraid."

"Have you been feeling well?"

Perlman laughed again. How was one even to measure? "Not particularly, but they made me eat flower petals."

"Who did?"

"The Madame, the girl. Arthur, it's a long story."

"So it would seem. I'm looking forward." He checked Perlman's eyes again. "You look all right, though, considering."

"I'm fine."

"You know there are guests downstairs."

"I thought I heard bells. Who?"

"I don't know. Two men."

"Lord Stanley?"

"Who is Lord Stanley?"

"Alfred Stanley. From the Lyric."

"Is here?"

Perlman nodded. "He's the Madame's uncle. Uncle Al."

Benjamin stood back.

"Yes, I know. The whole thing is preposterous."

"You must be in heaven."

Perlman began laughing again, a giddy laugh, every little heave of which was exciting another throb in his head, so that instead of sounding 'ha-ha-ha,' he actually sounded 'h-ow, h-ow, h-ow', which under the circumstances seemed not inappropriate.

The two of them were silenced by a knock at the door.

"Yes." Perlman collected himself. "Who is it?"

"Me." The girl. The door opened. She stood still in the frame, in the slim white dress with the square collar and the same canvas slippers. "Are you coming down?"

"Nina, did you meet Dr. Benjamin?"

"Yes." She curtsied, entered, then sat in a chair against the wall. "How long are you going to be?"

"Miss—" This was Benjamin's first real encounter apparently. "You might want to wait outside. Dr. Perlman isn't feeling well."

She looked up at him as might a colleague, and one better trained in the field. "He'll be all right." She turned to him. "How long?"

"Miss—"

"Arthur." Perlman sat up straight. "Trust me, there's no real fighting it."

"You're sure?"

"Look at me." He swung his legs over the side and stood. "I'm tired of bed anyway." He felt his empty stomach, then staggered over to the mirror and saw the bandage above his ear. "But I can't go like this."

The girl stood. "Let me see."

"Miss—" Benjamin tried intercepting her, but she was too intent.

"Have *you* looked?" she asked.

She stepped aside and let Benjamin pull back the dressing. The two of them leaned over to inspect.

"It's not so bad," said Nina.

Benjamin agreed. "Just a little welt. You'll be fine."

"Do you have a comb?" asked the girl.

Perlman didn't. He looked at Benjamin, who handed over a small mustache comb—tortoise-shell. Perlman ran it through his hair, and covered over his wound. The girl lifted his jacket from the chair and helped him on with it; then he checked the mirror one more time.

"You're fine," she said, "except for your collar." She straightened it.

Perlman turned. Arthur was watching, amazed.

"I'm trusting this goes nowhere."

"Of course."

The girl took hold of Perlman's hand. "Come on." She gave a tug, and the two men followed her down.

## CHAPTER 31

**M**iss McCumber had been far from idle since flogging the intruder by the fireplace earlier in the afternoon. The whole first level had been transformed—disrobed, dusted, polished—and was now gleaming. Flowers and candles were everywhere.

As Benjamin had warned, there were two new guests—both men. Perlman recognized the first. It was Mr. Rowe, from the premiere party, Mr. Lullaby, looking primped for the occasion. His suit was a better cut, a brown wool with an ocher windowpane stripe; he'd swept a finer-tooth comb through his hair as well, to tame its luxuriance. The second gentleman he'd not seen before—a fair and serene presence, standing by the mantel with his hands behind his back, examining Nina's painting with an intensity that a curator might focus on a museum piece, or a dog on a duck.

"Dr. Perlman." Madame Helena was looking resplendent in a dark ensemble, a deep and velvety-brown—an antique folk necklace scattered a lattice of opals and agates across a solid and slender vestment; a high choker collar; and ample, cloud-billow sleeves. Her hair was high as well, more so than usual, which plucked a jealous string—would he alone have merited such altitude?

She welcomed him and Benjamin, who'd already been introduced. Nina too; she passed discreetly through to the Music Room, where it appeared this evening's scene was to take place.

"Dr. Perlman, you remember Mr. Rowe?"

Rowe turned dashingly, mahogany hair bouncing in the lamplight, quick smile and overexuberant wit.

"Dr. Perlman, fancy seeing you here."

Perlman was thinking the very same, boosted by the near-certainty that his pretext for being here—the girl—was surely superior to Rowe's, which he assumed must be the gentleman over by the mantel, to whom Madame Helena was now handing a stein of beer.

"And Nicholas. This is Dr. Perlman."

The stranger turned. A high round forehead, scant hair about the top and temples—young though, early thirties, with a flaxen Van Dyke and light blue eyes, sensitive and intelligent. "Dr. Perlman, Mr. Roerich."

They shook hands. "Roerich. What is that?"

"Swedish," the Madame answered. "Means 'rich in glory.' But Mr. Roerich is from home, actually." The two of them shared a patriotic glint. "I am so glad Andrew thought to bring you by."

Roerich smiled with his eyes.

"So did she tell you?" Rowe leaned in. "Dr. Perlman here is a mesmerist."

"*Mesmerist.*" That was his second demotion in two days—from therapist to hypnotist to mesmerist; tomorrow he'd be reading palms. Roerich nodded without judgment, though, and won points right there for being the only man in all Europe apparently who was capable of hearing Perlman's occupation and not mentioning the Rachmaninoff concerto.

Benjamin sidled up with two glasses of sherry, one of which he handed to Perlman, for show. Both understood that he probably shouldn't drink.

Rowe took note. "The Madame says you've been under the weather, Doctor. I'm afraid Nicholas might have been hit by the local complaint as well. Seems it's everywhere."

Perlman turned sympathetically. Mr. Roerich did look a bit pale. "No, mine is a more individual affliction, but I'm actually feeling much better, thank you." He asked Madame Helena, "Is Lord Stanley here?"

"Getting ready," she said, still cold.

"Yes." Rowe lifted his glass. "I was saying, what an unexpected pleasure—to come for a meal and get a show."

"I hope you don't mind," said Perlman

"Not at all. My cup of tea. And Nicholas is a man of the theater as well."

"Is he?" This slightly disappointed Perlman. Mr. Roerich seemed a man of nearly monkish dignity.

Just then three chimes sounded in the Music Room. The Madame took Roerich's arm and they started for the French doors together. Rowe let Benjamin go next; he wanted a word alone with Perlman.

"Anything I should know, Doctor?"

"About?"

"You and the Madame."

So it was true, Rowe was nothing but an old dog who'd caught her scent. "The coast is clear, Mr. Rowe."

He smiled, squinting. "Well, we'll see, won't we?"

The bell sounded again, and Rowe nodded Perlman through.


The Music Room was hardly recognizable, and happily so, after so many years of neglect, finally to be put to its intended use again. All was dark but for the stage. The two pianos had been slid to opposite wings and covered. The set in between was simple: upstage center was the steamer trunk, and beside it was a much more exotic piece—a black sedan chair, like a small booth on wheels, leaning back against its rails.

The audience had been provided five pretzel-back chairs, set in a shallow arc back a ways from the stage. Roerich had already taken the outermost. A clasped fan reserved the next for the Madame, who at present was standing beside the girl over in the left wing, waiting. Rowe offered Perlman the seat to her left, but he declined, so Rowe took it. Benjamin sat next to him, then Perlman assumed the flank.

Once they'd settled, Nina escorted the Madame to the center of the stage, then returned to her place without a word. The Madame took a moment to let her gentlemen guests drink her in. She was a vision there, alone in the light—the height of her hair accenting the natural balance of her posture, the length of her neck, and the size—the sheer openness—of her eyes. She directed them at Roerich, Rowe, and Benjamin in order.

"I have been asked to give an introduction. I will try to be brief, though it should be said, our story this evening is one for which any number of explanations might be given. I would apologize in advance, then, to Dr. Perlman, for those respects in which the account I shall be offering now contradicts his understanding of what we have had the pleasure so far to witness."

She looked at him—really more playful than terse. He replied in kind, like a flirting bird, puffed by the public allusion to their weekend together, and his initiate status in the home.

She clasped her hands in the manner of a soprano, turned her attention back to the three neophytes, and began the recapitulation:

This is a story which takes place long, long ago, back at a time when the boundary between heaven and earth was not as fast or forbidding as it is today. So it is that our heroine is a young demigoddess named Oona, the daughter of a divine mother, Artemis, and a mortal father, Malachai. Oona has never seen her mother. Artemis left long ago, in favor of a realm more native to her divinity, and so it has fallen to Malachai to raise their daughter, to teach and to protect her.

But these are troubled times. As hard as Malachai and the other high priests have tried to preserve the memory of the One Spirit from which they and all things are derived, the people have begun to forget. They are praying to false gods, they are worshipping idols, they are practicing Black Arts. In fact, recent talk of sorcery in the hillsides has prompted Malachai to send Oona high into the mountains, to the temple of his brother Aram, in the hope that she will be safe there.

Rowe raised his hand here, a sarcastic schoolboy. The Madame merely shook her head and resumed.

Unaccustomed to such confinement, Oona has been languishing, a reluctant captive in her uncle's tower. She has endured a lonely winter with just Aram and her nursemaid Porphyry, but the cusp of spring tenders hope, for every year the sun's return is celebrated by the Feast of the Thaw, which takes place not far from Aram's temple.

Oona has been looking forward to this. Finally, after such a long and lonely winter, there shall be people coming with gifts to offer, and there shall be music, and dancing. The sun will be warm again, and best of all, her father is coming, to help conduct the Rite with her.

And yet something strange has occurred in the days leading up—or nights, I should say. For two nights in a row, a curious trail of smoke has appeared just outside Oona's balcony, rising from the river that runs beside the temple. When Oona looks down, she can just barely see—there is a large dark shadow gliding through the water below. It looks like a whale, swimming round and round in long, slow circles, except that it seems to be breathing smoke.

Oona has heard of this, of a man who lives inside the belly of a whale. Y'aromel, the whale is called, and the man's name is Thaire, but no one has ever seen them except at night, when Y'aromel swims up near the surface to vent the smoke of Thaire's evening fire.

The first night this smoke appears, Oona lets it pass; it is too strange. When it returns a second night, however, the temptation is more than she can bear. Oona jumps from her balcony, flies out over the river, then dives down in to see this thing, this shadow, but when she comes up next to it, she discovers it is no whale at all. It is a vessel of some kind, gliding beneath the waves. The hull is made of glass, and when she looks inside, she

sees that there *is* a man, but it is so dark, all she can make out
are his eyes. They are staring back at her, and so she flees. She
flies up to her tower again. Those eyes. They were like ash.

Here she took a well-earned moment. Perlman's attention had been
divided, in fact, between the quality of the Madame's description and
the reaction of the girl as she stood listening. Nina was still over in the
corner and, though solemnized by her duty as Chorus, could have
shown no more satisfaction at the Madame's effort than if she had broken into a dance. Her eyes were steady on the floor in front of her, but
the corners of her mouth were ever so slightly twitching. She had chosen well.

The Madame continued:

It is the following morning that the first rite of spring is conducted. Oona's uncle Aram opens his gates so that all the people
who've come to observe the feast may bring their gifts inside the
temple, the last of their winter store—dried fruit, flowers, and
grain. They present them, one by one, to Aram in order that he
may bless them.

It is a grand and joyous affair. Aram sits on the terrace of the
temple courtyard, and Oona stands beside him, very happy. The
sun is high. The people are jubilant. There is music and dancing, and she knows her father is on his way.

But then she notices—out in the middle of the throng there
is one man standing alone, with a hood over his eyes. She
cannot see his face, but he is staring back at her. Aram notices,
too. Who is this man? he asks, and why is he looking at you
that way? Oona says she does not know, but still Aram is
concerned. He makes her promise to tell him if she sees this
man again, but before Oona can ask why—why one man
should strike such fear?—a balloon appears from around the
mountainside. Her father is here. All the people rejoice. They
stand back and await his descent. All but one, that is—the one
in the hood, who seems to have vanished.

Once again Rowe raised his hand for attention. Once again his gesture was cut short by the Madame's glance.

That night, after all the high priests have convened, Oona meets her father alone in the temple library. It has been too long since they've seen each other and she has missed him greatly, but this evening Malachai bears some very grave news: The augur has had a premonition. He says that before the new season is through, a Lord of Darkness shall descend upon the earth, bringing deluge in his wake. This has long been foretold, but now the prophesy is upon them, and Malachai cannot help blaming himself for failing to preserve the memory of the One Spirit from which all nature springs.

Still, he is taking measures. To ensure that something of their faith survives the flood, he shall be moving the sacred arcana, six scrolls which record all the most ancient wisdom. He is stowing them in the casket you see here before you, which he intends to bring to the ritual site and hide inside the catacombs that run beneath. To this same end, he will be sending the other priests away as soon as the feast is over. Oona he would like to go east with Aram. As for himself, he says that he has grown tired—of this fight, of this flesh. Should the waters come, he does not expect he shall resist.

Oona is very upset when she returns to her tower. She cannot sleep, thinking of all her father has said. She sits out on her balcony, grieving, and there is no trail of smoke that night. But when she finally goes to bed and lays her head against her pillow, she finds a small gift underneath.

The Madame now raised her hand to show the white crescent shell the girl had found. She held it between her thumb and index finger, and guided it in a slow arc for them to see.

The following day the rites are conducted, the same as every year, at three different altars ascending the mountain—one at

daybreak, one at noon, and one at dusk. The last grain, the last
fruit, and the last flowers are offered in turn, while Malachai
leads three prayers in thanks and praise to the sun, the one and
only God.

The third and final altar stands near a dry bed of stones.
Once the flowers have been offered and the prayer has been
sung, Oona ascends to the first stone of the bed, just as she has
done every year since she was a girl. She opens her hand, and
just the same as every year, the first water of the season flows
out into the bed. So ends the fast. The people come to drink. So
begins the feast.

All this is as it has always been. When all the people have
filled their bowls, Oona goes to look for her father, to offer him
his share, but he is nowhere to be found. There is only Aram,
very grave. But what has happened? she asks. Is something
wrong? He tells her, yes: They have been followed, he says, and
a prisoner has been taken.

The Madame retarded this last phrase, then turned to Nina.
"Which I believe brings us up to the present moment."

Nina confirmed, nodding her thanks. The Madame returned the
shell to her, then descended the stage to the grateful, if respectfully
quiet, reception of her audience. Rowe shifted cheerfully, nudging the
knee of his friend Roerich. Benjamin sat straight in his chair, agog.

None of them was quite as impressed with the Madame's effort here
as Perlman, though, he being the only one who could fully appreciate
what a remarkable display of dramaturgical prowess this had been—
to have taken the jumble of scenes and ideas with which they'd been
buffeted the last three days and with a few nips and tucks, some
subtle excisions and transpositions, distill them into this very clear, and
to that end rather compelling, liquid narrative. Though on the other
hand, what was the wonder? Did it not settle the fact of the Madame's
role in all this, that she should be able to present such a lucid account?
Indeed, to hear it coming from her mouth was to recognize its obvious

kinship to the shows that she and her brother had concocted on their private stage at Sonskovo. All that was missing was the music.

The gas lamps flared again to reveal the set more clearly—the steamer trunk front and center, the sedan chair slightly to the right. It was an even more exquisite piece than Perlman had first allowed, like a nobleman's rickshaw, but enclosed, piano-black, with a delicate gold trim, an Eastern floral pattern that he guessed was also carved into the wood. It was turned away slightly so the audience had a slanted view of its back window, which was draped with black velvet curtains.

Nina took a long wooden match from the stone bowl and lit it. Like the Madame's speech, her movements were all very precise and economical. In bare feet, she crossed to the rear wall, where hung a single-spired sconce. She plucked the candle—ivory white—and turned to her audience calmly, the dry wick in her right hand, the burning tinder in her left, like a fork and knife. As the flame crept closer and closer to her fingers, she spoke:

"Oona went to look for her father in the catacombs. She returned to the vault where the arcana had been hidden, and there she found a prison cell."

She turned her head. The booth of the sedan would serve.

"She was about to look inside when she heard her father's footsteps and disguised herself as a flame."

She now lit the candle and brought it back over to the piano, stage left, where a small tin holder was waiting, with a finger clasp. She planted the stick, rounded to the bench, and right on cue, just as she sat down, there came a voice from behind.

"Where is he?" It was Stanley, entering through the French doors. "In here?"

He made his way around the left side of the audience and entered the light. He was dressed as he'd been the night before, in a purple cassock, but he was wearing a grape-leaf garland as well, and his manner was much more grave and agitated.

He paused above the steamer trunk and took count of what was inside. It did not please him. With a glance he dismissed the unseen guard: "You may go." He waited till he was sure he was alone, then stepped up to the window of the booth and parted the black curtains.

His eyes confirmed the presence of a prisoner, but barely. "Awfully dark in there. Can you see?"

Behind him, the candle on the piano beckoned. Malachai turned. Unwittingly he took it from its place and held it up to the window; his daughter flickered. "Let me see you. Down with the hood." He pushed the candle farther through; the satin walls inside flared a golden orange.

"Ah, you don't like the light, that's what they said." He pulled back out. "Do you know why you're being held?"

There was no answer.

"I assume you do. Is that fair?" He looked in again and waited, but still there was no answer.

"I'm not sure silence is going to serve you, friend. Silence is a scoundrel's refuge."

He waited, to give him one more chance, but there was no reply, which finally Stanley seemed to accept. "Very well. You are silent. I will speak." There was a stool against the back wall. He set it beside the sedan and sat as comfortably as he was able; the seat was rather small. "I will tell you a story. It's one I used to tell my daughter when she was a girl." He set the candle down on the floor and looked at it, almost as if he knew.

"You've seen my daughter—today. She isn't like you or me. She is not so bound by flesh. What Oona's spirit desires, she can do by mind alone. This has always been true, even when she was a girl, so often I was called upon to rein her in, to see that she did not abuse her gifts. And when she asked why she could not do this or that, this is the story I told her."

The candle flame hovered, attentive.

"There once was a boy who lived alone with his mother. One day he found a small wooden box beneath her pillow, which he brought to her and asked, 'What is this I found?' And she told him, 'That is a gift from your father, a jewel he gave to me the day that you were born, and I keep it beneath my pillow so that every night I might look at it, to be reminded of him and of the power which brought you to me.'

"The boy had never heard his mother speak of his father, and he asked if he could see this jewel, but she said no. 'It is better you find on your own the meaning of which this gift is a token. Then I promise, I will let you see what's inside the box.'

" 'But when will that be?' asked the boy.

"His mother replied, 'When you are a man.' "

Stanley sat back, hands on knees. " 'When you are a man.' You can imagine, this was frustrating to the boy. Now every time he passed his mother's room, he would think of that box beneath her pillow. And any time he proved himself at anything, he would go to her and say, 'Mother, today I won the footrace. Today I climbed the highest tree. May I see my father's gift?' But she would always tell him no. 'You may have won a footrace, you may have climbed an oak, and I am proud of you, but these things do not a man make.' And so he had to wait.

"Now, in time it happened that the leader of their tribe, the one whom they called Lord and Master, Oman'en, built himself a fleet. His domain had long since reached the shore, and Oman'en wanted more, so he prepared a campaign for which he would need men. Our friend, the mother's son, was still too young—the hair on his cheek was soft—but he decided he did not care. He would stow away. The day the fleet left, he found a hiding place inside the largest ship, and he was not discovered till they were well away from shore, too far to go back.

"At first, of course, the men gave him all the lowliest, filthiest jobs they could find, cleaning their fish and buckets. But the sea is an unpredictable home. The vast skies, the teeming waves, and the unfathomed deep all will test a wayfaring fleet, and so it was that before they reached their first foreign shore, the boy had ample cause to prove himself. Every storm they met, he battled most fiercely; every serpent from the deep, he challenged and slew; every foe, he vanquished. Before a season had passed, the mother's son, the youngest among them, was given a ship of his own to command—and he was feared, and he was followed, and there are many stories of his heroism on the sea, and on the islands that Oman'en's fleet then conquered, one by one.

"They were away nine seasons in all, but when at last they returned to their native shore, hulls heavy with all the riches they'd won, first thing they brought the young brave to their Lord and Master, Oman'en. They told his story, and Oman'en was impressed. He asked if there was some reward that he might offer, but the young brave said only that he wished to see his mother, that she might know her boy was now a man. Oman'en was pleased by this. He asked what was his mother's name, but when the son replied, Oman'en grew suddenly grave.

" 'Now I am not surprised to see that one so young could be so lion-hearted, knowing the blood which runs in your veins. I have known many concubines, but none whose beauty possessed the power of your mother's, or whose power possessed such beauty.

" 'There was just one pain that she could not endure, and that was the disappearance of her son nine seasons ago. So sudden the loss, so profound her grief, the light soon left her eye. The color vanished from her cheek, and it was a mercy when the winter came and took her.' "

"The young brave did not understand. 'This cannot be,' he said, but then Oman'en's second, the necromancer Vordenuel, held out his long white hand to show him: there in his palm was the box, the wooden box he'd found so long ago beneath his mother's pillow. And now he knew that it was true. His mother was no more.

"In grief, he took the box to where the fleet was moored. He wanted to throw it in the sea and boil the oceans to nothing. It was for this he'd gone to prove himself, to face death and taste blood and become a man, but now his mother would never know. He hated this box, and what was inside. But before he cast it into the waves, he had to see—what mere stone could have caused such pain and sorrow? He opened the box and looked inside, and do you know what he saw?" Stanley leaned in to the window and spoke the answer slowly.

"Coming from the box was a light so bright, so gleaming white, it burnt the young brave's eyes. He could not see."

And now he sat back again and spoke the rest slowly, as though each word were a razor-sharp knife. "No mother. No man. Oman'en's son returned to the sea that very night, alone. Some say it was to perish there, while others claim he made the deep his home, for only in the bowels of the ocean could his tender eyes bear the light, and there no one need see his shame."

Stanley paused a moment to let this last phrase settle, burrow, and sting; then he looked back through the curtains. "So? Is this a story you know?"

Silence.

"I think you do. And do you know what else? I think Oman'en's son has yet to learn his lesson. I think that once again he wants to see before he's ready." Stanley slid the trunk up to his feet.

"Last night I placed six scrolls inside this casket." He began removing them now, one by one, to show. When he came to five, he looked inside the trunk again. "But that is all. Someone has taken the sixth—"

The Madame's head gave a slight turn; Perlman sunk imperceptibly in his seat.

"It is gone," said Stanley, "and as I think of all the people I have seen today there is only one whose presence I suspect, only one who shrinks from the god we celebrate." He leaned in. "Does your father know you're here?"

No answer came, and finally it seemed the prisoner's silence was frustrating Stanley. His face began to flush with anger.

"I'll take mercy on a heart confessed. But to a heart stone silent—to a heart stone silent I am tempted to do as you. Yes, I know your way. What if I should do the same?" He picked up the candle and held it to the curtain. "What if I took you to the highest altar that I could find and pulled that hood down from your eyes?" Again he guided the flame inside the booth, whose satin walls once again burst orange-gold. "Because you know my god shall be much stronger than this. If this is a tear, my god is an ocean, and far more brilliant than any sorcerer's stone. Don't doubt me. If I must, I'll tie you to the highest rock and slice those lids from your eyes myself, that you might look upon the light which so offends you."

He pulled the candle out and sank back in the chair. "But night falls. Even after all your treachery, the sun is your friend. It grants you one night to consider your confession. But consider well, for my god will return at dawn, and I shall, too, and if you've not come round, be warned: I'll see that no hood, no cloud, nor sea ever comes between you and the truth again."

He was done. Stanley stood and looked off, presumably to the guard who'd shown him in. "Make sure he's fed." He started for the small door leading to the back stairs, but then remembered the candle in his hand. He set it down on the piano, and made his exit.

Nina, who'd watched all this from her seat on the bench, gave the audience a moment to observe the flame alone. Then she stood: "As soon as her father was gone, Oona returned to the cell and revealed herself."

She took up the candle and crossed the stage again to the window of the sedan chair. She held the light up to the curtains, and for a moment all was still. Perlman couldn't imagine what she was waiting for, but then the curtains stirred—once, twice—as if a draft had entered. Then something began emerging from between them: it was the hands, the cast, with a coarse rope tied around the wrists.

Perlman slid his eyes over to the Madame. She was blocked from view, but her hand was to her mouth.

"And Oona helped the prisoner escape," said Nina. She slipped the rope from the wrists and let it fall. The bronze hands hovered a moment longer, then, just as slowly and evenly as they'd appeared, withdrew again behind the curtain.

Nina turned. She looked out beyond them, and the flame danced gently as she spoke.

"She poured sand into the eyes of the prison guard and led Thaire through the catacombs to the lake. Y'aromel was waiting, and Thaire was going to leave—he did not mean for her to come—but when he knelt to offer thanks, he saw that hanging from Oona's necklace was the gift that he had given her."

The girl held out the white crescent again, just as the Madame had, between her thumb and index finger, turning it slowly for them all to see.

"So he let her inside Y'aromel; they sank down in the water, and became one."

The gas lamps dimmed to nothing. For several moments there was just the candle flame hovering alone; then, from behind, the French doors slid wide, and the parlor light slanted in.

"Dinner," said Miss McCumber.

# CHAPTER 32

**M**iss McCumber's announcement only served to confirm what had been Perlman's creeping priority over the course of Stanley and the girl's scene. Not that he'd taken their efforts for granted, but this latest installment—with all its twists and turns and origin stories—had signaled a level of convolution more than sufficient to warrant his final and abiding impression, which was that he was very very hungry.

The dining room was candlelit, the table set in observance of the same dual influence that marked everything else in the house, subscribing in detail to an English sense of what was so, or should be so—white china, lace, silver, an arrangement of autumn flower—while around the edges, and at length, there could be detected what Perlman was coming to think of as a certain "Russian" laxity creeping in. Not all the glasses matched, for instance, and there were age-old and never-to-be-removed stains on the runner.

There were six settings. The five of them took their places without apparent calculation: the Madame at the garden end of the table; Rowe to her left; Benjamin to her right; to his right was the Russian, Mr. Roerich; at the opposite end sat Perlman. The vacancy waited between him and Rowe, who was first to speak once they'd all settled in.

"Absolutely astonishing."

"Take any notes?" The Madame smiled.

"Yes, my God. That sedan chair, was it always here?"

"Upstairs."

"And do you think that was just Lord Stanley and the girl?"

"I assume. It's possible Miss McCumber had a hand. We'll have to ask Stanley."

"Who was marvelous, as always."

"Wasn't he? Good part, though."

"Yes. A real treat." Rowe took another moment to process. "But I've never heard such a curious story. Where did it come from?" He looked at the Madame, who answered with a highly disingenuous shrug, the point of which he seemed to gather nonetheless.

"All right, where did *she* come from? Whose is she?" He looked at Perlman dubiously. "Not yours?"

"She is in my care for the time being."

"But where is she from?" He looked back at the Madame. "Pskov?"

"Vienna."

"Vienna?" He scowled. "How strange. Where did she school?"

He looked back at Perlman, who glanced at the Madame before answering. "These are matters of confidentiality."

Rowe gave a look of open intrigue—the gauntlet thrown. He took up the wine bottle from its dish. "Drink?"

Rowe actually stood and started around, in what seemed to Perlman an overtly territorial gesture. He covered his glass, on account of this and the fact that the day-long hum in his head was just now fading to a dull throb. Then Stanley entered.

"There he is." Rowe straightened, graced. "Good show."

Stanley bowed humbly to gentle applause and took his seat, once again attired in customary cuffs and collar. Rowe poured him a generous glass, then noticed all the chairs were taken. "Won't the young lady be joining us?"

Stanley shook his head. "She said to go ahead. Miss McCumber is bringing her a plate."

Rowe clucked, serving himself now. "Too bad. I have some questions. Would you be at liberty to help us?"

"I'm under no restriction that I'm aware of."

"Good." He took his linen and sat. "So first, may I ask, was that just the two of you?"

Stanley smiled. "Peeking behind the curtain, are we?"

"Professional duty."

"Maybe afterward."

"There's more?"

"After dinner, as I understand."

"Excellent."

Miss McCumber came in with a rolling tray of platters—English fare, roast beef and cabbage and boiled potatoes. She played her part discreetly, offering no sign as she served Perlman of having so much as glimpsed him before.

As soon as she was gone, Rowe held his drink aloft. "A toast. To our absent auteur and chorus, Nina . . . ?" He waited for the name. Madame Helena glanced at Perlman to cite the matter of confidentiality.

"To Mademoiselle Nina," Rowe left it.

"Mademoiselle Nina," the party seconded.

"And whatever has possessed her with this genius."

"Hear, hear." They clinked and drank.

"And a word of thanks," the Madame reminded. Stanley bowed his head. The Madame said her prayer in Russian, for Mr. Roerich's benefit presumably. He, the Madame, and Stanley crossed themselves. Rowe kept his head low, more out of respect than devotion, then, as soon as it was appropriate, took up his fork and knife and began to carve his meat. "Well, I suppose the first question is, do we trust this man, the hooded one—what's his name?"

"Thaire."

"Do we? I mean, do we think he stole the scroll, or was he there for the girl?"

They all looked at one another. "That's the question," concluded the Madame. "Could be a combination."

"Could be," said Rowe. "Still, I'd like to know whose side he's on."

He took a bite. "I mean, if he didn't steal the scroll, why didn't he just say so?"

Because he didn't have a mouth? thought Perlman.

"Well, because his alibi isn't very good," replied the Madame.

"What's his alibi?"

" 'I've been following your daughter for the last two days.' "

"Good point." Rowe took another bite. "And do we think there's any chance *the girl* might have taken the scroll?"

No one seemed to think much of this idea.

"Well, but then why do we think she was so quick to help him escape?"

"Because she likes him?" said the Madame.

"But he might be a thief."

"Act of faith," she said.

"And getting in the boat?"

"A bigger act of faith."

"I should say."

"It always is," she smiled.

Rowe smiled, too. "And by the way, were those the 'Nonsense'?"

The Madame nodded, and Rowe sent a wink across at Roerich, Perlman a glance at Benjamin. Yes, *the* "Nonsense."

The Madame tried changing the subject. She turned to Roerich and began asking him about some art show in Paris. He had apparently just had some pictures in an exhibition there, historical paintings. Roerich was an archaeologist, it turned out—expert in "pagan Rus"—as well as a painter and set designer. Impressive fellow for one who spoke so little—Rowe did most of his boasting—but Perlman was only paying half-attention. The Madame's comment about the girl's getting in the boat—the "act of faith"—had cued his imagination. He gave his mind to it for just a moment, but the vision appeared with a suspect readiness: through the window of Y'aromel, an amber-lit pane gliding evenly through the deep blue and framing the image of a man and a woman, "becoming one," as the girl had put it. He saw it with a surprising clarity—the man's back arched and rolling, and she beneath him, lithe and white. And yet it wasn't only for the prurient swoon that Perlman let his mind linger. It was more to do with a curious recognition. The man he couldn't see so well—he assumed it was Alexander; they'd been Alexander's hands. But it was the girl that gave him pause, for this wasn't just some faceless heroine, a vague conjuration of flaxen maidenhood; nor was it Nina, as one might have thought; nor even the Madame as a girl, as also would have made some sense. This was another someone, he recognized from just the legs— how they came so slim from the hip, how they bowed at the calf and pointed at the toe. He'd seen those legs before, many times, and that pale round face against his shoulder; those wide-set eyes, an ocean blue, rising up in ecstasy—

". . . I think you're in for a treat, Dr. Perlman." Rowe was looking at him from the other side of the candle.

"Excuse me?"

"Diaghilev," he said. "He says he wants to do the same thing next year, but with the composers. Apparently he's going to try to get them all—Scriabin, Rachmaninoff, Rimsky-Korsakov."

"In Paris?"

Rowe nodded.

"Well, if anybody can do it—" the Madame intoned.

"I wouldn't bet against him." Rowe clued in Roerich. "Dr. Perlman is a fanatic about Russian music."

Roerich turned to Perlman and smiled with his eyes, almost as if he'd seen, too. Had that not been his sweet Anitra, the street urchin from Leipzig? Perlman tried wiping the image from his mind.

"Well, I think it's all to the good," said Stanley. "The artists coming west."

"It's all to the good if they go back," the Madame answered. "I just worry the rats might be leaving the ship."

"That's a bit rash," said Stanley, sounding very much her uncle.

"I don't know. I don't know that I blame the rats. I may be one of them." She looked at Roerich. "Nicholas, you're going back?"

He nodded.

"Good." She returned to her food, head shaking faintly. "It's just never an encouraging sign when the artists start leaving. Whom was I speaking to the other day? A woman somewhere. At Mrs. Besant's. She was talking about the Renaissance, saying how odd it was that all this genius should have just spontaneously appeared like that. Have you heard this, as if Florence were some sort of unaccountable blossom?"

"A sport," said Lord Stanley.

"Yes."

"But isn't that the point?" asked Rowe, the willing fool. "Or at least that it was a rebirth? *Renaissance?*"

"*Italian Renaissance,*" said the Madame. "The only reason the Italians got their Renaissance is that all the artists had left Constantinople."

Perlman couldn't help a smile. The authority with which she spoke. Had she read this in one of her books?

Rowe checked the facts. "And when exactly did the godless Turks climb the walls?"

"Fourteen fifty-three. But the artists were long gone by then. I suspect they started going after the Romans took her, which was 12 . . ." She looked around the table. No one knew. "Early 12-something. You give them a few hundred years to set up their easels, and that's when you get your Sistine Chapel."

She made it sound rather easy, but Rowe was buying, rolled the idea around his mouth. "Never thought of that, but I like it."

"Do you see?" Madame Helena looked back at her uncle now. "This is my point. You'd think the place never existed."

"Constantinople?"

"Byzantium. The whole thing. Don't you find, Dr. Benjamin, Dr. Perlman—there is a conspiracy of silence among the English?"

" 'O Solon, Solon,' " replied Perlman.

"Yes." The Madame turned to Rowe. " 'You Hellenes are but children.' " She took a sip. "The point is, there's always been civilization thriving somewhere, and before it got to Florence, it had been in Constantinople."

"Second Rome," Stanley threw in.

"Exactly." The Madame nodded. "And do you know what was to be the third Rome?" She looked about the table. " 'Two Romes have fallen, but the third stands, and a fourth there will not be'?' " She waited. No takers. "Moscow."

Rowe laughed, very inappropriately, which was her point.

"I'm sorry."

"No, you're right. It is laughable. Sorry Nicholas."

Mr. Roerich did not seem to take offense, but Rowe moved to save himself nonetheless. "Madame, I have to say, I think I agree with Stanley here. You're painting an ugly picture. I was under the impression that matters had more or less been quelled over there."

"That is the impression, yes."

"I mean, I can't imagine there's any other outcome one could have hoped for. They certainly couldn't just keep on."

"No, that's true," she said. "And I've no quarrel with the workers. I think the existing order is an embarrassment. I think the Tsar and the police have behaved miserably, and that reform is long overdue. All true."

"Well then, what's the problem?"

"The Socialists."

Rowe laughed through his nose. It was this sort of thing, this bluntness, that apparently delighted him. "What about the Socialists?"

"Honestly?" She poked her roast beef. "I suspect it's the fact they're atheists."

This word sent a sudden charge around the table, it was so unexpected; Perlman nearly dropped his fork. Rowe swallowed his chin. "Madame, some of my best friends are atheists."

"Well, I'm sure they make good friends. It's when they get in the business of running governments that I take issue."

Again Rowe grinned, an awfully condescending expression for one treading on such thin ice. "Oh, I don't know, Madame. I might sooner live in a country run by atheists than by the Orthodox."

"Atheists *are* orthodox," the Madame replied, flatly enough that even Rowe could tell, if his purpose was to ingratiate himself here, he'd chosen a bad tack.

"Very well," he conceded. "Still, we can take heart. Russia is a long way from being run by Socialists."

"They've got their foot in the door," the Madame rued, "and I wouldn't put it past them, blasting their way in."

"Oh, but, Madame," said Rowe, "you're sounding awfully dramatic now. And suppose they did, suppose they got their way entirely, you don't actually think they'd impose some atheist regime."

"Have you spoken to them? They're fairly hostile about religion."

"Hostile about religion doesn't mean hostile about God."

"It shouldn't," she said; she'd just about had it with him. "The point is, Andrew, they have a model in their minds of how nature and man and history operate. And it is a model, one can't help noting, in which no consideration whatever has been given to an Almighty or an Unknowable Creator. As far as they're concerned, God was conceived by kings to pacify peasants. Now, you can call that anything you like—atheist, agnostic, secular—you could call it humanist. I'd still say, if there is no God in it, then the model must be hollow. And that hollowness, as they say, will out."

Rowe paused. It seemed he hadn't known till now the level of her religious commitment.

Benjamin dabbed the corners of his mouth. "And would you direct this objection to any view that doesn't include room for God?" As usual, he'd said this with just the right tone—interested, but somehow blessedly impersonal.

The Madame treated it in kind. "If it is presuming to describe the nature of things, then yes, Dr. Benjamin, absolutely. For if the model does not admit to a Creator, then it shall be absent what, for me, is life's essence. And so yes, of course, I am bound to wonder what insight it could possibly hold, or why I would ever think of entrusting my future to it."

She had not so much as glanced at Perlman during all this, but the effect was conspicuous. Finally, she turned. "Yes?"

"Nothing," he said. "You're just starting to sound a bit like Malachai."

Admittedly, she smiled. As did Stanley.

"Speaking of which," said Rowe, "can I just get in one more question about this story, if now wouldn't be a bad time?"

"Now would be a good time," said Stanley.

"It's actually not too far off the subject, but it's something that occurred to me during the Madame's introduction. The girl Oona? You said she was a demigoddess."

"Yes."

"Meaning she is the offspring of a god and man."

"Goddess and man, in this case."

"All right," said Rowe. "But her father, Malachai—he sounds to me like a rather strict monotheist. If I understood."

"Yes."

"Well, I was just wondering, how can someone who believes in only one God have a demigoddess for a daughter? Wouldn't her very existence argue to the contrary?"

This was a good question, thought Perlman, which even he might have posed if he'd been willing to dignify the story with that much scrutiny.

The Madame allowed, "The language gets confusing."

"Doesn't seem to me a question of language," said Rowe. "Either you believe in lots of gods, or one, or none. No?"

"Well"—she thought a moment—"no. All it really means to believe in one God is that you recognize that all things are ultimately grounded in the same being, that they emerge from one and the same unifying force. That doesn't necessarily rule out the idea that within a given plane, you still might encounter various levels of divinity, higher and lower frequencies of that force."

He laughed. "Madame, *what* are you talking about?"

"Well, demigoddesses."

"But didn't we just establish that that's a question of parentage? You know, the Greek idea."

"Yes. I'm not excluding Greek cosmology from what I'm saying. I'm actually trying to make some sense of it for you."

"Yes, but—" He stopped, pressing his lips in frustration. "But you

see, even those—the myths—I have to say, I've always had trouble
with them."

"How do you mean?" This concerned her.

"It's embarrassing to admit, I agree—but you know, a certain kind
of myth I understand well enough. There's a volcano. The father tells
his son the God of the Mountain had a hiccough. That's reasonable. It's
just another way of describing a natural event. But when you get into
this 'Greek' area, with the gods and beasts all sniping at one another
and copulating—that's when I run into trouble, just because it's never
clear what I'm to take literally and what is more figurative. Do you see
what I'm saying?"

"Perhaps an example."

He searched a moment, but came up blank. "Well, any of them really. You know, they draw us in with these very human tales about lust
or jealousy or some such, and then at a certain point, one of the characters will go and do this completely confounding thing, because he's
a god—give someone the ears of an ass—which only reminds me that
at any point he could have turned them all into chickens, so what the
devil do I care? Do you see?"

The Madame nodded indulgently.

"Or here, you've got some of the same problems, if you don't mind
my saying." He pinched the air. "A little crit: We have this Oona, who
seems capable of doing anything she wants, yes? She can fly, presumably she can breathe under water, assume other forms, while at the
same time there's her father, Malachai, who's riding in on balloons and
hiding tablets for fear the secrets might get out, and making sure his
daughter is safe when it seems to me she could do them all in with a
swipe of her hand if she wanted."

The Madame nodded. "More or less."

"Yes, but don't you see—and I'm not criticizing, mind you. It's wonderful stuff—" He leaned around to make sure that Stanley wasn't
taking offense. "I'm only saying that, for me, when you've got a very
real element in play—a prison cell, say—and you put it together with
something that's clearly unreal—the business with the candle—"

"Oh, I liked that."

"I did, too. I'm only saying it becomes difficult for me to know where to invest my feeling. It's difficult to know what's at stake is what I'm saying—when the rules seem so arbitrary. Am I wrong?"

He looked to Perlman, sensing some support, and in fact, the doctor had been taking a kind of sadistic pleasure in this, the torturing of the Madame's fantasy with a level of analysis it simply hadn't been conceived to withstand; yet it occurred to him that she might be operating at a disadvantage, if only because there were clearly several fundamental aspects to her defense that she was for some reason not admitting.

"Madame, if you're withholding on my account, I hope you know you needn't."

She had to lean around the candles to see him. "Excuse me, Doctor?"

"Withholding?" Rowe sat up. "What are you withholding?"

The Madame didn't say, and the entire table was looking at Perlman now.

"Well," he said, "just that Mr. Rowe is trying to understand the rules of the story, how all this works together. It occurs to me that you've a fuller explanation than the one you're giving, but that you may not be offering it on my account. I am thanking you for the consideration, but in fact I see no reason that any of our guests—your guests, excuse me—should be excluded."

"Excluded?" Rowe mock-pounded the table. "I demand to know what you're talking about. Madame, what is Dr. Perlman talking about?"

"Doctor, what are you talking about exactly?"

"Well," he shifted, still pleasant, "I'm not going to pretend to be any kind of expert on the subject, but I have been given to understand that our story this evening bears the earmarks of Atlantean legend."

"*Atlantean?*" Rowe couldn't place the word. "What the devil is that?"

"Atlantis," the Madame helped.

"Atlantis?" He looked at her, then Perlman, then back at her. "You must be joking."

"There are elements," she said; she wasn't about to apologize.

"Stanley, is this true?"

Stanley glanced up from his plate to nod, and Rowe took a moment to digest—detected no immediate objection, and so let with a slow and sumptuous grin. "Atlantis it is." He thumped the edge of the table with three fingers. "I'm afraid you find me at a loss, though. I don't know a thing about it." He took up the wine bottle and replenished the Madame's glass. "Isn't it supposed to be under the sea?"

"Lately," she said.

Benjamin slid his own glass forward for a refill. "It was a whole civilization, wasn't it? Lost in the flood."

The Madame turned. "That's right, Dr. Benjamin."

"What else?" asked Rowe.

"Well"—Benjamin slid back his glass—"I don't know much more than that, but it was supposed to be quite advanced apparently." He turned to Perlman, sensing dismay. "Plato, no?"

"Very good, Arthur."

"Plato?" Rowe snatched back the table's attention. "When was this—this flood?"

Benjamin wasn't sure. He referred the question to the Madame.

"Depends whom you ask," she said. "There were supposed to have been three separate cataclysms, actually, but the latest would have been in 10,000 B.C. or so."

"Hm." Rowe saw no problem with this. "All right, but then tell me, what's it got to do with gods and goddesses? That doesn't sound like Plato's territory."

The Madame looked across at Perlman to see if he wanted the question.

"Oh, I'm over my head."

She agreed. "Well, I suspect the reason Dr. Perlman brings it up is because there are those who'd contend that, in addition to what Dr.

Benjamin was saying, that Atlantis was a very advanced civilization, it also for a time played host to god and man alike."

"What?"

"Yes, that the Atlantean epoch coincides with that period where what had been divine—or purely spiritual, if you will—descended into flesh."

"Hold on." Rowe looked as if he'd tasted something sour. "But are we actually supposed to believe this?"

"We're not *supposed* to do anything, Andrew, but I'd say that yes, in order to understand the story, you'd probably do well to set aside your assumption about how we all got here and consider an alternate possibility—an alternate myth, if you will." She glanced at Perlman. "Not incompatible, mind you, but one which ventures to explain our presence here from a more spiritual than purely biological perspective."

"May I have a moment?"

She granted one. Rowe took up the wine bottle again, filled his glass all the way to the brim, took one theatrically dainty sip, then cleared his throat. "Fire away."

"All right. Very good, Andrew." She took a moment herself to choose her route, and as Perlman looked over at her, absently stroking the opals of her necklace, once again he was struck by the impossible combination this woman represented—manifestly keen mind, a razor-sharp intellect, and canyons of retention, all squandered beneath a regime of criminal indiscrimination, which was itself redeemed by a mystifying capacity not to take itself too seriously. What did this woman actually believe?

She released her necklace and turned to Rowe. "This would be a view," she said, "which understands the universe to be an essentially spiritual entity, of which this world and our lives represent a kind of experiment—a 'coagulant sojourn,' if you will—which different aspects of that one Spirit have gone to explore, but in which, alas, most of *us* have gotten stuck."

Rowe shook his head. "You've lost me."

*Coagulant sojourn.*

"Well, really it's not so different from the cycle we complete in a single life," she said. "At least in the view of those who so believe. Spirit becomes flesh and then eventually returns to spirit."

"Familiar with the notion."

"Well, here the idea is simply extended to describe the life of mankind: that we are all descended from this one unified spirit, and that we must have developed into our present form—this distended, diasporic taffy—over time; that is to say, by grades. Does that make sense?"

"Suppose I said yes."

"Well, if you accept that—that it must have been a gradual process by which Spirit became Flesh, or One became Many—then surely you can see that at any given point during that transition there were bound to have been entities who were more 'of spirit'—that is, who managed to preserve the memory of the One Force from which they sprang— and those who were more 'of flesh'—that is to say, who forgot, or who never knew."

"Beasts," said Rowe.

"If you will. The point is, when we speak in terms of goddesses and demigoddesses, we're not necessarily calling into question the idea that all things are One, we're simply referring to those beings who, by virtue of parentage or practice, or whatever the case may be— gift—are more celestial in nature, more closely allied with their spiritual origin, and therefore not as subject to all the . . . mortal limitations."

"Which is why they get to fly and turn into candles," said Rowe.

"Yes. And inaugurate seasons."

He shook his head. "And this is Atlantis we're talking about?"

"Well, Atlantis is hardly the only place you'd find such a mix. Over in the South Seas you had Lemuria—"

Rowe raised his hand. "Madame, one at a time. Just let me understand, what we're talking about—this Greek configuration—that's Atlantis?"

Still the Madame hesitated. "Well, I suspect that the stories we're all most familiar with would hark back to a rather early stage in the development, which is why the distinctions tend to be so stark—who is a

god and who a man. In Nina's story, my sense is that we're dealing
with a slightly later stage, which is why I think you're right, there's
such an unusual mix of the material—the technological even—along-
side an admittedly more subtle variety of magic."

Rowe's head was still. "Madame, I'm speechless."

"You asked."

"I did." He thought; he frowned. "And who is this girl again? Are
you really not going to tell me?"

They both shook their heads.

"All right, then at least let me know—how much of this is coming
from that Blavatsky woman?"

The Madame shrugged. "She's one, but there's a whole crew of
them now. Steiner."

"Pfft." Rowe dismissed the difference, the same as that between a
rotten apple and a rotten onion.

The Madame was not offended. "You gentlemen are awfully quick
to judge ideas on account of their source. What if I'd said Ovid?"

Rowe reached for his glass. "I just think you may know too much,
Helena."

"You're not alone." She glanced across at Perlman.

Rowe turned. "No. You don't go for all this, do you, Dr. Perlman?"

He shook his head. "I got thrown back at 'alternate myth.' What's
the prime myth again?" He looked over at Benjamin, who lifted his
shoulders.

"Darwin?"

"Oh, good for him," said Perlman, at which Rowe laughed out loud.
Rowe really wasn't so bad.

"But is she immortal?" asked Benjamin, quite out of the blue.

The Madame leaned forward. "Excuse me, Dr. Benjamin."

"Oona. Did we establish whether *she* was immortal or not?"

The Madame sank back slowly, as did Perlman. That was another
dignifying squint. But for once, the Madame didn't appear to have a
ready answer.

"Well, she certainly was," she said finally. "But I suppose I'm not entirely sure anymore."

No one pressed—Rowe had raised his flag—but Perlman understood. She was referring to the "act of faith" again.


That was the last that was said of the Oona story. The conversation
drifted more peacefully from there. By Perlman's count, five bottles of
wine came and went, even though Roerich was sticking to beer and
Perlman was abstaining. Sobering up, in fact. And the more the others
drank, the more distant he felt from their conversation, which was too
bad, they spoke of so many things that interested him so keenly. They
toasted Rimsky-Korsakov for his kindness, then forgave him his pre-
sumptions. They toasted Mussorgsky as well (Roerich, it turned out,
was related through his wife). They spoke of the ballet in Paris, and
what was becoming of Scriabin (left his wife and daughter for a young
student), all the sorts of things that Perlman always dreamed of dis-
cussing, and with people who seemed to *know*, but he was nearly as
silent as Mr. Roerich. With some food in his stomach and his head
clearing up, and following that rather sobering dip into the Madame's
well of lunatic notions, the reality of the situation descended once
again. What was his plan? Was tomorrow not Monday? What was he
going to tell Herr Blum? Where exactly was the girl? (Three times he
asked Miss McCumber to check on her.) And what the devil was
Anitra doing there underneath the man? Every time his eye passed by
the candles, the thought of her recurred—vividly, lest he forget—that
for all the Madame and her uncle may have contributed the last two
days, this was clearly his doing as well, more so than he could ever have
knowingly conceived.

Stanley excused himself just after the salad course. Dessert was
served—a simple plate of butter biscuits, sliced pear, and cheese. They
drank a sauterne—Perlman had a glass as well, to be polite—then Miss
McCumber entered, not with coffee, as might have been appropriate,
but with a single covered dish, which she set before the Madame.

A giddy silence fell. All understood, this was the start of the second
act. Madame Helena removed the top; there was a demitasse and a leaf

of the Madame's stationery, covered with writing. The Madame passed
the demitasse to Roerich, but kept the letter for herself. She began
reading it silently.

Rowe watched her, eyes glazing to adoration. "Madame, I really
must say"—he'd begun slurring his words two glasses ago—"it is good
to have you back."

She said nothing, and from a distant corner of the floor came the
soft knell.

"Coffee?" She lifted her head, only half-serious.

Rowe's chair barked out his answer—why ruin all the good work?
He rounded to her side. She stood. She took up her letter, plucked a
candle from the table setting, and led them out into the hall.

Benjamin stopped Perlman at the door, to play doctor.

"And how are you doing?" he asked.

"Little headache. You?"

"I'm saving mine for the morning."

"So it would seem. I wasn't aware you were so versed in Plato."

Benjamin grinned—a heavy-lidded, catlike grin, unlike any Perlman had ever seen cross his face.

"Gentlemen?" The Madame beckoned. Perlman stepped aside, and
Benjamin staggered out into the hall.


The others were clustered together just outside the dining room. All
the doors had been closed, which made of the space a long, narrow corridor, vented by the staircase leading up to darkness on the right. To
the left, at the deepest, farthest end, and the only lit corner of the hall,
were the girl and Stanley. Stanley was back in costume, kneeling on a
pillow and surrounded by several bowls with pestles. They were filled
with spice-like ingredients, which he was pouring back and forth with
a clearly ritual air, the intended effect being that he was performing
some sort of "Black Art," though to Perlman it looked more as if he
was making a bundt cake.

The girl stood just behind and to the right, as might a guardian angel. With a nod she signaled the Madame, who lifted the page up to her candle. She paused, looking at it. The penmanship wasn't very good—Stanley's, it appeared, with cross outs and lines arrowed in. She counted a rhythm in her head, then lifted her chin and began reading aloud. Her uncle Stanley joined her for just the first line, then left off while she finished the rest.

*"O Calliste, O Ariste, mi-Bedisu, ay-Selene, mi-diana, mi-Ardemis. Our darkest night has fallen, I look to you for light. Know I have tried with all my earthly means to do thy will, to keep your gift to me, our daughter, safe and pure. Know she has done your will as well. She brings joy and serenity where she goes. In these days of preparation, my one solace has been the thought of her, that there is good which should survive, and that is why I'd offer all our wisdom in return, would burn it on the pyre, if I could know that she was safe tonight."*

Down at the far end of the hall, Stanley finally seemed to be satisfied with his concoction. He swiped a dark thumbful and smeared it across his forehead like a Catholic. Then he leaned down and touched his head against the floor. Palms flat, he held the pose without apparent strain, and once again joined the Madame for just the opening line of the remainder:

*"O Calliste, O Ariste, mi-Bedisu, ay-Selene, mi-diana, mi-Ardemis. Forgive the meager and infirm world which you have left. I have summoned all the priests and Timmon's guard, and they shall lead us to Oman'en's lair. But I fear the winds and waters may be slow, and so I pray. Hear my despair and know I would not call you otherwise:*
*Oona is in danger."*

So ended Malachai's entreaty. At the far end of the hall, the girl extended her hand, and the Madame started down. Stanley did not move or raise his eye, even as his niece handed the note to Nina. And here Perlman suspected another sleight of hand—during the exchange. The page was now a paper cup, which the girl held to the Madame's candle. As soon as it caught, she set it down on one of the dishes on the floor. They all watched as the fire devoured the paper. It flared bright, then started floating upward, ascending in a remarkably straight line up the stairwell, and turning to ash just as it left sight. Before it could descend again, the lamp below went dark, and Stanley and the girl had slipped out the door in back.

Three stern raps then sounded just the other side of the wall, as from a pair of sticks. Roerich was nearest the parlor door. He turned the knob and leaned in, but it was the Madame once again who led the way.

# CHAPTER 33

The room looked like a crypt. All the shutters were closed, all the sconce candles lit. There was no live stick of incense that Perlman could see, but the scent was ambient.

The furniture had been radically rearranged, with one obvious purpose in mind. Everything had been pushed back against the walls except for the drop-leaf table, which now stood dead center and was opened to a full circle and draped in a dark brown or black woolen tablecloth; Perlman couldn't tell in the light. This was surrounded by a circle of five mismatched, but no less insistent, chairs, while five select items had been set out around the table, one at each place. Clockwise from the southernmost, they were:

*a comic mask*

*a monocle*              *a quill pen*

*a paintbrush*          *a watch*

At the center of the table stood a lone silver candlestick with one white candle, the same as had provided Oona's disguise in the Music Room, still lit, the golden-white flame wavering expectantly.

Benjamin crossed to the monocle. "I assume this is me."

The Madame looked. "Well, the brush is Nicky."

"The watch," said Perlman, "is mine."

Which left the quill and the plaster mask, which seemed fairly obvious. They all took their places. Against the western wall the clock tocked patiently while the heavy, comforting scent of drunk wine mingled with the incense. No one spoke, perchance the girl might enter. They glanced variously from the flame to their oblong likenesses in the silver base of the candlestick, then up again to each other's glowing face. The Madame's showed equanimity. Rowe remained in the throes of a blindfolded giddiness. Benjamin may have been the most comical sight. His pince-nez was halfway down his nose, and his brow had assumed a height that Perlman had never quite seen before, but he appeared to be as open as ever. Roerich sat sphinxlike, eyes piercing the flame.

It was Rowe who relented, broke the metric silence with a quelled belch. "Do you think she's going to join us?"

"I'm not sure," the Madame answered softly.

Silence again. Another thirty painstaking tocks, syncopated by the stray clearing of a throat, a shifting seat, the gently tapping foot or finger.

After a half minute and no sign of their escort, the Madame spoke. "Perhaps we should hold hands."

More shifting seats, then compliance—on Perlman's part only because the hand on his left was that of Mr. Roerich, far and away the most acceptable male instance in the room, and the hand on his right was hers. They became a circle, and just like that, as if to approve the gesture, there came the most gorgeous and ghastly sound from the next room.

Roll six—Perlman recognized it instantly. The girl was playing the Welte, and he nearly pulled away right there. He looked over Rowe's shoulder through the small opening between the French doors, but all was black. There was just the *lento* lofting out its fragile chords, one by one, descending on their ears, and in Perlman's case, down his spine as well. He didn't like the reminder. His palms began to sweat.

It was the Madame, oddly, who stayed him; she, who had much

more reason to protest this, being made to sit and listen to the sound of her brother playing the piano in the other room. A discernible pang of sympathy was rounding the table, yet she answered it—and Perlman's more selfish resistance—very simply and directly. She squeezed his hand, and there was nothing either scolding or remotely suggestive in it. Only music, she seemed to say—to all of them. His music. And because it was his, it shall be fine, because he was fine, he was good. It was a touch intended to calm, and for a moment it succeeded.

Perlman listened, in fact. The *lento* was just now ending, descending like a stream, from shelf to shelf, into the more flowing, more rolling *allegro*. But it seemed so much simpler now. What eleven hours ago had chunked and splattered against his ears, a gnarl of clusters and convolutions, arbitrary counterpoints and random syncopations, seemed to have been leavened by a good meal, by candlelight, and the evening air. With the Madame's hand in his, Perlman followed like a fallen leaf on the surface of the sound, while it wandered, shifted, swirled, turned, eddied, and then finally, with a deft *ritardando* on the part of whoever was manning—or girling—the pedals, came to a gentle stop; a quiet pool to rest.

The company all eased in their seats. The Madame gave another squeeze. Not so harrowing, was it? No. The clock resumed its regular dominion, and Perlman tried pulling his hand away—assumed they all would—but the Madame and Roerich both denied; the circle was to remain unbroken. They set it down on the table, a garland of knuckles, and took a collective breath.

Rowe was first to speak. "Well, I know what I think." He looked around from eye to eye, but there were no takers. "It was the two of them, yes? In the boat. Dr. Perlman?"

Perlman kept his head perfectly still.

"Dr. Benjamin, what about you? I've a feeling you're with me on this."

Benjamin nodded. His eyes were still closed.

"There, see?" said Rowe. "I'm right, aren't I? It was the two of them. Afterward."

Benjamin nodded again, and Perlman shot him a glance this time—

that wasn't going to help, encouraging Rowe like that—but as he looked over at his friend now and saw how contentedly his lids were resting, he was reminded that Benjamin was quite drunk.

"All the blue," he said, scribbling the air with his hand, the one holding Rowe's.

"What do you mean 'blue'?"

"The blue," he said again, more lazily.

"I suspect he's referring to the water," the Madame offered softly. "Through the window."

"Oh." Rowe turned back. "Is that right, Dr. Benjamin? Did you actually *see* the water?"

Benjamin nodded firmly, and now it occurred to Perlman that his friend might be more than drunk—

"And fish," he said proudly.

"And fish! Why, Dr. Benjamin, I'm impressed." Rowe looked across at Perlman now and grinned. On some level he understood, too: Benjamin was in a trance. "Let me ask you something, then. We agree it was afterward"—the candle wavered coyly—"and yet didn't it seem to you that they were headed somewhere? I mean, that that wasn't just pleasant . . . drifting."

Benjamin shrugged at the self-evidence. "Well, he was showing her."

"Showing her what, thought?"

"The fish."

Rowe laughed out loud. "The fish." Rowe was losing Perlman here.

"Well, and the rocks and the plants and things," said Benjamin, oblivious, and sounding a bit more French than usual. "I gather the point was that for everything up here there was something down there, and vice versa. Horse for seahorse."

"Star for starfish," volleyed Rowe.

Yes, Benjamin nodded, that was good. His expression had taken on a kind of idiot grin. Rowe admired it for a moment, then moved on.

"Well, why don't we save that for the ballet version. What I'm getting at is that I think they might have been going somewhere."

Benjamin nodded. "That's true, too."

"Yes, because unless I'm mistaken, I'd say that at the end there, they arrived."

Benjamin agreed, absolutely.

"And I don't think it was back at the temple."

No, Benjamin shook his head.

"So where was it?"

Benjamin thought back, retraced as many steps as he was able, but then shook his head. "Don't know. That's where the music stopped."

Rowe tsked his disappointment, while Perlman more quietly heaved a sigh of relief. Quite enough of that, but just then—

*bum bum bum*

—a timpanum sounded softly in the parlor, and the piano resumed. Of course. All hands lifted compliantly. All eyes narrowed on the flame—all but Perlman's—then gently closed.

Damn the girl.

So this was how she wanted to play it, eh? Let the music lead? Let the drunken guests make up the rest themselves? He wasn't sure how he felt about this. Of course, on a certain level, one had to admire the cunning of the gesture—enlisting the stolen arcana to guide them through the pass. He didn't know that it completely made sense, but it was certainly clever, nicely barbed, and no doubt the music would turn up something—

There, for instance, that was a gorgeous phrase. Perlman didn't remember that from before, but that was exquisite.

Still, there was something that made him uncomfortable here. If he didn't know better, he'd almost have said he was feeling protective of the story, because for some reason the idea of just giving it away like this disturbed him deeply. He'd have much preferred that it stay with the girl. At least with her there was the intimation of some guiding intelligence—and the hope of an end. But leaving it with this crew—what could it possibly matter what they thought, particularly in this condition?

He looked over at Benjamin. His eyes were rolling beneath their lids like a nightmarish dog.

*Oh, but come now, Arthur, don't.* If he could only have his hand, whisper a single word—but Roerich was sitting in between them, and with the Madame on his right, Perlman felt as if he'd been deliberately cut off.

No, he didn't like this combination at all. He didn't trust it; or the music, frankly. The roll had reached the primitive bit again—with the steady drumbeat bass—but it seemed to have taken on a distinctly sinister tone this time around. The girl let it play once through, just long enough for them to hear the cadence, then she stopped. Silence resumed, and the circle set its hands down on the table.

Again, Rowe was the first to speak. "Lovely." He turned to the Madame as if she deserved some credit, too. "But I'm afraid I couldn't make heads or tails."

She shook her head; neither could she.

He turned. "What about you, Dr. Benjamin?"

Benjamin's eyes were still closed.

"Doctor?"

"Hm?"

"What about you? Did you see anything?"

"Oh." His head tilted, and Perlman could tell right away his trance had deepened—level two, it looked like. "Yes."

"I'll bet you did. What? Say."

His brow furrowed, looking for his answer. As a friend, Perlman prayed he wouldn't find it, but unfortunately the images were still too fresh.

"Well," said Benjamin, "there were two things actually. But the first was a . . . bathing spring."

"Bathing spring?" Rowe straightened, delighted. "What were they doing at a bathing spring?"

"It wasn't they," said Benjamin. "It was she. All the rest were women."

"Mmmmm." Rowe's eyes bounced. "I like it. In fact, I think I may have heard that part—'Maidens bathing in the moonlight.' "

He was making fun, but Benjamin didn't notice. "No moon," he said. "But there was Oona—and did you know she glows?"

Oh, that was unfortunate, thought Perlman.

Rowe could barely contain himself. "Like a firefly, you mean?"

"Well, no, not on-and-off like that, but yes—"

The Madame cleared her throat, admonishing Rowe. "Dr. Benjamin, I'm not sure I understand. How did Oona get to this bathing spring? Where was Thaire?"

Benjamin pursed his lips; that *was* the question. He didn't seem to have an answer, though.

"Well, why don't we back up a bit," said Rowe. "Now before, where we left off, you said they'd just crested, yes?"

Benjamin nodded.

"Did you get any better sense where?"

Benjamin tried to think.

"Upstream? Downstream?"

"Oh, down. It was a hillside."

"Good, a hillside, downstream. And was it still night?"

Benjamin nodded, squinting. "But there were . . . fires."

"Fires. Meaning people."

Benjamin nodded.

*This was ridiculous.*

"Do you have any sense who these people might have been?"

Benjamin pursed his lips again. He was struggling.

"The father's tribe?" suggested Rowe.

Benjamin considered; it seemed possible. "But it's not a village," he said. "It's just a hillside."

"Perhaps it's their rite," the Madame put in.

"Aaah," Rowe turned. "Yes. Because someone said they prayed to night, didn't they? Does that make sense to you, Dr. Benjamin, that this might be some sort of nocturnal rite that Thaire was taking her to?"

This made sense to Benjamin.

"Interesting." Rowe's eyes narrowed. "I want to get back to this bathing spring, though. Now, tell me—when Thaire and Oona emerged from the lake—I assume they emerged from the lake together."

Benjamin allowed.

"Was there anyone who might have met them?"

Benjamin shrugged at first. He hadn't actually seen them emerge, but then he paused. "There might have been an old woman."

"What makes you say that?"

"Well, there was an old woman at the spring. Did no one see this?"

"What did she look like?" asked Rowe.

"Well . . . old. And blind, I think. And it's possible she had a bundle of sticks beneath her arm."

The Madame nodded slightly; Rowe noticed. "Did you see?"

"No, but—" It was too complicated to go into, but she recognized the reference clearly. "Oldest and wisest," she said.

Rowe looked to Roerich, who nodded as well, and suddenly it occurred to Perlman that the fair young Russian might be playing a part here, too. For Mr. Roerich wasn't just an artist, remember—nor a set designer. He was an archaeologist as well, the Madame said, expert in Pagan Rus. Perlman hadn't lent the claim much credence before, but now he wondered if it weren't true, or if Mr. Roerich might not be a more effective communicator than he let on. He felt his hand. It was suspiciously still—inert, in fact, as if all energies were flowing left into the open trough of Benjamin's defenseless brain.

"All right," said Rowe. "It sounds as if you may be on to something here, Dr. Benjamin. But let me ask, if this 'oldest and wisest' woman brought Oona to the bathing spring, what happened to Thaire?"

"He went with the ashman."

"Ash-man?"

"Shaman?" the Madame tried.

No, this was a terrible combination, thought Perlman. These people knew far too much, and far too little.

"The one with the box," said Benjamin. " 'The long white hand.' "

Rowe didn't appear to make the connection, but pressed on. "Very well. So Thaire goes off with this shaman-ashman, and Oona is taken away by the 'oldest and wisest.' Question: She's blind, you said?"

"Yes."

"How is it she leads?"

"Well. Oona glows."

"I'm sorry." Rowe grinned. "That's right. Oona glows."

*The prick.*

"And floats."

*Arthur, stop!*

And Benjamin did, to Perlman's surprise. He jolted slightly. "Sorry."

The Madame looked up, concerned. "Dr. Benjamin, is something wrong?"

"I should stop."

"No," said Rowe. "No, old boy. You're doing well."

"You're doing very well," the Madame agreed. She gave Perlman a firm squeeze. None of that.

Perlman squeezed back. "Arthur, are you sure you're all right?"

"I'm fine."

"You know, if you don't want to, you don't have to go on."

"No, August." His eyes remained closed and comfortable. "I appreciate your concern, but I did see this."

"Yes, come along, Dr. Perlman—" Rowe was looking at him around the side of the candle, the flame shying from his breath. "It's just a story. Don't be such a . . ." He left off. Perlman would have bet his life the waiting word was "Jew," but Rowe did not speak it and Perlman did not take offense. He couldn't, but decided now to wash his hands. These people were on their own.

"I'm sorry. You were saying?"

"We'd got her to the spring." Rowe gave Benjamin's arm a shake. "With all the other maidens."

"Yes," said Benjamin, "and, August, I doubt you missed this—" He turned; even in trance a gentleman, making sure everyone was included. "A very handsome modulation—Schubert—as she entered the water. And they all laughed, because it began to glow like her."

*Glow like her.* "Thank you, Arthur. That's very nice."

"So she was happy, then?" asked Rowe.

"Oh, very," said Benjamin. "They were treating her like a queen, it seems to me."

"How is that?"

"Well, washing her hair, her feet, that sort of thing. And feeding her—"

"What?" asked the Madame incidentally.

"Oh, I don't know. Fruits, nectars—and they dressed her as well." He paused again—a detail. He slowed. "There was one, in fact—one of the maidens had a long white gown, the one who *had* been chosen. But they took it and gave it to Oona, which didn't seem fair. She said no, but the old woman told her it was right. 'All this time we have been praying, and you are the answer.' "

"Wow." Rowe sat back. " 'We've been praying, and you are the answer.' I like this, Dr. Benjamin. This is very good." The Madame agreed. "So they give her the gown, then what? Or do you think we should wait for the music?"

He turned to the Madame, but she denied any guiding influence. "I suspect the music will know when to enter." She waited a moment, lest it decide, but all remained black and silent behind the door, so she proceeded. "Dr. Benjamin, you said there were two things you saw. Have we come to the second yet?"

Benjamin shook his head.

"What was it?"

He squinted, less certain. Perlman felt Roerich's hand: nothing.

"A tent," said Benjamin finally.

"A tent?" said Rowe. "They brought her to a tent?"

Benjamin nodded.

"Was anyone else there?"

Benjamin thought again, though what for Perlman couldn't imagine—the answer seemed fairly obvious. Finally: "The men," he answered.

"Mmmm, yes, of course." Rowe nodded; Rowe liked.

"Thaire?" the Madame asked.

"Yes, I think so."

"What makes you hesitate?"

Benjamin grimaced. These things were like dreams. The longer you let them sit, the harder they were to retrieve. "I think because she wasn't allowed to go to him. They had to show her first."

" 'Show her.' " Rowe leaned in. "Do you mean to the men?"

"Yes." Benjamin nodded, more certain; it was coming now. "The ashman came and he took her hand. And he was leading her around for them to see."

Rowe closed his eyes to picture it. "That's very nice. I even wonder—do you mind?"

Benjamin shook his head.

"Well, I've got all the men sitting in a circle, yes? And the ashman's leading her by the hand—she's floating?"

"Yes."

"Yes, well, I wonder if it isn't possible that while this was taking place, the maidens might have been dancing—some sort of a ritual dance."

"No, that's right!" Benjamin sat up. "That's absolutely correct. They were, or they'd started."

Benjamin was very excited now, collaborating with the theater folk. The mind was a wonder.

And here, of course, the music started in again. It picked up right where it had left off, at the beginning of the primitive passage—the newly titled "Maiden Dance"—and Perlman had to admit, the rhythm did possess a certain folk-y sway to it, well suited to puppeteer a band of dancing maidens. The five of them sat listening, conjuring the image together, but as the tune turned over and over again, this simple yet exotic phrase, Perlman found himself focused on the Madame's hand. Her touch seemed to be withdrawing almost, pulling farther and farther away with each refrain. He wondered, was this her brother calling, asking Helena to play. By the fifth return, Perlman could hardly feel her fingers at all, then—*bum bum bum*—the timpanum concluded the episode and she was back; firm.

Rowe took a deep, satisfied breath and opened glassy eyes on Perlman. "Happy?" That was his cup of tea, wasn't it?

Perlman said nothing, offered nothing, so Rowe turned briefly to his right. "I'm guessing that was all fairly clear to you, Dr. Benjamin."

Benjamin nodded.

"Yes, I wonder if we shouldn't open things up a bit, though." Rowe

wheeled to the Madame; he must have sensed it, too. "I wonder in particular if there's anything that Madame Barrett has to offer."

"I?" she feigned.

"You." He held her with his eyes. "You seem to have an insight."

"An interest."

"Serve it."

Well said, Rowe. The Madame paused a moment to consider the
question—what had she to add?—and Perlman felt another surge of
apprehension. Benjamin as guide was one thing; the Madame, quite
another. And he wished that he could caution her, tried oozing
through his fingers that she please be careful here. She was more powerful than the others, and this was an ominous trail they'd chosen. He
had to think she sensed it too, and perhaps she did. Perhaps she simply couldn't resist. Perhaps this was the flame she could not keep her
paper wings from, and who was Perlman, this day, to chide her weakness? He had a handsome welt above his ear to show for his.

She began modestly. "Well, I think she was simply wondering if
these could possibly be the people her father fears so much."

Rowe agreed. He wanted more, though.

"They have been so kind," she said. Her eyes were on the flame
now, her every syllable causing it to shift and sway. "Bathing her,
clothing her, feeding her fruits and nectar which her father has only let
her sip. When she thinks of how he treated Thaire, she feels
ashamed—imprisoning him like that, and threatening him—while
here the ashman leads her around to meet their elders. They bow their
heads, cast flowers before her, and gold."

Rowe was openly enamored. "Tell me about the ashman."

She paused; her eyes narrowed. "She can't quite see. He wears the
head and the hide of what was once a great brown bear. His hair is
long and gray, his body is frail. She can see his ribs, and his skin is covered everywhere with ash and paint, but she can feel the strength in his
hand, that he has magic. She can hear him without his using words.
And he can hear her as well . . ."

"That she is thinking of her father, that she is thinking Malachai
must never have come this far, for if he could see the maidens now—

they are like feathers dancing—or the fires outside, how they light the low-slung clouds, the birds circling in and out, the black boats sliding back and forth along the lake, and everywhere the drums. She can hear them all across the valley, and the people singing their prayer, and she knows that if her father could only hear them too, he would be consoled—there is no wrong in this. What is wrong in this? . . .

"The ashman says, 'If the sun should hear our prayer, so should earth.'

" 'And if the earth should hear our prayer,' she says, 'then so should water.'

" 'And so should fire,' he replies. 'And wind. So should every shape and shadow.' He gives her more to drink. 'And if we praise the day,' he tells her, 'then we should praise night. The night should have its god as well, shall name its god tonight' . . . And she knows that what the ashman says is true, but more than anything she wants to be with him again, with Thaire." Her eyes relaxed.

"But?" asked Rowe.

"But when the music ends, she is standing before Oman'en and Oman'en is standing before her."

There was a moment's silence. Perlman wondered if the music shouldn't enter. He looked to the doors, but then their arms all began rising. He turned. It was Benjamin, lifting up his hands, and his trance had deepened drastically this time. He'd gone all the way to level four, it looked like, thanks to the Madame. His eyes were rolled up in their sockets, and he was opening his mouth to speak, but Perlman knew already this wasn't going to be his friend. His lids fluttered momentarily, a flash of white, then from some completely foreign region of Arthur Benjamin's throat there spilled an equally foreign incantation; nothing which made sense, of course, though the sound of it was awfully familiar. The Madame recognized, too.

Rowe was the most disturbed, though. He wouldn't even look—he turned away—then as soon as Benjamin was silent again, he leaned in to the Madame. "That wasn't Russian?"

The Madame shook her head.

"Then I'm wondering if maybe we shouldn't pause a moment."

A bit late for that, thought Perlman.

*Bum bum bum*—the timpanum agreed. Rowe was not director here.

"I'm just thinking for Dr. Benjamin's sake—"

*BUM BUM BUM*, the drum repeated sternly, and Rowe sat back, a scolded dog. It didn't seem he'd realized till now what a willful fire he'd been teasing this evening.

"It's all right," the Madame tried consoling him. "It was only a prayer."

Rowe looked across at Perlman now, with deepening concern. Not the Madame, too?

"He was only offering thanks," she said, still gazing at the flame. " 'O blessed night, the river returns my son, and my son should bear this—' "

And suddenly Roerich came to life. Just as the Madame said the word "gift," he yanked his hand free from Perlman's grasp and smacked his knuckles on the table with such a loud crack the candlestick jumped in its place. The flame flickered wildly, then he began snaking his fist back and forth along the cloth, where in its wake he left a serpentine design—a trail of something gray-white and dusty.

Rowe leaned around to see. "What is it?"

"Ash," said Perlman vaguely, stunned.

"What?"

"Flowers," said the Madame. "Leading outside."

And now the piano joined, came chiming in with a high and eerie anthem. Roerich took hold of Perlman's hand and sat back in his chair. They were to listen, but Rowe was on the verge of panic. He was looking across at Perlman, shaking his head. They should stop this, shouldn't they? Benjamin and the Madame were much too deep, and Roerich—Rowe's eyes rolled—Mr. Roerich over there was capable of anything now that he'd been roused. The things Nicholas knew . . .

Perlman didn't deny, and might have added that the music presently striding through the French doors was an equal unknown—this was farther along the roll than he'd gotten this morning. Yet he had no intention of stopping it, for though this sudden surge in their momentum was unnerving, finally it signaled to Perlman the imminence of some conclusion. For the first time since entering this home, he felt that tug again, the gravity of their destination pulling at them inexorably, like five leaves in a gutter stream. And so with a nod, he advised his anxious acquaintance across the table against resistance. These currents were awfully strong. One need only look at the Madame between them, upon whom the triumphant discords of this ancient Lydian processional were acting like pure oxygen.

Finally she could not contain herself anymore. "It is a sea of torch-light!" she exclaimed. "They've come from all across the hillsides."

"I'm sorry," said Rowe, a nervous twinge teasing the corner of his smile. "I'm afraid—I just need to know, where exactly are we headed?"

"Up!" said the Madame.

"No, I mean—are we all right here? Doctor?" He looked across at Perlman again. Rowe clearly did not like seeing the Madame this way, but Perlman actually found himself more moved. How she had missed this, hearing someone else so exactly. Her eyes were alive beneath their lids, like children under bedsheets.

And Perlman could see as well, if from a more remote perspective. The girl was like a fallen star, rolling up the dark hillside, dividing the torchlight as she passed. She was indeed the one that they'd been wait-ing for. He only wondered, Did the Madame not hear the menace, too? Did he not? Or was that just the question which had been nag-ging him ever since they'd left the tent: Where in the world was Thaire?

The Madame turned her ear. Now she heard it. Somewhere strewn inside the chords a splatter of false notes had sounded—a handful of stones—which just that quickly turned the pageant-stride into a stalk. There was no denying now. This child, this gift which their long-lost prince had brought them from the river, was not theirs to keep. She was theirs to offer.

"This is too far," she said. "They've gone too far." Her hand gripped tight, but she was right. The music had grown even darker, was lead-ing through a grove of black trees. She didn't know where she was anymore, and the notes were just as lost, a weave of unrelated lines scattering manically above the steady pulse.

"The lights are falling back," she said.

And so they were, dispersing like a nest of snakes till there was just the one remaining; a frightened figure, syncopating timidly to the same persistent bass as had measured the whole ascent—shying, shying, and now joining it for one last measure, four last paces, before coming to a stop.

All was silent, even the clock.

"What is this place?" the Madame asked.

Rowe's eyes were bugging. He was looking over at her, cringing almost, but she appeared to be waiting now. Her head was tilted back, swaying slightly. Benjamin was more hunched and squinting; he had nothing either. Perlman glanced to the French doors, but there, too, the space between was hollow and expectant. And so it fell to Roerich.

"A circle of standing stones," he said, his voice more resonant for the silence it had been keeping up to then; his words more plain and clear for the slightly Slavic accent with which he spoke them. "With five tall stakes standing just inside."

"Nicholas," Rowe tried cautioning, "are we absolutely sure about this?"

"The ground is soft beneath her feet," the Madame said.

"The ground is covered in ash," replied Roerich. "And at the center is a large flat rock."

"Nicholas—"

"What has happened here?" The Madame tilted back her head. "And what are those at the tops of the stakes? It feels as if they're looking at her."

Us, thought Perlman.

"Skulls," said Roerich. "Horse."

"Nicholas, please. Madame," said Rowe, "there are no skulls. We're all just sitting in your parlor. My goodness. Tell her, Doctor."

Rowe looked across at him again, but Perlman felt his eyes deaden. He had tried to tell them—before. He pressed the Madame's hand. "Are you all right?"

"What is this place?"

"Is the girl all right?"

She shook her head. "What has happened here? And what is *that*?" Her expression twisted.

"It's nothing," said Rowe. "It's your imagina—"

"No, what *is* that?" She reared. "Beneath her feet, the ash . . . is soaked . . . and black—"

"It's blood," said Roerich.

"NICHOLAS!" Rowe shot forward. The flame licked. "Please! I'm going to have to insist this stop right now." He tried pulling his hands free, but neither Benjamin nor the Madame would let go. "No, I really must—"

"Mr. Rowe," said Perlman, "please be quiet. Madame, is there blood at her feet?"

The Madame was trembling, but managed a nod.

"Whose blood is it?"

"DR. PERLMAN!" Rowe leaned across and glared at him, clench-jawed and impotent. "What *are* you doing? Ow." He winced. Benjamin was mashing his knuckles from the right.

The Madame gasped.

Perlman turned. "Madame, what?"

"It's a body," she said. Her hand was like a vise. "Behind the stone, there's a body."

Indeed, thought Perlman, and at that moment he had no doubt whose body it was, or the name that he'd been going by, or why the Madame should have been the one to find him.

She was arching out of her chair, pulling away and moaning. " 'Please . . . Don't let it be . . .' " She didn't want to look, and Perlman understood—why subject herself again?—yet he felt his compassion strangely governed, for there was still the girl, and there was her best friend, Oona, standing in the circle, standing by the stone with fresh blood soaking the ashes at her feet.

" 'No.' " The Madame shuddered. There were tears on her cheeks. " 'Father, I am sorry. Mother . . . forgive me . . . forgive us. Just don't let it be—' "

"Madame." Perlman took firm hold of her hand. "She must see who."

She nodded, she knew. She leaned forward, catching her breath, but even then she could not bring herself; her head turned away. Just her pupils slid beneath her lids, over and over, and when they met the candle's light again, she let out a sudden burst of emotion, an expulsion that scattered Roerich's ashes across the tablecloth, but Perlman couldn't tell if it was horror or relief. She seemed confused.

"Madame?"

Her mouth was open, but her voice wouldn't come. ". . .—sh."

"What? Madame, who is it?"

". . . h-sh . . ."

". . . Ash?"

Yes, she nodded.

". . . The ashman?"

"Yes."

. . . *The ashman?*

Before Perlman could even begin to make sense, there came a shock of sound from the parlor, a chord so sudden and jarring the entire circle jolted in their seats. Perlman recognized it instantly—it was the fourth time he'd heard it now—and the following cluster, struck with equal passion, left no doubt. These were from the beginning of the roll. This was the opening statement, the soft caresses of the *lento*, come back with stunning exultation.

And now the Madame's breast turned up. Her face began to light. "There he is!" she cried, with a failing voice. She lifted her hands. Rowe actually turned to look over his shoulder, and just then a thunderous smash shook the ceiling from above; the beams all quaked. There came a second crash, and Perlman tried pulling free—that had sounded dangerous—but now the French doors burst wide and a dark, cloaked figure came harrowing in. Rowe shrieked and cowered, and even Perlman closed his eyes, as the howling invader descended upon them, swooping around the table like a swarm of bats, thumping and thrashing. The piano had gone completely berserk. It sounded as if someone were attacking the keys with fists and elbows. There was a tug and snap among the arms—someone fell—the intruder fled by the front hall, and it wasn't much longer after that. The piano hammered

out the last of its savage coda. The final chord spiked down murder-
ously, hovered a moment, and only then, as the dissonance began to
fade, did Perlman feel his shoulders ease again. The muscles in his eyelids all relaxed, and finally, when quiet had resumed, he opened them.

The lamps were lit. Rowe was down on the floor, and the table had
been cleared of the blanket and the candle. There was just the flat
wood top and the two splayed leaves. The Madame's eyes were open
but vacant. Roerich's, too.

Benjamin was the only one who had yet to emerge. His left hand
was still suspended in the air where Rowe had let go. The expression
on his face was tight and twitching.

"Dr. Benjamin," said the Madame, "look away."

He didn't respond.

"Arthur," tried Perlman, "it's all right."

Finally Roerich reached up to tap his shoulder, and Benjamin shiv-
ered awake, as from a nightmare. He took in the room, the light, the
table, then looked back at the four of them—his hair askew, his pince-
nez crooked on his nose—and answered their vague, spent attention
with just a single word.

"Carnage."

# CHAPTER 34

Rowe was the first to stand. In the electric light he was absolutely blanched. They were all a slightly paler shade—but Rowe, cocksure Rowe, was most visibly rattled; and outraged. Rowe's line had been crossed.

"Madame, I trust you're all right?"

She did not look at him, but nodded.

"Good." He straightened himself. "Then I think I may be leaving." He started for the front hall. Roerich followed after him, not that he seemed so upset, but one leaves with one's partner. The Madame rose next for somewhat the same reason, decorum; she went to see her guest out. Perlman and Benjamin straggled after, more like filings after a magnet.

It was drizzling outside, they could see through the transom. Rowe had already taken his coat from the closet, but was struggling to get his arms through the sleeves.

"Dr. Benjamin." His voice was trembling. "I fear I may have been cavalier with you. I apologize. And you as well, Dr. Perlman. I suspect you were probably right." He misbuttoned himself and turned to the Madame, though it didn't seem he knew quite what to say to her. "You'll give best to Stanley." He tipped his hat awkwardly and lifted and umbrella from the stand. "Nicholas?"

Nicholas was coming. He exchanged a more cordial, more Russian, farewell with the Madame, then followed his shaken companion out into the night, for the pregnant-silent walk back to their own parting.

The Madame stood a moment, out of sorts. She dabbed at the corner of her eye with the base of her palm. "Dr. Perlman, it seems I may have caught your bug." The rims of her eyes were thick and dark. He'd never have imagined he could see her this way, so vulnerable. "If you'll excuse me." She passed between him and Benjamin and gingerly headed up the stairs.

There were just the two of them now.

"Are you all right?" asked Perlman.

"Fine."

"You were fairly deep there, Arthur."

"Yes."

"Have you any memory?"

"Oh yes."

Perlman started him back to see about the girl. The French doors were still slid wide from Stanley's ambush, but it didn't appear there was anyone in the Music Room. He pointed Benjamin to the Welte-Mignon. "Did you get a chance to see that?"

"I'm surprised it's still standing." He went to take a closer look, while Perlman checked the corners and beneath the tables. "I did some asking around, incidentally. About Barrett."

Perlman opened the door to the back flight of stairs leading up to Alexander's room. "And?" It was all black. He didn't want to go up.

"Doesn't sound like syphilis. Dr. Weston said he knew the man they used to use. A homeopathist. Apparently there was a quick downward spiral, emotionally, then I gather it was self-inflicted."

Perlman stepped back out. "Blood?"

"I'd heard laudanum, but I suppose the two aren't mutually exclusive."

Perlman nodded. "Well, there's a great deal more here than meets the eye." He wondered if the girl was upstairs taking a bath somewhere.

"So what did you make of the end?" Benjamin asked, a propos.

Just then Perlman noticed a light in the Madame's office, beneath the door leading to the breakfast nook. "You said, 'Carnage.' "

"No, but before that, on the stone. Did she say it was the body of the ashman?"

"Yes."

"Well, how does that work? The ashman had been killed?"

"Yes."

"By?"

"Thaire."

"You sound awfully sure."

Perlman nodded. "The music. There was a reprise of the opening theme."

Benjamin smiled, impressed. "Good ear."

"Well, I'd heard it already, remember." Perlman looked back through the office again, at the light. He was almost sure that was she.

"So when Madame Barrett said, 'There he is,' she was referring to Thaire?"

"Yes."

Benjamin laughed at himself. "I thought it was her brother."

"Well, I wouldn't necessarily mark you wrong for that, but within the context of the story, yes, I'm fairly sure she meant Thaire."

Benjamin nodded, reflecting. "So he was a hero?"

"By certain interpretations, I suppose yes."

"But then her father came?"

"Yes. Malachai arrived, and the priests, then I think 'carnage' fairly well sums it up."

Benjamin's face curdled at the reminder. "But what about Oona, though? Do we know if she survived?"

"That I'm not sure of." He motioned to the breakfast nook. "I could probably check, if you like."

"Please."

"If you'll wait here." He made his way through the Madame's office and tapped the door.

"Yes?" came the girl's voice, calm, assured.

He opened. She was sitting on the window cushions, with a pitcher and two glasses of water.

"Are we ready to go?"

"Not yet."

He paused. "There can't be much more."

She shook her head. "Thank Dr. Benjamin, but tell him he doesn't have to stay."

He looked at her. She was rather cool, but he supposed that wasn't the worst answer. And strangely he had begun to feel a kind of ease again, since the end of the scene really—a certain bygone confidence returning—as if with the end of the roll a fever had broken.

Benjamin was still sitting at the Welte-Mignon, examining the spool. "Yes?"

"I gather she survived."

"Oh. Well, good."

"And you may go."

"You're staying?" Benjamin looked at him as though he must be mad.

"I'll explain it all to you. Don't worry, I'm fine."

Benjamin clearly wasn't so sure, but relented. "All right, then. You needn't see me out."

Perlman agreed; he didn't want to stray too far from the girl.

No sooner was Benjamin out the door than someone else came tramping down the back stairs, someone heavy. It was Stanley, out of costume, face scrubbed. "Where's Helena?"

"Her room, I think. I'm afraid she seemed a bit undone."

"Yes, well, I hardly think she could have anticipated all that."

Perlman detected a curious note of reproach in this, but let it pass.

"Stanley?" called the girl, a calm summons from the breakfast nook.

Stanley excused himself and went to receive his orders. They spoke briefly behind the door, then he emerged again, looking relieved. "I am dismissed."

"Your part is done?"

"Is done."

"She didn't give you any hint how much more?"

He shook his head. "Pray not too much. Better bring this to a close."

Again it sounded as if Stanley, of all people, was placing the responsibility with him. Perlman didn't protest, though, for he did feel distinctly—he wasn't yet sure why—but that he might have stumbled on a trail out, a gentle downhill slope.

"I couldn't agree more."

"Good, then. I'll see myself out. Tell Helena I'll come by tomorrow." Stanley turned to leave, but Perlman stopped him to his own surprise.

"Do you mind if I ask—when you came in there at the end, that was to save her, yes?"

"Yes."

"From?"

Stanley thought, not long. "Thaire, I suppose."

"Well, then what was Thaire doing?"

Stanley looked at him, and a slow smile crossed his face. He set his hand on Perlman's shoulder and leaned in to his ear. "Stop deferring, Doctor. No one knows any more than you." He pulled back again, still smiling. "I'm off." He offered one last bow and made his exit—blustery, mysterious, moving, and absolutely daft Lord Stanley; without whom, none of this.

As soon as Perlman heard the front door close again, he went to check on the girl. She was still in her seat, with the two glasses in front of her.

"I believe it's just us now," he said.

"Except for Miss McCumber."

He felt his wound, then noticed the samovar on the far table. "Is that warm?"

"It just started," she said.

"Very good. Then I'm going to straighten up a bit. I won't be far."

He decided he should try to return as much as he could to its original station, to leave things more or less as he'd found them. He rewound the piano roll and set about moving all the parlor furniture back into place. He hauled the drop-leaf table over to the corner again and felt better for the physical exertion, more aware than ever of the unusual calm spreading through him, an inner stillness returning, which seemed to be drawing strength from Stanley's admonition. No doubt he was right. Who knew more than Dr. Perlman? He arranged all the cushioned chairs back around the hearth and returned the tea table to its place. There was no reason he couldn't end this himself. He sheathed the sixth roll and set it back inside the steamer trunk with the others, then shoved the trunk up against the wall, now convinced that that's what the girl was waiting for.

He returned to the breakfast nook. She was still there, still quiet— holding her glass of water with a combination of authority and reconciliation that he recognized from their walk around the hospital fountain.

He stood at the window. "This will be the last," he said, "what's coming up."

She shrugged, the same as then.

"And I'll lead."

"You and Oona," she said.

"Of course."

They were silent a moment. Outside, the garden stirred restlessly in the wind. Tomorrow would feel like autumn.

The girl slid something out on the table beneath her palm.

"What's that?"

"You're supposed to take it," she said. It was the white shell. "Oona says that's all you need."

"Then we'll be done?"

She nodded.

Perlman felt the samovar. The water was ready. He poured two cups and set them on the same tray as yesterday. He cut two slices of lemon as well, and packed a spoon with the Madame's evening leaves.

"You'll be coming up?" he asked.

"As soon as Miss McCumber's gone."

He took the shell. He placed it on the Madame's navy linen and started for the stairs.

He could see beneath the door that the Madame's light was on. He knocked.

"Yes."

"I brought you some tea."

"Oh." He could hear her rise and shift.

"I can just leave it."

"No, thank you. You may come in."

He opened her door. Her room was surprisingly white—all tans and blues in the evening light. She was sitting in a slipper-chair by the window. "You can set it there." She motioned to a table by the bed. "And there's a chair for you."

"Thank you. Don't get up."

In the corner was an armless Windsor chair with a cream-colored satin cushion. He took it and set it beside the table, not quite opposite hers.

"Stanley said to say he'll see you tomorrow."

She barely registered. Her cheeks looked soft.

"And everything's in order."

"I heard. Thank you." She smiled faintly. "I should get a key for that cabinet."

"Madame, I hope you'll accept my apology—"

"You've nothing to be sorry for, Doctor."

"Well, I am the one who put the roll there. I shouldn't have. I shouldn't have touched it—"

"Oh, Doctor, it was there. And who's to say . . . It seems to me you did just fine."

Like Judas, he thought, the necessary evil.

She smiled sorrowfully. "It's interesting, though—and this has been true." She paused; as always, rhythm a consideration. "I don't mind the photographs. I don't mind seeing his books or his instruments. Even the hands—for some reason they don't bother me. It's the music." She paused. Her lashes were heavy with tears.

"It was always there, you know. I can see his head in Mother's lap, covering his ears—'Make it go away.' He was like a little hole in a dike, a little chink, and the whole sea trying to get through. All I ever wanted was to give him something, something he could pour that music onto. A canvas. That's all I wanted."

Only from the Madame's mouth could this have sounded so much like a plea of innocence.

"I'm sure you did very well," he said, intending no irony. "He didn't sound like a tortured soul."

She smiled. "Sometimes, no." She shook her head, uncomprehending. "Do you know, there are some people in our lives—I don't know if they're supposed to be the ones we love, they're the ones we must be with, I don't know—because it seems to me that every day, everywhere we look, we look past such misery without a thought. We are steel. But then there are some people where you just cannot bear their pain, do you know?"

He didn't really.

"And of course, they're the ones you cause the pain."

He thought of going to her side, but to offer what possible consolation? He passed her his handkerchief, and there came a knock at the door.

"Nina?"

"May I come in?"

"Of course," the Madame answered. She was standing, wiping her nose daintily. "Come and make yourself comfortable. The doctor has brought tea." She noticed there were only two cups. "Did you want some?"

The girl shook her head.

Madame Helena dunked her spoon, and watched a moment absently as the tea bled into the water. Then she stood and excused herself.

The girl had seen her distress, but refused any blame. She stood against the bedpost, waiting.

"If I lit a candle," said Perlman, "would that make it easier for Oona to hear?"

The girl nodded. There was one on the mantel, a short white candle in a tin saucer. Perlman brought it back to the Madame's table, and as he lit it, for the first time he let his mind turn to the questions that now faced him—how, in fact, he was going to do this. He still had no idea, yet he wasn't concerned, for more than ever he felt suffused by an almost preternatural sense of calm.

The Madame returned, recovered somewhat. She noted the girl's slippers. "You look as if you're going to bed."

"Are you ready?" the girl replied.

"I suppose." The Madame took her seat and looked at Perlman. "Ready for what?"

"The end," she said.

"The end," he echoed. "And I believe it's my turn."

The Madame was neither surprised nor averse. She seemed relieved.

"I'd like us all to get comfortable, though. Madame, you're fine in the chair there. Would it be all right if Nina lay down on the bed?"

"Of course."

Nina climbed up. The Madame helped, arranging the pillows around her like a throne. As Perlman removed her slippers, he had the strange sense of preparing a body for burial, but he would not let himself be dissuaded, not while he could smell that scent, the fresh draft of an open door.

He asked the Madame, "You haven't a metronome?"

"I'm sure we do. Do you want me to look?"

"No, no. In the reading room? In the cabinet perhaps?"

"Yes, I think so."

He'd seen it there. He took the white shell from the tray and started down the hall.

The floor of the library was covered with books. Someone had indeed toppled the western shelf. He'd have to clean this up as well when they were done. For now, he simply stood among the rubble and opened his palm to consider the one clue he'd been granted. The shell:

—which Thaire had left beneath Oona's pillow

—which Oona had been wearing when he let her come inside his boat.

He considered the shape, the crescent. Or was it a sickle perhaps?

—with which one might entrust the farmer but not the thief?

All this was true, but not quite right. There was something he was not seeing. He looked at all the books surrounding him, and his heart sank. Was the answer somewhere among these? Was there another page he'd have to find?

But then a breeze shifted outside, and a faint light flickered in. The leaves of the Madame's pear tree sounded as if they were whispering to him, calling for him to look, but he didn't even need to, for as he felt that gleam against his cheek again, the hairs on the nape of his neck all began to thrill—the same as when he was sitting in his seat at St. James's Hall, when each successive note was the fulfillment of his every hope and expectation. He turned and there it was, looming through the spindly branches, hanging high above the Thames—the sliver that she'd drawn four nights ago, now grown into a silver crescent.

He looked down at his hand again: the shell was the moon.

Because there had been no mention of a moon, had there? Not in the girl's first painting, or even during the rite. Benjamin had said, *No moon.* Now Perlman knew why.

He looked back out the window and was sure—that was the augur's

dream out there. That was the Lord of Darkness, yes? That was the
Light from Light.

"Dr. Perlman?" The Madame was calling down the hall. "Were you
able to find it?"

"Yes, I did. Just a moment."

And now the image came to him—of how he should begin; as clear
as if the girl had framed it for him. He would simply have to make her
see, or make her dear friend Oona see. Then rely.

He took the metronome from its shelf and started back down the
hall as if he were gliding forth on the soft palm of a giant, guiding
hand.

The girl and the Madame were both settled in as he had asked—the
girl lying flat, her head upon a single pillow; the Madame in her chair,
hands in her lap; the candle on the table between them.

Perlman set the metronome back on the mantel and adjusted the
tempo to 120 beats per minute. A little faster than usual, but he would
speak in half-time.

"Are we all comfortable?"

They nodded.

He started the pendulum and returned to his chair, sliding it just a
touch closer to the bed. He could tell already that the rhythm would
help—was placing him back in his element even now.

"Now, before I start, I'd like for us all to breathe for a moment—
deep. Could we?"

They did.

"Deep," he said again, relaxing himself, finding that depth in his
chest; he felt as if it had been years. "We'll count down from ten . . .
nine . . ." He let the tocks syncopate. "Eight."

The girl joined at "seven"—*tock tock*—"six"—*tock tock*—"five."
Perlman left off at "four." They could barely hear "three . . ." and by
"two" she was ready. She didn't say "one."

"Good. Good." He paused. "Now, you wanted to hear the end?"

She nodded faintly, lids placid.

"And I will tell you."

He would. He took a sip of his lemon water. Still warm, tart. As always, he reminded himself, begin with the senses. Find the moment, through the senses. He took one more sip, then set his cup back down beside the candle.

He shifted in his chair to face it. The metronome was tocking steadily, offering him chance after chance to enter. He checked his pocket watch. It was nearly 11:50. He waited for the second hand to pass the twelve, then turned his eye to the flame and began.

"... She has been asleep ... But even before she opens her eyes she can feel ... she is in her bed again, in Aram's tower ... The down is soft against her back, and she can smell the river.

"... She opens her eyes and looks out across the balcony ... It is night ... The sky is black ... but there above the ridge of mountains is something she has never seen before ... A great silver sickle is hanging in the sky ... glowing, like a giant lantern.

"She rises from the bed ... She walks out to the balcony to see it closer ... She can feel the cold stone beneath her feet ... the damp night air ... When she comes to the rail, she looks down ... The river is higher than she has ever seen ... The strand is gone ... The water is nearly halfway up the cliff, and out in the distance, where the hills used to roll into valleys, she can see that the horizon is like a pane of glass stretched out beneath this great silver beacon ..."

Perlman waited now. The metronome beat out the time, while she pictured it. Finally, she stirred.

"... 'Hello?' " she said, in a higher register than he was used to. " 'Who is there?' "

"Oona?"

" 'Who is it?' "

"Oona?"

"... 'Aram? Why am I here? What has happened?' "

" 'I brought you,' " said Perlman, leaning forward. " 'But we must go now.' "

". . . 'When did this light appear?' "

" 'As we returned,' " he said, " 'but it has seen what we have done, and now it is calling all the waters to rise and wash the land, which is why we must go.' "

She was silent awhile, trying to fathom the enormity of his words. ". . . 'My father is gone?' "

" 'Yes.' "

". . . 'And what of Thaire?' "

Perlman hesitated. He didn't know.

". . . 'Did you see him?' "

". . . 'Thaire won't harm you anymore.' "

" 'Did you see him?' "

" '. . . Oona, we have to go.' . . ."

Again she chose silence, but for an even longer, more stubborn, while this time.

". . . 'Oona, the water,' " he said.

" 'I am not afraid of the water,' " she replied, and it was almost as if he'd known she would. *I am not afraid of the water.*

". . . 'No, but I am, Oona . . . And the others, and we cannot wait much longer.' "

" 'Then go.' "

There again. *Then go.* It was as if the rest was clear somehow, was merely theirs to play.

". . . 'But you know that I can't leave without you—' "

" 'You *will* leave without me.' " She turned her wrist, in search of his hand. He gave it, and the rhythm of the metronome belonged to her now.

". . . 'You see this light up in the sky." Her words sounded calm and even. " 'I know this light . . . This light has lived within me all my life. It is my mother—Artemis—and she has come to rule the night, forever now . . . She shall hang above the dry land and the sea, and look on all that turns below . . . What day forgets, the night will remind, in spells my mother shall cast, and this now is her first.' . . .

" 'You will leave this place, Aram. You may take the arcana with you, and you may go . . . and someday, you and all who go with you will find the land again. You'll build homes, and sow fields, but look upon my mother, Aram, and listen to me . . . You will remember nothing of the world you leave behind. Whatever these waters have touched, that shall be washed from your mind as well. You will not remember these hills, or the river that once divided them, or the temple that was your home. You will not remember my father, or me, or what has happened here tonight . . . You will remember one thing only.' "

He waited.

". . . 'All is One,' " she said, and then she pulled her hand away.

Perlman looked up at the Madame. Her hand was on her cheek, and her eyes were closed, but she was listening. Waiting.

He turned to the flame and the words came easily again, as if he'd spoken them countless times to sleeping children.

". . . So Aram left the temple, and there was only Oona in her tower, and her mother looking down. And while the tide drew higher and higher, Oona searched the waves for a shadow or a plume of smoke—some sign that Thaire was there, that he had come for her . . ."

He paused. The girl was breathing deeply, slowly, in a kind of serene suspense. The end was here, he knew, awaiting his word. He only wondered, would he be a coward for saying it? Was he only managing his escape, or was this what was so, what was true? Was there even such a thing in this place? He looked at her—sweet girl, her hands lying flat across her belly—and he did not know the answer: only that the door was open and he must take it.

"But there was no shadow," he said, "nor any plume of smoke." And now there came a thin sucking sound from the girl's throat, but no protest.

". . . Just the water rising," he continued. ". . . It came up to her tower first, then to her balcony . . . It came up to her ankles, then her wrists, and then at dawn it finally reached her lips, but Oona did not resist . . . She let it fill her lungs and swallow her . . . That is where she died, on the balcony of Aram's tower . . . and that is where she remains, at the bottom of the sea . . ."

In a moment the girl fell silent again. There was just the flame, hovering. Perlman leaned down—and here the moment he would never confess to anyone. He was about to blow it out, he'd drawn his breath, when the light seemed to snuff on its own.

He looked up at the Madame to see if she'd seen, but it was too dark. There was just the smoke and the metronome, and he supposed he would never really know.

He took up his watch. A minute to midnight. Madame Helena stood. She returned the candle to the mantel and stopped the pendulum, for silence.

Perlman felt the girl's forehead. Warm. "She's all right," he whispered, all instinct, all confidence now returned; the certainty of what was to come. He held her by the wrist and spoke into her ear: "Nina?"

Nothing. He let a moment pass, then brought his mouth up close again. "Sylvie Blum?"

She was still, breathing faintly. He set two fingers in her palm and repeated more slowly, "Sylvie Blum?"

Three silent tocks elapsed, and then he felt it distinctly. Her hand gripped his.

He had done it. He was safe again.

"Good." And all tension eased. All the muscles slackened. "Good. Sylvie Blum, all is well. It is now midnight. You will remain like this, asleep, till morning. At nine o'clock you will awaken at the clinic, with no memory of this place or ever having been brought here. Do you understand?" Her grip tightened. "Good." He looked up at the Madame. "You'll get us a cab?"

She was already standing at the door. "Of course." She started out.

Perlman remained. He opened the window just a crack, then sat back down. He took the girl's hand, lowered his head against the blanket, and simply breathed.

Just as Perlman had instructed, Sylvie Blum awoke Monday morning in her room at the clinic, oblivious to everything that had happened the last seven days. Her father arrived for his appointment promptly at 10:00 to find her both physically robust and unmistakably herself.

Dr. Perlman offered only a brief explanation, the same as he reported in the files that he handed over to Professor Bernheim later that afternoon. The episode which had so upset Fraulein Bauer the week before—the appearance of the "false identity"—had been a result of the girl's anemia and an unwarranted barrage of morphine. Rest and a few intensive sessions with Perlman, subsequently erased from her memory, had been all she'd needed.

Blum respectfully did not probe, as if to question were to doubt, and to doubt might break whatever benevolent spell Dr. Perlman had managed to cast on his only daughter. For this same reason, he agreed that Sylvie be withdrawn from Miss Mobley's and enrolled at a day school in London, in order that she be near Dr. Levitz, a generalist to whom Perlman referred the case. Sylvie left the clinic at noon, and Perlman heard nothing more of her until some six years later, when by grapevine came the news that Miss Blum and her father had both died a while back of syphilis, in Berlin, months apart.

That he permitted the case to close in such an orderly, expeditious, and frankly dishonest manner was a liberty Perlman permitted himself on two counts. First, he had done as asked. He had delivered the girl in good health, and the proximate cause of her trauma—her mind and body's concerted refusal of water—had been corrected. Second was his conviction that whatever the future held for Sylvie Blum, the period of his usefulness had ended. Sylvie was not the girl he knew, and in the brief time they spent together before Herr Blum came to pick her up, her sullen glare confirmed the impression he'd formed early the week before: that he frankly preferred the other one, the one who was gone.

As for the meaning of the episode itself, Perlman's initial inclination was not to pay it much heed. Now that he was free from the grip of its remarkable momentum, he wrote it off as an anomaly, something like the man who'd played the *Goldberg Variations* back at Nancy. If there was a lesson to be learned, he suspected it had less to do with Irving Blum's daughter than with his own weaknesses, and with the hollow lives of London's artistic elite, upon whom he was now also inclined to close the drawer. He did this literally, in fact, filing the Barrett songbook away in his closet, where he wouldn't have to see it anymore.

The episode would not go away as quietly as he might have wished, however. In the ensuing days and weeks, the deliverance of Sylvie Blum became the subject of much impressed cooing and chuckling in and around the hospital. This was principally due to the rumor—whose source could only have been Sister Antoinette—that Dr. Perlman had actually taken the girl away for two days. No one knew where, only that she'd been "split" when she left and cured when they returned. This, combined with the impressive donation Herr Blum forthwith handed over to Mr. Shepard—Perlman refused any part—only reconfirmed the doctor's reputation as the shaman of Little Britain.

Perlman knew better, of course, and as those first few days passed, buffeted by nudges and winks, knowing smiles and pats on the back, he found the lie increasingly difficult to bear. He was no healer. He'd narrowly escaped professional ruin by a means he did not understand and did not really care to. What he'd managed to do there at the end—

drowning Oona in the rising tide of her mother-the-moon—had been capitulation. The Madame and the girl had gotten him to play *their* game, by *their* rules. All he'd done was give in—played well but, in so doing, violated every principle and conviction he'd entered with. For that, it seemed he'd gained Sylvie Blum, but lost forever any sense of worthiness or enlightenment. He felt as if he'd finally awakened to his own ignorance and never would sleep again.

The third week of October, roughly a fortnight after the girl's discharge, Perlman stopped taking new cases. The reason he gave was ill health, which was true enough. A thorough physical examination confirmed the presence of several minor ailments—a heart arrhythmia, fatigue, and a mild anemia. By early November the clinic had for all intents and purposes closed.

Perlman's musical life suffered as well. He attended nothing that whole fall season. Not his brother Leonard's recital at St. John's. Not even Diaghilev's production of *Prince Igor*, which came to town in late November (the one for which Roerich, the dinner guest, had designed the sets). Messengers came bearing three separate pairs of tickets— from Madame Helena, from Irving Blum, and from Mr. Shepard. Perlman turned them all away. For three months he sat alone in his flat, trying to forget—the *Times*, the *Spectator*, and the *Pall Mall Gazette* his only real companions.

Come winter, his spirit had fallen so low that Leonard prevailed upon him to travel south. They got as far as Italy together, but without his musical appetite to guide him, Perlman proved to be a restless, fitful traveler. In early March, Leonard went on to Palestine without him, and Perlman spent two rainy weeks alone in Milan.

The one boon of his protracted convalescence was the fact that, for those three months, he did manage to remain more or less sober. In Milan the cumulative effect of extended temperance finally kicked in. He'd been managing to resist the hottest ticket in town—Mereschi, the last castrato—when by chance he noticed on a billboard that an unknown pianist named Brazzi was giving a performance of Schubert's last sonatas at the conservatory. Perlman had never heard either 959 or 960, and so for that, and the likelihood there wouldn't be a crowd, he attended. The concert began at 7:30, and by 10:00 Perlman's torpor had lifted like old dead skin. Those eight movements and a subsequent conversation with a fellow lodger at his pensione so revived the doctor's taste for life that he started back for England the next day, fueled by the idea that he might finally dust off the Chroniks; get around to organizing them, decoding them, whipping them into presentable shape.

He arrived back in London the last week of March, still reasonably intent, but wisely staked his hopes in habitual behavior. He didn't go so far as to reopen the clinic, but did agree to resume rounds at the hospital five days a week, as before. He worked in the early afternoons exclusively, setting aside his mornings for the Chroniks and twilight for walks.

The first he saw the Madame again was early May, a raw and rainy Wednesday. He had taken his afternoon constitutional to a teahouse over by St. James's called Mallory's. There was an open stove always burning, and the windows looked out on the street.

Perlman sat at his usual table by the stove. He ordered a black currant tea, loaded his pipe, and opened the little book Bernheim had pressed on him so many months ago—the dream book by Freud. As usual, however, the combination of the walk, the tea, and the warm air of the fire had a lulling effect on him. He drifted in and out of the words, nodding here and there, doubling back and starting over.

He was in a thorough murk, reading the third paragraph of the introduction for what could have been the fourth or fifth time, when he was jolted upright by a tap at the window, the sharp chink of gold on glass.

She was oddly lit. Behind her, a murky twilit blue outlined her figure. She was in the black hat with the ostrich feathers, the cape—primed to make a graceful entrance wherever it was she was going; and though she was a silhouette he could still see her face, lit a warm amber by the stove fire.

She did not come in. Just a brief look in the eye was all—"You," it seemed to say—then she moved on down the street. "You," as if she'd been thinking of him, as he had been thinking of her, on and off, every day since September.

In all that time, however, he'd never known how he would react when he finally did see her again. Would he feel anger? Guilt? Horror? He did not expect to be reminded so quickly. For even in the glimpse—"You"—Perlman remembered. Or forgot. What horror? Who else in all the world could so effortlessly, by tapping a pane of glass, lift his heart so.

He did not rise to follow her. He kept his seat, finished his tea, and left soon after. But the following day, Thursday, he made sure to be at Mallory's again, at the same hour, in the same chair, sending up the same smoke signal, just in case. But he did not bring the book, and she did not bring the ring.

## ACKNOWLEDGMENTS

My gratitude extends to more than can be named, but among those who can, and in particular, I offer my sincerest thanks:

to Jonathan Galassi, for his commitment; to Paul Elie, for his standards; Lynn Warshow, for her diligence and care; and to Amanda Urban, for continuing to clear the way;

to The New York Public Library; The Nicholas Roerich Museum; The San Francisco Public Library; Stage Left; and belatedly to Golden Gate Park;

to Étienne Baxter, Dennis Russell Davies, Annabel Lee, Elizabeth Meryman, Andy Tyson, and Ward Williamson, for a miscellany of help;

to my readers—Adam Guettel, Sam Hansen, Hope Hansen, Peter Hansen, Maud Bryt, and Emily Woods—for all their kind and frank input; and to Virginia Medellin Priest, the best unpaid editor in New York, for the continued generosity and severity of her criticism;

to Whitney Hansen and Kate Robin for waiting;

to Domenico Scarlatti, Franz Schubert, Frederic Chopin, Richard Wagner, Edvard Grieg, Modest Mussorgsky, Alexander Scriabin, Jean Sibelius, Béla Bartók, Dmitri Shostakovich, and, most of all, Sergei Sergeevich Prokofiev, for their example and inspiration;

and finally, of course, to my wife, Elizabeth, for home.